SEMIOTEXT(E) NATIVE AGENTS SERIES

Published by Semiotext(e)
PO BOX 629. South Pasadena, CA 91031
www.semiotexte.com

Special thanks to Robert Dewhurst, Cayal Unger, and John Ebert.

Cover: Hector Mata: "Poster of Andrew Cunanan," West Hollywood, CA, July 17, 1997. © AFP PHOTO/Hector MATA.

Back Cover Photography: Gary Indiana
Design by Hedi El Kholti

ISBN: 978-1-58435-198-6
Distributed by The MIT Press, Cambridge, Mass. and London, England
Printed in the United States of America

THREE MONTH FEVER

THE ANDREW CUNANAN STORY

GARY INDIANA

CONTENTS

CUNANAN / BOVARY

Every century has seen its share of sodomy and mass murder, but in the twentieth century, butt-fucking and genocide reached an industrial apex, making them special objects of fascination. It's the peculiar genius of *Three Month Fever*, Gary Indiana's peerless encapsulation of the American *fin de siècle*, to gather the century's major themes and knot them together in the figure of Andrew Cunanan, an insolvent social climber and homicidal sodomite who, in Indiana's account, is thrillingly recast as an American everyman.

Writing from the turbulent vantage of early 2017, there's an irresistible urge to revisit the pathologies of the late nineties—the pinnacle, in many ways, of the long Reaganite epoch now coming to an end. The murder of Gianni Versace, nuzzled between the worst years of the AIDS crisis and the rise of the Internet, prominent in a series of blockbuster deaths stretching from Nicole Brown Simpson and JonBenét Ramsey to Matthew Shepard and Princess Di, provided a febrile opportunity for journalists to workshop the era's main theological scripts: the relentless focus on success and fame; the corresponding preoccupation with drugs and self-destruction; the siren song of easy credit; the cultural aggrandizement of travel and vacation; the urban renaissance; the triumph of liberalized marriage markets; the simultaneous worship of complexity and venality—scripts all doubly important for the gay community, which was settling into its first period of bourgeois normalcy. For Gary Indiana, Cunanan's spree provided an opportunity to stress-test popular mythologies.

The great pleasure of reading Proust, a critic once asserted, is that he relieves you of the anxiety that you might be smarter than the author. Gary Indiana, whose writing sparkles with extravagant insight, pounding the reader with an endless succession of triple axels, affords the same pleasure: in his books, art dealers hawk work with "the mentality of pork butchers who keep both thumbs on the scale," a reticent witness speaks to the FBI about a murder with a "serene detachment...as if an appliance he had once leased were now suspected of causing a warehouse fire." No, you don't write like this, whoever you are. Gary Indiana is the Eminem of American prose.

Despite his virtuosity, or perhaps because of it, Indiana has had the bad luck of being misidentified as an "experimental writer," even though his most important work is formally conventional by the standards of the post-war avant-garde. *Three Month Fever*, his greatest novel, aspires to a kind of realism. Propelled by penetrating observation and telling details, the text is intermittently embellished by orthodox techniques that have been in wide use since the 19th century, like free indirect discourse and documentary collage. More accessible than experimental, the novel is also shriekingly *pertinent*, not only to a gay or niche or "downtown" audience—the kind that thrills to the slasher edginess of a writer like Dennis Cooper—but also to the wider "general reader" who has heard of Brett Easton Ellis, and who sustains corporate media and the mainstream elite. Saddled with an enthusiastic cult, *Three Month Fever* would have found its natural home in less delusional times among readers like Cunanan himself—that is, among conscientious disciples of general-interest magazines, which barely noticed the novel when it came out. On the other hand, if the world had been less delusional in 1999, Versace might never have been killed, and the book might never have been written.

"Major" American postwar fiction, the kind written by authors like John Updike and Richard Ford, and reviewed, sometimes by those same authors, in places like *The New Yorker*, tended to focus on suburban dads; its more recent practitioners, plying a diminished successor genre marketed as "literary fiction," have dwelled on similar characters, though now the men are often childless and live in cities. Andrew Cunanan, parodied by journalists as a rakish SoCal psychopath, cuts a different figure. A steely cipher with moderately good looks and encyclopedic knowledge of useless worldly details, Cunanan emerges not as a postmodern reboot of Harry Angstrom but as something much larger and more portentous: an American reincarnation of Emma Bovary.

Like Flaubert's Norman housewife, Cunanan is a restless striver from the provinces ("credulous San Diego") burdened by a writerly imagination and an unquenchable thirst to circulate in high society. Like Emma, he racks up enormous debts in his quest to project a golden aura, credit arrangements that gradually unwind in a paroxysm of mania and death. Both characters are preoccupied with fetish objects—Andrew with designer clothes and watches, Emma with bracelets and bangles—and mesmerized by the coded signals they believe such objects emit ("Andrew thought you could tell how someone voted," Indiana writes, "by their choice of an olive or a beige refrigerator"). Like Emma, Andrew is simultaneously a fabulist and a compulsive consumer of fables, a "prosumer" sponge for media clichés and also a sensitive observer of things he cannot name, like the "pattern of flesh on a person's hands" or the "grain of an uncooked steak." Both Emma and Andrew stand in for their readers, their authors, and the psychic desperations of their eras.

As Indiana intuits, gay men, with their zeal for status-seeking and talent for false posturing, are the rightful heirs to *Bovarysme*. Given that the most admired heterosexual relationships in the United States are infected by austere moralism, prime-age gays are the closest thing we have to would-be courtesannes. In *Three Month Fever*, Andrew is not a "flaming queen," but he does have "that hyperbolic theatricality, everything calculated to amuse or impress." Everybody in society pretends to be richer and happier and more successful than they really are, Indiana seems to tell us, but gay men, still paradigmatic outsiders, perhaps most of all. Whether this is a consequence of years of practice at subterfuge, or, alternatively, of the intensity of intermale competition, where every rival is a potential lover, the novel doesn't say. *Three Month Fever* features a gay world where solidarity has been replaced by a brutally enforced pecking order from which individual relationships are no refuge. Everyone belongs to "the community" more emphatically than they do to one another. Andrew's paradox is that he is *entirely* public—"a sort of human special effect—a walking gay bar." He exists only in the telling: the sum of his own lies, the lies told about him by acquaintances, and the fresh lies dreamed up by the press. Like Emma Bovary, he lacks true interiority.

The critic Peter Brooks once provocatively charged that *Madame Bovary* is "the one novel, of all novels, that deserves the label 'realist.'" Brooks felt the novel had earned the label because Flaubert, ideologically committed to piercing popular illusions through withering description, had successfully conveyed that narrative was itself a lie and a dead end. Storytelling, in Flaubert's famous formulation, depends utterly on the "cracked kettle" of "human speech...on which we tap crude rhythms for bears to dance to, while we long to make music that will melt the stars." Brooks considered Flaubert an apocalyptic writer, a man so bereft of faith in the sovereignty of the imagination or the goodness of people that he wielded his pen as a world-destroyer, accumulating broken language and descriptive details as a brief against reality, which he considered irredeemably corrupted by cliché. Flaubert was put on trial for *Madame Bovary*'s alleged obscenity, but also for his poison-tipped promotion of "la littérature réaliste," which Flaubert's prosecutor called an affront to art and human decency.

Like Flaubert, Gary Indiana has a congenital urge to debunk. He practices what we might call "deflationary realism," a craft distinct from the so-called "hysterical realism" of writers like David Foster Wallace and Zadie Smith, whose imaginations are more powerfully laced with sentimentality. Although Indiana's novels have not led to any legal indictments, they have often led critics to accuse him of immorality or cynicism. *The New York Times*, for example, in reviewing Indiana's earlier novel *Resentment*, a work of speculative fiction loosely based on the Menendez brothers trial, took Indiana to task for "his absurdist bleakness" and "alienating nihilism." The novel's "densely written pages are so relentlessly focused on the catastrophic side of human nature," the *Times* wrote, "that one is driven to ask, what's the point?" In 2015, the literary magazine *n+1* complained that Indiana's cynicism and "blasé knowingness" left no room for the "traumatic," the "tragic," the "romantic," or "the revolutionary."

Certainly *Three Month Fever*, like *Madame Bovary*, is too preoccupied with cliché to embrace the mawkishness demanded by critics. Trauma, tragedy, romance, and revolution might be themes that appeal to Bovary, but they are less relevant to Cunanan, who, instead of taking cues from novels, bathes in the secular clichés of magazine journalism. Far from a romantic, Indiana's Cunanan is an incandescent source of "hot takes," learning his best tricks from the fatuous storytellers of *Vanity Fair*. He is especially hot for "turning points." As Indiana writes: "Andrew collected 'turning points,' recounted them gravely in heart-to-heart conversations—*the real turning point for me was getting involved in AIDS prevention work*, Andrew might say, or, *I think Iran-Contra was a major turning point for a lot of people.* In spells of fabulism it might be, *The big turning point was when we left Israel.*" Where Emma focuses on primping her appearance, "filing her nails with the care of a metalsmith," Cunanan primps his backstory, embroidering his personal history with ever-more theatrical details: a wife and child left in San Francisco, a bisexual father working for Ferdinand Marcos, a career in the Navy. In letters to his ex-lover and eventual victim David Madsen, Andrew effectively publishes an epistolary issue of *Vanity Fair*, loading his dispatches with witty aperçus about bullfights and vomitoria and Corsican manners and Saint-Jean-Cap-Ferrat. When Cunanan closes his eyes and sinks into "reverie," the phrases that fill his mind's void are headlines: "*Merger of Nynex and Bell Atlantic Clears U.S. Hurdle… Trial begins in the Okla-homa City Bombing Case.*" Abjuring the labels "true crime" or "nonfiction novel," Indiana has declared *Three Month Fever* a weaponized "pastiche"—an attempt to dissolve those "unsatisfying modes" by reproducing an episode warped by journalistic nos-trums and therefore "inextricable from its own hyperbole." Holding the line against "fake news," the novel embraces realism as an assault on the world's unreality.

It's tempting to believe that Indiana undertook the project of *Three Month Fever* as an enraged response to a very specific jour-nalistic inaccuracy: the thoughtless canard, widely circulated at the time of Versace's murder, that Cunanan, who had physically ballooned in the weeks leading up to his killing spree—and whose credit card bills betray ravenous feasting at restaurants such as Denny's—was in the throes of a crystal meth binge. "One indisputable characteristic of people on crystal meth," Indiana notes in pained exasperation, "is that they don't eat." But the average journalist, whose range of earthly experience turns out to be startlingly restricted, has no way of knowing this.

Indiana claims to have written *Three Month Fever* as "a propaedeutic lever with which to bury the consumer" in "indeli-ble abjection." And yet Indiana is plainly not oppressed by language or reality to the same dark extent as Flaubert, despite any cranky protestations. For one thing, he is palpably tickled by Americana, and especially by the stern officiousness with which names and concepts are paraded about ("the so-called Rumpus Room" in *Resentment,* the "trite decadeism of Joan Didion"). And while *Three Month Fever* might not contain enough of a moral to clear the considerable hurdle of millennial gushiness, the novel does exalt a recognizable ethic: the ethic of "worldliness" itself. As Indiana writes in his introduction to *Three Month Fever*:

> I have, in my lifetime, known five murderers (that is, five that I know of), two of them documented serial killers. With one exception, I knew these people either before they killed or before their crimes were discovered—in other words, knew them as normal people in the world rather than as murderers, and although I have lived a rangier life than some, it's my suspicion that this is not *such* a bizarre circumstance.

Of course, Indiana's unusual closeness to mass murderers is a very bizarre circumstance indeed. The function of his revelation is to hector the reader, as if Indiana can barely imagine how one could go through life without at least once crossing paths with a multiple murderer, or going on a meth binge, or selling one's body for money. The complaint is justified. Why *doesn't* the reader know any serial killers? What kind of lives *have* we been living? Not modern ones—not most of us.

Aside from looks and cold-hard cash, worldliness is the most valuable currency among homosexuals, conferring an aura of hard-boiled acuity that can substitute, if need be, for classical markers of masculinity. Just as Cunanan matter-of-factly glosses European capitals for non-initiates like David Madsen (and just as Flaubert, the son of a Norman doctor, pulled back the curtain on dreary Rouen for readers of the *Revue de Paris*) Indiana positions himself as a seasoned insider explaining the facts of life to the cloistered masses.

Indiana's exaltation of worldliness and rage against naiveté has scandalized innocent reviewers, but hidden beneath his prose's urbane exterior is a Proustian generosity. While Indiana's literary method is to deflate the world he depicts, that world starts off considerably inflated, with ordinary people having thoughts and leading lives as complex and textured as Indiana's own. The world that Indiana presents as *fait accompli*, is, in fact, a sci-fi of intelligence and erudition, a fantasy realm where sugar daddies riff on soybean futures at champagne-soaked soirees while their charges debate the aesthetic merits of *To Die For*. Such a scene has never occurred in recorded history—not in San Diego—but it suggests deep wells of magnanimity for Indiana to suggest that it might.

The world's complexity is an astonishing thing to apprehend, and most people don't apprehend it all, except to denounce it. At the moment, it looks like the populist revolt against complexity is perhaps the defining struggle of the coming new era. Gary Indiana, to an almost unique degree, is neither frightened of complexity nor seduced by it. His gift is to imagine a world where intricacy trickles down, not as a hysterical detail or an apocalyptic omen, but as a vector of empathy. Everyone's life is complex, whether they realize it or not. Not everyone is a spree killer, but at some subterranean level everyone wants to be.

THREE MONTH FEVER

THE ANDREW CUNANAN STORY

For Emma Sweeney

"To agree to explain homosexuality to heterosexuals is like explaining the Gospels to children addicted to television: all that sticks in their heads is an ox, an ass and Mickey Mouse in the midst of it all."

—Aldo Busi, "Sodomies in Elevenpoint"

Last night I found obscenities Scrawled
across my wall
I swear I can't repeat
The filthy words that I recall
And then the most immoral
Damned insulting thing of all
As I read each line I noticed
His handwriting was identical
With mine.

—Dory Previn, "Doppelganger"

ACKNOWLEDGMENTS

This book has its point of literary origin in a long investigation into an entirely different case, namely that of Charles Sobhraj, the so-called Tourist Killer of Bangkok, Nepal, and Varanasi; since many of the psychological materials gleaned for that unwritten book found an unexpectedly appropriate home in this one, I (belatedly) want to thank Richard Neville, and also to thank my many friends at the Press Club in New Delhi for their generous help in that Byzantine inquiry three years ago. The press corps of India, wildly variegated and politically contentious as it is, has, I'm sorry to say, a considerably larger spirit of collegiality than its counterpart in the United States. The contrast is so striking, in fact, that the *only* American journalist I can thank here without reservation is Eric Zorn of the *Chicago Tribune*, who did not add much to what I already knew, but offered what he had with good will and no proprietary reservations.

In contrast to journalists who worked this story, the police departments of Minneapolis, San Diego, and Miami were unstintingly helpful, and I owe a special debt of gratitude to Det. Lt. Collins of San Diego, Det. Lt. Dale Barsness, Det. Sgt. Robert Tichich, and Det. Sgt. Mark Lenzen of Minneapolis Homicide, and Det. Paul Scrimshaw of Miami Beach Homicide, for sharing their theories of the case as well as their investigative data; the Sheriff's Office of Chisago County, Minnesota; Dr. Lindsay Thomas, the Chisago County Coroner; and the Miami Beach Police Department.

Thanks to the many people who helped collect information: Robert Glück and Chris Komater in San Francisco; Tim Loftis in Philadelphia; Richard Flood of the Walker Arts Center in Minneapolis; Kay Rosen in Chicago; Steven Lafreniere and John Sanchez in New York; my agent, Emma Sweeney; Matthew Stadler and Steven Zeeland in Seattle; my brother and sister-in-law, Kent and Shirley Hoisington, and their son-in-law, David Makowicz, in Annapolis; and Steve Lindsey in San Diego, who also provided a place to stay, numerous free meals, and crucial assistance in some unbelievably stressful situations. (In connection with the latter, I must also thank here Jim Hinchee, Billy Sullivan, Carol Steinberg, Susan DePalma, Frank LoScalzo, Elena Ackel, and Marilyn Holle.) Howard Frisch and Fred Harris dug up many useful reference works and provided relief from the long country isolation in which this book was written. Thanks also to the Tyrone Guthrie Theater in Minneapolis for making an apartment available during the early stages of my research.

Further thanks are due to Rich Bonnin, Fred Robertis, Monica Salvetti, Matthew Janjeski, John Cook, and Don Buchwalter in Minneapolis; "Jay" in Seattle; Art Thompson, Nicole Ramirez-Murray, Ramon Jimenez, Tony Valenzuela, and "Eric" in San Diego; Jerry Douglas in New Jersey, and Rob Davis in Washington. I also thank the many informants who specifically asked that their names not appear in this book. I realize that many people who allowed me to interview them will not be especially pleased by the frame I've drawn around their information or the conclusions I've reached about certain aspects of this story; it shouldn't be assumed that my ideas about the case reflect theirs.

I am very grateful to Beth Neelman, the legal counsel on this book, for making the vetting process a fair, reasonable, and expeditious experience—and, in this connection, want to express very belated gratitude to Victor Kovner, who rescued my last novel, *Resentment*, from legal euthanasia. For brilliant advice and unflagging encouragement, I thank my editor, Diane Reverand, whose subtle guidance was exactly what I needed to get this book written.

Finally, I want to thank the friends who discussed this book with me as it was written, shared their opinions, offered useful criticism, listened to endless recitations on the phone, and generally helped me survive a daunting, frequently miserable period of trial and error: Larry Johnson, Lynne Tillman, Linda Yablonsky, Michael Tolkin, Sharon Niesp, and Barbara Kruger.

GI
January 1999

PREFACE

Unless you were personally involved in it, the scariest aspect of the Andrew Cunanan story was the insensible proliferation of media coverage of it following the shooting of Gianni Versace: the killer, widely ignored while he left a trail of bodies from Minnesota to New Jersey, became, abruptly, a diabolic icon in the circus, of American celebrity, and virtually any scrap of information about him, true, false, or in between, got reported as breathless fact along the entire spectrum of "news providers." Egregiously, with little or no regard for accuracy, Cunanan's life was transformed from the somewhat poignant and depressing but fairly ordinary thing it was into a narrative overripe with tabloid evil: ugly sex, drug dealing, prostitution, et cetera. The boilerplate figure of the serial killer, familiar by then to most Americans, was extracted from specious accounts of Cunanan killing small animals as a child; innocuous remarks he may or may not have made, to people who may or may not have known him, chitchat overheard by restaurant waiters, and a portentous quote from Louis XV in his prep school yearbook were rushed into print and onto the airwaves as evidence that Cunanan was a true sociopath, yet another wearer of "the mask of sanity" who had passed among us, in this transient society where no one really knows anybody else, without detection.

One could usefully argue that many of American society's most admired figures, its so-called role models, from CEOs to movie stars, including some of Versace's most audible mourners after the event, could easily qualify as sociopaths, the culture of narcissism having segued some years ago into the culture of total-self-aggrandizement-by-whatever-means-present-themselves. America loves a successful sociopath. We are not so much a society where nobody knows anybody else as we are a society where only media celebrities are considered to have actual existence. Leaving that point aside, I was astonished to discover, soon after starting research on this book, how little of what had been reported had better than a fanciful relationship to reality. The most insistently highlighted points of the story seem to have been hallucinated, or bribed out of what one generously would call unreliable witnesses. But even the rare scrupulous reporter must have found himself stymied by the impossible tangle of myths Cunanan wove about his person. Once Cunanan became a media star, people told other people what Cunanan had told them, which tended to be whatever had popped into his head on a given day. Even the less impeachable stories, in the particular worlds that Cunanan inhabited, were, and are, ultimately unverifiable, for several reasons. In large part they concern the most private and fiercely guarded kinds of interaction, among people who are almost the opposite of public figures. And something in the nature of this story produced, among those most likely to shed some wayward illumination on it, an impenetrable reticence.

There was, I believe, "something about Andrew" that made what he did, to those who knew him, amazing and completely unsurprising at the same time. I have, in my lifetime, known five murderers (that is, five that I know of), two of them documented serial killers. With one exception, I knew these people either before they killed or before their crimes were discovered—in other words, knew them as normal people in the world rather than as murderers, and although I have lived a rangier life than some, it's my suspicion that this is not *such* a bizarre circumstance. As Gore Vidal says somewhere, if you want to see the face of a killer, look in any mirror. There are deeply criminal people who will never kill anybody, and perfectly nice individuals who one day will run amok with an AK-47. Until a person goes postal, he just looks like part of the landscape. Sometimes an eccentric or disturbed part, sometimes not.

For two decades, we have been deluged with narratives about serial killers (particularly in the form of the "true crime" saga), which invariably lay out the full pathology of a given miscreant and assure us that there are "signs to watch for," that if only we paid attention in the early stages, society could prevent serial murders and related unpleasantness. Interestingly, Cunanan didn't experience the early traumas or manifest the egregious childhood behavior that experts tag as typical of the serial killer. More interestingly, in adult life, he did have enough of a screw loose that plenty of people noticed it, and often found it amusing. What can we conclude from this about experts? Or about life? In those days of high drama between the Versace killing and Cunanan's suicide, after the serial killer paradigm failed to match the case, numerous moldy "profilers" turned up hourly on cable news, groping for some ingenious synthesis between "the classic serial" and "the classic spree" killer: Cunanan seemed less a threat to the general public than to familiar narrative genres and their claims to classicism. (He didn't quite fit the "spree" pattern, either; he finally became a mixture of two things he didn't resemble.)

It isn't my desire to add word one to the "true crime" genre, or to the "nonfiction novel" à la Capote or Mailer. *Three Month Fever* is a pastiche with which I would like to dissolve both of these unsatisfying modes, concerning as it does a story that is itself a pastiche, and in many respects inextricable from its own hyperbole. And here I would evoke a different pedigree of hybrid nonfiction (that is, a hybrid of narration and reflection, fact-based, but with no pretense to journalistic "objectivity," the journalistic mode, or any of its normative moral aporias) which includes Emlyn Williams's *Beyond Belief: A Chronicle of Murder and Its Detection*, James Baldwin's *The Evidence of Things Not Seen*, Alexander Kluge's *The Battle*, and, to cite an earlier example, Curzio Malaparte's *Kaputt*. I have tried to fashion a credible, but hardly seamless, documentary from the most reliable sources in the case—police and FBI materials, witness interviews, selected reportage, the usual legwork—bridging substantial information gaps with my best surmise. Yes, some novelistic techniques are employed. For example, the italicized notebook entries that punctuate part 2, chapter 5, were written by me, as stipulated in the text. (All other *writing* attributed to Cunanan in this book was, in fact, written by him.) A few minor characters who perform no important action are composites of two or more informants, else the reader would be in for a great deal of expository dreariness. Several names have been changed, as Jack Webb used to say, to protect the innocent. It was clearly necessary to simulate Cunanan's mental state throughout the narrative, and to speculate, beyond the inferences evoked by forensic data, about the interactions between killer and victims between April 25, 1997, and the final act in Miami. It was, in fact, crucial to speculate about many quiddities of Cunanan's psyche and solitary behavior—I wanted, above all, to make this person palpable to the reader *as* a person. I do not know if Cunanan actually masturbated into Jon Hackett's shoe, or had the standard male tooth-loss castration dream when he left Norman Blachford. But I *feel* that he did, or at the very least that something analogous happened. Regarding the location of David Madson during Jeff Trail's murder, and the amount of time between the Trail murder and the killing of Madson, I have chosen what I consider the most plausible scenarios, based on voluminous police reports and interviews with homicide detectives, and with Madson's friends; there are, even among the police, diverse opinions about how Jeff Trail's murder went down and when David Madson was killed. Regarding the Miglin murder, and contrary to statements by the Miglin family spokesperson as well as Chicago Homicide, I find the rent boy statement summarized by the FBI, cited in part 3, chapter 17, entirely credible, as it was given long before the Versace killing brought publicity seekers out of the woodwork, was made by someone whose personal and legal interests would have been better served by *not* coming forward, and supports several off-the-record stories I obtained from disinterested sources. In any event, a careful consideration of all the crime-scene data—including the unlocked *front* gate of the Miglin home, the fact that the Miglin garage on the rear alley has no obvious connection to the Miglin home, and other, even more telling circumstances such as Marilyn Miglin's absence from the house, which could not have been assumed by a stranger whose victims were exclusively male—makes the notion of a "random killing" unbelievable to anyone who is not predisposed to believe it. And so on.

There are, alas, many unsolved mysteries connected to this story, and since the task of piecing together a life from the snippets available was daunting enough, I have not pursued all the alluring sidebar items. Yes, there was a dead mourning dove found near Versace's head, its tiny brain clipped in midflight by a bullet fragment that ricocheted off the wrought-iron gate. Does this mean the Mafia hired Cunanan, perhaps in exchange for safe passage out of the country? Or that Cunanan himself was bumped off in the houseboat, that Versace was a professional hit by a Cunanan double? I don't think so, but I don't know. Then there is the matter of Torsten Franz Jacob Reineck, owner of the houseboat, also owner of the Apollo Spa, a gay bathhouse in Las Vegas, where several neighborhood bartenders and shopkeepers swear they served Cunanan in the middle past; Reineck was known to these neighbors, and in Las Vegas generally, as Dr. Frank Mattias Ruhl, a nonpracticing ear, nose, and throat specialist. After the discovery of Cunanan's corpse on the houseboat, a Dr. Frank Mattias Ruhl presented himself to the Miami Beach police, along with a warranty deed and bill of sale indicating that Ruhl had recently purchased the houseboat *from* Torsten Reineck for $10.00; it was subsequently reported that Reineck was wanted in Germany on a number of fraud charges, including, suggestively, former possession of a printing press capable of manufacturing passports. Weirdly, before Ruhl supposedly purchased the houseboat from Reineck, Reineck answered a summons concerning the leakage of effluvia from his septic tank into Indian Creek by claiming diplomatic immunity—he was, he said, an attaché of some sort, from a country called "Sealand," and displayed a passport from this country, which is, in fact, not a country at all, but a World War II antiaircraft emplacement on a rock in the English Channel. Are Reineck and Ruhl the same individual? Did they, or he, know Cunanan, and provide ingress to the houseboat? The lead homicide detective in Miami Beach does not entirely buy the well-known story of the houseboat caretaker, i.e., that he entered the houseboat and saw an unfamiliar pair of sandals, then heard a shot, then ran and called the police, et cetera. But the case is closed, and, contrary to popular belief, the police do not generally trouble themselves tying up loose ends on a closed case. At last report, "Reineck" was thought to have returned to Germany, to face the music there, while "Ruhl" has simply vanished from the screen.

It might have been tempting to follow these threads. For all I know, there may be more connective tissue between the six events that made Cunanan famous than anyone has yet discovered. In starting my own investigations, I did not reckon on the extreme difficulty of getting *anyone* involved with Cunanan to talk; for twenty years or so, I had been intermittently reporting stories of considerable complexity, some arguably more gruesome and tangled than this one. I had interviewed hundreds of people all over the planet on every manner of charged subject, but in this instance, and truly for the first time, I encountered a kind of phobia-laden mendacity among potential informants that startled me. It may simply be the case that Cunanan had, with some remarkable exceptions, ghastly taste in picking friends; at any rate, some made it plain that whatever tidbits they had were only available for great sums of cash. Even the people he had no choice about picking implied the same thing. Strange to say, the quality of observation that many of these people have exhibited in paid TV appearances has been stunningly impoverished, imprecise, almost amnesiac in its generality; as I discovered over months of research, the most sensational of these tabloidal revelations were freely invented.

While I did, in the end, glean enough information, from enough helpful people, to see most of this case in the round, the wariness and cunning I found directed at me as a "journalist" bodes nothing good for that profession. The arrogance and inanity that fuels a twenty-four-hour news cycle has earned an amazing amount of contempt in the country at large—like the Andrew Cunanan story, amazing but unsurprising. People may be entertained by the mindless, predictable, redundant, distorting, and meretricious techniques currently used to cover news, but at heart they despise them. This makes any search for the truth of things something terribly close to folly.

ONE

FLIGHT DATA

1

On Friday, April 25, Andrew got a ride to San Diego Airport from Kenneth Higgins, a cute blond friend of fairly recent vintage who later described the ride as uneventful, involving scant conversation, San Diego Airport being only a few minutes from Andrew's apartment at 1234 Robinson and practically in San Diego itself. You can, after all, drive from downtown straight through the airport into Point Loma without crossing such epic wastes as separate most cities from most airports. Aside from the brevity of this ride, Andrew had already talked himself silly in the days just previous, to Kenneth Higgins and Robin Thompson and Erik Greenman and various others, some of whom attended Andrew's so-called going-away dinner, about his imminent relocation to San Francisco, and what he termed *this little side trip to Minneapolis*, claiming among other things to have *excellent business prospects in San Francisco*, a new apartment, a new roommate, what amounted to *a whole new life* waiting for him in the city on the bay. These prospects were so auspicious that Andrew had declared his intention to *buy a whole new wardrobe*, consequently, in the days just prior to this little side trip to

Minneapolis, Andrew gave away Missoni sweaters and Dolce & Gabbana suits and Ferragamo shoes, Helmut Lang blazers and Prada jackets, designer clothing items from shops on Rodeo Drive, shops in Milan, shops in San Francisco, pricey garments acquired in the course of his incessant travels, some barely worn, gave them away in an access of insensible largesse, much to the distress of Erik Greenman, Andrew's roommate, who later complained that Andrew gave many items to near strangers that happened to fit Erik Greenman perfectly.

One of the themes Andrew had developed since his recent trips to Los Angeles and San Francisco was his *overwhelming love* for David Madson, a neophyte architect in Minneapolis whom few of Andrew's San Diego friends had ever met. According to Andrew, his affair with David Madson had started on a high note the previous summer but faltered and ultimately fizzled because of the long-distance nature of the relationship, and it was only now, when the spark had almost sputtered out entirely, that Andrew realized how much David meant to him. David was, he told Kenneth, *the only person in the world he had ever really loved.* He had managed to spend the week before Easter or part of the week before Easter in a hotel room with David Madson in Los Angeles, had wined David and dined David and even clothed David in an Armani suit and an Andrew Mark jacket courtesy of Andrew's platinum card, not just David but two of David's friends as well, a so-called model named Karen Lapinski and her fiancé, Evan Wallitt, a yuppie couple from San Francisco, *at the Chateau Marmont*, Andrew emphasized, which might not have been the priciest place in Los Angeles but was certainly one of the classiest, especially now that Eric Goode had done it over, yet none of this sumptuary excess had worked the desired magic.

Andrew said that his sister was an anesthesiologist who worked in Minneapolis and he said he wanted to *try again* with David Madson. He told some people that he had *unfinished business* with Jeffrey Trail, a friend of his who was, unlike David Madson, well-remembered in San Diego, an ex-navy heartthrob Andrew had stuck to like glue for years and years, who had, much to Andrew's dismay, moved to Minneapolis a few months earlier. But Andrew always said a lot of things. Sometimes he said he had served eleven months in Israeli intelligence and sometimes he claimed his family owned the Ace Parking concessions downtown. People liked Andrew for his brassy joie de vivre and his quick tongue and rolled their eyes at his stories when he wasn't looking. Andrew was not a flaming queen, but he did have that hyperbolic theatricality, everything calculated to amuse or impress. He usually gave his name as *DeSilva*, which didn't really sound Jewish, but Erik, who lived with him and had to know, said his real name was *Cunanan*, which really didn't either.

Andrew left San Diego carrying a single black nylon duffel bag, and as usual he was, in the parlance of the California Southland, "upbeat."

2

I'm of two minds about the future, he thought, having developed considerable uncertainty about his precise location on the map of his own existence. His sister Regina lived in San Francisco, not Minneapolis. They'd talked about Andrew moving in with her and Andrew, with part of his mind, was en route to San Francisco, but another part seemed to be traveling to Minneapolis, not for a little side trip, but to *set up shop*, as he thought of it, a thought having some reverberation in his childhood, when Andrew and a friend played a game called Store, in which they operated a miraculous store where they could *sell anything* a customer asked for, since at that innocent age he believed that anything demanded could be magically supplied. The smudgy landscapes of National City shimmered in his mind, drought-stunted jacaranda trees, a parched riverbed at the bottom of a hollow, ribbons of tarmac with minimalls and fast-food huts, loan offices and auto repair shops, the occasional fenced enclave of sedentary mobile homes. Trailer parks in National City usually resembled municipal dumps, littered with broken lawn furniture, tires, cinder blocks, and discarded propane canisters. The Catholic churches looked like Howard Johnson's. Everything in National City teetered between the organic ugliness of poverty and the antiseptic ugliness of Target stores and McDonald's franchises.

At the so-called farewell dinner he kept his ambivalence and his recent uncustomary depression in check, though the fact that the guests barely knew one another reminded him that his social existence here had always been disjointed, a matter of part-time residence in many different worlds, and that his friendships misfitted some bold image he held of his place in the cosmos. They *were* his friends, that moment's logical handful, yet except for Robin Thompson, whom he'd known for six or seven years, they weren't the ones he'd had a year earlier, and those, in turn, hadn't been the ones he'd cultivated a year before that. People floated into his life and floated out again, no relationship stuck, as if he, or they, continually outgrew the context of his friendships. It had something to do with "young and gay." Something to do with "no socially approved structures." Your most intimate pal of a year ago might stare straight through you in a bar, and it was startling how few memories stirred in either one of you. *I used to know him* was a line people uttered all the time, without any weight or irony, meaning anything from *I slept with him once* to *He used to be my whole life*. Andrew sometimes felt like a composite of all the people he knew at a given time, a composite that turned blurry below a certain depth. As people drifted out of his ken, vital parts of himself seemed to atrophy. Jeff Trail's leaving San Diego had unnerved him, because Jeff had been his friend longer than anybody, and the fact of Jeff had long seemed proof that it was nothing specific about Andrew that made his other relationships so transitory. He'd kept up with Jeff fervidly, arranging rendezvous in San Francisco while Jeff trained in Sacramento for the California Highway Patrol, flying down to Austin with him on the job search that ultimately landed Jeff at Ferrelgas, in fucking Bloomington. It now appeared that Jeff had had it after one brutal winter in Minnesota but he hadn't told Andrew that, Andrew heard about it third-hand. Well, they had gone through a sort of estrangement. But that happened in any enduring alliance, little things built up, you had to have periodic blowups to clear away the garbage.

The restaurant had been a favorite for years. He loved the expense of it, the extravagantly fussy appearance of the entrees, loved taking military boys from the provinces there to awe their Jack in the Box taste buds with minimalist food and his knowledge of the wine list. *The grape harvest was simply ravaged in '91, premature budding in April and crippling frosts in May, hailstorms in June, then a drought, I really don't think you want the '91 Chablis. You want a '92 Cote Chalonnaise. Trust me.* He brought all sorts of people there; he tipped extravagantly and knew all the staff by name, and their deference to him made its impression on people he wanted to impress. But the place now felt eerily hollow and unreal, like a stage about to be struck, his degree of connection with it and the people working there, as well as his companions, diminishing throughout dinner. *Grilled ostrich filet with leek risotto and marsala-garlic-rosemary glaze. Organic winter greens with focaccia croutons. Baked rainbow trout layered with smoked salmon, fresh spinach, scallop mousse, and braised celery.* Teeny portions on sauce-swirled plates like miniature abstract sculptures. The menu in California Cuisine usually seemed to him unutterably soigné, but on this occasion it reminded him of the food in *American Psycho*. The blood-rare ostrich slices on his fork looked human.

Andrew had carried off endless small retouchings of his back story in the sluggish circles of Hillcrest, tinkered with his pedigree, adding daubs of racy color in its bars and restaurants, not simply to foist between himself and people he befriended a cautious distance, but also to win their acceptance, to whittle a niche in the soporific local narrative, and Andrew believed himself, believed in the multifaceted characters he incarnated. Now, oddly, he had become conscious for the first time of spawning a deception, acting a role at odds with the natural scan of his feelings, for although the occasion itself proclaimed that he was abandoning Hillcrest, the restaurant, and everyone present, a fair chance existed that his disappearance would not be the gradual vanishing they expected, mitigated by phone calls and letters and visits that wove a slender but tangible cord of continuity, there was in fact a strong possibility that he might dematerialize more unaccountably, leaving a sour reek of failure or pathetic pretense behind, the nervous breakdown mess of an adolescent who leaves home too early, bottoms out, and moves on, never retrieving his remaining stuff from the apartment on Robinson. There was the possibility that his new life might involve a transforming struggle, producing total amnesia about his old life—in other words, that Anthony the waiter, George the manager, and Kenneth and Robin and these people gathered to mark his departure would, somewhere in the middle future, *think differently* about him, perceive themselves betrayed and negated by him, unraveling his stories without generosity and citing the abandoned VCR, magazines, old bills, and dirty socks in Erik's apartment as evidence of a disordered mind, the embarrassing residue of a fucked-up loser whose whereabouts nobody knew.

He imagined desultory, late-afternoon bar chatter, the sloppy talk of people complacently going nowhere, watery happy-hour cocktails in big plastic tumblers, the sharply angled shadows on the pavement outside the bars. In the tropical anomie of this slow, easy town, Andrew DeSilva would persist as an assortment of knowing anecdotes, until the people he knew grew older and forgot about him, speculating on rare occasions when his name came up that he'd probably died. He reminded himself that dear as these people were, they did not really matter. If he walked into Flicks, or some other Hillcrest gay bar, ten years from now, he would find them exactly where he'd left them. At the so-called farewell dinner Andrew said it was a *bittersweet occasion*, said that everyone had his own ideas about him, but nobody really knew him. It was the sort of maudlin thing most people said when leaving one place for another, and nobody thought much about it at the time.

3

On the plane, flipping through a two-week-old *Time* spread on the Hale-Bopp Comet–Heaven's Gate suicides ("Special Report: Inside the Web of Death"), Andrew considered the great changes coming over him, changes that had really begun, he realized, almost a year before, when he moved into Hillcrest from Norman Blachford's condo in La Jolla. Norman had wanted him to stay, had offered to pay his tuition at UCSD, was even willing to let Andrew live by himself in the place at 100 Coast Boulevard, since Norman owned another condo just down the cliff. Norman already spent much of his time at the other place, to dilute whatever unwelcome implications the fact of them *living together* might have for Andrew, Andrew thought. The relationship didn't have a legible noun. There were delicate suggestions built into its outward presentation that Norman was Andrew's "sponsor," that Andrew was Norman's "decorator." Out of perversity Andrew later put it around that he'd left because Norman refused to buy him a Mercedes, but mainly Andrew chafed at the image of himself as a *kept boy*, an image Norman assiduously avoided making present to Andrew's mind, but one necessarily suggested to anyone who saw them together, since Norman was three decades older than Andrew and had little to recommend him besides a blandly genial personality and a large personal fortune. Andrew did not mind telling certain younger men that he *was* kept by Norman; Andrew even gave out the story that more than one rich old man paid for his favors. In New York or Los Angeles the claim that men who could afford the pick of any litter would just naturally pick him might have met with considerable skepticism, but in credulous San Diego it led people to suppose that Andrew carried a much stronger sexual charge than anyone suspected, perfumed him with a mist of sophisticated eroticism, even persuaded some who actually knew better to imagine that when Andrew's clothes came off an unexpected god of love revealed himself. On the other hand, really being bought and paid for irritated him. However generous and undemanding Norman tried to be, he took various things for granted, expected certain pleasures, needed company, wanted to arrive in distant cities, at cocktail parties, at preview evenings of philharmonic orchestras, at benefits, et cetera, as the elder member of a "couple," and this meant, of course, that Andrew was widely regarded as the colorful, surprisingly well-spoken *companion* or, among Norman's peers, after a few drinks, *trick* of Norman Blachford, a *spicy little number* in the saga of Norman Blachford, unformed youthful clay, a sunspot of carnal energy, a possession that Norman's friends Norman's age often coveted and flirted with and sometimes, behind Norman's back, made serious attempts to steal.

The vulpine attentions of this older crowd, at their Queens of Yesteryear Republican soirees in La Jolla and twee junkets to faraway capitals, gave his lack of romantic success in Hillcrest a bitter taste. Andrew could manage his role in Norman's life with the solemn poise of an undertaker, but he also needed to breathe. During his time with Norman, another myth he'd spread to make himself more alluring in Hillcrest had proven useful. There were, he told people, a wife and child in his life. As proof Andrew gingerly slid from his wallet a cropped, excessively happy-looking snapshot of LC and her first daughter, their eyes demon-red from the camera flash. LC had gone to Bishop's School with Andrew; she was the type of horsey, honey-fed fifth-generation Californian

Bishop's pretended to attract in droves, from a family full of corporate attorneys. After Bishop's she'd inherited a house in Berkeley. Andrew lived there for nearly two years as a sort of housekeeper and nanny, him and LC and LC's husband and LC's kid, part of the time holding down a clerical job at the Bank of California. For many fags a man who'd fathered kids was automatically more virile, more potently loaded with spunk than another fag. Or so many fags said. The story didn't really lure much more action Andrew's way than his occasional disclosure of multiple sugar daddies, but Norman, at least, accepted Andrew's familial obligations without question. When Andrew began slipping off on weekends to meet David Madson in San Francisco, he supposed it gave Norman a little charge to tell friends that his boyfriend was *away visiting his ex-wife and their daughter*, it had such a grown-up ring to it, and made Andrew sound such a stud.

4

The plane climbed over Serra Mesa, Tierrasanta, the Miramar Naval Air Station. Andrew knew the route: Escondido, Black Canyon, the brooding gloom of the Santa Rosa Mountains, Rancho Mirage, Indian Wells, Thousand Palms, the whole ragged canvas of weird geology between Interstate 15 and Joshua Tree, the dry alkali lakes of the Mojave. Lightning strikes in a dry lake fused the sand into glass rods. He knew the ground route, 15 to Ontario, Ontario to Victorville, Victorville to Barstow, Barstow to Vegas. He knew the ground route and the dry lakes on the Nevada side, because the Nevada dry lakes were smack in the middle of the underground testing range where Pete, his father, worked as a paramedic the year before they moved to Bonita. If you were right there at the site, a fifty-megaton event caused localized ground disturbance roughly equal to a magnitude 5 quake. Interstate 8 or the 10 would get you to Scottsdale and Phoenix, places he knew because of Norman and couldn't feature going back to, desert necropolises verdant with aqueduct water and full of retired opera queens. He had "adored" the Southwest on first exposure, when things with Norman seemed to be leading somewhere hopeful. The banality felt extreme enough to qualify as exotica. But the desert excited his allergies. The queens told the same Lenny Bernstein stories at every party. There was too much flocked wallpaper in Scottsdale, too many escritoires tucked in cerise-painted alcoves. Too many Met souvenir programs and playbills from the original Broadway productions of *House of Flowers*, *Sweet Bird of Youth*, and *I Can Get It for You Wholesale*. Too many Japanese fans under glass, jade elephants on Stickley sideboards, too many turquoise-and-silver bracelets. The redemptive irony never surfaced. *Scottsdale leisure lifestyles* had pretty much been Norman's thing when Andrew met him, *keeping active in the golden years*, not that there was anything besides beach to distinguish La Jolla from Scottsdale in the leisure lifestyles department. It was all money and it was all good and it was all boring as hell if you stopped to think about it. The great advantage of life with Norman, for a while, was that Andrew didn't have to think about it; it had been an easy, floaty time filled with soft, pleasant sensations, as nuanced and meaningless as the surface of a stalagmite.

He could not, in fact, recall a specific turning point when the spell broke (though Andrew collected "turning points," recounted them gravely in heart-to-heart conversations—*The real turning point for me was getting involved in AIDS prevention work,* Andrew might say, or *I think Iran-Contra was a major turning point for a lot of people*; in spells of fabulism it might be *The big turning point was when we left Israel*), only a scattering of discomforting moments: an evening in Seattle when he found his eyes following a boy much younger than himself in company with a man much older than Norman, and realized that he'd said *After all, there's nothing wrong with being taken care of* as often as he'd heard it. Or the parties where Andrew and his "age group" milled around in brittle camaraderie, drinking and nibbling canapés on the fringes of conversations about the prime rate and where the NASDAQ had closed that afternoon, conversations that, unlike gab about politics or the World Cup or where to buy Cuban cigars in Vancouver, excluded the young and charming as firmly as such talk in a different setting would freeze out wives, mistresses, or hookers. You were never to know too precisely where the money came from or how it circulated and accrued, though Norman, from time to time, did mention his business ventures, the sound abatement company he'd sold off in Arizona, or the balance of stocks and bonds in his portfolio. At the parties, though, money spoke a secret language, a crisp Masonic shorthand that Andrew couldn't follow without egregious effort. Like fault lines, all the vectors of money connected deep down in the earth's roiling magma, soybean futures and silver prices and light sweet crude oil from the North Sea, IBM and Microsoft and merging pharmaceutical conglomerates, ten-year treasury notes, currency valuations, short-term parking areas for cash; housing starts and unemployment figures and corporate earning reports and Alan Greenspan swam around in this linguistic broth while waiters plied the rooms with trays of tapas or dim sum and newly popped bottles of Mumm or, on a lucky night, Veuve Clicquot, in which case the trays would feature Sevruga and toast points. The young men he was thrown in with on these occasions followed sports, and Tommy Hilfiger, and TV shows like *Seinfeld*. They tracked the careers of certain actresses with an avidity verging on desperation. They read novels by Anne Rice and amused themselves by casting the movie versions. They were studying to become "professionals" in one field or another in the middle future, invariably something lucrative and unimaginative that required computer fluency and reflexive avarice. Andrew hated everything they liked, and sometimes unsettled them by smuggling the details of some sensational murder or the finer points of *Pulp Fiction* or *Shaft's Big Score* into the conversation. "He's a sweet guy," they reported later to their patrons, "but he sure has kind of a morbid sense of humor."

5

The geography of the Manson Family unfurled beneath the clouds, somewhere high in the Panamints. Andrew was born the year of helter skelter, the year when Squeaky Fromme and Sandra Good and Leslie Van Houten and Patricia Krenwinkle scrambled around Death Valley looking for the omphalos, the bottomless hole in the earth, churning up dust storms in chop-shop dune buggies. Wherever Andrew went to school, wherever the family moved, there had always turned out to be, maybe five streets away, or four seats back in English class, somewhere in the immediate region, an unlikely person who was nebulously related to someone who'd been in the Manson Family, someone with vague bloodlines to a wayward dentist's daughter or the son of a preacher man run awry. People then believed in utopia, he'd seen some modest residue of long-ago idealism in the parents of his friends, their political opinions, streaks of it anyway. Andrew thought you could tell how someone voted by their choice of an olive or a beige refrigerator, but when he watched the parole hearings of Van Houten and Krenwinkle on afternoon TV, their descriptions of a world many people had thought possible—not bloody-brained Manson himself, but the dippy Love Children he'd harvested off the streets of San Francisco and LA—corresponded to nothing he knew. Andrew found the sixties almost unimaginable. His parents had obviously missed the fun parts of their own youth, despite his mother Maryann's claim that Pete had been a great dancer, like she was some kind of expert. When other people were snapping the chains of received ideas, his parents' minds had contracted instead of expanded. The family's houses were solemn and hushed and haunted by Jesus Christ and his sour blessings. A palpable depression lodged deep in his parents' marriage like a petrified cyst. His father had gone to Vietnam, an Asian fighting other Asians. *Twenty-three years in the US Navy your father and this is the miserable thanks he gets*, Maryann waving the first of the pension checks signed over by power of attorney. After they moved from the Rancho Bernardo house to the Rancho Bernardo condo overlooking the golf course. The affordable condo in the not-so-great part of Rancho Bernardo that was going to be as good as it was ever going to get. However opaque Vietnam might have been to millions of college students, Pete had viewed it as an opportunity; in some skewed way it advanced the status of Filipino-Americans, or one particular

Filipino-American, anyway. The irony was that Pete was now back in Plaridel with his thirteen siblings gibbering in Tagalog and had been for years, skipping out after Andrew's first year at UCSD. Pete figured he'd done his paternal duty, hung in there long enough, all he could say about it now was "I married the wrong gal," kind of a pathetic statement in view of the facts. In his second or third year at Bishop's, Andrew's suspicion that his father was a loser turned into a depressing certainty, long before Pete got caught with his hand in the till at his brokerage job, sold the houses, and signed over the pension, leaving them with a view of the golf course and no prospects.

Andrew started to see, all those years ago at Bishop's, the toilsome upward lurch into upper-middle-classdom and Pete's little ventures along the way—the pedigree-dog-breeding idea, the at-home used-car dealership—as exercises in futility, even though they brought in cash, because Pete, whatever he did, was always going to bump his head on a pretty low glass ceiling, master's in business administration notwithstanding. Other Filipinos became doctors or lawyers and for them the money never dried up, but Pete had worked his *ass* off becoming an amorphous nothing, and one day, Andrew knew, everything would come crashing down, and eventually everything did. *I'm too old to go to jail*, famous last words.

The illumination didn't make him love Pete less. He began to love his father differently. Protectively, melancholically. Before he was even noticeably in the world, Andrew had the aching sense of a world already lost. His father became small and vulnerable and touchingly deluded, a tough guy in a small grifter's universe. Andrew began separating himself from what he saw as a specifically Filipino fate, assembling a new background from what he read in books and saw around him. The world of difference between *Hispanic* and *Spanish*, between *Filipino Roman Catholic* and *Sephardic Jew*, well, it didn't take extravagant subterfuge to morph from one thing into the other, a piece at a time, if you had the brains to back it up, to supply the right detail at the telling moment. It helped to study people, learn their interests, make the conversations about *them*. He learned that flattery will get you anywhere with nine persons out of ten, and it cost you nada, zip, *rien*. A time came when he could walk into any rich-kid-from-Bishop's house and have nobody notice the slightest resemblance between himself and the Filipino maid.

Not that people *asked* about things like that, in La Jolla they didn't, in La Jolla people *assumed* things, or didn't assume them. The trick was to slip the right assumptions into people's minds and neutralize the wrong ones before they found occasion to be curious. In San Diego you were generally all right, and would never be questioned about anything, if people assumed you had money. You could say you were a Saudi prince or the man who invented Chia pets if the money was there; if the money talked out of your clothes and your table manners, no one ever raised an eyebrow. Later, when Andrew traveled, he realized that people in other cities often asked what you did for a living, whereas San Diegans never did. The more pointedly idle you were in San Diego, the more other people took your success for granted. It was a city where the retirement age could be twenty-five—maybe you'd worked out some software for Bill Gates, or parlayed a modest inheritance into an equities fortune. A little older, you were maybe retired from the marines or the regular navy. Or just got handed everything at birth, like LC. Among many strata of San Diego society, the work ethic was viewed as an amusing aberration. People went to the office out of some perverse lack of interest in golf, or surfing, or betting on the World Cup.

6

Inside the Heaven's Gate web of death was this Marshall Applewhite geek who segued from musical theater ingénue to messianic cult leader and called himself Do or Bo, ruling over intergalactic phenomena with a bulldyke registered nurse named Peep who died of cancer, and a cabal of flauntingly insipid followers, reminiscent of opossums and other small-brained creatures stunned by onrushing headlights, some of whom "had chosen to have their vehicles neutered." Andrew had to wonder what that signified, a polar reversal of the sixties, apparently. Instead of controlling people's minds through desublimation, sucking and fucking all day until their boundaries dissolved, Do turned them into castrati and gave them a minute-by-minute schedule for every little activity, a kind of *Good Housekeeping* version of S&M, and in Rancho Santa Fe, no less, in what *Time* called a "mansion," but from the pictures looked like the dormitory of a third-string business college, with a tidy, sneakered corpse in every bunk bed. In the spooked-looking video still of Do that *Time* had used for the cover, the green was dripping out of his corneas and changing into mascara. The kind of face you'd see on LSD. Pete was into some Weird God trip too, had segued after his troubles began from devout and unreflective Catholicism to a more energized and inchoate mysticism. He believed in something called the Great White Brotherhood of Ascended Masters, followers of a violet flame said to have originated on

Mount Shasta. Andrew had scanned the literature, which included volumes on the "missing years" of Jesus and related arcana. The Brotherhood worshipped a Ron Hubbard type named Elizabeth Clare Prophet, who'd moved the cult from California to Montana on some astral real-estate tip. Exactly how the violet flame had leaped the Pacific to the Philippines Andrew didn't know, contagion of madness no doubt. Yet Andrew could, with certain psychic gyrations, set his own mind shunting along supernatural routes. In the Philippines he'd sometimes heard voices and seen flaming icons in his mind, Technicolor scenes from the Bible, a whole panoply of arguably psychotic, somatized data that briefly inspired him with the notion of remaining in the islands as a missionary. Over there they had what Andrew called *Catholicism Super Unleaded* anyway, an infectious blurring of faith into everyday drama—mass sightings of the Virgin, weekly episodes of stigmata, and holy water cancer cures. Every capsized ferry and typhoon was laid out in the Book of Revelations as plainly as a turd in a toilet bowl. The irony of belonging to something called the Great White Brotherhood was wasted on Pete, the line being that *white* referred to a shimmering nimbus around Jesus Christ rather than the pigmentation of the Saved. Elizabeth Clare Prophet looked a little bit like Rue McClanahan, Andrew's favorite Golden Girl. Marshall Applewhite looked like the kind of old fag who sometimes drank in The Caliph in San Diego, a particular kind of weatherbeaten, alcoholic fag who wore very long hair, always blond, who you could tell wore it long thinking it gave a sassy androgynous pizzazz to an ancient pitted face: the World's Oldest Whore look. "The religious impulse sometimes thrives on false sentiment," the Heaven's Gate article concluded. "In its search for meaning, the mind is apt to go down some wrong paths, and to mistake its own reflection for the face of God." Andrew just loved *Time*speak. It said so much about everything while explaining absolutely nothing. Andrew's personal bouts of religious effulgence had never been a search for meaning but rather the opposite, flights from making sense of things. Because the true meaning to be found in a cold examination of one's life is the unbearable fact that life is meaningless.

They gave you something like a meal on the flight, a gray knob of beef that slid apart at the touch of a plastic fork, surrounded by tasteless carrots. Andrew normally blanched at inferior food because of contaminants, but airplane food, he thought, went through some sterilizing ray or intense heating process that killed all bacteria along with all nutrients. He drank two Stoli miniatures over ice. He didn't want to arrive hungry, or needing a drink, or off his rhythm in any way. Even though what he hoped to accomplish remained fuzzy he knew equilibrium was essential, he'd been weighing the pros and cons of telling David things about himself that had to be presented calmly, and the more difficult part would be fielding David's reactions, overcoming whatever problems were thrown up by his own candor, resigning himself, if he had to, to intricate repair work on their relationship. So many harsh decisions, so many ways of being hopeless, Andrew kept having to leap across a sinkhole of greasy feelings to stay on his feet. He wondered if the type of confession he contemplated making to David would work for him if he heard it from someone else, and reckoned he'd never quite been in the same position with anyone else that he was in with David.

7

Andrew tried to focus on the here and now, but since here and now wasn't anywhere, exactly, he sank again into reverie. *Merger of Nynex and Bell Atlantic Clears US Hurdle.* Utah or Colorado below, CNN on the video projector, a dinosaur fossil from China on the front page of the *Times. Trial Begins in the Oklahoma City Bombing Case.* When he left Norman, he moved into a hotel-style rooming house on University and then moved in with Erik Greenman, part-time porn star, a.k.a. Josh Connors, *who gets as good as he gives,* it said on a box cover, *in this kissing, cocksucking, toe licking, and ass-eating fuckfest from All Worlds Video,* around the corner from his favorite places: Rich's, Flicks, the Obelisk Bookstore, California Cuisine. He'd never lived with someone who wasn't financially symbiotic in some way. Things felt teetery and Andrew knew he'd reached another "turning point." There was the negative shift in his finances, Norman's four thou a month no longer coming in, and he knew he'd miscalculated or more simply not thought about how things would be when he ran through his credit and the money he'd made selling his Infiniti, that it was all expenditure and no income, *not good.* On the counter side, far more crucially, his consciousness had started expanding. Way beyond what it had been. His whole being became energized, almost radiant with possibilities. It was now a matter of selecting what to do, where to channel the unbelievable fertility of his brain.

He knew that outwardly this inner growth, accelerating throughout the fall and winter, appeared to be simple weight gain and too much drinking and sudden bursts of ill temper. At times he'd fallen prey to self-pity, for instance moaning (half comically, he hoped) to some of his bar mates that nobody wanted to date him. An old rival in Numbers, hearing this, japed that on the contrary Andrew looked extremely dated to him, and this of course got back to him, and stung. He had numerous violent mood swings and even assaulted a few people in an ambiguously playful manner, and these episodes puzzled him afterwards, as if someone else had stepped into his body for a time while he hovered outside it. He told himself these were queasy side effects of a dramatic positive change. You couldn't evolve without pain and strangeness. The fact that he *could* drink after years of ordering cranberry juice in bars, decanting the morose and angry sides of his nature, was actually an improvement over his former compulsive, downer-induced sanguinity, more honest—you couldn't be *on* twenty-four hours a day, unless you took crystal, and then you rode the drug to a world-annihilating crash. He was becoming who he really was, unlocking his vast potential while riding out the wiggy parts like a captive spectator.

Andrew had goofed a little with testosterone, shooting it into a muscle every three days using squeezed-out insulin IVs he'd written up as damaged inventory and pocketed from Thrifty years ago. You were supposed to build on the steroid effect by pumping iron at the gym, and he'd been so busy wooing David and scoping out his prospects in San Francisco that he'd found no time in March or April to work out. Two or three tennis games with Bruce from the bookstore hadn't dented his flab. The hormones made him puffy and bleary-looking, his nuts had shrunk a little, what of it, he pictured him and David laughing about it, when they'd been truly together for a while, heard David solemnly telling him, *My love for you isn't based on what you look like*, as if Andrew didn't know. *At least not entirely*, David might add, cracking them both up.

When he thought about how it would finally be with David, all these transient worries about money and where and how to live shrank to their proper, tiny dimensions. He'd released his feelings in discreet bursts, in the margins of postcards, sometimes wistfully, sometimes with jokey bravura, as a charm against rejection. In Los Angeles, David had vetoed most of Andrew's sexual agenda, but *not all of it*. David needed Andrew's steadfast influence to really open the floodgates. Andrew now felt it was time to step into the full role of lover. He felt a tenderness so implacable that it swept aside all the obstacles presented by David's life in Minneapolis: his job, his friends, the damned neurotic dog he was so attached to. The dog could stay, he supposed, he'd pampered Erik Greenman's Rottweiler long enough without bashing its brains in, had even cooked dinners for Erik Greenman's Rottweiler, had even told people he'd miss Erik Greenman's Rottweiler more than anything else in San Diego—in a way it was true, Andrew was always good with people's dogs and people's children, it bonded him in a fairly direct way to the people themselves, and yet he felt jealous of the dogs, the children, these creatures that were never judged, never tested on their morals or whatever, yes, David's dog could stay, but the rest of it had to go, he decided. It would be a matter of helping David see these attachments as transient and somewhat beneath his potential. David *malingered* in Minneapolis, Andrew thought, to be close to his roots in Wisconsin, yet David was almost as estranged from his family as Andrew was from his. No doubt David made the best of a second-rate situation, scaling the ladder at John Ryan Co. several rungs at a time, but the whole package was provincial, in some respects perilously close to pathetic—for instance, David's attempts to cultivate an edgy cachet by dating black guys. Andrew figured David's black thing was his way of tweaking Minneapolis's vaunted liberalism. Andrew didn't consider these black boyfriends any real threat, maybe they provided a certain sexual novelty, but David tired of them quickly. The only semi-long-term one, Rob Davis, who'd gotten on Andrew's nerves back in January, was already history. He remembered catching that smug bastard trying to dish him to Jeff Trail, and the guilty look on Jeff's face when Andrew stepped between them. Jeff had been saying something about *law enforcement*, Rob Davis had rolled his eyes. Andrew wiped the memory away with a pleasanter image of David naked, handcuffed and hog-tied in the Chateau Marmont, David begging *Popi* to do ... whatever.

8

The past scrambled when he searched it out, moments lay in shadow or evaporated like mirages on Interstate 10. Somewhere he'd been marked, somewhere in the vanished narrative he'd learned a guilty secret, one that at first seemed a faint hairline fracture in his sense of belonging to this family, these people, he did not know why it was a secret, or how he'd recognized it as such. It could've been the way familiar gestures of affection were that taught him he couldn't stare, couldn't touch, couldn't smile a certain way at certain things. He recalled in a general way a thousand little incidents of cruelty but could not bring a single one into focus. As far back as memory would go, he'd been suspected of things never named in his presence, by playmates and playmates' parents and relatives and his sisters and brother and his parents, too, suspicion leaked from people like gas, it flashed in an adult's glance, a child's giggle, filled strained silences in a room, suspicion struck and moved on, slashed without lingering to watch the wound it opened bleed. Since he was a small child he was suspected before he himself knew, became complicit with the suspicion aimed at him and tried to deflect it onto others, though without the conviction of instinct, the names that were chanted had a different flavor in his mouth, the mocking gestures and knowing signals of eyes and mouths, the whole repertoire of exclusion resisted his attempts to reproduce it, he simply wasn't mean enough or thoughtless enough or normal enough to grasp the point of making another person feel like shit, like a freak, like a queer.

9

In a recurring dream, they still occupied the house on North U Avenue, two blocks east of the 805 overpass, a neighborhood of Mexicans and Filipinos. There were also a few white families that had skidded off the Monopoly board into the darker regions of the golden dream. Some of the houses had fences and lawns and some had wan little gardens or trellises of bougainvillea and some were painted candy pink or apple green and they all had ten-year-old cars patched with primer in the driveways and bald patches of dirt in the yards. At certain hours you could smell which kind of people lived where by the odors on the sidewalk, at their place you'd smell spaghetti sauce or cabbage or chicken adobo. It didn't look like a slum to the untrained eye, California slums never do, but the dream brought back the suffocated atmosphere of life under a bell jar, whiffs of mildew and dog poop out back, a sandbox he'd played in forever until one day he didn't. Pete had built a tree house in one of the pepper trees, with a trapdoor, that became a spaceship speeding above the earth, the deck of an ocean liner, the home they would live in in a new life. In the tree house, he saw how scary everything down on the ground was, how frozen in place by gravity and habit the forms of life and relationships were. He didn't have words for his intuitions.

Pete built and fixed things in the dream, not as he often really had wreaked improvements on their houses, but in a trance of incessant repair, as if the house were a leaking dike or a flooding riverbank, its structure continually battered by calamity. He nailed up rooms inside rooms, sawed passages in walls, dug hurricane basements and bomb shelters under the crawl space. He strewed accordion-wire barricades around the property, which was menaced by wild beasts—coyotes, mountain lions, feral dogs, rattlers, rabid skunks, an especially plentiful type of evil goat, sometimes sightless zombies that would chomp your arm off. The house kept expanding, closets were suddenly discovered to be hidden entrances to vast mirrored chambers, whole uncharted wings of the house opened up and routinely caved in, cutting him off from the others, trapping him in mazes of underground tunnels that sometimes turned into regular streets and minimalls and parts of the Hotel Del in Coronado, famed for its Christmas lights and Marilyn Monroe. Things broke for no reason, picture frames shattered by themselves, tables and chairs collapsed mysteriously. Playing cards changed into photographs, photographs turned into landscapes, the sodden palmy archipelagos his father came from or places shown on television wracked by typhoons and amazing floods. In the dream, he was *not suspected of anything* and they were safe there. Not all the time, for peril was the very substance of the dream, but dangers always neutralized themselves and melted into happiness.

The actual house on North U Avenue was laid out in such a way that people moved in it guardedly, with a ceremonial avoidance of ruckus and noise, no stampeding feet on the stairwell, no arguments above a certain decibel, Maryann had "nerves," the way richer women had "migraines," but the house itself dampened any nerve-challenging exuberance, an obdurate sullenness had soaked into the walls and the molding, only a certain kind of statement ever occurred to anyone inside that house, words of a measured inflection, a studied weightlessness. Warm colors registered as gray. The rooms did not get light and were full of sad objects, chairs covered in abrasive fabrics, loud ceramic lamps, melancholy knickknacks his mother used to "brighten" things. Little sculptural displays of her feelings, devotional or maternal, set on tables and shelves over discs of artificial lace. Like all American living rooms, theirs was never lived in, and when it was, a forced gloomy festiveness agitated its dead air, enervated its dull surfaces, birthdays and Christmases cranked up its deadness into a rhapsody of alienation, gifts given in that room invariably revealed what utter strangers they all really were to one another. Somehow the right gift, the actually-wished-for gift, revealed this more powerfully than the absolutely wrong or unwanted gift. The right gift was the one you thought you wanted and the way you thought was always wrong. Had the others really felt this, had he felt it himself as early as that? Andrew couldn't be sure, couldn't be sure they'd ever found all these things painful or even that *he* had before he knew himself different than them. He had always dissembled his unhappiness and assumed that they had, dissembled to the same degree, but perhaps they couldn't recognize unhappiness in themselves or maybe religion or an unbroken sense of belonging made them give the horror a bright remedial twist.

His mother's voice droned through all the rooms, like the gurgle of plumbing, the plash of Moorish waterworks, inexorable, tireless, as if her ability to talk renewed its surprise for her with every sentence. *My Andrew*, Maryann called in the dream, for he had always been hers, their attachment a fierce, clinging, almost desperate business quite different from the proprietary emotions she directed at the others, my Andrew, believe it or not, six years old and he reads the entire Bible. Maryann saw portents in every small manifestation of intellect, Chris and Elena and Regina were more your average kids, not dumb by any means, but none of them a brain like Andrew. The last baby she would have, apotheosis of yearning. Not just her baby but their baby, cynosure of their collective eyes, the science project they were all collaborating on. He had not in fact read the Bible all through, he'd skimmed for the good parts after the point in Genesis where Uz, Hul, Gether, and Mash are enumerated as the sons of Aram, he could not care less who begat whom *ad nauseum*. He memorized, recited proudly for visitors, things like *Thou didst make my enemies turn their backs to me,* other people's attention ran through him like electricity, *and those who hated me I destroyed.* To be gazed at in wonder gave him delicious feelings. *They cried for help, but there was none to save.* The crude awe of his family would eventually serve as antidote to their suspicion. *They cried to the Lord, but he did not answer them.* He had the precocious wisdom not to recite the passages he most often puzzled over, which ran more to things like, *If a man has an emission of semen; he shall bathe his whole body in water, and be unclean until the evening. And every garment and every skin on which the semen comes shall be washed with water, and be unclean until the evening.* The power of Maryann's longing made it easy to confuse this gifted child with Jesus among the learned men, whatever that was, some faded oleograph or prayer card from Sicily or Manila where Teenage Jesus confounded the Syrian soothsayers or Roman philosophers or what have you, great things of a Christ-like prodigality would emanate, from Andrew Phillip Cunanan one way or another, when you looked at it squarely this kid's presence had a miraculous quality, consider the time Chris opened the encyclopedia at random, What's Bolivia, he says, Andrew tells him Bolivia, an inland republic of South America, once a part of the Spanish vice-royalty of Peru and known as the province of Charcas, or Upper Peru. It is the third largest political division of the continent, and extends, approximately, from nine degrees forty-four minutes to twenty-two degrees fifty minutes south latitude, and from fifty-eight degrees to seventy degrees west longitude. Okay, what's *Bourse*, Bourse, the French equivalent of the stock exchange, *Borelli*, Giovanni Alfonso, 1608–1679, Italian physiologist and physicist, *Bore*, a high tidal wave rushing up a narrow estuary or tidal river. *Borku*, a region of Central Africa, *Boris* Federovich Godunov, tsar of Muscovy, *Brigandage, Barratry, Bismuthite*, the list goes on and on. A kid with this type of potential is truly a gift from God, no two ways about it, you don't deprive a child who has these startling capacities, you are really just a caretaker for a higher power and have to ride with the punches.

With the launching of this myth that he had read and comprehended all fifteen hundred pages of their tattered Old and New Testaments and had a whole encyclopedia lodged in his brain, a myth that seemed to spring from Maryann's peculiar optimism and spread through the family like influenza, Andrew began shaping himself in the form of other people's desires. He was tender and vulnerable with his sisters, who protected him out in the world and treated him with the elaborate care and curiosity a young girl might devote to a miniature, malleable replica of her father. With Christopher he became the smaller, weaker adversary who outwitted his gentle boxlike opponent in games of combat. Andrew transformed them. The slightly different characters he incarnated subtly coaxed them into roles they were destined to play. Gradually the roles became their personalities. Caring for this strange special child made them ordinary in their own eyes, destined for the ordinary varieties of fate. Andrew secretly felt more like a girl than a boy. He experienced a confused thrill glimpsing Chris's balls where the legs of his shorts made gaps. His femininity was read as the normal delicacy of vast brainpower. When he realized that Chris's body arrested his gaze and stirred inchoate wishes to see and smell and taste the unmentionable mystery of various parts, he stopped letting Chris wrestle him or hoist him around on his shoulders, afraid his little prick would stiffen as it had started regularly to do, and expose his secret.

He had his face in a book every possible minute, but books consumed him quite aside from curiosity because the printed word obliterated the house on North U Avenue and its intricate tensions, removed him to a place where his family was not an assortment of competing expectations but a warm ball of fuzzy feeling in the next room. His brain became an independent country they knew less and less about as time went on. Maryann and Pete shared practically nothing, the house was a minefield of unacknowledged problems, but both held in awe "education" and the advantages it supposedly brought. This obscured Andrew's withdrawal from family life behind his bedroom door—he was, after all, *in there reading his books*—a withdrawal he further veiled with brief but unctuous displays of affection. He refined the actor's craft, projecting a sensuous warmth disconnected from his feelings, a warmth he poured more generously as people became transparent and vaguely repellent. He did not know why any of this was happening to him. He felt important and worthless, invisible one minute and the center of all life the next. He sensed that he could overturn everything, destroy the whole structure, just by speaking in his real voice the things he had hidden in his mind. His voice froze in his throat. He did not want such obscene power over everything but feared that its absence would erase him. He swallowed it and kept it inside him and waited for fate to reveal its purpose.

In the dream, they had never moved from the house on North U Avenue. Somehow Bonita hadn't happened, Rancho Bernardo hadn't happened. The money hadn't come and gone, Pete hadn't run out on them, Chris and Elena and Gina had stayed on there with him and his mother and father. They'd all grown up and gotten married and stayed there growing old, trapped like fossils in the sad rooms.

10

Childhood friends: Once he showed me their backyard out his bedroom window they had Venetian type blinds out there it was almost all dirt Andrew said it was where his father did target practice for the Philippine Mafia you know every kid makes up stories I don't know what his father did but he told me it was Special Ops he'd somewhere picked up that phrase reading a book on the CIA as far as I know his dad worked at the amphibian base or whatever you call it in Coronado Andrew had two sisters his brother must have been in high school or left home by then I remember the mother all the time going to church we would see her at the bus stop I think we were five six seven years old who remembers that far back I do remember him wearing dress slacks really what I would call dress clothes all the time the button shirts the ties particular about his shoes you never saw him with sneakers on and very conscious of things like how his hair was parted and fussy about his clothes and Andrew spoke very very correctly always extremely polite and a little standoffish or snobbish I recall but sweet too in a way always interested in you what you were doing oh also a collie I think they had two dogs a collie and some other kind that were their dogs and their dad had a kennel at one point selling dogs breeding dogs I seem to well vaguely dogs barking a lot and the mother you know it was generally known I think if he had been out playing the minute he came home it was all who were you with where were you playing what did you do this that and the other questioning him on every trivial little thing just incredibly overprotective possessive in that way you often hear about and even at that age I think she drove him crazy this shy little boy she um combed his hair in front of his friends straightened his cuffs or his collar he could never walk past her without her grabbing him and fussing she dragged him to church practically every day I think he found that environment completely stifling he just uh withdrew into his imagination with all his stories and so on because I think he couldn't stand it really.

11

Maryann came from Hornell, New York, and still she had a Sicilian accent. By the time he entered the scene, Maryann's lift didn't seem to reach the top floor; they soon had a Japanese nanny, Mrs. Miki Brown, to help hold things together. Maryann was sensitive, she viewed Andrew as sensitive too, a fragile prodigy, *My Andrew, he's such a quiet kid, so well-behaved, Pete never has to raise his hand.* By the time they moved to Bonita, he'd become a cult, an object of reverence, bright as no one before had been bright, Andrew's "giftedness" was a capital investment, like the hunting dogs and holding on to the property in Bonita after they moved to Rancho Bernardo, the Little Prince, *I have to make the Prince his French toast*, sometimes *little monkey*, when he got into Chris's stuff Chris called him things like *dickweed*, but he was mainly *the Prince*, or *Schmoo*. Gina named him Schmoo one day and it stuck. Schmoos were these cuddly creatures in the *Li'l Abner* funny strip shaped like hams or bowling pins, all eyes and hairs, that sporadically poured into Dogpatch like manna. The hillbillies of Dogpatch kept them as pets because schmoos gave so much affection, and when food got scarce Mammy Yokum or Daisy Mae might slice the hindquarter off a schmoo and throw it on the frying pan. Love and sacrifice weirdly went together, if people loved you they might eat you, look at Jesus, the love of Jesus could lift any soul and cleanse any sin, Jesus had to be the schmoo of schmoos and every Sunday at St. Rose of Lima in Chula Vista they ate His body and drank His blood, the highest love obviously involved cannibalism on some level, *Accipite, et manducate ex hoc omnes: Hoc est enim Corpus meum*, love meant giving and giving and Andrew gave. He watched and listened and figured out what other people wanted him to be, and became the particular Andrew each one wanted. It was his way of making himself adorable and it was their way of eating the schmoo.

12

Childhood friends: Andrew always had nice clothes, nice shoes, brand-name clothing, he'd let you know he had on a Polo shirt, a tie from Brooks Brothers, this is a little kid we're talking about, if you went over there you saw by the way they all were with him the sisters particularly he was treated as special, he was in a special preschool program which, this is so long ago, El Toro Tiny Tots, and after that the enrichment program at Sunnyside Elementary, kind of an emphasis on audiovisual I mean in the enrichment no computer instruction was a few years down the road, more like closed-circuit learning programs, wore his hair kind of, like a shag, dark curly hair, it's strange to remember this but he had beautiful hands, really delicate little hands and pale little nails he talked with his hands all the time so you noticed the hands, I guess his mom was Italian so, the father was only there on weekends, he, am I thinking he worked in Nevada? Something in Clark County, some paramedical, out on the testing range, I can't remember if Andrew ever told me, a Chevy Vega station wagon comes to mind, funny I even can—the hands if you were hearing music he'd conduct the orchestra he knew who people like Andre Previn were he'd talk about paintings in the San Diego Museum can you see this tiny kid who isn't even this tall talking all about I don't know what Monet or Expressionism Renoir Picasso I was baffled by Andrew to tell you the

God's honest truth where he got his information about things I never heard of at that age but there was something I don't want to say sad because he wasn't sad he was just the opposite but kind of I can't think of the word like what some kids will do to try to get accepted by their peers or whatever is like baffle them with bullshit which isn't the best way because one day somebody is going to know a little more than you do if you see what I mean, and they're not really accepted that way anyway, I mean in California, a place like Bonita, it's not as if brains, you've got the beach and the mountains and the whole car culture lifestyle the emphasis is more outdoorsy, this region, it's surfers, it's horses, it's windsailing on the bay, it's Jet Skis, what kind of car, not at that age, but in terms of status, like bragging about your older brothers and sisters and you'll do the same in a few years, get the same goodies, the same cars, I know he got picked on in preschool kids threw sand on him in the schoolyard his sister Gina was always coming down to sit with him at recess he was just incredibly passive and never fought back, that was in El Toro not in Sunnyside I think more than anything Andrew got confused when people didn't just love him other kids in that situation he just didn't know how to handle himself, were there racial tensions I don't think so, I mean definitely not, I mean who knows he certainly never said anything to me, I know it's politically correct to always bring that up in a case like this, but I mean, it's not like their family is black or anything, it was like with the Mexicans, I don't mean in National City because there you know you have a preponderance of ethnic but take an area like Bonita or parts of Chula Vista some Mexicans are Mexicans and some are Mexican-American, you have the border fifteen miles away so there's plenty of Mexicans speaking Spanish all the time and being Mexican I mean really living the Mexican lifestyle twenty in the apartment or what have you lots of illegals and there, believe me, you do get some prejudice from various segments don't forget San Diego spelled backwards is Orange County whereas Filipinos, well yes you do find some attitudes because so many people in Bonita have Filipinos working in their houses so you tend to find stereotypes along the lines of Japanese make the best gardeners and et cetera although at that point actually the Japanese owned every major building in downtown San Diego but Andrew, it was a mixed family anyway, his eyes maybe his eyes looked a little Oriental I should say Asian from a certain angle but from what little I know that was never a problem.

13

There was never enough that was truly first-class. Never a snap-shot you could take that said *this really hangs together*. Pete was going to get it for them, the golden life, though as it turned out Pete's clock was ticking, Pete's involvement had a hidden expira-tion date. Maryann did the best she could with the money Pete brought in, which was plenty, really. Other people's money, as it turned out, but what the hell. For years, Pete had clung to some stubborn Filipino ideas and harsh old-fashioned village notions of family, ridiculously strict about Elena's dating and curfew and grounding the kids on the faintest pretext. Now he decided if they were Americans they ought to live like Americans, not permissive per se, not bringing up the spoiled brats that you see in the media and what have you, but keeping both eyes on the main chance and making less fuss over trivia. In this age of Reagan, only a deaf dumb and blind person couldn't clean up. Maryann liked this shift, she noted that modern American kids needed certain sybaritic evidence of their families doing well, needed to dress hip, Chris should be allowed to grow his hair long, they pick things up from the television, they see things at school, what can you do? Andrew has more feminine hormones, he can't be expected to play rough, go out for sports, look how advanced he is, these books, *The White Notebook* by Andre Gide, *The House of the Seven Gables*, way beyond me, *The World According to Garp*. Andrew needs to develop his mind, Pete easily saw the sense of that, Andrew was his favorite anyway from day one. When this child came, the mother had so many problems, Pete picked him up and held him at three A.M. if he cried, changed the diapers. Mrs. Brown helped of course but she wasn't full-time, wasn't live-in. Pete had never been physical with the other kids but in this case, with the mom so often disabled, the hugs and what have you that every child needs, for a long time, Pete had to do that and therefore the strong bonding between them and so on. Plus Pete sometimes was very strict with the others but never with Andrew, Andrew never made trouble anyway, and when he did, you could see it was bad influences, other kids, behavior he picked up, monkey see monkey do type of behavior he really wasn't responsible for.

But never quite enough stuff, never a completed picture, even when everyone had what he needed, even when there was plenty of what people wanted, when every kid for example had a new car, certain other things were missing. If the point was to move out of National City, in Bonita they didn't have the horses or the swimming pool that people who really belonged in Bonita just naturally had. The tackiness of North U Avenue fell away, but it left holes. You couldn't have the best of everything because the best of everything cost millions. In Rancho Bernardo there was even less than there had been in Bonita, if you looked closely, less furniture in the house, less atmosphere, less this, less that. There seemed to be more, but there was actually less. And the lack wasn't money really but some failure of daily living to cohere, a failure of plans to materialize. It was as if moving to these places made it easier to pretend they had always lived in similar places, that enough was just around the corner and not an impossibly long way off, yet some key little piece of the puzzle remained missing. It didn't bother Chris or Elena or Gina, and, in fact, they seemed unaware of it, same thing with his parents. Andrew always got a little more, usually a lot more than anybody else, yet he was the one who saw that there wasn't enough, that the whole thing did not hold together, that everybody had missed the expiration date so clearly stamped on the package.

14

A childhood friend: I remember he came to my house and got upset because we didn't have any Perrier, which, if you're thirteen, Perrier is like Alka-Seltzer, I thought that was, you know, pretty bizarre, Andrew always projected the image that he came from a wealthy family, he'd do anything to be one up on everybody else, he was the most status-conscious person I've ever known in my life, he was the type if everybody else put pennies in their penny loafers Andrew would put dimes, just to be different, he was constantly trying to give the image of having all these things and I knew it simply wasn't true.

15

He kept his eyes open. He saw things he couldn't name. The pattern of flesh on a person's hands, the grain of an uncooked steak. The expressions that became fixed on facial muscles over time, so that faces became trapped in them. He saw fear behind his mother's smiles, despair and rage in his father's silences. He saw these things but couldn't name them. He so often had been told that the way he perceived things was not really how things were that when he saw fear he told himself it was imaginary fear, what he saw and interpreted as despair was a sick tendency of his mind to twist very ordinary and innocuous patches of uneventful time into storm warnings. In the privacy of his mind, he was sometimes unreasonably paranoid and at other times unreasonably self-assured. He thought people were making fun of him when they weren't, and when they were, he missed it. Maryann brought him to church so often he began giving hints of a religious vocation. Priests lived well, even in Chula Vista. He became an altar boy. He learned the lugubrious gestures and movements and vestments, the imperious rituals used to turn very inferior Napa red and tasteless wafers produced in bulk into Jesus's flesh and blood. It was a miracle of true faith because nothing whatsoever happened. Transubstantiation taught him stagecraft. This empty platform is really the Cherry Orchard. He enjoyed displaying himself in his tunic and handling the priest's somber drag and serving Mass, liturgical ceremony suited him, he liked dressing up, he enjoyed the seriousness of it, the endless boring ceremony the parishioners had to sit and stand and kneel there and endure, his favorite part was holding the gold disk on its handle under the chalice gazing into people's mouths as he trailed the priest along the altar rail, the way they stuck their tongues out and shut their eyes to receive the host made them childish and vulnerable, exposing all the mysteries of their dental work. Sometimes, for no reason he knew, a stiffy sprouted in his pants as he stared into these trusting open mouths.

16

In seventh grade at Bonita Vista a tall skinny older boy whose name he later remembered as Bobby or Mike, an eighth-grader, a kid from an upper-middle-class progressive family who sensed in an occult way that Andrew's experiences all came from books, a transfer student with a long face thick eyebrows Irish name like O'Donnell O'Powell showed him how to "make cream," demonstrating on his own frighteningly thick member the proper motion and velocity, lecturing more and more breathlessly until his voice disintegrated in gasps and moans and finally one long tortured-sounding grunt as spunk shot out of him, *Okay, now you do it.* From an early age, Andrew had given himself unbelievably pleasant sensations "climbing in place" against the frame of a swing set, wrapping his thighs around the metal bars. Later he'd gotten the same result using the sturdiest furniture legs in the house; spurting a thin ejaculate that stained his under-pants. The canary yellow stains never quite laundered out. If Maryann asked where they came from, Andrew told her they were stray drops of pee. He was family champion at diverting Maryann from her own cunning baleful knowledge of the world. She spent her days in a spiritual miasma where the workings of the Holy Ghost were entangled with shopping lists and menu planning, where come stains on her son's underpants constituted fatal proof of Satan's earthly dominion. Though several school friends had expounded the standard technique of jacking off, Andrew had failed to cream himself that way until this encounter with Bobby or Mike, whose mouth lapped away all the evidence in tremulous excitement.

He had only vaguely understood that climbing in place, making your willie cream had anything to do with "sex." Sex was what he figured Chris did with his girlfriends, you stabbed a girl's vagina with your stiffy, somehow it sank in and got sucked deeper by the goop in the vagina and you moved it around in there a long time and the cream went inside her. He suspected having semen licked off his balls involved him in some type of mortal sin, and just to be safe he confessed it the following Saturday, using the formula the priests at St. Rose of Lima seemed to prefer, alluding to an "impure deed" and letting the priest infer he meant "touching himself." The priests did often ask if you'd "done this with a friend," whispered a few phrases about the dangers of impurity if you said yes, really the same phrases they said if you said no, in a graver tone of voice, how displeasing impurity was to Our Lord and how it gave more pain to Jesus and added more weight to His Cross. Most intense pleasures and even many mild ones were said to drive the spikes deeper into Jesus's palms and feet, to squeeze the Crown of Thorns deeper into his forehead. In this instance Andrew was fined thirty Hail Marys and ten Our Fathers and given absolution. Thirty was a lot, anything where your banana came into it brought a miserable number of prayers into your penance, and of course you had to kneel down and say them right then in a pew, picturing Christ getting triage in Paradise Valley emergency room for the trauma you'd given Him, because you might walk out of church and get killed by a truck. If you had an incomplete penance, your soul went to Purgatory for hundreds and hundreds of years, a drop in the bucket of eternity but really a long time for you. Purgatory was almost the same as hell, only temporary. Yet supposedly preferable to Limbo, where unbaptized souls went. In Limbo they got most of the benefits of Heaven but were forever denied the ecstasy of seeing God. Andrew felt the first little chink in his armor of faith over just this issue, for he couldn't conceive that seeing God, in and of itself, would be such an amazing pleasure it was worth burning in Purgatory for a thousand years, when souls in Limbo immediately enjoyed a fairly lavish existence after death that went on forever without getting worse.

He couldn't imagine a bigger pleasure in Heaven than the pleasure Bobby, Mike, *the tall kid*, had given him the week before, that Andrew had given himself really, except maybe the pleasure of doing it with a boy Chris's age who was fully developed, a high school kid who already fucked girls as well. Chris himself was out of range. Andrew didn't feel right admiring Chris's lanky body or thinking about Chris's stiffy. There had been that time when Chris or for that matter Pete gave off the same hypnotic and dangerous funk as boys at school or men he noticed on the streets, but the curiosity he'd had about them changed irreversibly, they became his brother and father again after this period of being something else. The same thing with his Schillaci cousins in Long Beach, Joe and Tony. With them, the attraction lasted much longer and was even more confusing because each of them had a female twin. If he pictured doing the not-quite-picturable things he wondered about doing with Joe, Andrew pictured doing them with Joe's twin Ruth too; if he daydreamed about kissing Tony, Tony's twin Angela would appear in his mind, sometimes both kissing him. What he pictured most was being in bed with another boy, both with no clothes on, kissing and feeling all over with hands, rubbing the parts down there against them. He imagined in that situation you could get the thrill of creaming without having to handle yourself, it would just happen, the kissing itself would be thrilling, the other boy would love you and you would love him. Of course this new angle, putting your thing in his mouth, could be part of it too, and more like sex, if you squirted your cream inside the other person.

17

Maryann: I just want to remember the good things. And that's what I remember up until fourteen, he and I were inseparable, but then when he became a teenager, he cut the apron string, naturally, doesn't want to be seen with his mother at the mall or at the movie, but we went to dinner. I used to take him to get his hair cut, just like a typical Jewish mother would with her son. Then I was not the, I mean, I was his caretaker. I could no longer keep up intellectually with him, because he was so far superior.

18

"I had long looked forward to my tour and interview at Bishop invisioning [*sic*] ivy covered walls, spacious classrooms and teachers the like of Mr. Chips and Miss Jean Brody. I imagined it as the

West Coast version of Groton, Deerfield and so on. When I came for my visit I was not disapointed [*sic*]. The previous evening a student at the school suggested that I go with him to school sit in at his classes and tour the grounds with him first so that I could have a better view of what being a student there was really like and afterwards I could go on the [*illegible*]

"The next day I took up his offer and saw the small classrooms cracked sidewalk and old buildings. But I also saw the small classroom size with more individule [*sic*] atention [*sic*], religious study and high quality students that attended the school.

"Afterwards I went on the school tour which was far more sheltered. I viewed the newly refurbished library, the computer room, rooms used especially for entertaining and walked through only the well kept grounds.

"That day I realized the real reason for going to a private school, for an education."

(*Essay accompanying Andrew's application to the Bishop's School*)

19

He smiled easily and often at Bishop's, and sometimes believed he had reasons for smiling. He'd shot up several inches and shed the baby fat in the face that made him look Filipino. He liked this sleek Mediterranean Andrew-ness he carried around, svelte-fied himself running cross-country for Bishop's. Guy Fleming Trail, San Clemente Canyon, Azalea Glen Loop, Batiquitos Lagoon Ecological Reserve, in five years he ran every lagoon and trail loop in the county. He knew he was one of the cute ones and high school belongs to the cute. He was also one of the smart ones, pride of the GATE advancement program, 147 on the Stanford-Binet. Smart plus cute, a formidable combination. But he was not really one of the rich ones, and he was becoming one of the queer ones, and so saw how easily all might be lost, a dark area presented itself in which being Andrew cute and smart would not get him through. The big world he found in books easily layered itself on La Jolla, but could not be imported into the large, inert, barrel-roof-tile dreamhouse/dungeon in Rancho Bernardo. He realized that his parents couldn't turn into great figures on the world stage by a magic wish. They couldn't change even slightly, their personalities had petrified over decades of stifled antagonism. He looked in his mind and in magazines for better parents with better histories. He decorated the flat family saga with meaningful touches. *No one in my family ever looked at a price tag.* He turned the queer thing inside out, made it as chic as a Xanax prescription by throwing it in people's faces. *You know you want a piece!* With unerring prescience he singled out the jocks who really did want a piece without knowing it, jocks who could never cop to it and would always want it and would figure it out at forty when it was too late for any fun, jocks so terrified of AIDS that the decade robbed them of what would have been many piquant years of wow-was-I-wasted-last-night blow jobs before they segued to UCSD or Pepperdine and married the sixth or seventh girl who put out for them. The cool people loved Andrew's japes, the cool people had fingered the same jocks as closet cases, they quoted the same movies Andrew knew backwards and forwards—*Black Mama, White Mama*; *Pink Flamingos*; *Touch of Evil*; *All About Eve*—they read the same magazines, followed the same scandals. Andrew only had time for cool people, not the obviously cool, not the vapidly cool, but the secretly, slightly nerdishly cool, the ones you recognized as raving beauties, only after they took off their glasses. Diligent students often carried the best weed, stolen from their parents. Andrew didn't really want sex, except as a sophisticated conversational abstraction, the hint of a darker knowledge of people's natures. He said he was saving himself for the Boise Cascade heir. He knew about the scene, the San Diego gay paper came free in every convenience store. He knew the types of things men did with each other from years of reading and knew there were dozens of bars and stores where people into oral, anal, FF, B&D, and *meaningful relationships*, et cetera, got together, but he'd also seen countless walking skeletons in Hillcrest, guys twenty-five who looked eighty wearing pancake over their lesions, wasting leather queens wheeled down the sidewalk by AIDS Foundation volunteers, still camping in a macabre fashion. Andrew was in no hurry to do the wild thing or come down with the even wilder thing, he wanted other things. He wanted "a tightly knit group of friends." He cultivated a following, a claque of like-minded intellectuals, sophisticates who could talk about Gaultier and Madonna in the same breath as Baudrillard, Gehry, and Baldessari, and important issues such as inherent evil versus upbringing. His claque changed every few months. Not all at the same time; Andrew ensorcelled and disenchanted people at varying rates of consumption. At Bishop's he was known as *a real character*.

By then, Pete was working in the brokerage downtown; it took an hour to drive Andrew to La Jolla and get to his job. La Jolla was far enough from Rancho Bernardo for Andrew to reinvent himself, pieces at a time. He commuted between his supporting role as Andrew *in the Rancho Bernardo television series* and the daily rewritten starring part of Andrew *in Bishop's, the*

Major Motion Picture. The series was scripted, offering few surprises for his character. The movie called for a fantastic amount of improvisation.

20

Class of 1987

Summary School Report

End of Junior Year for <u>Andrew Phillip Cunanan</u>

Andrew is a true intellectual with a ready sense of humor and concern for others. He relates well to adults, discourses brilliantly about culture and history and is capable of profound thought. He is independent, occasionally self-indulgent and at times only interested in pursuing areas that truly interest him. A fascinating individual in every way, Andrew can't help but enliven a college campus!

Most of his teachers describe Andrew as absolutely unique in the classroom. He does excellent work on the Advanced Placement level (three 5s to date) with the exception of mathematics which doesn't intrigue him in the least. His study habits and organizational abilities are not as honed as many students, but in many ways that is his nature and his strength. As one of his English teachers notes: "He reads widely but not always the assigned material. He appears to have an international and extremely broad background. He writes with style and breadth—never misses the point of a question, although he may not have all of the factual information to address it." Andrew can miss weekly and monthly requirements yet be fully prepared and achieve a 5 on a AP examination. This first-rate mind will be appreciated in every way by college professors. He has remained in the top twenty students in the class and has compiled an excellent record despite the tendency at times to follow his own imagination in academic pursuits. I would think that college professors would cry out for students like Andrew Cunanan.

Andrew's intellectual activities outside the academic day are as varied as his interests. He took a humanities course at the University of California last year simply for the love of learning. He has studied art history on his own for many years and received the school's art history award last year. Our teacher in this field (an expert of long standing) describes Andrew's reading and background in this field as one of the finest that he has ever encountered.

Lettering on the cross-country team for the past three years among other activities, Andrew is extremely involved all around the campus. He has been active in the Beyond Bishop's Council, the Peace Club and has worked with young children in the pediatric ward of a local hospital. Andrew has done much for our literary publications editing and selecting material.

Finally, Andrew should not simply be viewed as satisfying the intellectual quotient at a particular college or university. Another faculty member states, "He is able to take an idea and follow all its ramifications (implied and explicit) without losing the train of thought." All of us applaud his originality, his fascination with ideas and his imagination. However, beyond all of this, he takes an active and integral role in his senior class at all times. He is an individual in every sense of the word and he will enrich a college campus immeasurably. He receives our enthusiastic recommendation.

21

Pete gave him a MasterCard. Andrew added to the blandishments of his company free dinners at Yen's Wok on Pearl, Sammy's California Woo. His powers as a raconteur grew with each semester. It became a famous thing, having dinner with Andrew and listening to Andrew's stories. Andrew's stories usually started out true, almost always he began by sticking to facts, and when he pasted in a vivid, spontaneously invented detail, he surprised himself more than anyone else was surprised by the story. Small fibs mingled in his speech like a stutter, unintended, flaring from an independent region of the brain. He soon resisted any scruple about it. If harmless lies entertained people, at least he knew he was entertaining them. Inevitably he made friends outside school, friends who didn't know he was not one of the Scripps heirs or the scion of the DeSilvas, a Fortune 500 family residing in Rancho Santa Fe. The DeSilva thing started as a goof, he and LC booked reservations at the Laurel with it to impress the maître d', sometimes they said DeSilva, sometimes *Baron Ashkenazi*, but Andrew had a darker use for DeSilva, dipping his toes in the murky waters of fagdom, the places where he wasn't known, where his true history had nothing much to recommend it. DeSilva was brash, announcing yourself as a Jew posed a challenge, becoming a rich Jew made him an enviable oddity. These fabrications felt real, in more or less exact proportion to how firmly they were believed, but had the odd effect of making the people he told them to a little unreal, as if he had invented them, too. *Never kid a kidder*, he liked to say when someone bullshitted him, meaning it, but Andrew had no idea how many of his pals embellished things as much as he did. In his darker moments he wondered if he was the only born liar in the world.

He borrowed a red leather jumpsuit from Chris and wore it to a school dance, a famous Andrew thing, like whistling at the water polo team and carrying a teddy bear to class. Despite his renown running cross-country, Andrew conceived himself as an infinitely fussy, femme neurasthenic like Sebastian in *Brideshead*, doomed like Sebastian to burn out in some complicatedly sacrificial form of homoeroticism. *I hope to see you before you get AIDS*, someone wrote in his yearbook. *You sex god you! You art stud you & Dude, take care & don't die until you're at least 25*, wrote another. *Promise me you won't contract AIDS while I'm gone.*

TWO

SATAN'S BREW

1

In the depths of the fait accompli, metonymic details, like charms on a bracelet, cast a heady voodoo spell over the press, the fact that *ostrich and beef tenderloin* were consumed at *that final dinner in San Diego*, for example, *all washed down with Veuve Clicquot champagne* was thought to illustrate a minatory decadence completed by *a tragic ending to a tragic life*, the smallest memories began birthing kernels of premonitory horror, before long the inexplicable took on the livid tint of inevitability, of *a ticking time bomb waiting to go off*, Andrew's former friends reported early evidence of trouble, "He's shameless, he could lie to his best friends for, you know, seven years and have no remorse for it," said one acquaintance who planned, three weeks before the so-called *killing spree*, to share an apartment with him, "I told my friends I met someone that was very interesting, and had— it's left me with an uneasy feeling, definitely," said another who regularly joined him for dinner, the implicit feeling was that the story should yield some instructive cautionary wisdom, impart an improving lesson about the cardinal virtues and the dangers of tolerating too much eccentricity. Siblings dutifully trotted out their ordinary spouses, their standardized children, as examples of the route not taken, while the route that was taken emerged as a malefic choice, a perverse bid for attention, the natural culmination of *laziness*, of *wanting everything without working for it*, perhaps, too, the predictable outcome of *an interest in extreme sadomasochism*. It was noted with asperity that *Andrew enjoyed watching violent movies*, most damningly he *especially loved the scene in* Pulp Fiction *where a man's head is blown off by accident*, and, of course, the unstated, the truly resonant thing about the scattered anecdotes and stray observations, endlessly recycled in various states of embellishment, was that they were so few, so disjunct, so impoverished in contextual detail. It was never learned, for instance, what his companions at *Pulp Fiction* talked about before the screening, or where they went afterwards, or how they happened to know Andrew in the first place. *I met him two or three years ago, I met him five or six years ago, I used to have dinner with him, I used to run into him in San Francisco*, Andrew wafted like ectoplasm in peripheral zones of perception, a free-ranging phantom whisking in and out of other people's dinner plans and movie dates, a kind of vibrant and vaguely disruptive smudge in an otherwise orderly universe.

2

Every crisis is an opportunity for someone. For Karin Lapinski and Evan Wallitt, the couple who stayed at the Chateau Marmont with Andrew and David Madson during Easter Week, 1997, David's murder brought the opportunity to sell their snapshots of Andrew and David to the tabloids. Erik Greenman,

Andrew's roommate, marketed his candids of "the serial killer's apartment" for eighty thousand dollars, providing, with help from editors, a grim yet zany account of Andrew's obsession with Tom Cruise. Andrew, vide Greenman, planned to *kill Nicole Kidman* in order to make Tom Cruise his *S&M sex slave*. Vide Greenman, Andrew *built a shrine to Tom Cruise in his bedroom* and announced whenever he left the house that he was *going Tom Cruising*. In an interview, Greenman substituted himself for another friend of Andrew's in a true story about Andrew mutilating a little sea creature, perhaps reasoning that it might as well have been he, Erik, who witnessed this, since it really did happen. (For the author of this book, Andrew is a propaedeutic lever with which to bury the consumer's blood-twiddled nose in an indelible abjection which our society manufactures with the same indifferent butchery as sausages.) For less enterprising souls, the Andrew saga simply offered the mesmerizing chance to be seen in public, to mint a sound bite, to strike a pose. They dressed conservatively, with taste, sweater sets for girls, blazers and turtlenecks for boys, assuming airs of ruminative detachment learned from years of watching Dan Rather and Peter Jennings, depositing the news that "Andrew was always pulling little pranks" and "always seemed to have a lot of money," sometimes adding such valedictory conclusions as "He's nothing but a common thug." Between each talking head bulged pockets of silence, an impression of missing parts, a jittery woeful suspicion that something terrible about the people talking would reveal itself if the camera simply kept recording, if more specific questions were pressed, if the indefinable notion of taste deployed were suddenly jettisoned. *Did you ever suck Andrew's cock?* might constitute such a breach. *Did you ever do drugs with Andrew?* might be another. But absolutely no one who got as far as *Larry King Live* had ever done a drug, or seen Andrew with his pants down, or even briefly visited the *dark world* he was said to inhabit.

3

In 1987, 1988, the darkness hadn't settled in. Andrew entered UC San Diego, where he earned, for the most part, solid grades, A minus in writing, B in ancient philosophy, A minus in the origins and consequences of underdevelopment, B in European social thought, A in nineteenth- and twentieth-century art. Andrew's mind wasn't entirely a chimera invented by head-waiters and barflies, its contents the arbitrarily ingested conversational camouflage of the journeyman sociopath. Andrew really could *think* at least as well as your average statistician (there is no imminent *but* looming in this sentence). If thinking in the abstract counted for nearly as much as the ponderous brainstorm of wreaking a dress out of safety pins, the book you are holding would turn into a rare Madagascan orchid or a spray of jonquils. Andrew thought he might become an art historian, possibly a museum curator, something within that tweedy range of opportunity, a respectable hands-on sort of art job that allows for a dash of eccentricity. The modesty of this plausible ambition belies the cliché of the cipher driven to violence by impossible dreams of cosmic celebrity. That year he moved out of the Rancho Bernardo house and lived with LC in La Jolla, an escape from the collaborative craziness of Pete and Maryann. Elena married, Chris was surfing and managing the Shore Bird Beach Broiler in Waikiki, Gina moved in with some family named Mayworm, none of them really copped to how messed up their parents were, but they all fled at the first opportunity. Andrew's arrangement with LC is heavily veiled. Peripheral sources indicate the kind of slightly unconventional ménage more frequent among affluent types than the straitlaced middle class, an outgrowth of their fast times at Bishop's. Elena later speculated that Bishop's was probably *the beginning of his corruption*, the proximity to rich kids, the moral laxity epidemic among the monied classes. Andrew himself must have viewed it as escape from eternal dreariness. UCSD and moving in with LC were further escape; he could live more completely in a world of his own devising, a world where nobody had to know exactly where you came from or how you got there, though Pete and Maryann tugged infernally at his inner gyroscope. By this period *being gay* was an insurmountable catastrophe in one world, an amusing peculiarity in another, *being gay* was a structural flaw that needed his parents' absolution and at the same time one he could never confess to. For one thing, the AIDS epidemic had bonded "gay" and "death" like white on rice; for another, Maryann would see it as another cross to bear and sink deeper into her punishing romance with Jesus Christ. For a third thing, Andrew could easily picture an indelible black cloud settling behind Pete's forehead. He anticipated *shame* and *doom* and *permanent bitterness* in his family, in bizarre contrast to the easy frank conversations he had with his *heavenly debutante*, a woman of striking looks, easy wit, and winning gestures, who knew how to sweep aside a day's accumulation of annoyances and freak-outs with a zaftig, determined stride in the direction of the wet bar. LC, they say, had a high, bright, metallic laugh, an openhanded acceptance of whatever came along that seemed like the California he should have been born into. LC and the people he met through LC had a way of neutralizing *old ideas* and *silly anxieties* by airing any supposedly dirty or taboo subject that drifted into their heads. After a date with an available male of their circle, one of the women told him, *You know what drives them all crazy, when you let them fuck you in the ass.* And sometimes, not often, he allowed one of these women into his actual back story, brought her home to what he considered the dire pathos in Rancho Bernardo. A series of beards that forestalled conjecture about his sexuality. His actual home, his actual parents became a plangent secret he shared as a revealing intimacy. They did not find his parents as horrible as he did. They thought Maryann was a little overwrought. "Intense" was the word they usually settled on.

4

LC dated, she had plans. Andrew felt they had a charmed friendship and experienced pangs of jealousy. They looked nothing alike, but Andrew imagined he was LC's astral twin. He could tell, for example, when LC was getting a headache, when LC was getting her period. LC's money, like all money, was shrouded in protective mystery, its presence spoke in the bank-fresh currency in Tiffany blue envelopes she handed him each week for keeping house, in the frequency with which the rooms of the apartment were repainted and rugs and chairs and table linen got replaced, Andrew often came home to find new glass tables, new candlesticks for the honeycombed scented candles, new throw pillows on a new sofa, perhaps a gold ashtray simulating an oyster shell or a Diebenkorn silk screen above the fireplace. The presence of money spoke in the rapidity with which these things were found wanting, were sent back and exchanged for almost but not quite identical things a slightly different shade or shape, or were given away to friends who didn't have money, friends who were waiting for their trust funds, friends who'd decided to become "artists" and had been cut off, some major infusion of this spectral yet omnipresent money stuttered on the horizon. They talked of *a house beside the sea*, Golden Labs, sunlight streaming through shelves of Depression glass. LC wanted marriage and children, but conscious of his feelings, said it wouldn't be the kind of marriage that would affect their friendship in any way, she hated that sort of thing, get married, lose your friends, she would find someone who wouldn't mind sharing their life with Andrew, this had a serendipitous ring, a wistful hint of the never-never, but it kept the charm going.

Andrew's mutation into Jewishness inflected his UCSD period; if he perceived a slight from someone his response would be, *What am I, chopped liver?* People who'd met the Cunanans were sometimes surprised to learn of their secret Jewish past, their expedient conversion to Roman Catholicism. Among acquaintances with no clue to his background, the family's hegira from Tel Aviv to New York to San Diego became a familiar travelogue. If pressed, Andrew admitted his ties to the Mossad, his work for Shin Bet in the early days of the Intifada. He alluded to undercover operations in Gaza, listening posts in Tunis. Encountered on a Saturday night, he was likely to claim he'd spent the afternoon *in temple*. Nobody doubted the Judaism, but the way he insisted on it was too much. *Who's kvelling*, they said when they heard the laugh, *that has to be Jewy Andrew*.

5

LC got married. Had a baby. Moved to Berkeley. Andrew was the godfather.

Pete flew away to his islands.

I'm too old to go to jail.

Andrew finished his semester. He could not, would not, deal with the mess.

He flew to Manila. He stayed for a month. One family source claims he "went with the intention of becoming a missionary." Another says it was a just a vacation, he wanted to see Pete, he never complained of any "squalid conditions." On the contrary, he later spoke of "beautiful foliage."

Every evening at precisely 8:50, he wrote in the missing manuscript (Andrew attempted a book about his sojourn in the Philippines, he showed it to friends, but since it is missing, I have rewritten it for him), *General MacArthur accompanied Miss Jean Faircloth to one of the movie theaters on the Escolta, one evening to the Lyric, on another evening to the Ideal, on still another evening to the Metropolitan, and along the Pasig River Japanese lanterns bobbed in the trees,* he saw General MacArthur in his mind, at a reception for Clare Booth Luce, ordering a gimlet that he never finished drinking, Andrew envisioned the two- and three-story Spanish Colonial buildings of Old Manila, their balconies sagging, distempered stucco water-mottled by monsoons, colored lights threw fiesta colors from bushes and sidewalk utility poles on the passersby, *Asia shock hits the moment you step off the airplane, the insane density of people everywhere, the unbelievable poverty right on the sidewalk in front of you, the thick smells of broiling meat and burning rubber, beggars in rags, naked children, mounds of rotting garbage along the roads, shantytowns with the streets full of craters and mud and raw sewage, at the same time everything runs according to its own logic, everything that looks disorganized is really highly organized, everything that seems grotesque and unbelievable turns out to be a venerated institution, a way of life for millions, the strange thing is people seem happy, if you're in a space with them they see you, they talk to you as if its natural, as if it would be unnatural not to talk to a stranger, you get on a bus that's painted and decaled like a carnival float packed so tight with people you can't breathe yet they all smile and squeeze in to make room and it gets everybody where they're going,* Andrew sometimes referred to his book as a "sweeping narrative," a sort of *Ragtime* or *Nashville* of the archipelago, *the Catholic faith isn't just people's religion here its a cult that everyone belongs to, many people have crosses tattooed on the flesh between their thumbs and forefingers, cab drivers wrap rosary beads and scapulas around their rear-view mirrors,* and it would be, he thought, if he could ever thread together the myriad non sequitur opening lines and middle paragraphs and floating motes of observation that filled his Clairefontaine notebooks, *Legua con Setas, boil ox tongue until tender, drain, fry in oil until brown, slice & marinate 2 hrs in white wine, saute onion and tongue, add chick peas and tomato sauce,* in which he imprudently entered at random data having nothing to do with his book, in his bedroom in the house off Claremont Avenue in Berkeley, recording in wet black ink of a disposable fountain pen whatever he needed to hold in his head, *wallpaper, paste, cardboard boxes, glue, knife, ruler, scissors, needle and thread, thumb tacks, pencil, varnish stain, waxed paper, paper straws, sheet wadding,* for example, material he needed for the dollhouse he was building, *Met Kevin after work at The Stud took two Vicodin for terrible headache*, when Andrew glanced through the Clairefontaine notebooks the references to headaches jumped out at him like an encoded cancer diagnosis, *bought codeine from Frank for crushing headache, took Tylenol and Valium for headache, Chez Panisse with Richard from the White Horse, hideous onslaught of migraine in the middle of dinner*, the alien's face that greeted him in mirrors was a rubber mask thrown over a migraine, these headaches flared from "stress," he'd been told, yet never or seldom ever when he perceived any stress, just the opposite, in fact, the headaches struck precisely when Andrew believed he'd started to "relax," it seemed that his body regarded as stress the very situations his mind associated with an absence of stress, when he studied his favorite painting in the fine arts museum, expecting the soothing effect of contemplation, the veins in his temple might commence hammering and a nerve-pinching band of pain closed around his forehead, attacks even surged in his sleep and ruined the night, he'd seen specialists, there were *no organic causes* and seemingly no reason for headaches, because there was no cause and no reason he felt that some trick of will should stop a headache and instead of lying down or swallowing an aspirin he went on with whatever he was doing when a headache came, becoming more and more abstracted, less and less responsive to the circumstance around him, or else unnaturally keen, unnaturally present, intent on every tiny nuance of a conversation, at times his voice grew loud and rapid and almost shrieking and anything anyone said made him laugh uncontrollably, the pains in his head turned any serious thought into an absurdity, the pain itself was absurd, like some overpowering drug it preempted the world of appearances and took center stage, in the theater of Andrew's psyche, lasting anywhere from five minutes to five hours, switching off abruptly like the barely heard thrum of an appliance that brings voluble silence when it stops, *headache at* La Bohème *in second act, finished in fourth act,* the happier type of headache entry in his Clairefontaine notebooks read, *went afterwards wearing suit & tie to Powerhouse on Folsom.*

As well as he remembered the headaches began when he came back from Plaridel and moved to Berkeley. *I slept well every night in the islands under a mosquito net a candle burning beside the bed the rustle of monkeys and bats in the banana trees.* LC and her husband lived in a house that LC had inherited, a beautiful house by all reports, big enough for the family and Andrew and a succession of long-term guests. *Reefs have formed for scuba diving in sunken wreckage from World War II, the memory of WWII lives on, Pete killed 4 Japanese soldiers who tried to molest his sisters.* Everyone was young and everyone was busy and everybody did his thing. *In the streets I see young men wearing my face, I see myself doubled everywhere.* If they all happened to land in front of the TV at the same time so much the better, *my own eyes staring back at me from the face of another,* hanging loose was better still, the worst was to have the outside world up your nose, unpleasant people in your face, the pronouncement of choice about egregious bad behavior was *if somebody did that to me I'd go on a five-state killing spree,* they all said it all the time. LC paid him for housekeeping, and to look after her daughter. He felt a special connection to this gifted child because she had the kind of enlightened parents he would have wanted. *Pete says he knows that I will do well of all the kids I'm the one with the most "promise." I know I'm the one who got the most promises and now all the promises are broken so how can I go by what Pete says.* She wouldn't grow up a conundrum or an oracle, her parents could engage her imagination without turning her into a freak. *He tells me not to listen when my mother goes on about feminine hormones she doesn't know what she is talking about.* When she learned things her parents knew what she learned, the aesthetic sense developed as naturally as her limbs or her nose, and she was too small for Andrew to feel envious of her good luck. (Years later the family moved south to Pasadena. Andrew remained on familial terms, became godfather to the second child, drove up for the christening. On that occasion he left his shaving kit, forgot it on the fireplace mantel while packing his bag. They kept it there for two years as a sacred totem, like Trobriand Islanders worshiping a Coke bottle, hoping he'd come back and live with them again.)

As soon as he got to the Bay Area Andrew's hopeful streak revived, his sense at any rate that things would turn a corner, he couldn't visualize the future but supposed that he'd finish college, he resumed after a long fallow spell spending many hours with his books, reading histories, the history of Carthage, the history of Athens, the history of Asia Minor, he haunted the museums and galleries and took in lectures at the Asian Art Museum and Pacific Film Archives, any fact Andrew registered stuck in his memory forever and he filled his brain with names and dates and periods and eidetic images of antiques and masterpieces of painting and movies from the time of Edison to the present day, if you showed Andrew a mask of coconut husks from the Cameroons or a Sisley painting or a still from *Tillie's Punctured Romance* he could tell you precisely what it was, reciting the salient facts about it that would prove, if you looked in the right place, to be the verbatim verbiage of a ten-year-old Christie's catalogue or an essay by Berenson or Kenneth Clark—you wouldn't look, no one ever did, most though not all of Andrew's brilliance was akin to the bizarre skills of an idiot savant, but Andrew also had the shrewd habit of picking friends from among the nominally bright, mentally torpid ranks of the indifferently educated middle class, people who were thrilled to hear bells go off when a name or a date was correctly assigned to some stray bit of cultural overreaching. He wasn't legal age and didn't drink but got into the bars anyway and his face became familiar in the Castro and the bars below Market and the White Horse in Berkeley, he met others "on sabbatical" from the cycle of school and careers, other bright people who had hit an impasse and nonetheless seemed to "function," Andrew understood "functioning" as participating in life above a certain class threshold, exhibiting competence and fluency in the issues of the day, the trends of the hour, above all avoiding any untoward outward self-absorption, above all never asking for help or displaying self-pity, and though the first thought of every day, *I don't know how to live,* swirled mantralike through his mind whenever he had no one to talk to or no book to read or nothing else to distract him, Andrew did know how to paint cheerfulness over despair and paste a brassy smile across a headache, around this time Andrew began stealing things, CDs from Tower Records, shirts and trousers from Nordstrom's, books and magazines from A Different Light, on his shoplifting forays he sometimes wore in his underpants a demagnetizing pad he'd whisked from a drugstore counter to thwart the store alarms, in Nordstrom's and Macy's dressing booths he usually razored the plastic-covered sensors free of the seams they were clamped to and sewed up the damage later, or balled the sensor up in a wad of aluminum foil, apart from petty larceny Andrew amused himself by scoring with strangers, more for reassurance than sex, picking up like-minded guys on Polk Street and doing whatever deed in their apartments. Andrew's partners this time were absurdly driven, nondescript men who simply needed a witness to their abject fantasies. The contrast with the tasteful household in Berkeley, and with his middle-class gay friends, gave him a sense of amplitude, of inhabiting many worlds at once. The "sex," if that was what it was, interested him in an academic way. By this time Andrew knew that he thought about having sex rather less than most males his age. Instead he thought about other people having sex, and what a curious compulsion it was, how the wish of it twisted their lives into funny shapes. He studied them like museum exhibits, for the information. He never felt involved, his infrequent arousal was a purely hydraulic, technical process. He made the encounters friendly and even said the nice things people yearned to hear, but his detachment, he realized, had a blank yet satisfied quality that irritated them. He was not really a good slut.

6

He signed up with Kelly Temporary Services as a clerk. At Bank of California, he filed. *I'm a Kelly Girl*, he sometimes lisped at an interested older party in Badlands or P.S. Piano Bar. *I'm a lemme*, he told Chris on the phone. *Lemme get that for you, lemme file that for you.* Back and forth from Berkeley on the BART. It became a year of giving presents; his expenses were few, and the city had the character of an immense cluttered gift shop, a hospital gift shop if you factored in the Castro, where so many walking dead propelled themselves from bar to bar that it really felt like a spectrally swinging ghost town. Despite omnipresent and no doubt salutary propaganda about *living with AIDS* and *living with HIV* the billboards and bus shelter posters and flyers and flimsy-looking rainbow flags merely lent a benign hospital softness to a plague city. Andrew bought and shoplifted precious and prescient objects, *perfect* for almost total strangers he'd met a week before, strangers whose routes and routines he studied, queried bartenders about, strangers who, if their lives had been different, might have felt uneasy about Andrew's altogether premature *admiration* and the intensity with which he'd focused on the meager personal information they'd shared on an idle weekend afternoon, imbibing to no great purpose at a discount Beer Bust or grimly festive Happy Hour launched to commemorate some fictitious gay holiday. As it was, these new friends were startled to receive a titanium cigarette lighter or a millefiori paperweight, or an obscure, first-edition homoerotic novel, a set of handcuffs, a handcrafted bullwhip from Image Leather, but flattered that they'd left such vivid impressions on a young attractive well-spoken thing, a boy really, almost jailbait, really, *I'm Drew*, he said ceremoniously, with antic yoo-hoo eyebrows raised above the rims of his gogglelike glasses, *Maybe you don't remember me but you sat on my face a few days ago*, the bar howled, the present whisked into view, drinks all around were ordered, and that voice, not exactly queeny, rather deep but grained or greased with a staccato insistence that could only issue from a homosexual in flight from social convention, *I got you this because I think you're a great guy, and I would really like to be your friend.*

If they did become friends the gifts kept coming, not always lavish ones, sometimes trivial office or household staples that simply reinforced the idea that *Drew was thinking about you*. It didn't seem creepy, just an offbeat aspect of Drew's personality. If you knew Drew he gave you things, ran across things while shopping that made him think of you. Drew could be especially thoughtful this way when it came to acquaintances on AZT, friends living with the illness, he didn't act at all squeamish, if anything he seemed to have a clinical fascination with the minutiae of other people's sickness, *how long has he had the lesions, when did he get the neuropathy*, Drew showed up at the memorials, he sent flowers, he helped sew panels for the AIDS quilt. Sometimes he was Drew Cummings, Commodore Drew Cummings, with a whole career of naval intelligence work already behind him, more often plain Drew or Drew DeSilva, the résumé really didn't need to make sense, Drew never lingered long enough to inspire the task of deciphering it. Anyway, there were plenty of less personable people around claiming to be reincarnated deities or witches or avatars of Vishnu, and nobody questioned *them*. Drew was there in your life very vividly for a week or two, and after that, Drew vanished from your screen for a month. When he popped up again, he had a gaggle of new people in tow. Drew *touched base* after you knew him a little, waved and sent you drinks from across the bars, whipped in and out of places with ever-unfamiliar companions who appeared from all their physical cues to know him as well or as little as you did. Sometimes they were young sexy druggy-looking studs festooned with tattoos and piercings, other times middle-aged leather ladies decked to the tits in chaps and harnesses, bear daddies with beards, preppy types in blazers with secret nipple rings begging a tug behind the lapels, Drew ran the gamut. Perhaps after months of perfunctory contacts, Drew swooped again into close-up somewhere you were drinking near closing time, leaned into you intimately and struck up a long heart-tweaking conversation in which the rueful vicissitudes of existence, the ironies and epiphanies of life in general, and gay life in particular, figured rather beautifully, and you were reminded that despite the wrenching randomness of this friendship and so many other friendships there were people in the world you cared about, and who cared about you, even if these empathies were doomed to track through empty ether like so many scrambled radio signals. In this respect Drew was no different than a lot of bar people, easy come, easy go. There were bars for cruising and bars for conversation, but in either kind of bar the restless hunt for something besides conversation gave friendships an ephemeral fluidity that alcohol rendered even looser and more transient. You could "know" many people for many years without knowing a single hard fact about their lives, a glimpse through the keyhole into their reality might be offered once or twice in a decade. The rest of what you knew was a compost of gossip and inference and whatever the person told you.

1

He had hardly any idea what he was doing at the bank, numbers and figures had always eluded him. He had absorbed several internal centuries of handicapping stocks during Pete's foreshortened tenure as a financial wizard, but Andrew could never balance a checkbook or perform any mathematical operation beyond long division of simple numbers. As it happened, the bank required more than any numerical aptitude an absence of color blindness, hard-copy documents in triplicate came in white, green, and pink, sometimes white, yellow, and pink, sometimes white, yellow, and green, a particular type of mortgage got recorded on a color the bank called "salmon." A working knowledge of the English alphabet also came into play, bales of completed forms already entered in the bank's computers materialized in his cubicle every morning to be sorted and sown through immense metal hanging files, work arrived in batches, batches of cards, batches of applications, batches of long sheets. All he needed during the day was a modicum of energy and this minimal competence, clean clothes, an air of eagerness. He pressed his hours into three-copy Kelly Services time sheets with a B of C ballpoint every Friday, raced across the teeming Chinese chaos of downtown at five to turn them in, collected his check on Wednesday lunch hour, no benefits, the bank hired temps for these go-nowhere jobs to avoid all the technical and legal complications of insurance and automatic pay raises and step promotion, the downside was guaranteeing thirty-six or forty hours work in a given week when the actual work manifested in fits and starts, the low-end clerical work ebbed and flowed throughout the week and throughout the day, *it's either a feast or a famine*, the supervisors said inanely of work no sentient person not recovering from stroke or catalepsy could possibly regard as providential. The temps of course lived for puddles of downtime, the longueurs of nail-filing and personal phone calls, though empty minutes had for Andrew a bilious existential edge. It was bad enough to be doing something meaningless but even worse to have time to contemplate how meaningless it was, anticipating more of it and knowing how few minutes owned by the bank could actually be obliterated by slurping a sixth cup of percolated Folger's with an island of lumpy Cremora, dissolving in it and scribbling furtive Philippine reflections in a steno pad, to be marooned in this way in what was merely an arbitrary pause of irritation was a lowering reminder of the dead loss all the so-called productive time on the job constituted on the broader calendar of wasted hours that charted, in effect, his life. However ingeniously Andrew beguiled himself during his morning walk to the BART into believing the bank was an acting job, a performance of something *not him* for eight hours that produced revenue and motivation, the belief never carried him through an entire day, one of the job's insidious effects being a Shakespearean range of unarticulated and unperformed inner states that cried out for truly monstrous expression, the baring of genitals, or the random discharge of a semiautomatic weapon, or, for complete monstrosity, a sudden braying of show tunes, whereas the permissible outward evidence of incongruence never rose above the slyly challenging and self-defeating display of a consciously miserable fashion sense or the puerile gesture of a "sophisticated" *New Yorker* cartoon taped to the opaque glass of one's work cubicle.

He never sleeps enough, his nights have become compensatory voyages into the city's cottony fogs. When he does go home, he spends hours fashioning small blocks of wallpaper in rosettes and chinoiserie for the rooms of a miniature chateau that stands on a plank table in his room like a courtroom exhibit, ostensibly a gift for LC's little daughter Dee Dee, but in fact the balsa pentimento of a nightmare in which he was urged by a sinister double of his brother to purchase a villa adjoining his own, a place that proved upon entering to consist almost entirely of puzzlework staircases traipsing down to the basement and zigzagging up to the attic in the horrible manner of M. C. Escher. After six months in San Francisco, Andrew is tired of climbing everywhere.

After work, he hops a trolley that takes him up Market and deposits him at Eighteenth and Castro, where he wanders down to the first of several bosky, sour-smelling bars on his route, washing the first Percocet of the evening down with some iced Ocean Spray, spotting a friend, Tim Sanders, a short guy with slight features and albino hair Andrew met on the Berkeley campus, when they were both gaping at an outdoor class in chorus-line dancing, who works in a design firm and likes talking about movies. Andrew knows everyone in the bar by name and knows at least a little about all twenty-odd people drinking there after work, but Tim, at that hour, is the only patron who thinks of himself as a friend of Andrew's, because they met somewhere else and have eaten burgers together at a place down the block and once hooked up on a Saturday to go clothes shopping. They have a spirited and totally forgettable and now forgotten conversation, and Andrew, who's feeling flush, buys Tim a second and third Bacardi and Coke before moving on to another bar, where he bumps into Don Setterfield, a tall, skinny, soulful-faced math nerd he knew in seventh grade and a few years later at Bishop's, who now works in market research. Even at Bishop's Don was wary around Andrew, skeptical of Andrew's big talk, but willing to find him amusing when he was, as he is now, ridiculously mannered and talkative on subjects other than himself, now it's musical events he's supposedly taken in at the San Francisco Opera, *La Bohème*, *Norma*, recent cultural stuff Don knows nothing about but thinks he should, Andrew interrupting himself to say *You're familiar with the plot of* Norma, when Don says No, he's kind of forgotten it, Andrew recounts the plot of *Norma* in exhaustive and colorful intricacy. Don finds himself warming to Andrew and wondering if he isn't mistaken to assume

Andrew's full of shit and disreputable in some hard-to-identify but scary way, certainly Andrew's *suit* is a little pretentious and out of place, he's being a little grand about ordering Don's drinks and his own cranberry juices, and the static hazel eyes belie the laughing mouth and pattering voice. Andrew's eyes have always seemed fixed on something entirely out of range of any conversation, reminding Don of certain cunning predatory lizards he's seen in *National Geographic* documentaries. No, he isn't mistaken. Andrew changes before his eyes into a Komodo dragon scenting its dinner and swishing its massive tail while pretending to talk about the challenges *Norma* presents to the aging soprano. And then he vanishes. Exactly as if the visibility of his metamorphosis had become apparent to him.

Andrew swings through numerous bars, encountering all sorts of people he's introduced himself to and made idle chatter with in the past, introducing himself to still more people, introducing the new people to the previous people, Andrew scatters in each musky saloon the largesse of his own avidity, following a finely honed instinct about who wants to talk to whom, it's something he's already noted for, hooking people up who're cruising each other. Invariably Andrew knows both and derives deep yenta glee from a successful pairing. If one of his matches mulches into couplehood, Andrew *kvells*, almost gloats, to the mild embarrassment of everyone, for it is somewhat daunting to suspect that this raving asshole operates with more acuity in matching compatibles than any number of delicately disinterested tacticians. Andrew is known everywhere, but not particularly liked by just about everybody. He has a loud queenly mouth and cooks up a different story for himself every night, not that every Castro bar hasn't seen his kind of queen a million times, yet

Andrew has forged an impressive array of sexual alliances between people who could barely stand him, in the process ensuring that they thenceforward would stand him a little better.

He is still *Jewy Andrew* in every sense, a refugee from *Funny Girl* who can't stop invoking his Hebrew Franks pastiche of ethnicity, who nevertheless sometimes pops into Nuestra Senora de Guadalupe for Mass when he hears of someone dying or feels that his own little wishes for the future might not pan out: then he asks God, that fraudulent puppeteer, to cut him a deal. There's just too much silly awfulness built into being a queen. *If You make me powerful and good*, he always begins oxymoronically, *I will stop*—but he never says stop what, because he would really have to stop everything.

8

At least 112 people were killed on November 14 when a typhoon with 150 mile per hour winds struck the central Philippines. Andrew disliked reading fiction. His own made-up stories entirely satisfied his need for fantasy. Or almost entirely. *Soviet President Mikhail Gorbachev met with Pope John Paul II in the Vatican on November 18, then signed a Soviet-Italian friendship treaty with Italian Premier Gulio Andreotti.* What he read habitually were works of art history, theories of color, price guides for antiques, *Architectural Digest. In New York District Court on November 21, Judge Kimba Wood sentenced Michael Milken, a former employee of Drexel Burnham Lambert, to 10 years in prison for securities fraud.* He read Suetonius and Livy and Gibbon, and *The Rise and Fall of the Third Reich*. He read *Variety* and *Billboard* and the book reviews in the *New York Times*. When he read novels, his tastes ran to historical fictions like *I, Claudius* and *Burr*, political stuff, Disraeli's novels, Henry Adams's *Democracy*. He got impatient with secular fiction, but had a warm spot for the ploddingly carnivalesque: John Irving, and an abiding favorite, *A Confederacy of Dunces*. He wasn't fat and he didn't fart in company but he "identified" with Ignatius, the monstrously obese hero, who talks in overblown, elliptical sentences and afflicts the grotesques around him with a kind of godlike sadism. It was a book published after the author's suicide, on the insistence of the author's mother.

One aspect of Ignatius meant to charm is quality of stubborn anachronism. He is out of step with today's world, repining for an earlier, ostensibly more gracious era. He can't abide or comprehend the existence of stupidity. He wages a daily, quixotic war against it. This has the paradoxical effect of making him stupid, though the book's many fans tend not to recognize this, and it may have escaped the author himself. Andrew considered that his mental gifts were, like Ignatius's, wasted on the world, and he found in the book an oblique endorsement of his gathering alienation. He began collecting people who were slightly out of it, who felt some essential disconnect between themselves and the culture, who sensed that their talents and aptitudes were simply too good for a mediocre society. He looked for an embattled and subtly self-pitying habit of mind among his bar acquaintances. In the year before he left San Francisco, a certain type of too-well-dressed and too-well-spoken, stuffy sort of queer became legible as belonging to "Andrew's crowd," though Andrew remained, even to his crowd, an ephemeral presence who preferred to "run into people" than make concrete appointments, whose movements seemed excessively dissembled in fishy accounts of business trips and social engagements, a sort of hologram with the tinny effect of canned entertainment.

At the same time, Andrew discovered another novel that answered, he felt, many questions that had hung suspended inside him for years like hibernating bats. It was called *Mr. Benson*. Andrew did not have sex often and had only occasionally experimented at causing or receiving pain, his "types" tended not to wear leather and signaling handkerchiefs so their tastes had to be figured out in conversation or in bed. The characters in *Mr. Benson* had no such ambiguity. Jamie, a twink, tries to make himself interesting in a gay bar to a mysterious, handsome stranger. The bartender warns him "that one's too heavy for you; he's looking for more'n you have to offer." Heedless, Jamie goes home with Mr. Benson, who trains him to be a perfect slave. Not just a bedtime role-playing playmate, but a full-time human toilet who's not allowed on the furniture, cleans Mr. Benson's boots with his tongue, services Mr. Benson's friends on command, keeps his hole and his privates assiduously shaved and wears Mr. Benson's brand on his butt. Mr. Benson puts him on a leash. Mr. Benson lathers up his arm with Crisco and plunges it up Jamie's ass and makes him beg for more. Mr. Benson hangs him on the wall, tortures his nipples into monstrously swollen erogenous cones, whips him with riding crops, stretches his balls, fills his throat whenever the urge strikes with a golden shower of his *manwater*.

As a sort of instructive garnish, the novel puts Jamie through a number of "imperfect" S&M encounters with persons other than Mr. Benson: a master who *simply uses him* and dumps him unconscious on a stoop, a stranger who fists him in a sling at the Mineshaft and leaves him to be pissed on by dozens of anonymous daddies. Least satisfying of all, he goes home with a clone who *rolls over* and expects Jamie to play top. The pure slave becomes contemptuous of anything soft in himself or his master: theirs is an exchange between masculinities, informed in the ideal situation by the most literalized sense of *tough love*. Andrew recognized *Mr. Benson* as a utopian work, like all pornography, but it clarified what he'd been seeking in sexual liaisons, the role that he felt suited him. He wanted to be Mr. Benson. As he could not very well construct a dungeon in LC's house, he looked for submissives with their own Rube Goldberg home entertainment centers. There were private piss parties and slave auctions advertised on fliers, enclaves of sometimes twenty or thirty intricately involved lumps of flesh snorting amyl and working their will in a room. It was a scene in which the standards of beauty prevailing in regular bars were somewhat beside the point, but looks helped, verbal skills helped too. Of course it fell short of the Mr. Benson ideal, with HIV rampant you couldn't piss *inside* someone, it wasn't smart to draw blood, getting rimmed was a gray area, and the script never carried into ordinary life. Andrew never found anyone he could walk down the street on a leash, or anyone waiting at home with a TOILET sign happily hung round his neck. When he went to the trouble of torturing someone, he often felt used and discarded afterwards because nobody ever became devoted to him the way Jamie devoted himself to Mr. Benson, no one called him "sir" on the street or scrambled to light his cigars in the Eagle, or really showed him any sort of deference at all unless he had them hog-tied or slung up in their apartments. For him, the fun wasn't so much inflicting pain or inserting stuff into their bodies but simply *immobilizing* a person, preferably someone larger than himself, having that person totally under control. If it only lasted an hour or two, this control was an illusion, a piece of theater. Andrew yearned for the kind of sincere domestic horror show photographed by Robert Mapplethorpe, a partner in a zippered hood groveling on the wall-to-wall near a Coromandel screen, and wondered as he had so many times in so many situations if there was something peculiar about *him*, something indefensibly off the norm even among people who fed their boyfriends from a dog dish.

9

Don Setterfield thinks he saw him on the famous evening of *Capriccio*, October 21, 1990: Don Setterfield remembers walking up Market Street past Zuni when a black limo pulled over and a tinted window rolled down and there inside in boat-light phosphorescence Andrew grinned his scary grin and said hello, sunk deep in the cushioned seat. Don Setterfield swears he saw Harry de Wildt and Gordon Getty, the dowager empresses of the city's haut monde, all en route to an unimaginable feast in a fairy-tale castle, having just streaked away from the opera house after a gay evening of Strauss with costumes by Versace, *Hola! Ihr Streiter in Apoll!* Others recall actually witnessing an exchange between Andrew and Gianni Versace in some unspecified area of the opera house, one witness claims Versace said *I know you, Lake Como, non?* and that Andrew simpered *Thank you for remembering, Mr. Versace.* It's purported by still others that Andrew and Versace had different words with each other, more familiar words, that Versace's *look* was a look of attraction, that Versace was *cruising*, how might we ever know the searing truth behind this idiotic anecdote, one person claims that he saw Andrew afterwards at a discotheque and that Andrew said Versace introduced himself and that Andrew replied *If you're Versace I'm Coco Chanel.* Despite ample evidence that Andrew had never been at Lake Como it was later supposed that he had been, it was also hypothesized that Versace thought he remembered Andrew from Lake Como but actually remembered him from somewhere else, or from nowhere else, that he simply mistook Andrew for someone else, or that Andrew, in fact, had approached Versace, had said *We've met before, at Lake Como*, or words to that general effect, in some tellings of the story Versace and Andrew did not encounter each other at the opera, but at a reception after the opera, at the so-called *Colossus* discotheque, perhaps in a so-called *VIP area* of the *Colossus* discotheque, in still others Versace was in the limousine with Gordon Getty and Harry de Wildt, en route to the so-called *Colossus* discotheque from the opera, or en route to a dinner party from a reception at the *Colossus* discotheque after the opera, of course it is also possible that a limousine containing Gordon Getty, Harry de Wildt, Andrew, and Versace carried them from the opera to a dinner party and after the dinner party to the *Colossus* discotheque, if indeed any of these people were together in a limousine on the night in question; in the made-for-TV-movie version we're propelled back in time to Lake Como where Andrew auditions for a Versace print campaign and takes his rejection badly, in all these endless retellings of the Versace anec-dote Versace is cast in the role of JFK meeting Lee Harvey Oswald on the campaign trail, it's assumed that Andrew's later disappointments coalesce around the figure of the mythical dressmaker, that he imagines some close personal connection to Versace and feels betrayed by him, or bitter over Versace's fame and his own insignificance, that Versace comes to represent everything in the world that Andrew himself can never be, that Versace owns everything that Andrew himself can never own, that Versace and his fantasies about Versace filled Andrew's brain for seven years, that Andrew felt Versace owed him something, that he felt used by Versace, in other words that this conceivably spurious encounter in the opera house or the discotheque or the limousine or wherever *triggered an assassin's bullet* and therefore qualifies in an especially satisfying way the conventions one would naturally find in *a chronicle of a death foretold*, but this nugget like so many things produced by journalism is a bit too tiny and thinly charged for an entire person to orbit around it from 1990 to 1997, however deranged and ridiculous he may turn out to be. There are people so smitten with celebrity that they're driven to kill it, journalists conspicuous among them, but in my version of the story Andrew got the same little thrill from meeting a big shot that a waitress gets from serving a sandwich to Milton Berle. As Marilyn Monroe is supposed to have said, *They say Milton Berle has the biggest one in Hollywood, but I mean, who cares?*

THREE

HAPPY TALK

1

Exhibit A: From the old vulgarian who brought you *Superman*, an unwatchable series of face-offs between some snarling swish plucked out of a Kmart underwear ad and numerous older, more conservatively dressed gentlemen who have, it seems, in the middle past, "tried to help" this guttersnipe kamikaze, who nances through large, noisy restaurants tossing prescription bottles at selected tables, smashes television sets in other people's houses, and runs over one of his victims no fewer than three times, at great speed, in the victim's own car, failing even then to silence the oleaginous kvetch, who must finally be gagged with packing tape and strangled manually; intercut with Franco Nero, incarnating the slain designer as a spiritually wise, protean ravioli, roaming the muraled interiors and soggy escarpments of Viscaya Mansion as he drops little road apples of enlightenment in the path of his dumbfounded entourage. His lover, whose noggin looks tiny atop his pumped-up frame, worries that Gianni's going too far in his fashions, and lives too much with his head in the clouds: he adores this starry-eyed dreamer, frets over him with truly civilized emotion. Should he read Proust to him aloud tonight? Too heavy. Truman Capote, then. For the genius's death scene, he gets a vertiginous set of stairs, like the entrance of Valhalla, instead of the barely palpable steps separating his actual gate from the actual sidewalk; for him, everything must be rendered on a heroic scale, the crass shopkeeper sensibility glorified into da Vinci–class visionary boldness, the male hookers ordered in bulk and screened by a ponce for that *je ne sais quoi* required to lubricate his *long-term relationship* airbrushed out of the portrait, because what we are watching is A Tale of Two Fags that illustrates, in no uncertain terms, which sort of whore it's appropriate to boo-hoo about, and what sort of fag you can safely invite to dinner.

It would be lovely to insert some incongruous footage at arbitrary intervals: Versace, perhaps, masturbating frantically while gazing at a creased photograph of Yves St. Laurent, or better still some fabulous fatty of the culinary arts, or, God forgive him, Eva Perón, *in the casket.* Or we could splice in a hotel banquet room, way up north in Seattle, circa 1994, on one of those magical nights known only to the blessed initiates of Gammu Mu, the gay travel club of which so much was made, that hush-hush fraternity of wealthy closeted older et cetera, the vast majority of whom are well past fifty, though a scattering of gym-hewn acolytes and ephemeral principessas lends spicy savor to the so-called *fly-in.* The world-famous Space Needle parts the nocturnal mists beyond the panoramic penthouse windows, coffee and Courvoisier are poured at all the round, candlelit tables, precious memories are being suppressed even as they're being minted. Our antihero, of course, is seated beside La Jolla developer and bon vivant Lincoln Aston, Andrew's older buddy, one of a clutch of La Jolla older buddies Andrew cultivates in his spare time. Lincoln

Aston who's about to be bludgeoned to death by a bad piece of trade (or is he already dead? happily, dates don't matter in the movies), a coy-looking retiree, we might as well cast Paul Sorvino in the part. If this were a film about a reporter's odyssey into Andrew Cunanan's *dark world*, we could zoom into a brandy snifter and ripple back to the present, to the tables and chairs stacked in clumps bathed in cold grainy daylight, a face-lifted matron made up like an Argentinian drag queen the day after Carnival stands quizzing the very waiter who just placed a little silver thimble of half-and-half beside Andrew's demitasse cup, her steno pad clenched in grimly determined fingers, the nails lacquered in *maroon*, what the waiter recalls, natch, is that *laugh*, that inimitable cackle, *kind of like Tarzan being goosed with a feather*, as another waiter put it, *Yes yes the laugh*, says our intrepid Brenda Starr encouragingly, *but did he ever mention crystal meth?* The waiter, a bit long in the tooth for a Gamma Mu function and even older now, a scattering of gray hairs marking the inexorable passage of time, scratches his scalp in bewilderment. *I only served him coffee*, he says. *Did he ever say where he got the crystal meth?* The reporter presses as only a crack reporter can press, moving closer to the window to angle her long, ethical profile into visual parallel with the Space Needle.

Now the camera slowly zooms straight into the waiter's head, parting the scalp and puncturing the cranium, embedding itself directly into his brain so that we *see everything he saw* on that long-ago night of homophile enchantment. The flickering candlelight. The flame-licked faces of wrinkled men in unwrinkled suits, more wrinkled men in Sea Island shirts and funny hats, mouths mouthing, fingers prying cellophane off cigars, here and there the sultry eyes of a young companion, and onstage—yes, there's a little platform stage the hotel keeps for string quartets and jazz bands and the occasional group-booking *bal musette* like tonight—we are suddenly far from rainy Seattle, several of our gamier sexagenarians have slipped off to the green room and now reemerge in sailor suits, likewise some of the younger talent are strutting forward in bright yellow hula skirts and varicolored leis, the little orchestra that beguiled us earlier with its Burt Bacharach medley strikes up feelingly, we're not in Washington State any more, farewell drizzle and fog, these gals are on their way to Bali Ha'i—*There is nothing like a dame!* Andrew feeds his burgeoning migraine a Xanax. *There is nothing you can name*—a San Diego city councilman in Mitzi Gaynor drag plops down at their table, awaiting his moment to proclaim himself only a cockeyed optimist. The sailors clumsily march back and forth on the cramped stage, island girls weaving between them on big mannish feet. There's a little bit of everything here tonight: bankers and brokers and a manufacturer of fiberglass cigarette boats, travel agents, restaurateurs, agribusiness insurers, owners of sports equipment franchises, soup to nuts really, *we feel every kind of feelin' but the feelin' of relief.* In the mind of our protagonist, whose mental furniture is only beginning to take definite shape in these pages, the proximity of the city councilman, by 1994, must certainly seem a good augury, like the fact that soon-to-be-murdered Lincoln Aston is picking up the bill for this entire weekend, an indication that other people's discretionary income will rub off on you if you spend enough time in its company.

Andrew now lives with Maryann in the Rancho Bernardo condo, and spends most of his days managing the Thrifty Junior Drug Store across the street, a job he started as a part-time clerk after moving home from Berkeley to reenroll at UCSD in the fall quarter of 1991. Andrew makes it through spring quarter 1992, mixed grades this time, and drops out again, Thrifty Junior then becomes a full-time thing, a daily crucifixion for which the only balms are Vicodin, Xanax, Percocet, and other peacekeeping members of the popular downer family. He shares a twenty-year-old T-Bird with Mom, which she drives to her endless church functions and Andrew takes to the Hillcrest bars, there are frequent arguments about the car and even more arguments about Maryann rummaging through his belongings in search of damning evidence about his personal life. She's already traced one matchbook cover to a gay establishment on University and shown a pile of cryptic snapshots to Andrew's visiting siblings. Last year Andrew shoved this implacable detective against a wall in the apartment and dislocated her shoulder, threatening to kill her, as he drove her to the emergency room, if she blabbed about it to anybody. Of course she did, but not then. She told her priest. She offered her sufferings up to God. She told the neighbors. However, she continues whipping up Andrew's breakfast, lunch, and sometimes dinner, and pressing his Thrifty Junior uniforms. "I fixed his spaghetti every day." But enough of this strange, long-suffering lady.

Gliding into view, on stage, from *Chicago*, in the role of Bloody Mary, bedecked in a coconut brassiere and citrus green acetate hula skirt, is the imperishably handsome and *very* fetching Windy City songbird and pioneer real-estate developer, Gamma Mu's own successor to Juanita Hall, *let's have a nice welcoming round of applause for the musical stylings of Miss ... Lee ... Miglin!*

Is it here, the reporter wonders, that these star-crossed whatever you call them first conjoined in unholy matrimony? *If you don't have a dream, if you don't have a dream, how you gonna make a dream come true?* I would guess yes. Some enchanted evening in Seattle, or in a more pedestrian banquette in Numbers, the old Numbers on Sunset in Los Angeles, where Andrew, like any bored stud from San Diego, occasionally made himself available for consultations. *Talk about things you like to do.* But let's not conflate this and subsequent meetings with *prostitution,* a word that drags along its own confessional and crucifix and hardly conveys the lighthearted entrepreneurial spirit in which these transactions are accomplished between men. Sufficient to say that if Miglin liked getting bound and gagged and vigorously whipped and was also a devoted husband and father, this statement contains no intrinsic contradiction.

2

The Soviet Union collapsed. The Gulf War came and went. Andrew C. cultivated a presence in various circles. There was an older crowd he saw in their homes in La Jolla and in restaurants. A younger crowd of military and ex-military types in Hillcrest. There was a leather crowd in Point Loma. He kept these relationships "compartmentalized" in a mental sense, but they intersected in space and time and there were, not infrequently, awkward and puzzling collisions of Andrew's various worlds, nothing drastic, nothing Andrew couldn't finesse, but curious enough to fuel a general perception of something hidden, possibly sinister. He traveled on weekends with Lincoln Aston: Cabo San Lucas, Two Bunch Palms, Miami, New York. He kept up intermittent contact with friends in San Francisco: Tim Sanders, Don Setterfield, LC. On a weekend trip up north he told Tim, over seafood risotto at Café Luna Piena, that his mother had died after a long wasting illness. Maybe it sounded awful, but her death was a relief, he could finally live his own life without her constant interference. Tim recalled hearing the same thing three years earlier. He doubted his own memory. Had Andrew said his mother was about to die, and had she then lingered all this time? Or had her death affected Andrew so profoundly that it still felt as if it happened yesterday? Meanwhile Maryann continued ransacking Andrew's drawers and closets for some key to his inner life. He sometimes tranquilized her by going to Mass.

As ever people saw him in flashes, a dinner here, a party there, drinks and a movie, always smiling, always happy, always talking the happy talk.

For the larger share of every week, he shelved inventory at Thrifty Junior and slipped out at night for the standard ghettoized escape from dullness. Being what one generous soul called "a Walter Mitty type," he enlarged the little events of his life for the benefit of people who might otherwise have viewed him as ordinary. If he spent the weekend in San Francisco, he might later say he'd been in Spain or Morocco. He was good at disappearing, and his acquaintances were good at forgetting. When he traveled to a new place, in the retelling it became a place he had "always" enjoyed visiting, having spent many months there in the blurry past.

He tit-tupped through the Hillcrest bars like a lounge comic honing his routine, all the theme parties and disco nights and discount beer busts and drag galas and lip-synching contests and charity balls and holiday fund-raising raffles, wherever gay people swarmed, Andrew materialized. For every person who will tell you that he danced every night with his shirt off and always bought drinks for the bar, there's another who swears Andrew never danced and never picked up a check. He laughed his insane laugh, gathered his hearties about him, held them spellbound in his orbit, became the cynosure of any room he entered. Or else he was morose and alone and sort of pathetic in his craving for attention, pulling crude pranks and alienating everybody. *He'd pick a baseball cap off somebody's head and run with it and put it on somebody else, so the first person had to chase him across the room to get it back.* Beloved local or space alien? Any true queen can do both parts at the same time, or in alternating bars on the same evening. *What I would love to do to you, baby,* Andrew liked telling new, cute faces, parting imaginary cheeks with his fingers and licking the invisible crack. *I wouldn't throw him out of bed for eating crackers unless he fucked better on the floor,* he said of various comely ectoplasms who never learned of his lustful designs. With twinks he butched it up, with "alpha males" he bent over in submission and backed his ass into their groins. No one saw him go home with anybody.

Most of the drug-dealing stories lead nowhere very special, the trail if there was one went stone cold the minute Andrew cooled, unless you count the Filipino dealer in Miami who swears he was selling Andrew crack and crystal meth *before Versace but after the three-state killing spree.* It *seems* that during his glory days in Hillcrest Andrew maintained a certain level of chemicals in his body on a daily basis and like any low-maintenance addict found wholesale suppliers through trial and error and was thus able to supplement his income by sporadically selling pills. This requires a sophistication possessed by vast numbers of American schoolchildren rather than the Fu Manchu–like duplicity of the master criminal. There was more to it, later on, but how much more? If dealing enabled Andrew, through gestures of troubling largesse—twenty-dollar tips for the bartender, expensive presents for friends, picking up a five-hundred-dollar restaurant bill—to verify his pretended wealth (and what sorts of rich people throw it around? What *did* he think people were thinking?), the idle gossip of a provincial backwater quickly multiplied the most extravagant of these gestures into nightly manifestations, for Andrew was hardly San Diego's solitary fictioneer.

While living with Maryann and working at Thrifty Junior between 1991 and 1995, Andrew inscribed himself as a *figure* in other people's templates, as he had in San Francisco, a figure detached from everything except a certain intense audiovisual immediacy. When he was in your face he was amazingly in your face, and when he wasn't, you forgot him. He had a real life and a dream life and a secret life that was half real and half a dream, or perhaps just a little real and mainly a collage of wishes. Some people half-believed Andrew's stories, if they liked him, assuming some prosaic measure of reality behind his gilding hyperbole, and others, who didn't, thought him an unbearable fraud. It's doubtful he ever forgot he was Filipino, that people glimpsed exoticism in his face and felt their racist reflexes twitch before he laid on his history du jour, a trace of difference always lingered, if not in their minds in his, some inchoate threat that he'd never get any further, than Pete, that whiter, richer, slower boys would pick up all the prizes. He tried to level the playing field with an uncanny mimicry. He hypnotized navy boys with little treats and endless questions about themselves, agonized over their problems and took them in hand, and before long could let them know and have them believe that he'd been in the navy, too. Andrew drafted and redrafted his résumé on the palimpsests of new people.

He never gave himself the benevolent long-mirror view that would make him doubt the need for a cover story. Instead he fashioned a fresh lance every day to poke in the world's eye with the idea, *I'm this. I'm that. I'm not myself.*

He met Jeff Trail in a bar in Coronado. Jeff had just served in the Gulf. He looked incredibly cute and hadn't a clue about civilian gay life. He had the weird vulnerability of military boys, naive idealism crossed with ego starvation and a nervous worship of masculinity. Andrew fastened on Jeff as a person he could mold into an ideal friend. Jeff was kind to a fault, gullible, and playful enough to view Andrew's weird shit as harmless foolery. Jeff supported his fantasies and to some degree facilitated his routines by endorsing or laughing off anything Andrew said, in return he got endless praise and attention, which he craved with puppylike simplicity. They sailed down to Baja in rented sailboats. Went skeet shooting in Oceanside. Andrew squired Jeff around Hillcrest, showed him off at Friday parties at Top of the Park. He discovered extremely junior members of the gay community for Jeff to have sex with, Jeff's tastes running as they did rather close to the age of consent. Andrew idolized him. When Jeff volunteered at the AIDS Foundation, Andrew seized the occasion to strike noble poses and soon was handing out condoms in bars, really feeling galvanized by the spirit of public service, even going so far as to organize a seminar aboard somebody's sailboat, a disaster, nobody came except some AIDS Foundation staffers and the whole thing degenerated into a party. Jeff was the only man whom Andrew let penetrate him (which, when it happened, was strictly a fuck-buddy kind of thing, no Mr. Benson trip, no tit and ball torture, no cups of Crisco), and if he had entered Andrew, not with his penis, but headfirst, inserting his entire body until Andrew was only a wrapper of skin stretched over Jeff, Andrew would've felt complete. To have one real friend can seem like ample defense against all manner of disappointment.

3

D.B.: Andrew and Jeff were very close, I'd say. It maybe wasn't as close as Andy wanted it to be. I haven't seen Andrew since 1994. I moved to Boulder in 1994 and after that I couldn't afford to go on vacation to San Diego any more, so it was probably on spring break, but we spoke on the phone, the last time I heard from him was on my last birthday, the twenty-first of September. I don't want to say he was obsessed with Jeff. Maybe on the verge of being totally obsessed. He really tried to emulate him in certain ways. I guess in the most important ways he couldn't, but he thought Jeff was very attractive.

The way I understood it, his dad was pretty strict, but I think that was just part of the line he gave certain people. I think he told people stories that he thought would generate the most awe or the most sympathy, depending on the feeling he got from you as a person. He did tell me his dad was pretty strict, but he never said anything about being beaten or abused. In hindsight I get the idea that he was ill-used, and probably abused, but I wouldn't want to say by his father and mother, but sort of by life in general.

I don't think he ever had any sort of over-the-top celebrity-worship thing. He always wanted to be wealthy. I got the impression he was dissatisfied because he was in high society but just on the fringes, he wasn't really there, and dependent on what he could get out of people, but I don't think he was so heady as they made it out, being obsessed with fame.

He spoke a little Italian. I never heard him speak more than a few little things in any language besides English. A little Spanish, a little Italian, but I couldn't say if he spoke enough to get along if he actually went to those places. I think that's a story he might have told himself, that he spoke all these languages. He never spoke anything big in front of me.

He was smart enough to change his identity with various people, but I don't think he could've pulled it off in such a small place as San Diego. Yes, he altered his history a little, but the idea that he stole little bits from other people's lives and made a new persona out of those, I think that's blowing things out of proportion quite a bit. He liked military guys, he liked blondish guys, after I came back in '92 and finally met him and Jeff he'd sort of changed a little because he was more into guys who looked like Jeff Trail rather than the sun-baked blond kind of thing, but I think that was a way he could, it would be easier for him to pretend he was with Jeff if he was with somebody who resembled him.

He could pull off being Hispanic. I thought he was Hispanic, I didn't know he was half-Filipino until afterwards. He didn't have typical Mexican-Hispanic looks, he had more like Spain Hispanic looks. When he was trimmer. He was a good-looking guy, but I can't say if that was because he could pull off being ethnic. If you saw him in a certain light he looked really Hispanic, but if you saw him in a different light he just looked like he had exotic eyes and a tan. It was hard to say exactly. There were plenty of guys who liked him.

He talked about Europe a lot. The way he threw money around, I thought, If anybody around here is going off to Europe, he could certainly do it, but I think that's a little exaggerated too, I don't think he would like spend half the year overseas or whatever, he might have gone once in a while with certain guys—I don't even know to what extent he was involved with—you read these articles that there were scores of older guys, but that wasn't Andrew. I think he'd probably been in Europe, but I don't think it was quite as extensive as they said, and I don't think it was a different guy who took him every time he went.

He got a huge-limit credit card for sex on demand from some guy, it was reported. I doubt if that's true either. He might have got a little spending cash and nice clothes, I get the idea it was expected he live there with Norman, but I don't think he got that much cash. That would give them too much hold over him.

That's another one, that guy in *Newsweek* or *Time*, what a liar. I don't believe that story at all. Possibly he spent the night with Andrew but the rest of it, that he was drugged and strangled and so forth, that's phony baloney. I could've made up anything and told it to the *Enquirer* or whatever, I felt there was enough dirt about all three of them already, I didn't want to shovel another bunch onto it.

4

Steven Z.: I had a lot of nightmares for a while, as did Jay, who spent a lot more time with Andrew than I did. Jay went back down there for their pride thing, which was after Andrew's death.

He said it had become almost the de facto motto for the pride event, "Andrew was not representative of the gay community in San Diego," and I wanted to say what a lot of them realized, that Andrew was a lot more interesting than the gay community in San Diego.

San Diego is a kind of slowed down LA, but the military thing also influences the gay scene there, makes people more secretive and conservative than they might otherwise be. The military, they don't wear their uniforms off duty any more, pretty much not since Vietnam, anywhere. That's weird in San Diego, because there's always been this trend of people imitating military people, it's become ever more extreme, I hear about people who will actually get military tattoos. People like Andrew developed narratives of supposed military careers, which are completely fabricated.

Andrew and I were on a kind of parallel track for a year or two. I was trying to interview military guys for a book, and he was there, courting them for whatever it was he wanted from them. It was strange for me to realize that both of us were out there doing this, neither of us especially wanting sex from these guys. It's something I never understood. My information about Andrew is pretty much limited from fall of '93 to fall of '95, that's when Jay was hanging out with him, pretty much every weekend, he'd call the house for Jay, he'd come by and pick Jay up, sometimes I'd see him in the bars, but I wasn't going out much. And then there were the occasional drug transactions. But what I noticed was the guys I met almost never asked any questions of me, it was something about taking the interviewer's role, paying attention to these military guys. They were so starved for anybody to actually listen to them that they never thought to ask me anything about my background, and I assume that must have been somewhat the case with Andrew too.

I always knew him as Andrew DeSilva. My contacts were limited to the few overlapping friends. I did hear at one point that he'd had a different name, but I didn't think so much of that, I wrote under a pseudonym so I had a different name too. He told Jay his mother lived in La Jolla, he said he only gave him a pager number, he was never invited to his home, somebody said that's because he's Jewish, Andrew was always saying to this Jewish friend of ours, Oh you should come and meet my mother, she'll be so impressed to meet you because you're Jewish and so on, but it never happened.

The time he sent me the Xanax through Jay, it did cross my mind that it might be poisoned. I knew he didn't like me. I always thought there was something shady about him, and I cautioned Jay about his association with him, but I never had any idea what would happen, obviously. I just had a weird sense about him. I can't tell now if that was just antipathy because he was able to spend all this money on Jay and offer him things I couldn't, it's hard to know what was rivalry and how much was dislike. I think I met him before Jay introduced me to him, but I wouldn't have paid attention to him. I was looking for military people, and aside from any claims he made, he just wasn't the kind of person I would've noticed.

I never considered him attractive. I thought his whole look was sort of silly, calculated to impress. I think all people noticed was the money. Twenty-dollar tips, and things like that, that got people's attention.

He wasn't known as a drug person. Other people who spent a lot of time with him didn't seem to know about that. His attitude toward me seemed to change after he gave me drugs, sold them to me, but I can't say in retrospect how much that had to do with our rivalry for Jay's attention, or his way of dealing with dealing. Other people he sold drugs to were people he hung out with, I can't imagine that would be all of it, but some people were very surprised when I told them he'd sold me Xanax.

I asked a dealer down there about it, he was very skeptical. He thought Andrew would have to be in with a crooked doctor or moving things over the border from Tijuana.

He didn't have the reputation of going to bed with a lot of people. Between Jay and me, we were pretty busy in different kinds of marketplaces. Jay was a regular at all the bars and some of the bathhouses, and I preferred video arcades and tearooms and such, and nobody we ever knew secondhand saw Andrew in any of those places, ever. And most people showed up in one of those venues, you heard about people having sex through those meeting places.

Jay said there was one person Andrew did have sex with, and Andrew became very uncomfortable whenever the guy came up to him or showed up. Andrew shut him down right away. Jay told me this person was not attractive.

Jeff Trail, with whom I had fleeting encounters, was very pretty. Not everybody ages well. My encounters were … early '95, probably.

I had the sense that Andrew wasn't all that smart, but he had an incredible memory. He could recite the kind of details that somebody who was very smart wouldn't bother memorizing. He could remember the names of everybody he met, and … I once mentioned some very obscure assistant professor of gay studies somewhere that nobody would've heard of and Andrew knew all kinds of things like that.

I always thought of Andrew as a dangerous person. Although not necessarily as dangerous as some of the other crystal fiends and people Jay hung out with who I'd guess to be more capable of murder than Andrew.

All these little things that would potentially seem to be clues, seem too easy. Even sillier, I took Jay to see *The Wonderful, Horrible Life of Leni Riefenstahl* and Jay came out chattering away, asking me all these moral questions. "Can you call something great art if there's this moral taint to it?" And I gave him my argument, he wasn't satisfied, he kept going on and on about it. Most of his buddies in San Diego didn't want to talk about those kinds of questions. And then he asked Andrew, who said something like, "Greatness is beyond good and evil." Which in retrospect you can read all the Dostoevskian implications vis-à-vis him as a murderer, whereas it might have been a commonplace.

5

Jay: The thing with San Diego apart from priding itself on being America's finest city, everything down there, they try to keep this fantasy world of everything's wonderful, it's always sunny, everything's great, the beaches are great, I went down there for Gay Pride last July, that coincided with Andrew killing himself, right before that he was still a threat, basically people were groaning, "We don't want this to rain on our parade." There was speculation among all my friends, "Oh, maybe he'll gun down people at the parade," and after he killed himself it was a totally different attitude. The bucket of water was thrown on the Wicked Witch of the West and all these little munchkins could have their stupid parade.

That's exactly how they act, they're your best friend when things are great, when you're tipping them well, when you're paying attention to them.

Andrew did have an aggressive side. He had a violent side. The thing that shocked me was that he killed Jeff Trail. It didn't make sense. If you met them together, they were just, Jeff was really a supernice guy, a real sweetheart, kind of insecure, but a really really sweet guy, a totally loyal and devoted friend. If he gave you his word, that was as good as gold. And Andrew, even though I experienced a few fits of his rage and all that, he was a nice guy. I still don't think of him as a monster.

The whole thing contradicts how Andrew was. He was incredibly smart. He was easily the smartest person I knew in San Diego, that's not maybe saying much, San Diego's known for its surfers and real-estate agents and stuff like that. In San Diego, it was easy for him to carve out a territory because he was different, he was smart, he was very gregarious and amiable, he could draw you into a conversation, he had an incredible memory. If you told him something, he'd remember it years and years later. If he met a person once he could pull out all that information. He was extremely analytical. He was good at problem solving, good at figuring things out, good at making associations. I don't think he didn't know what was going on, that might've fed into why he killed Versace. The Versace camp says he never met Versace. But Andrew told me that he had met Versace, before I left San Diego. Not right before, but while I was hanging out with him. He might've been miffed, or—

I think it was more than a casual meeting. The way Andrew described it. He said he talked with him and everything. But Andrew—I kind of talked it up because Andrew prided himself on who he knew. I was just a Midwestern bumpkin when I got to San Diego, and after I met Andrew, for a while he told me so many things, it was just one of those things where if you're not familiar with that kind of society or that kind of culture, it's kind of like, Okay, I believe you because you said it, but it's kind of unbelievable. He said he had dinner with Versace, not just the two of them alone, but a dinner, something like that, I chalked it up—like when he said he was going to date the future Boise Cascade heir.

I only knew him as Andrew DeSilva. He never indicated that his family lived in the San Diego area. He was good at covering his tracks, that kind of tied in with his good memory. He told me he was Jewish, his parents were Jewish, they lived in New York, they'd emigrated from Tel Aviv. They went to New York and made a fortune in I forget what, they were poor to begin with and then worked their way up. He said he had a daughter with his wife who he's married to in San Francisco, he called her a harpy, though, I'm not even sure, so ... and that was basically it with his family life. He said he had one brother, but I think it was some sort of cover or smoke screen, because the guy lived in San Diego, and he just made allusions to him being his brother. I'm not sure if I was supposed to believe that or not.

He said he went to some prestigious college, because when I told him I was worried about not being able to get accepted into San Diego State, he sort of jokingly said we couldn't be friends any more if San Diego State wouldn't accept me ... because he'd attended some Ivy League college or something like that. Actually, you know what, he did say he went to school at UC San Diego, that he was sent out from New York to go to boarding school in La Jolla, now I'm remembering that. And I get the—yeah, because he said he was still going to UCSD part time, that he was working on his doctorate. I'm not sure what he said he was studying. He was just so learned, not learned but knowledgeable in so many different things, he could switch between biology to political science. Anyway, the thing that was so amazing, that really shocked me, a lot, was that he wasn't Jewish. He pulled off the whole Jewish thing, he knew everything about Judaism, he knew the holy days, all the details about the religion, and it turns out he wasn't Jewish.

I think it might've been a sore spot with him, that he had no ambitions. Right after my announcement about going to San Diego State, I said I wanted to teach and everything like that, and he wished me luck, he said he'd be able to come visit me at Yale or Harvard or wherever I'd be teaching, and I think he basically hoped everybody else would succeed, but he never displayed any ambitions.

He projected that he had plenty of money. In San Diego people think how well you're doing is based on money. He had money coming out of the ying yang. I think everybody thought he was at his last stop. He'd succeeded in life because he had enough money to do whatever he wanted, to flit around, have fun all the time: The whole ambition in life in San Diego is to get that money. It's kind of superficial and vacuous. But that's why it wasn't such a big deal in anybody's eyes that he wasn't aspiring to any sort of management position, or associate professor, or anything, because that's not what's on people's minds.

I didn't go to his house. He kept that pretty tightly under wraps.

I knew Jeff through Andrew. We'd go to the beach and hang out. There was a great admiration for Jeff Trail from Andrew. Jeff liked being fawned over. He was insecure. You can tell if some-body's insecure even if they swagger about a little bit. Little things in their behavior. That's the way Jeff was, insecure, and he appreciated Andrew's attention. Andrew built up his ego.

Andrew was usually in a good mood. Always very witty. He was good at keeping that kind of behavior up, loud, flamboyant—I mean there were times he was thoughtful and somewhat more reserved, I wouldn't want to say melancholy, that's too strong a word, but quieter, to get that side of him you needed to get him alone, which, he didn't like being alone, he always surrounded himself with people. But he was calmer one-on-one and a little less mannered. He wouldn't necessarily make jokes all the time. I can think of one day at the beach when we had a pretty serious conversation, and then we went to Wienerschnitzel, that hot dog place, we got these chili dogs, at first he didn't want to go, then he decided he'd slum with me. I came from a very, very poor background, so for me this was like going out, and we got orange drinks to make it extra trashy, and were sitting eating these hot dogs and then he divulged to me, I said, well, I complimented him, I thanked him for showing me—this was only a few months after I met him—I thanked him for taking me under his wing and taking me out to places I would never have gone like Cali-fornia Cuisine, I said I never got to see these things when I was younger because I was so poor, and he then told me he came from an extremely poor background too, he knew how it felt, so that was kind of touching, to offer that, when he said it I knew on some level he was telling the truth. Andrew was really good at hiding, or fogging up what he said so you were kind of skeptical whether he was telling the truth or not, but at that moment I knew he was telling the truth.

There was the popular conversation that he was selling crystal and using crystal, I never saw that, I know what people on crystal look like, I lived in San Diego long enough to see that. It's not like a caffeine buzz, caffeine people get chatty and very verbal and eloquent in their speech, but on crystal they're just stupid. I'm not sure where he got money from. All I know is he had a lot of money, I know you don't make a lot with prescription drugs. He did have prescription drugs available.

He didn't like people to treat him. I always perceived it as a power thing. If you treat somebody, they're at a naturally lower position.

If he didn't like you, you knew it. You were shut out of all the circles Andrew was friends in, you were shut out. Andrew would make it known, "I don't like that person, he thinks he can use me." One thing he complained about, one person he said was trying to use him to get to someone else. He had a perfect memory, if you slighted him, he'd remember exactly.

He liked going to the beach. He never went in the water. Movies. He didn't drink. He always had cranberry juice or soda. He took downers. Painkillers. One day at the beach I stepped on a stingray, out came that whole drugstore he carried around.

The Tom Cruise stuff was just too unbelievable. It would've been hard to want to kill Nicole Kidman, especially after the fabulous job she did in *To Die For*, which was one of his favorite movies.

6

Eric: I met him after I got out of the navy, which was September of '94. When I was working in Hillcrest at the Obelisk Bookstore.

When I stopped working in Hillcrest, I'd' still run into him all the time, but I didn't know him as well then. I could tell Andrew didn't have many close friends. I knew him as well as anybody else in San Diego, we would talk, but not about anything important. Any time you would ask him anything of any significance he would quickly change the subject and walk off to talk to somebody else. I knew him as Andrew DeSilva.

He always gave the impression that he was a rich little Jewish kid. That's the image he presented. He did make some interesting comments here and there about "this is pharmacy stuff, pharmacy knowledge." Everything he ever said was vague. He never really answered any questions. I always knew there was something wrong with him. Fred, my husband, knew him before I did, and he and his friend always used to joke about Andrew being the classic serial killer. This was long before, Fred has a psychology degree so he's always making comments about people's deep inner character. Joking, but "if this were to happen I wouldn't be surprised." Andrew introduced Fred and I, at Rich's, on Christmas Eve. I saw Fred across the bar and had no idea who he was, Andrew happened by, I thought "Oh, Andrew knows everybody, I'll ask Andrew." Christmas '94. Then forever after, if he saw us, he'd have to tell the world he introduced us. He never let us forget it.

He talked about how rich he was and how he was always doing things for other people. He told Fred that a good place to stash a body here in San Diego would be in the rocks behind Mount Cuyamaca. He said, "Vultures will pick a dead body apart within hours." He was always commenting on, "Oh, we just got back from dinner," usually at California Cuisine, or whatever trip he'd just taken. He'd stop and see me at the bookstore. It was one of his nightly stops between Rich's and Flicks and the Alibi. I guess he used to hang out at the Alibi, he was always kind of aloof why he went to the Alibi, I think it was for business reasons. The Alibi's a straight bar.

He never bought a book. At least not from me. He'd stop to say hi and be social, to socialize with whoever was there. I didn't pay that close attention to him, because I really didn't trust him. He was an acquaintance I saw all the time and talked to all the time but never about anything of any significance. I took everything he said with a grain of salt. There were so many times I attempted to ask a question that I didn't get an answer from him, it left me with, "This is totally superficial." The story I'd gotten was he was living home with his mother in La Jolla and that's where he got his money.

If it ever came up about him going out with somebody rather than him setting somebody else up, if you tried to set him up? He'd say, "Oh no, he's your type, not mine, I like the bondage type or whatever, I like them a little rougher." He did talk about that a lot. Bondage. How he liked that. Our relationship was always kind of playful. I was on the hunt. He thought I was so cute, he always tried to set me up with people. If I played with *him*, though, he'd say, "You're not rough enough for me." I never saw him come on to anybody. I saw him hugging people but he hugged everybody. That laugh.

I never saw him get angry with anybody.

I never would've invited him over for an evening, I wouldn't have felt comfortable divulging inner secrets or anything like that. It really all stemmed from the fact that if you tried to have a meaningful conversation he'd turn tail and go cackling off into the distance, "Oh, there's so-and-so." So I thought, if you're not even going to acknowledge who you really are, why should I trust you? I asked him point blank once, What do you do, where do you get your money? He just wouldn't answer. I think he got some of his money from selling drugs. Not all of it. I don't know how much money he really had, a lot of that may have been a facade also. I think he got some from there, because I saw him once, going into the Alibi, I said why are you going there and he said, It's a dark place for business.

He would never buy a drink for me. Here he was supposedly throwing out all this money, we'd be hanging out some place for the evening, and he never bought a round of drinks for anybody. It could've just been where I placed on his social network, I didn't rank high enough to get a drink from him. He was *known*. I don't know that he was *popular*. He was a contact point. He knew everybody. So he was a good person to know in that way, if you ever needed to know anybody else, Andrew knew them, you could always get introduced that way. I didn't know anybody who knew him as a close friend. We'd run into him everywhere, actually. We'd see him in La Jolla, all over the city. Popular, I don't know.

He was compulsively introducing himself to people. If there was someone cute around that he didn't know, he made it a point to meet them and find out who they were. But I don't know anybody who ever had sex with him. He never seemed to have a boyfriend. Occasionally he might introduce somebody as his boyfriend but it was just somebody he was with. When he came into the bookstore he'd be with different people every night. I just figured, "that's your story for the night." What's the name of that guy who got killed, Lincoln Aston. I do know he and Lincoln were relatively close. I heard that the place Lincoln was killed was the same place where Andrew lived with Norman afterwards.

I only met Jeff Trail once before I left to go to Japan, and that was it. From what I remember he was a great guy, real nice guy, but that's all. I could see him being close to Andrew because he was very social, that's the impression I got. These two social people. It's like that whole bar scene where everybody knows everybody and if you don't know them you want to know them because they're fresh meat. After I met Fred I stopped going to the bars and that's when I fell out of contact with Andrew because that's how I knew Andrew, from that whole scene, University Avenue.

I think the general reaction when it all came down was "Did you really know anything serious about him?" And everybody would be, "Well, no, not really." People were freaked out but, in a funny way, no one was really surprised.

Fred was the doorman at Flicks for a while. He says it said DeSilva on his license.

7

Statement of Sgts. Tichich, Lenzen and Gordon.
Given on 5–25–97.

Tuesday, 5–22–97, Investigators traveled to St. Diego in further-ance of this investigation.

Sgt. Lenzen contacted one of the individuals whose name had been supplied by one of the investigators of the FBI named PHILLIP DOLES. Phillip was contacted by phone. He has known Andrew Cunanan for approximately six months. He met Andrew when Phillip moved in across the street from Cunanan. He states that Andrew was popular in the clubs in the Hillcrest area of San Diego. He described Andrew as the type that would walk into a bar, give the bartender two hundred dollars to run a tab, then walk out after having spent only a fraction of it without getting any change. He states that Cunanan told him he was a computer consultant and that he would often travel around the country on business trips. He states Andrew did drink but he never saw him drunk.

Phillip advises he and the friends he hangs out with all wear their heads shaved. He noticed that in early April Andrew shaved his head also. He said Andrew dressed very well wearing expensive clothing and he also noted Andrew paid with cash rather than credit card. He also said he knows of no one that was sexually involved with Andrew.

After speaking with Mr. Doles Investigators then went to the California Cuisine restaurant located at 1027 University Avenue located in the Hillcrest District. It had been previously learned that this restaurant had often been patronized by Andrew Cunanan and his friends. At this restaurant May Papas, who is the daughter of the owner, Stele Kellemarais, was interviewed briefly. She was reluctant to discuss her knowledge of Cunanan and his associates but did state that she is aware that he often visited a very wealthy man by the name of Doctor Willis. She states Willis was not a medical doctor and that he is the former owner of the Park Manor Hotel in San Diego. She mentioned that Willis previously lived at 700 Front Street, San Diego however does not know his current address.

At approximately 1500 hours Investigators went to 11099 North Torrey Pines Road, the business address of Daniel Stih, the purpose of this visit was to interview Stih and follow up on information that had been previously obtained.

Daniel Stih advised he has some what limited knowledge regarding Cunanan as he disliked him. He said Andrew was fat and therefore he was not interested in him. He said to his knowledge no one that he knows of was involved romantically with Cunanan. He described Cunanan as asexual. He only knew Cunanan for six months. Stih did state that his friend Bob Belmont liked Cunanan.

At approximately 2200 hours Investigators returned to the California Cuisine restaurant and spoke with Robert Belmont. Belmont acknowledged that he knows Andrew Cunanan well. Robert advises that he met Jeff Trail when Andrew tried to set he and Trail up together, but it did not work out as Robert was not interested in Trail.

At approximately 1145 hours on Saturday, 5–24–97, Investigators went to the residence of Erik J. Greenman, dob 6–29–72, 1234 Robinson Avenue, Apt. 6, 619-692-4424. Greenman stated that he is the roommate of Andrew Cunanan and that he has known Andrew for approximately three years. He states that he has been living at this address the past fourteen months and that Andrew moved in approximately ten months ago. Erik is employed as a waiter at Mixx Restaurant, 3505 5th Avenue, San Diego, 619-299-6499 ....

Erik stated that he believes that Cunanan at approximately this time became involved in the sale of pharmaceutical type drugs that were stolen in some manner. It is Greenmans belief that Cunanan was involved in robberies of trucks that deliver pharmaceutical supplies to drug stores.

Erik states that on several occasions he observed Andrew to come into the residence with a suitcase that he believed contained pharmaceutical drugs and that he would take the suitcase in the bedroom where he would change clothes into business attire and then immediately leave the residence with the suitcase and Greenman's rottweiler dog. Andrew would return later and on several occasions Greenman observed him to be in possession of large amounts of cash. Greenman tells that on one occasion after Andrew returned that he stated something to the effect of "that's the quickest three thousand dollars that I ever made" ....

Greenman also stated, although he has no direct knowledge as to Andrew's role in these apparent robberies, that he believes that he was acting only as a middle man and that other persons unknown to him actually committed the robberies.

Greenman did recall seeing some of the prescription bottles and noticed that they had a label of Thrifty Drugs on them. He does not know if this could be related to the fact that Andrew once held a job at a Thrifty Drug Store in the San Diego area ....

At approximately 1430 hours, 5–24–97, Investigators went to the law office of Richard G. Mr. G. advised he would prefer if only one investigator interviewed him and Sgt. Lenzen did the interview.

Mr. G. advises that he met Andrew Cunanan in early 1993. He states that he met Jeff Trail just after this when Cunanan introduced him to Trail. He was unaware of any problems between the two of them. He states that when he first met Trail, Trail was still in the Navy. He states that his relationship with Trail was very casual and he could not provide much insight into Trail's life. He did recall an incident while Trail was in the Navy in which Trail was criminally charged for failing to report the presence of marine paint on a ship's manifest. G. states that he believes that there was some kind of trial which resulted in Trail being found not guilty, however Trail felt the incident would be a blemish on his record thus harming his chances for advancement in the Navy so he decided to resign his commission ....

G. states that he always knew Cunanan by the last name of DeSilva until when G. purchased a plane ticket for DeSilva as a gift so that DeSilva could accompany he and several other friends for a week end excursion to Vancouver. When he told DeSilva about the ticket, DeSilva told him his name on his passport was Cunanan and the name on the ticket would have to be changed. G. never inquired as to why Cunanan had two names ....

Lenzen asked G. if he had any knowledge of Cunanan being involved in the sale or transportation of drugs. G. states that he did not have any information about this, however did advise that in 1995 and 1996 had sustained a nagging neck injury which eventually resulted in surgery. He did recall that when he was having chronic neck pain that Cunanan provided these pills (3) for G. to try because the medication prescribed for G. was not eliminating the pain. He did not recall if the pills were contained in a prescription bottle or not.

G. describes the rather extravagant taste in clothes and dinners that Cunanan apparently enjoyed. Lenzen asked G. if Cunanan seemed to have a lot of money prior to Cunanan entering into the relationship with Norman Blachford. G. stated that Cunanan always threw around a lot of money both prior to Blachford and during the Blachford relationship ....

G. advises that Cunanan told him that he was born in Israel and had served in the Israeli Navy. He also stated that he had attended Yale University Graduate School and attended Graduate School at the University of San Diego with a Major in History.

G. believes that if his name is publicly brought into this case he will lose his job.

G. states that since the murders he has spoken with a friend, Joseph W. G. said W. is also a friend of Trail's. W. told him of two unusual incidents which had been told to W. by Jeff Trail. The two incidents involved dinner parties that had been organized by Cunanan and attended by Trail. G. did not feel comfortable relating the stories to Lenzen and recommended Lenzen talk to W.

Lenzen subsequently contacted Joseph W. by telephone. Lenzen asked W. if he would relate the dinner party stories as told by Trail.

The first dinner party was one which was thrown in San Diego by Cunanan. It was a birthday party for Cunanan in which Cunanan was apparently attempting to impress Norman Blachford just prior to Cunanan and Blachford entering into a relationship. Andrew Cunanan apparently went out and purchased himself several expensive gifts, then gave the gifts to the friends who would be attending the birthday party. He told the friends to wrap the presents and bring them to the party. Trail apparently believed Cunanan's motive for doing this was an effort to impress Blachford by showing Blachford that Cunanan's friends liked him so much that they purchased expensive gifts for his birthday.

The second incident was a dinner party which apparently took place in San Francisco. At this occasion Cunanan was apparently trying to impress two unknown individuals from either Chicago or San Francisco. Prior to the dinner party Andrew approached Trail (who was at the time a Cadet at the CHP Training Academy) and asked him to tell the other people at the party that he was really an instructor at the Academy rather than a trainee. Andrew apparently approached another friend who was attending the dinner party and asked him to present himself as a country western singer, instead of his actual employment as a steward for Southwest Airlines.

8

Andrew won Jay a melon baller at a Hillcrest Tupperware party, and in May 1995, a "mentally disturbed drifter" named Kevin Bond bashed in Lincoln Aston's brains, supposedly with an *objet d'art* in Lincoln's home. Kevin Bond ran as far as Utah, then thought better of it and turned himself in. Jeff Trail cashiered out of the navy after appearing, heavily veiled, on a television news program, weighing in on the "don't ask, don't tell" policy for gays in the military. Somewhere in the summer of 1995, Andrew kissed Thrifty Junior and Mom good-bye and moved in with Norman Blachford at 100 Coast Boulevard. Weirdly, the condo they lived in had been purchased from Lincoln Aston. If you believe just anything, Blachford was one of a long line of rich men whom Andrew exploited after carefully researching their careers and interests, their fondness for orchids, for example, but if this were true, the world being what it is, the gay world and journalism particularly being what they are, the proper names of Andrew's other paramours would by now be as familiar as the post-Onassis escorts of Jackie O. It's plausible that Andrew did a lot of detective work on the rich, to move among them easily and comfortably identify, as if born to it, the luxurious junk with which their lives and their homes are so often stuffed. The rich are different from us, different anyway from him, as a magic charm against death the rich fill their houses and private airplanes and seasonal hideaways with incredibly precious and intimidating versions of the everyday objects ordinary people have, plates and flatware and furniture and flush toilets, in addition they fill all available space with every imaginable and unimaginable aesthetic object, creating an aura of awe and grandeur around the invisible Freudian fecal pile that makes it all possible. The horror vacuui sensibility of the rich is a form of voodoo against the inevitable neoplasm, coronary episode, renal failure, diabetic amputation, prostate malignancy, cerebral incident, or mentally disturbed drifter that arrives, voodoo or no voodoo, exactly on time in every life but Leni Riefenstahl's. There's good evidence that Andrew liked moving through the sorts of rooms that *Vanity Fair* writers live to describe, though his actual relationship to objects, and to physical reality in general, may have been more complicated, more inflected by magical thinking, than even the most ardent debutante's. What isn't plausible is the notion that Andrew sunned himself on the Riviera and regularly fleeced little fortunes out of lonely millionaires while managing a drugstore and living with his mother.

Miss Blachford isn't spilling. His statements to police and FBI suggest a serene detachment from the case, as if an appliance he had once leased were now suspected of causing a warehouse fire. It may have been Norman, and not Lincoln Aston, who flew Andrew up to Seattle and introduced him to Miss Miglin, but Andrew's sister Elena recalls being shown a photograph, long before Andrew and Norman cohabited, in which a man she later recognized as Miglin sits in some watering hole with Andrew's arm draped around his shoulders, both looking groggy.

Blachford told police that he "always" knew Andrew as DeSilva, never as Cunanan, despite having traveled with him on numerous flights that required the presentation of passports and the entry of one's legal name on the air ticket. Andrew may, qua Eric's Fred, have had a driver's license under DeSilva, but the only two passports ever issued to Andrew were issued to Andrew Cunanan. (The mystery of the DeMarrs passport reportedly used to register at the Normandy Beach Hotel is easily cleared up. There was no DeMarrs passport. No passport or other ID was presented to the hotel. Andrew may have been asked for it and later given the desk a passport number without the passport, but this writer checked in there without being asked to present anything.)

We know precious little about their domestic arrangements, only what others observed or thought they observed or heard other people observe, enough perhaps to conclude that Norman's physical demands on Andrew weren't egregious, didn't involve the elaborate use of implements or prostheses, and that there's quite a lot of truth to Maryann's assertion that Andrew was employed *as a companion to the elderly.* We know that Andrew was *paid a salary* to be free to travel with Norman at any time. In the period immediately prior to Andrew moving in with Norman, Andrew persuaded Norman to shift his base from Scottsdale to La Jolla. Andrew accompanied Norman back and forth between Arizona and California many times, for much of the year they spent together the couple was in transit, *on vacation* essentially, soaking up atmosphere, dining in wonderful restaurants, consuming cultural goodies in fabulous settings, mingling with other well-off people Norman's age who had earned the good times they were having while waiting around to kick off.

Andrew loved it, just loved it, and spent a fair amount of energy dissembling his surprise and pleasure, since all the places he was seeing for the first time were places he supposedly had been a million times before.

9

Now he has exactly what he wants. It's no longer important to impress people with millions he doesn't have. Now he can spend freely instead of strategically. He even can be candid about where the money comes from, like a deb who's married well. Not candid with everyone, not with the people who "matter," but within the disposable circles of Hillcrest friends, cigar store clerks, headwaiters and bartenders, it's a good joke that Robin Hood swoops down from La Jolla when he's in town to blow his rich hubby's money on clueless servicemen and hangers-on. Money makes him glow. Years of pretense have been magically ratified. The manic, antic Andrew people remember is this Andrew, bubbling over with nouveau riche *jouissance*. The twenty-dollar tips become forty-dollar tips, he's even been known to tip 100 percent on meals for six or seven friends where the bill ran over a thousand dollars. The clothes are all top designers and Andrew's fond of giving away thousand-dollar jackets, five-hundred-dollar pairs of shoes after wearing them once. He gives away watches, cameras, calculators, bracelets, Cuban cigars, every imaginable and unimaginable pricey thing, he buys scarves and suits and silk shirts in Europe and finds them not quite to his liking when he sees them in California light, out they go. Andrew wants every little thing that touches him perfect, the highest possible expression of taste is barely good enough for him, Norman's condo isn't good enough, it has to be redecorated under Andrew's supervision, the Infiniti he's driving isn't really good enough either but he's confident he'll boost something grander out of Norman in the fullness of time. Norman has a tendency to *penny-pinch*, Norman has an old-fashioned habit of *nickel and diming* his companions that Andrew plans to cure him of, but no hurry, there's plenty of money and therefore plenty of time, time is money if you're hustling it, but if you already have it, money is time.

Another curious change: the Philippines are no longer terra incognita. Among selected new people, Andrew insinuates a connection to the Philippines, he's not even very emphatic about being *Spanish* Filipino as opposed to indigenous. Of course, his Filipino family is more exalted than most, *Think Imelda's Blue Ladies*, his father is a former general under Marcos, a bisexual roué cut from the same awesome cloth as Rubirosa, in fact, who always has the cutest teenage boyfriends, and owns an immense pineapple plantation, on the veranda of which Papa can be found any night polishing off a bottle of Jack Daniel's with his latest inamorato, *Think Tennessee Williams*, Andrew would instruct people, sometimes painting in the dire sexual depravity rampant in the tropics, the eternal machinations over family money and real estate, his mother the Dragon Lady, his father Burl Ives, sometimes he tossed Christopher in there as the hippie black sheep canoe-carving beach bum, his sisters of course were trapped in a glass menagerie, one anyway, the other had split to become a doctor, escaping the *island madness* just as Andrew had after years of working as a private pilot for a high government official … And more curious still, Andrew apparently drops these far-fetched visions into gatherings with Norman's friends, in Norman's presence, worldly people who've been around the block a few times and have plenty to protect, ergo good ears and noses for con jobs. Their verdict on Andrew: *charming* in his way and *pretty* at least in the beginning and *terribly bright*, probably *harmless* too, but completely *directionless* and a *compulsive liar*.

People will put up with anything from the young and beautiful. *Only God could love you for yourself alone and not your golden hair.* The morphology of appraising glances exchanged by aging homosexuals in the presence of junior flesh marks a boundary between species. The old know *everything*, including all the secrets of the young. Andrew seldom suspected that others saw more of him than he ever chose to reveal. And when he did, he hated them. His looks protected him from harsh opinions. Delusions nourished themselves on tactful silences. Among the rich and old, Andrew's looks deserved humoring and among the young, where the standards for flesh are more devastating, money insulated him from the usual acerbities and blunt reality checks. Friends did throw him over. Jay dropped him after Andrew blinded a small crab with a cigarette, ripped it still wriggling into pieces with his car keys, and fed its entrails into the weird maw of a pink anemone, one day at the beach in La Jolla. Andrew had already offered to murder Steven when Jay, in an access of paranoia, thought Steven had broken into his car. A joke, Jay thought, until the incident with the crab. Jeff still hung around with Andrew, haplessly, as if Andrew's fierce attachment could not be severed by any usual means, as if he had assembled Andrew from an ugly part of his own dream life and now was responsible for him, but even Jeff laid plans for his escape.

10

Witness: Karen Marie Lapinski
DOB: 042468
Address: 1750 Vallejo St., 104, San Francisco, CA 94123
Phone: 415-673-7360

On Tuesday, May 6, 1997, at approximately 9:40 a.m., I was contacted at the Sheriff's Office by Karen Marie Lapinski, DOB 042468, and Evan Wallitt, DOB 012060. In speaking with both Karen and Evan, they advised they had been faxed a newspaper article which talked at the death of David Madson, a very good friend of theirs. In speaking with Karen, she stated that she had previously lived in Minnesota, Duluth. Karen went on to state that she had worked with David at Donaldson's in Maplewood, MN. Karen stated that David had originally started law school at the U of M, him deciding to quit law school and go into architecture, which he did, him receiving a master's degree from the U of M. Karen stated that she has known David for approximately 15 years. Karen stated that in November, 1995, David was in San Francisco on a job related trip. Karen stated that while David was in San Francisco, he met Andrew Cunanan in a bar. Karen went on to state that David had told her that in meeting Andrew they hit it off together at which time David brought Andrew home with him and introduced him to Karen and Evan. Karen remembered that Andrew had told them at the time that he lived on Green Street in San Francisco, CA. Karen stated that David and Andrew stayed together at the Hotel Monaco or Oriental Hotel in San Francisco.

11

Notes of meeting with F: David Madson had an infectious laugh. He was flirtatious, sometimes giddy. Short, blond, not a beauty, but cute. He was a bit of an ass kiss. Very intelligent, almost intimidatingly so. He dressed expensively, even among expensive dressers: two-thousand-dollar suits, seven-hundred-dollar shoes. Never spoke about Andrew to his friends but referred to "someone in France," someone with money: F assumes this was really Andrew. He preferred black men, southerners he met on business trips. F. says he wasn't F.'s type, yet F. sometimes entertained the notion of having something more with him. David always got what he wanted and when he got it he didn't want it any more.

12

Andrew sent him a drink in the Midnight Sun, a bar in the Castro where the usual thing is to stand around gaping at video monitors planted high on the walls. Not unlike Flick's, Andrew's favorite bar in San Diego, which offers a more considered decor but no less than six screens that continually run music videos and snippets of ancient sitcoms, movies featuring men in drag, the campier moments of recent award shows. For gays of a certain age, such bars are waxworks simulacra of a former time, like the replicant shopping districts of Universal City and the theme bars sited outside the gates of various Disneylands. The same cock is served, but *nothing ever happens*. The radical energies of the past, the varieties of difference a living culture germinates in defiance of tedium have wheezed away their last breaths. What's left is a claustral normality without secrets, a subculture with the same tastes and icons as the culture at large. The average gay bar is no longer a place where the chaos of libido dissolves the ligatures of class consciousness. Even the scary trade of yesteryear, the semistraight proles with bad teeth and fabulous endowments, wouldn't be caught dead in such a place without the bands of their Calvin Klein underpants conspicuous above the beltline.

A lifeless scene, in other words. Andrew had flown up from San Diego for a little action, on the pretext of visiting his wife. David Madson was taking a break from job hunting in Minneapolis. One has to blame the braindead flavor of the ambiance for the fact that they found each other fascinating, enough so that David brought him back to the apartment on Vallejo and introduced him to his friends, then spent the night in Andrew's hotel room. Andrew gave his real name, which by this time felt like a pseudonym, or an identity he was resurrecting for some fugitive purpose. In the room, Andrew tried out his Mr. Benson routine, ordering David to strip, kneel before his master on the floor, and kiss his master's boots. Andrew called David "faggot" and "asshole," growling the words in a harsh manly fashion, as Mr. Benson was wont to do. David called Andrew "sir." Andrew wanted him to take his fist, when that was refused he ordered David into the bathroom and told him to get in the tub and "bathe in his manwater," that too was declined, and after some perfunctory humiliation they cuddled in bed and fell asleep. It wasn't Utopia, but Andrew had found Love.

13

In the weeks and months that followed David Madson became Andrew's Holy Grail, the Great Love he convinced himself he'd been looking for all his life. Andrew began sending him letters and postcards and phoning him regularly, to keep himself present in David's mind. *David, Thanks for making my time in the city so much fun. We made good memories. So, okay, as I write this I am watching a lecturer deliver a talk "Treasures of the Tsars" at the S.D. Museum of Art…. a slide of a little sleigh that the Tsar's children used to be pulled in by dwarfs! Pretty cool. I leave for NYC next week. This is the season to remember friends, both old and new. I hope this note finds you thriving…. I really do. Drew.* At Christmas a box arrived at the condo, containing a heavy book on Palladio and snapshots of David with his Dalmatian, Prints. *David, I knew in my heart "someday my Prints would come." Thanks for the care package…. I can't see your blue eyes because of the aviators…. The book is beautiful! I plan to leave it out in a conspicuous place as evidence of my high erudition & exalted taste—poor fools if they only knew, ha! Really, thank you. I think maybe you're kinda smart & I'm a little undone because your gifts were so sweet. They made me feel good about the world … I can't wait to see you. Until then I must content myself with these photos in hues of ice, pearl, mist, ash (not stark, stylish) and remember through-the-veil-of-imagination with them. Yours, Drew.* For New Year's he and Norman and twenty of Norman's friends flew to New York, not as a Gamma Mu thing but merely as a rich people's thing. They stayed at the Millennium and went on the Old Globe Theater tour. They saw *Miss Saigon* and the other big shows. They watched the ball drop in Times Square. They had dinner in Rounds, the hustler

bar and restaurant, rent boys spilling over the sides of their banquette. Norman liked a little extra spice from time to time, to
break up the monotony. Andrew jogged in Central Park. He
phoned David often. David knew nothing about Norman. By his
account, Andrew didn't "live" anywhere, he "stayed" in various
properties maintained by his businesses. David had a voice mail
number and a mailing address in La Jolla and no way to reach
Andrew directly, as far as he knew Andrew's businesses related to
the film world, film sets, some type of technical operations. He
heard noise abatement. He heard Churubusco Studios. The
operation whatever it was involved "meetings" that were also
pleasure trips, deals that closed in the world's pretty places just
for the fun of it. They hooked up again in San Francisco right
after the New York trip. Champagne and oysters at Zuni, Chinese nouvelle cuisine at Betelnut. Andrew prepared for the
rendezvous by memorizing a standard history of Western architecture as well as a work on local landmarks. During the weekend
he was able to casually point out and expatiate upon the Neutra
house on Calhoun Terrace, the Alcazar Theater on Geary Street,
and the weird little housing development in Presidio Terrace,
which Andrew called "Quaker gingerbread"; he just happened to
know that the Federal Reserve where Evan Wallitt worked was a
Skidmore, Owings, and Merrill Building, and that there were
two generations of Newsoms, and that Gilbert Stanley Under-
wood built the original Rincon Center as a post office. San
Francisco's literary heritage likewise held no secrets. Andrew con-
versed easily about Robert Louis Stevenson and Ambrose Bierce
and Lawrence Ferlinghetti and even Ina Coolbrith, or rather these
names floated in and out of conversations about other things,
about Robert Altman's comeback and Kathleen Battle's evil

temperament, and episodes of *Roseanne* and *The Simpsons* that they'd both seen, and this and that that reminded Andrew of something Nietzsche wrote and of course *The Fountainhead* came up and David had to confess that *The Fountainhead* was one of his favorite books even if some of the ideas in it seemed pretty cruel and unrealistic and Andrew informed him that Ayn Rand had lived in a Richard Neutra house originally built for D. W. Griffith, furthermore life is cruel, and different rules apply for exceptional people. The sex was better this time. Andrew had poppers and dildos and a zippered hood and a ball gag on a leather thong and David trusted him enough to use the dildos on him while he had the hood on, though he had misgivings about it, for David *being penetrated* carried with it all kinds of control issues and trust issues and safety issues, Andrew assured him that *the bottom is always in control,* David let himself get into it, nodded agreement when Andrew unzipped the mouth part and pushed his erection into the opening, it was like being meat, meat engorging other meat, the quiddities of their personalities falling away leaving warm raw meat sweating in the room. A week later David got a letter from the Halekulani in Waikiki, *Dave, It's beautiful here. The hotel's main building dates from the 30's. Five acres of beach front on a spectacular setting. I was going to send you a shell but it wouldn't go in the envelope.... If you have a chance, think of me. Miss you. Your devoted pygmie wife, Drew.* Two days later another note, on Mauna Kea Beach Hotel stationary: *Dave, This is the Brady Bunch "The Hawaiian Episodes." Even the hotel looks like a Mike Brady original. Never took to the skies but did go out on an outrigger (I suck).... At night they shine spotlights on the water and you can see giant manta rays! Very languid. I sleep 14 hours a day. Feel suspended between two worlds here.*

Not paradise, but not Miami Beach either.... Best sushi ever! You pick your dinner out swimming in a tank and then they scoop it up and sushi it. O.K. So much for the aloha spirit. There is fun here and much beauty, but I wonder if all the Howlii's (Mauuis) know how lucky they are. I'm sure I don't. Big kiss for Prints, Mahalo. Drew.
On the phone, Andrew filled in certain blanks with allusions to business partners, associates, visiting friends, the busy agenda of a slightly alienated but always bouncy socialite, the suggestion was that if only he were not enmeshed in the admittedly sybaritic atmospheres of what were, nonetheless, the responsibilities of capital, he would want to be with David every minute, and in fact, aside from Norman, who was utterly in the dark about David's existence, David was the only reciprocal "romantic" partner he'd ever found, though it didn't follow that Andrew truly repined for David's company, for what he really wanted was to go on living this endless vacation with Norman while making himself the object of David's heart. Andrew believed that his letters and phone calls were casting a magic spell over David and binding him closer. He considered himself a mysterious, charismatic figure in David's eyes, a romantic figure very much like Mr. Benson, whose actual sources of income are never revealed in the novel. In fact, he supposed that David felt highly flattered to know Andrew thought of him in so many different places. This was a little bit true. Of course some of the things Andrew said on the phone and wrote in his cards and letters David found offputting, unclever, tiresome in their self-absorption. Andrew seemed to think his whimsical remarks about his own fun-fabulous misadventures were inexhaustibly fascinating, or howlingly funny, and then too, David sometimes had the faintly disturbing only half-conscious sense that Andrew's missives contained an

essential falsity. David did not at first fully register these irrita-
tions. At first he banished them to Siberia in his mind as
unworthy of his strong affection for Andrew, David didn't allow
himself to think negative thoughts about people he cared about,
he stored them in a special place, froze them to keep them from
going rotten, he dismissed the infelicities of Andrew's letters as
the sloppiness of haste and distraction, at the same time David
felt there was not yet enough between them to constitute an
"exclusive" relationship, he had no thought of being "faithful" to
Andrew except in the sense that he never mentioned to Andrew
the men he dated and slept with in Minneapolis. David, like
Andrew, had a whole, full life to occupy him. *Dave,* came more
news, from Colorado, *The only card in Aspen without pictures of
skiers!* A tent designed by Eero Saarinen for the 1949 Goethe
Bicentennial. Andrew slouched in a lounge overlooking a chair
lift that Norman penguined towards on his skis. He sipped his
chocolate and rolled an unlit cigar between his fingers. *I have
decided to become a ski bum and live up the life of a wandering zen
monk. (But not before lunch).... My ski outfit is so cute. I look like
an eggplant wrapped for Christmas. My gout has kept me off the
slopes.... "Stop crying at your own movies. Make a new movie."—
Billy Wilder. I have decided this is good advice for happy living. Life
is good.* Fat clouds skated slowly across the blue sky. Andrew was
getting fat. Putting on pounds anyway. For some reason, he sent
the address of the other condo. *Andrew "I'm talking and I can't
shut up" Cunanan 7486 La Jolla Blvd. #498 La Jolla CA 92037.*
Aspen was full of people Norman knew from years of doling
checks to the Phoenix Symphony and other worthy causes. They
were all twenty or thirty years older than Andrew. David found
another picture postcard in the mail, "Dave and Dicky Durrance

ride the old T-Bar tow on Little Nell, 1949." *Dave, Went to party last night at "the magic mushroom house." An icon of the 70's design, it's shaped like a mushroom, man! ... The Audi drifted into a snowbank and got stuck (I was driving, O.K.) Local crowd.... Bought a t-shirt that reads "Just hand over the chocolate and nobody will get hurt." Very me. Very Boobstein. Last day today so will eat decadently. Yours most deliberately, Drew.* David puzzled over "most deliberately," it had the dyslexic ring of Andrew's pseudoprofundities, but he filed the note away with the others and fed the dog, made some phone calls, met some friends for dinner; he had a new job, a free-lance arrangement at John Ryan Co. had now become regular employment, David had new things to focus on and shunted Andrew over to a siding. Andrew was on his way to Europe. *Hi! Just had dinner here,* a card from Café des Artistes in New York read, *I'm beginning to think I squat over my meals too long.* Jesus, David thought, who cares? *Will you write to me?* Write where, exactly, David wondered. *Do your work & be all you can be (the two don't necessarily go hand in hand). Ciao, Drew.* Andrew pictured David hunched over a drafting board, busy, his time outside the office a static blur of listless socializing, Andrew's absence a throbbing lack, as Mr. Benson, far away, donned a black silk cape and domino in his Gritti Palace suite above the spectral gray Adriatic. *Dear Dave, Carnevale! Confused memory. Every morning I wander through a maze of streets & bridges to Florian's for coffee.* He really only had to walk a few yards down San Marco to get to Florian's, and as it was freezing in Venice, Andrew barely stirred from the Gritti before noon. *Sometimes bouncing over the lagoon in a riva on a stream of sunlit foam.* He and Norman had visited the cemetery island and the villa Wagner died in, tramped through about a thousand churches, ate lunch several times in tiny, hard-to-find trattorias on Guidecca. *Sometimes keeping pace with the Italians (very slow, like a gondola). I am such a tourist! Oh well. The sound of water lapping on stone is everywhere. Gardens hidden behind high walls. Lots of secrets. I kinda like it. The place is in decay. When the light is fading I look at the facades and they start to dissolve.... Woody Allen came after all! The name of his jazz group is Woody Days. What's he thinking? ... I am a cipher amidst the immense splendors of this place. I don't have a mask (but my natural one is so good!) More dogs. More than in Aspen even. They bring them to restaurants. Princeton would be very happy cause there are mostly Dalmations here. I did not send you a Valentine but I wish you were mine. I am enclosing the Florian logo which I think looks like a heart. "European men are sexy. American men are cute." John Faber the Pencil King.... Next week I go to Firenze incognito. Per bello uomo della mia mente, Drew.* They moved on to Florence. Andrew spent an entire day in the Uffizi, then another. Norman was, he considered, in many ways an ideal companion: urbane, erudite, curious, best of all uninsistent. Perhaps with some adjustments, some genuinely binding arrangement about money, the relationship could work itself into something permanent. He would have to be free to see other people, specifically David. Grand Hotel, Firenze.... *Watching the sunset over the Arno. I went to a cool house in Venice by Carlo Scarpa. 18th c, outside, inside contemporary & very good space. Yum.... "Mighty Aphrodite" is called "La Dea Dell Amore" here which means "The Goddess of Love." It doesn't rhyme, man!!! Can't wait to get back to the states. Florence is cold and metallic & very DeChirico this time of year. Arrived by train this afternoon. I ate at Harry's Bar in Venice almost every day & it really is the only good place. We had a high tide & I had to walk on wooden planks cause the streets were flooded.... Florence is one of Italy's gay meccas so I think I'll go out tonight. The local club is called the "Crisco" which is not encouraging (at least, not to me anyway). O.K. Nobody wears b-ball hats here & there are no blondes.... Later, will have dinner with some student friends at Enocoteca Pinchidri & I can speak American & be vulgar. Yeah! The shops here are not so good & I haven't bought a thing.... Bye for now, Drew.* Next came Milan, and then a short visit to Nice, and the villa Norman owned or leased, Andrew wasn't sure which, at St. Jean Cap-Ferrat. Yes. He wouldn't mind ten, even twenty years of just *appreciating* things and holding his own at dinner parties. There were far worse things in life than the twee faggots Norman enjoyed keeping up with in his travels, these little monied nobodies with their muscled bum boys in tow. Andrew had no trouble whipping up breakfast for six or planning pleasant surprises for Norman. He was having trouble keeping his weight down, Norman never said anything, but Andrew knew if his looks went no amount of sparkling conversation would hold things together. *Only God could love you for yourself alone and not your golden hair.* Amber: Window to the Past. Small gecko lizard, 23–30 million years old in Dominican amber. Hundreds of species of these kind of geckos are found throughout the Caribbean today. X rays reveal that its bones are still intact. The nearby leaf was chewed, probably by a leaf-cutter bee. Length of amber 1.7". The first card from New York had been bought at the Natural History Museum. *Just like Jurassic Park,* Andrew printed. *They also had works of art in an amber room created for the King of Prussia. The Nazis dismantled it in 1942. The walls were covered in a mosaic of 30,000 carved pieces.... It's cold here, but I had a jog in the park anyway. Tonight I go to see "Mrs. Klein" with Uta*

Hagen. Miss you, Drew. The second card showed a Roman fresco in the Metropolitan Museum: *Saw "Pergamon" show today. Nice if you're into gigantism. The Rockefeller Wing is reopened & looks out into the park. I think I'll move in.... I love the armor. I mean those gloves man! The articulation of the joints! Cool. Mrs. Klein very good.* Andrew found a weekend in March to fly in to Minneapolis, get the lay of the land, meet some of David's friends. The weather was blustery and Minneapolis struck him as a maze of weird Americana, he didn't get the point. He stayed at the Radisson and picked up the check at every meal. There was an awkward episode when Andrew borrowed David's car to go shopping at Mall of America, Andrew shoplifted a lot of clothes from Nordstroms and Gap and then forgot them in the trunk, where David found them and knew they'd been stolen because of the price tags and the way they'd been tossed, Andrew didn't understand why David got so exercised about it and David was flummoxed by Andrew's attitude, if he had so much money to throw around why did he need to steal clothes. With David's friends Andrew came across patronizing and arrogant, desperate to impress. David's friend Rich thought Andrew was "overcompensating," trying too hard, when Andrew told them at dinner that his family had a printing empire in the Philippines Rich said, Oh, you must speak Spanish then, and Andrew fumbled, admitted he didn't, and quickly changed the subject. Without really meaning to, Rich raised a lot of questions Andrew didn't have smooth answers for, rattling Andrew's international moneybags routine. Andrew didn't appreciate the slow, methodical niceties of Minneapolis. People there seemed indifferent to the wider, more colorful world he felt he represented.

Another quick rendezvous in March, in San Francisco: dinner at Sanraku on Sutter, and a surprise, Andrew introduces David to the legendary Jeff Trail, a pleasant enough, self-effacing guy who's training for the California Highway Patrol. JT and Andrew arrive at the restaurant together, and it's obvious they've known each other a long time, they have *key words* that come up in the course of the meal. JT tells some funny tales about the CHP Academy that illustrate the difference between law enforcement as people imagine it and law enforcement as it really is, there's also a fair amount of chitchat about guns, the three-shot bursts of a 9mm Heckler and Koch VP70 and the blowback design of the 7.65mm Walther PPK, the virtues and drawbacks of the .40mm weapons favored by the CHP, all this palaver about firearms is way outside David's range. It seems that JT and Andrew have this sort of jock bonding going way back, it's all convivial enough, but David gets the feeling that JT, at moments, is backing away from this intense rapport with Andrew, it's just an impression, almost nothing, a hint of reserve, a suggestion that JT isn't totally available to Andrew's promptings, and later on, in the hotel room they've taken together, Andrew throws out ambiguous asides concerning J. T., *he doesn't know what the fuck he wants*, Andrew mutters, scrambling in his travel bag for handcuffs and a pair of serrated nipple clamps he's eager to try out on David. *Worship Daddy's pecker*, he commands, tonight Andrew takes everything a whole lot further than before, especially in the verbal abuse department. The time just flashes by. Soon another letter, from the Ritz Carlton in Phoenix. *Dave, Phoenix is a large citylike area surrounding the Ritz Carlton. It's about 3000 miles from Manhattan. The terrain here is varried and ranges from clay to grass to composition, depending on the type of court you like. JT says that because Phoenix is on the large side it is advisable to play close to the net. People are supposed to come here because of the climate. The people at Canyon Ranch are all on special diets that restrict their intake of synthetic food. (Synthetic food?) JT says that organically grown fruits & vegetables make the cocaine work faster.... St. Jean Cap Ferrat is very cute. Lots of big white villas, pretty beaches, French actors, yachts, lavish parties and people who speak English. I can't wait to go back. People there spend most of their time having lunch, which is something I do very well ... Everybody on the Riviera is busy. The directors are busy trying to get something to direct, the producers to produce, the buyers want sellers and the sellers want buyers. And the waiters are very busy trying not to take your order.... Went to the new Museum of Contemporary Art in S.D. Very cool. Much cooler than the S.F.M.O.M.A. Met two guys that work with Robert Venturi ("Oh, Bob.") Whatever. I am now plotting revenge. Unfortunately the clock has just caught my eye. I must get going. I have decided against the half an orange and jar of peanuts in the mini-bar and on the spur of the moment have decided to dine out. I guess that's just the kind of boy I am—whimsical.... Yours, Drew.*

For most of April Andrew played Lady Bountiful in Hillcrest, sometimes he took Norman with him to the bars and restaurants and picked up his check, a nice gesture, even if the money came out of Norman's pocket in the first place. In Flick's and Rich's and The Loft and El Caliph and the Inn on the Park Bar there were always at least two little twinks who pranced in Andrew's wake scrounging beverages and hanging on his fabulous accounts of foreign travel, behind his back the same twinks noted that Andrew was *really letting himself go*. During April, he met up with David twice, once in Long Beach and again in San Francisco, more epic meals, more epic ruminations about architecture, painting, and the movies (Andrew's business brought him in contact with *everybody*), more incredibly intense sex. David voiced certain qualms about "getting involved." He described the fiasco of his long affair with Greg Nelson, a guy he'd lived with for two years in one apartment and then shared the lease on his loft with for about six months. This affair had started on a high, bright note, but Greg Nelson turned out to have problems. After a time, they fought constantly, Greg Nelson having fallen into a self-destructive spiral, it didn't help that Greg Nelson's mother committed suicide practically right in front of him. After months of trying to *get help* for Greg Nelson, trying to get Greg Nelson to *seek help* and so on, David had had to throw him out and change the locks and then this endless acrimonious dispute about the security deposit on the loft gave Greg Nelson an excuse to phone David and harass him by telephone, accusing David of assault and battery and psychological abuse and what have you, Greg Nelson claimed David owed him seventeen thousand dollars and what David owed him was nothing remotely approaching seventeen thousand dollars, in the long run David had had to *file a restraining order* and even then the manager of David's building kept getting intimidation from Greg Nelson over the alleged security deposit David owed him. Finally they gave him his half of the security deposit. Next David started getting hang-up calls, sometimes twenty or thirty hang-up calls in a single night, which was truly unnerving, the calls were usually placed from a phone booth and showed up on David's caller ID as "numbers not available" but one of the calls was placed from a country club that Greg Nelson's father belonged to, Greg Nelson visited this *reign of terror* on David for so long that David really

worried that Greg Nelson could turn out to be the type who'd *act
out*. The problem had finally solved itself when Greg Nelson
moved to Washington, DC, but this whole Greg Nelson episode
had made him wary of involvements and long-term relationships, not that he thought Andrew could turn out the same sort
of nut case or anything, he simply wasn't sure that this *playacting*
and *role playing* and *master-slave relationship* stuff, fun though it
was, was necessarily the best way for them to get to know each
other on an intimate footing. After all, when Andrew tied David
up and forced him to eat his cock and so on they were both
acting out a script and not really relating to each other in their
own personalities. True, they did relate to each other when they
weren't having sex, and David did like the sex, but it didn't feel
like the kind of sex he would want to have in a long-term relationship. He found all this rather hard to articulate and after
discussing it *ad infinitum* they had sex again the way Andrew
wanted it, brutal, Andrew beating David's ass with a leather belt.
On that particular trip David heard some confusing things from
someone his friends knew who said he'd gone to prep school with
Andrew in La Jolla, how Andrew had always been this outrageous
liar from a not-very-well-off family who claimed to be richer
than God and was thought to have stolen a lot of money on a
school trip, got accused of it, and somehow talked his way out of
trouble, but everyone knew he'd stolen it. The details were too
vague for David to credit but it disturbed him nevertheless. *This
is the lobby in its pre-makeover incarnation,* Andrew wrote on a
postcard of the Arizona Biltmore, *At the far end you see a glimpse
of the resteraunt (with the tree in window). Best room in this place
(the rest. That is). Drew,* it was already scorching in Phoenix,
Newboy, he wrote on another card, *This is the pool area. Amazingly,*

the surrounding hils look much the same today. (Due to strict building codes) weather is fine. Drew. He was beginning to think of David as his "secret love," and casting himself in a Danielle Steel miniseries of wealth and infidelity, he was somehow the beautiful young wife and the beautiful young husband at the same time, torn between the aging moneybags he did not love and the brilliant young architect who'd awakened unsuspected depths of passion. He imagined a chorus of concerned friends warning him not to let his head be ruled by his heart, that he had a really good thing going with Norman. Whenever Norman went over a restaurant bill or made the little face he made when he thought the price of something too high, Andrew folded the visual into his miniseries, cutting away instantly to David stepping off an airplane, David embracing him, David's mouth between his legs, *The picture doesn't do it justice*, he wrote on a card of the Frank Lloyd Wright mural in the lobby, *This is bea-ti-ful. The carpet is too. Love or what you will, Drew.* "What you will" gave everything that playful Grace Kelly touch of searing emotions held in check by the delicate game of love. *Some names of suites here: the Taliesen Suite, the Grossman Suite, the Goldwater Suite.... very Arizona.... Sheer bliss. Did I mention how much I love Phoenix?* There were no masked balls or impromptu picnics or suddenly flirtatious pool boys, the parties were the types of parties where middle-aged people surprised you by lighting up a joint or pulling out a little phial of coke but then failed to get interestingly stoned, maybe their eyes widened comically or somebody tripped on a carpet. Everyone in Phoenix was *nice* and Andrew didn't have to prove anything, though it was taken for granted by many of Norman's old friends that Andrew was a typical *parasite*, having no profession and no discernible goals and a way of carrying himself as if he thought he was a Calvin Klein model when in fact his body looked slack and unexercised in his clothes and his efforts to make himself interesting smacked of youthful egomania. Andrew noticed how little interested people were in his bids for attention, how they listened with one ear and watched other people when he spoke. Andrew had never in his life imagined it was possible that he could *bore* people, that men especially, but women, too, could walk away from him in midsentence with a little whispered *excuse me.* It happened several times in Phoenix, and when they left Phoenix that time, Andrew concluded that people in Phoenix were *weird* and *provincial. Dave,* he wrote from the Park Lane Hotel in Manhattan ten days later, *Met coolest woman ever on the plane. Think Julia Roberts' mom in "Something To Talk About" (the Gena Rowlands character). You're great! Love, Drew.*

14

Andrew told Jeff Trail "everything." But for Andrew "everything" included fantasies taken for reality and fabrications he was trying out like trousers, to see if they fit. And because Jeff alone was always there, sacrificially loyal and painfully aware that he incarnated Andrew's impossible ideal, Jeff knew as no one else knew the degree of dissociation Andrew reached when he took up with Norman Blachford. It began much earlier, no doubt, when Andrew discovered that his salary at Thrifty's and small loans from Lincoln Aston could be doubled and sometimes tripled by buying and reselling pharmaceuticals, and that the resulting "wealth" substantiated his claim to be scioness of the parking lot fortune, the sugar fortune, the pineapple fortune. What Jeff saw a little more clearly than others was that Andrew had taken up permanent residence in the house of make-believe. Andrew really believed that the pill money was a little sidebar effusion of his entrepreneurial genes, that pills or no pills a plump, safe cushion of money lay under him. And being with Norman made it so.

Some varieties of human ugliness so closely resemble sublimity that they cannot be recognized without extreme magnification. Andrew had dazzled Jeff for years in precisely those areas in which Jeff felt haplessly inadequate, boxed in by his homespun Midwestern tastes and narrow military education. Andrew'd read every book, seen every movie, heard every opera, reeled off information with such throwaway brilliance that Jeff considered him a "genius," and explained away Andrew's deficits in terms of the tormented gifted child, protecting its vulnerable treasure with a carapace of raving neuroticism. Over years of intense proximity, Jeff had witnessed not just once, but an unsettling number of times, the spectacle of Andrew caught, not merely in a lie, in even more embarrassing episodes where Andrew's knowledge of various subjects had been exposed as shallow or completely fraudulent. It happened typically when Jeff and Andrew did the bars, some stranger would drift into Andrew's ken and unlike the reliably stupid regulars they always talked to, the new person would actually know whatever topic Andrew decided to blab about. These episodes gradually undermined Jeff's belief that there was any *there* there, he began to see Andrew as something smaller and considerably more desperate than the urbane sophisticate who'd taken him up years before; he also began to see Andrew's sartorial and cosmetic emulation of himself less and less as the sincerest form of flattery, more and more as a scary kind of parasitism, it now alarmed him when Andrew showed up wearing

Jeff's baseball cap and *Jeff's* haircut and suchlike signifiers of *Jeff,* conveying as they did a delusion of twinship that seemed to implicate Jeff in Andrew's craziness.

Certainly this clammy unwanted intimacy weighed in Jeff's decision to leave San Diego, though it was hardly the main thing; Jeff needed to make a living after cashiering out of the navy. In the early part of 1996, he applied to train for the highway patrol, which involved moving to Sacramento. Andrew was *freaked,* Andrew had *abandonment issues.* Of course Andrew also had Norman and Norman's money and Andrew and Norman were flying all over the place and hardly *in* San Diego and Andrew really wasn't in the position to vent too egregiously about the *betrayal* he felt. Still he made his displeasure known, he spoke of *depressions* and *headaches* and a terrible *sense of loss.* In a murky, alchemical way, Andrew *tried to replace Jeff with David,* at the same time he tried hanging on to Jeff by *proposing they go into business together.* Andrew's reality testing had run so awry by the spring of 1996 that he started hatching plans to *expand his drug business,* to go professional with it. Andrew had some vague idea that Jeff, once he became a highway patrol officer, could facilitate the smuggling of *cocaine across the Mexican border.* Andrew also believed he could go on living with Norman and sleeping with David on occasional weekends and run a full-time drug opera-tion at the same time, of course Andrew had absolutely no idea where or from whom to buy large quantities of cocaine in Mexico, he had some idea how to move illegal cargo from Mexico to California by water, since everyone in San Diego has gone from California to Mexico and Mexico to California in a boat at one time or another. Exactly how the complicity of a member of the California Highway Patrol might come into play was a bit of a mystery to Jeff, Andrew's idea seemed to be that Jeff would accompany Andrew on a boat and show his California Highway Patrol badge to any inquisitive DEA or customs inspectors they happened to encounter on the high seas, unfortunately Jeff elected to *humor* Andrew and *play along* with this patently impossible scenario because it was *easier* and *less scary* than contradicting Andrew or telling Andrew he was full of shit. Not too many people had ever seen *the other Andrew* pop out of his box but Jeff had, not a pretty sight. When Andrew actually felt threatened, his face changed and his eyes especially became crazy and a stream of hysterical bile came pouring out of his mouth, on occasion Andrew spoke of *getting back* at certain people who had crossed him, Jeff figured Andrew's Sicilian genes from his mother's side had *vendetta* written into the program. When Jeff dropped out of the CHP Academy four months after signing up, it was mainly because he'd gone on a ride-along where full-fledged California Highway Patrol officers made constant reference to *faggots* and *cornholers* and *fudgepackers* and *shit-fuckers* and *AIDS-carriers* and *Non-Human Targets*. Four months of the CHP Academy had pretty much revealed the CHP as a culture of talking marmosets and baboons and gibbons who ran on incessantly about faggots and fudgepackers, furthermore these marmosets baboons and gibbons carried lethal weapons and Jeff could easily picture being hung out to dry by feckless colleagues in a dicey situation, but a fraction of his decision rested on this fearsome mental image, of Andrew persisting in his drug lord fantasy, compromising Jeff through sheer persistence and manipulation, and landing them both in jail. And once they were in jail, Andrew would turn Jeff like a doorknob and probably walk.

Jeff had too much macho written into *his* program to consciously *fear* Andrew, but he dreaded him. After CHP he moved in with his sister, Sally Davis, in Concord, rather than return to San Diego. In May, he met Daniel O'Tool in the Castro, in Badlands. Daniel O'Tool waited tables at Café Diem in Oakland and Jeff found him *muy sympatico* and made friends with Daniel O'Tool and soon went to live with Daniel O'Tool and Daniel O'Tool's mother, Karen, in a house on Potomac Street. It was at this time that Andrew introduced Jeff to David Madson.

15

Around the same time, Andrew slipped darkish hints into his meetings and phone conversations with David, suggestions that helped explain, for example, why Andrew had a voice mail and a pager rather than a regular phone number, and why David had been furnished at various times with four different addresses for Andrew, two of which had turned out bogus when David attempted to mail him letters. Andrew offered these confidences to show his growing trust, casting himself as something between Burt Lancaster in *The Killers* and the yakuza love-death victim in *In the Realm of the Senses*. There was more to his business than just acoustical environments or whatever. Financing didn't always come through completely legitimate means. He had dealings with all kinds of characters, and sometimes he ran only a few steps ahead of the law. Andrew fed this a little at a time, and David didn't know what to believe.

Eventually many people would find it important to establish that neither David Madson nor Jeff Trail did drugs or approved of drugs or would have involved themselves with drug dealing, many people felt obliged to construct ingenious psychological explanations of why David Madson and Jeff Trail would to whatever degree *tolerate* the presence in their lives of someone *involved with drugs*, the media narrative more or less demanded that even the coke-tooting designer be declared *drug-free*, or at any rate *mellowed out* from "the excesses of the eighties." These efforts somewhat missed the point that homosexuals are, in American society, widely consigned to the same category of things *as* drugs, the category of illicit dirty things that people have to be protected from, and that any homosexual however law-abiding and even puritanical in the conduct of his own affairs is trained from an early age to distinguish hysteria about sex from the realities of sex, and hysteria from reality about drugs, only *the homosexual hysteric* so completely internalizes the national discourse about sex or drugs or anything else that he stands up and salutes the flag whenever it goes past *without irony*, since the homosexual is continually taught by the world around him that his natural home is the sewer, the homosexual is uniquely equipped to discover what truly belongs and what doesn't belong in *the sewer*, and in this matter of drugs, the homosexual who doesn't take drugs is nevertheless able to view antidrug hysteria as the sham and hypocrisy it really is—I mention this merely because the peculiar vectors along which this story was hijacked have only the most feeble relationship to reality. Well before David Madson might have become *alarmed* by Andrew's insinuations about some dark business that may or may not have involved drugs, David Madson would have been *interested*, as in the unfolding of any mystery, and Andrew might even have correctly guessed that a clandestine aura about himself would lend a touch of sexy danger to an already fraying romance.

This is where you go when you're bad, Andrew writes him in late May from the Park Lane Hotel in New York, *The view's nice tho. Off to the continent. Hmm. I will miss you. Have the best summer and know "someone very far away will be thinking of you" (Sabrina) Truest, Drew*. If Andrew did miscalculate and misread David Madson, it was not in the slow leakage of allusions to illegal activity, but in the assumption that David Madson's libido had frozen in place while its supposed object jetted about the globe. *I took a walk in Central today and saw a stereotypical group of NY construction workers having lunch on the steps by Gracie Manor. No catcalls. Damn! Better hike up my skirt next time.... Miss you—Drew*. Andrew thought rough sex and "miss you," coming from him, were enough to claim a lover's fealty, as he had no experience of lovers and no idea how he really affected people. *Dave, Went to a show called "Rembrandt, Not Rembrandt" today. A lot of fakes.... Now I must go see Mimi expire in the snow at the other Met. Yours, Drew*. On the phone, he claimed he had assets trapped in Europe, money he couldn't bring in, "merchandise" moving across borders. *David, Leaving N.Y. always makes me a little sad. France is glorious but a little forbiding. I will see this arch* [View of the South and East Facades of the Roman Triumphal Arch, Orange]. *It shows the Romans conquering the Gauls. One relief has a Gallic slave kissing the boot of a Roman soldier (needless to say it is a favorite of mine amongst the ruins of antiquity).... Je t'adore, Drew*. Well, David wasn't going to be kissing any boots on Andrew from here on in, if they even kept seeing each other it would have to be a lot more reciprocal. The next thing was a card of *la maison carrée*, Nîmes. *Went to Arles today and wanted to imitate Van Gogh by cutting off not my own, but Mike's ear. He was a little cranky about it but when the bleeding stopped ... tomorrow Avignon & then maybe Orange. If I have to talk to any more Corsicans or North Africans I'll never stop throwing up. I tell my French friends about you and just like everyone else they say I made you up ... you're just too good for moi. Love you, Drew.* He had not in fact talked to any Corsicans or North Africans, he had no French friends, there was no Mike, he trailed about in Norman's wake and smiled politely at Norman's friends and attempted, now and then, a declarative sentence cobbled together from the phrases he knew, when he managed to make himself understood he couldn't completely grasp the responses he got, he complained to Norman that he'd lost all the French he'd once upon a time spoken fluently. *I'm very tan & I look like a granpa in my geriatric clothes. Is there any hope? Love, Drew.* But Nîmes was exquisite, the midday light filled him with a feeling of beatitude, he inhabited certain moments with his whole being as if no yesterday or tomorrow could trouble him. *David,* he wrote on a card of the amphitheater, *The exits are called "vomitoriums" no doubt because they spewed forth the great unwashed into the arena. The amphitheater is still used for bullfights! They take it very seriously. Little Nimoise kids dream of becoming torreadors. Major celebs. Think Madonna's "Take A Bow" video.... Love, Drew.* Next the Villa Orplid, with Norman's snotty chums, Andrew working hard to out-snot them with pricey purchases from the surrounding villages, tiny jars of incredibly rare honey and the like, genuine pig-rooted truffles, he decides to drop more hints of Cary Grant–type intrigue to thrill David, *This is the house. If you want to write (and please do) send a sealed env. With no name (yours that is) and no return address to: Andrew De Silva Villa Orplid Chemin du Phare 06 Pointe Malongue 06230 St. Jean Cap-Ferrat France Sorry to be secretive but it's very important. The situation in Marseilles has become extremely delicate and I may not be home in July. All my love, Drew.* It crossed and recrossed David's mind that Andrew was traveling with a boyfriend, he rather hoped that was the case, but what to make of the alias, of "the situation in Marseilles," and why pray tell could he not put a return address on a letter? It all sounded like a big indecipherable mess. Still he sent a letter in the stipulated form, *Our office is working with Wells Fargo Bank, so I have meetings with clients in San Francisco, I'll be seeing Karen & Evan & will give them your regards, do you know when you're coming home? I'm thinking of spending 4th of July weekend in Washington, maybe we could meet up*—yes, he wanted to see him, wanted to grovel at his feet, suck his cock—*I hope Drew you aren't involved in anything that will land you in trouble*, as soon as he sent the letter off he didn't want to anymore. Why have sex with a jerk. Stupid. Really stupid move. Another card, showing Pont Saint-Benezet in Avignon. *What's up? Hope you're having a great summer and that the furry monster is becoming a rapacious steak lover! Day after tomorrow its back to the Cote D'Azur. Till then its sing, sing, sing … Love, Drew.* And a letter, on stationary from Cloitre Saint-Louis Hotel, *This hotel is beautiful. It used to be a Jesuit cloister & Jean-Michel Wilmotte remodeled it. It's so chic I almost screamed. Avignon is still full of scamps & vamps, c'est moi, ne pas? Plus now they have great shopping. We picked up a hitch-hiker & he turned out to be cool & gay (quel surprise!) & to have lived in N.Y.C. Now he's a waiter and we're off to his restaurant tonight. Big kiss for Mr. Pink Fuzzy Lips. Love, Drew.* Another letter in the same day's mail, from Hotel D'Europe, four stars. *This town is deeply neurotic. I feel at home. Fine food, romantic views … who wouldn't miss California. Back to Villa Orplid tomorrow, as I have house-guests arriving on Saturday. You are the cutest, most adorable guy ever. Stay fun & have fun. Love, Drew.* David found himself unreasonably annoyed by the familiar references to his dog, then annoyed with himself for becoming annoyed, thinking he should find it thoughtful and touching that Andrew thought fondly of the dog, that he hadn't *deliberately* made Prints throw up, still he could not shake the thought that Andrew didn't really know him, not really, furthermore he didn't know Andrew, Cunanan one minute DeSilva the next, and what if there was absolutely nothing to all this subterfuge and intrigue about Marseilles and frozen assets and so forth and this guy just liked muddying things up, keeping people in the dark about … what? In some ways it was even worse if Andrew *didn't* have these shady deals going and simply fabricated underworld scenarios to make himself interesting, how pathetic would that be? *You can see the house on this postcard. Cool. Had my first run-in with a European hairdryer (which hurled me against the wall w/hurricane-like force). Love, Drew.* He supposed that Andrew fucked these hitch-hikers and "guests," he remembered Andrew saying more than once how he "loved using condoms," it was the nearest Andrew came to hinting that David's nix on anal intercourse frustrated him, David didn't know why he'd always refused with Andrew, he'd certainly done it with other people, he even felt jealous of the backpacking teenager he pictured Andrew mounting from behind across the hood of a rental car, both with their pants around their ankles, it was stupid to picture it and even stupider to wish it were him because he knew he would always refuse *that* to Andrew. Maybe Andrew was *getting* it up the ass and not the other way around, some of these references to his skirts and his dresses, and the postcard of Grace Kelly and Cary Grant in *To Catch a Thief*, *Here I am with Cary.... Don't know if I can be home July 4th. Don't worry about me tho cause I'm O.K. Love you, Drew. P.S. Small party here last nite for 200!* More sightseeing, rich food, cloudless skies, perfunctory sex, endless hours of grooming and dressing, walking his feet off, broiling himself on lounge chairs, undressing, sleeping, listless banter about other perfect places to be idle in, five-star restaurants in Portugal and Budapest, hard-to-book hotels in Turkey, Dublin, Paris, and the Azores, scribbling, *This is "castle hill" overlooking the "old" port of Nice. My hotel is in the "new" port. I climbed up here today to the fortified town & visited the cemetery & the Naval museum. Love, Drew the Eurotrash Boy*, feeling the passage of time, unsettled by Norman's small economies. *If I could hold you and sleep next to you I'd be a new man. I may finally get my Mercedes SL 600! (You can buy them a lot cheaper) I feel I deserve it, even if nobody else does. Tomorrow I go to Paris for three days with a business partner. (The world's most romantic city with the world's least romantic guy.) Oh well. Miss you & your laugh, Love Drew.* Certainly Norman didn't see where Andrew deserved a Mercedes or needed one. Andrew's whole attitude had been morphing from understated gratitude to a sense of regal entitlement for quite a while. He would even say right in front of company that his goal in life was to be taken care of by rich old men, things like that, and Andrew's ... *performance* was disinterested and intermittent at best, he cruised other men all the time and *yawned* expansively at the dinner table, anyway you had to pay import duties and shipping costs if you bought a car abroad, it really wasn't any savings, and could his ass be a little fatter? Did he have to stuff down every cream puff and brioche in the south of France? And those pills that made him glaze over and sit there grinning at nothing? *In this postcard you can see the turquoise tile roof Cary Grant scampers across in Hitchcock's "To Catch A Thief." Remember when they're walking in this garden & Grace Kelly says she knows the villa's owners? Or was that La Leopolda villa? Went to Monte Carlo & lost. O.K. Opera in Nice tonight was bitchin', Turandot, but tres avant garde. Food wonderful, company less so. Tomorrow AIDS rally-concert in Place du Ville. Tres cher, Drew.*

16

He dreamed that all his teeth fell out and he left Norman, when he ran it back on the flight to Minneapolis some pieces of it stood out strangely, "turning points" and impulsive moves geysered up from a brackish pond. They left France, flew into JFK, spent four days with a friend in East Hampton. At the East Hampton parties the boys all looked cuter and younger and in better shape than he, and something about the *way* they were kept, not for conversation, or beautiful manners, but strictly and blatantly as fuck machines, underscored disposability in an unnerving manner that made Andrew's own position feel highly untenable, contingent on Norman's goodwill, and Norman lately seemed cranky and meditative as if he were staring down the future and coldly appraising his options. Back in La Jolla nothing resonated, worst of all David told him he was dating someone else from Washington, DC, that he didn't think he and Andrew were sexually compatible, *I really think we should just be friends.* Andrew had heard this before from guys he'd had one or two dates with and some of them had in fact remained friends, sort of, but in this case he surmised that his duplicity, his situation with Norman, unknown to David but no doubt suspected by David, had put the kibosh on their very real love, besides that the condo depressed him, the rainy season had arrived and he felt surrounded by oppressive memories, often found himself, for instance, standing in the very spot where Lincoln Aston had had his head battered open. If he wanted to eat lunch or shop in La Jolla, he had to walk or drive past the Bishop's School, a pall had fallen over everything like fine chalky dust, whenever these glooms descended. Andrew fed his nervous system another Xanax, the Xanax after a while produced a euphoric feeling of omnipotence. In this omnipotent state he phoned people all over the United States, people he'd met at Gamma Mu fly-ins and people he'd gone to school with and LC and Jeff Trail and David of course and his navy friends and his Berkeley friends and his friends in Montreal and LA and he must have called Lee Miglin, too, must have kept in touch with Lee. Andrew kept these people on the phone for hours, communicating his bliss, his vibe of deep connection with them, sharing critical insights about himself and whatever "dynamic" had informed their relations in the past. Some of the people Andrew called could tell he was high as a kite, but others were startled by the keen analytical reflections Andrew offered, the cackling high humor that went along with them. Some felt the qualities that had endeared Andrew to them in the first place were now decisively coming to the fore, they heard a new maturity, a new resolve, the voice of someone finally *putting it all together* and their approbation in turn confirmed Andrew's sense that *everything was going to be all right.* He had his platinum card and his gold card and his MasterCard and his

Rolex and his Infiniti and a whole rich life ahead of him, he knew all sorts of classy people who would help him in a pinch, and though he couldn't fully imagine in every niggling technical detail how an entirely new existence might be fashioned from the plus and minus columns of his life to date the first thing needed was a change of venue. Andrew packed up a lot of stuff and left a note for Norman, expressing his regrets, he was sorry it didn't work between them but they were just too different, no hard feelings, later when he went back for some books he'd forgotten, Norman handed him a check for ten thousand dollars and wished him luck.

Jeff came to San Diego for a job fair and Andrew took him out to dinner, the long habit of their friendship was a thing Jeff couldn't shake, Andrew was like your crazy aunt or demented cousin whose welfare you had to care about. Jeff had an interview in Austin. Andrew decided he had to tag along, booked the tickets, flew in there with Jeff and had breakfast with Jeff's half-sister Candace and made himself charming and it all passed without incident but Jeff kicked himself, the more he tried detaching himself from Andrew the more attached Andrew seemed, Jeff realized that his own equivocation caused what someone had explained to him as intermittent reinforcement. Instead of giving Andrew clear decisive negative signals Jeff put out a mixture of positive signals and negative signals, sometimes refusing Andrew's insistent closeness but sometimes accepting and even welcoming it, Jeff couldn't help it, he was used to spilling his problems and doubts and anxieties to Andrew and Andrew always had infinite patience and often surprisingly good advice, he knew he let Andrew come to Austin because he was anxious about finding a job, he needed to be told how handsome he looked and how smart and competent he was and how any person in their right mind would hire him over a dozen competing applicants, the only off note the whole time was Andrew's suggestion that Jeff could earn a very enviable living if he moved back to San Diego and went into business with Andrew, an *import-export* business that sounded like the revival of his coke-smuggling scheme with period furniture and Peruvian antiquities thrown into it, probably looted from god knows where and just as illegal and imaginary as the coke. Jeff heard cloud-forest burial shrouds, he heard Chimu pottery. Once again he did not, unequivocally, say no.

Moving in with Erik Greenman brought a little shift in Andrew's social itinerary. Erik worked the friendly little front bar in Mixx, the front bar had shiny blond wood and five or six stools and neat gleaming rows of overhanging glasses and jewel-like pyramids of booze, three plain wooden tables near the stairs leading up to the dining room. The people who collected there had this easygoing upscale inebriate camaraderie and Andrew found it an island of neutral calm, handy for the space in the evening between dinner, which he often ate there, and the demanding nightly display of personality and affluence in Rich's and Numbers and The Flame on boy's night, the Brass Rail, Greystoke, Club Odyssey, Shooterz, if he timed it right Andrew could hit them all with an hour or two to wind down in Flicks before closing time. He slept all day most days, waking shortly before Erik left for work, just in time for *Roseanne* and *Jeopardy*, an ideal roommate arrangement. Erik introduced him to his porn colleagues. They had names like Bryan and Ryan and Tyler and Adam, all blond and built and cute as buttons, Andrew loved turning up in loser bars like The Loft and funky-piss-elegant joints like Bourbon Street entangled with two or three stud muffins whose filmed couplings half the clientele had whacked off to, Andrew winked and mugged and flashed knowing little smiles at creeps who hated him, like the bartender in the street-level saloon at Inn at the Park, while embracing their very images of perfection. The Bryans and Ryans and Tylers and Adams found in Andrew that rare listening board whose sympathy was more than the dutiful tariff preliminary to a paid-for fuckorama, he really soaked up their stories and seemed to care. They had all been sexually abused as children and subsequently used in one dire way or another all their lives. They regarded fucking on camera as a type of healing, prostitution likewise, in doing these things they were *taking control, making a choice* about how and where and with whom they had sex, of course having sex remained the absolute central activity of their lives, but then again it was *work*, they even sometimes spoke of it as their *craft*, and it was, Andrew learned, at least an art if not a science to maintain an erection under hot lights, with six to a dozen people looking on, and to fuck, say, one actor's ass while fist-fucking that of a second actor, or to switch between takes from missionary to doggy-style, keeping the spectacle of penetration *completely visible to the camera at all times*. Outside the context of their work, the porn people were peculiarly innocent about the world, much resembling the navy boys of yore, most of them had been navy boys, in fact, and had started their porn careers while still in the navy, to supplement their paychecks. They took Andrew to parties in Oceanside and Laguna Beach, introduced him to escort service ponces, directors, porn executives from the San Fernando Valley. Occasionally Andrew engaged the services of S&M bottoms who advertised in *Circuits* or *Gay and Lesbian Times* but few did in-calls and he never brought people home to Robinson Avenue, more typically he splurged and took the train to LA, having sold the Infiniti for twenty thousand dollars, checked into the Marmont or the Mondrian, and hired dates from the specialty columns in *Frontiers*. His porn friends would have gladly done him for the usual fee, he discussed the possibility with Bryan and Ryan (who were lovers, and between spells of work were restoring a farmhouse in Iowa), tying up and torturing Bryan and Ryan together, but these plans never coalesced. During this period Andrew's *mood swings* had started, probably from drinking alcohol on top of Xanax, an explosive combination. One time at a party Andrew accused Ryan of trying to pick up a boy Andrew was cruising, another time in Flicks Andrew suddenly lifted Bryan off the floor and set him down on the bar, Bryan poured a gin and tonic over Andrew's head, setting off one of Andrew's *rages*, not that Andrew hit him or anything but he *glowered* and spit out some nasty words and looked ready to kill, these episodes were becoming frequent and a little unsavory ....

By November, Andrew had run through ten thousand dollars on restaurant bills, trips to LA and San Francisco, clothes, phone bills, and absolutely insane bar tabs, to say nothing of *drugs*, pills of course but occasionally *cocaine* and *Ecstasy* and the odd hit of *speed*—not *crystal*, crystal was a ghetto drug, Andrew's croaker connections came up with much better, FDA-approved shit like *Eskatrol* and *Dexamil*—and despite the purchase of a Nordic-Track and sporadic tennis games, he was putting on weight and losing his muscle tone and passing way too much time lounging around in his room gazing stuporously at videos with titles like *Sex Pigs, Target for Torment, Grease Guns, Balls to the Wall, Thick N' Creamy,* and so forth. He really hadn't made any progress at all on his nebulous schemes for the future, to counter this stagnant dopey listlessness he called Lee Miglin and told him he'd be in Chicago around Thanksgiving, called David and said he was coming to Minneapolis to visit Jeff, Jeff having just moved there for this job with the propane company, finally he called Jeff to announce his visit. These plans galvanized Andrew into motion, he got his hair cut, had himself fitted for disposable contact lenses, tried to work some fat off on the NordicTrack, when that failed he went on a speed binge that killed his appetite entirely, ridding him of six or seven pounds and making him unbelievably avid.

17

Federal Bureau of Investigation
88A–MP–47461

The following investigation was conducted by Detective (Det) _____ and Special Agent (SA) _____ of the Chicago Division's Fugitive Task Force (FTF) on July 18, 1997.

At Chicago, Illinois:

Information had been received prior to this date from CHICAGO POLICE DEPARTMENT (CPD) Det _____, assigned to Area 3 Violent Crimes Unit, that an individual, _____ had contacted the CPD to advise that he was a male prostitute who had in the past had sexual relations with LEE MIGLIN and ANDREW CUNANAN. In response to this information, arrangements were made _____ for an interview to be conducted at his residence on _____.

Det _____ and SA _____ accompanied by Det _____ responded to _____ residence where an interview revealed the following information in summary:

_____ described himself as a male prostitute, using the word "rent boy" as a common term used in the "Gay Community" to describe a male prostitute. He indicated that he had been involved in this occupation for years and had used the proceeds from this business to pay his way through college.

As a matter of practice in this occupation, he placed an ad beginning in _____ in a magazine called the _____. This ad ran from _____ until _____. It cost $13.00 a week to place the ad. He could not recall the exact words of the ad, but believed it would have been words to the effect, "New in town, young college boy looking to meet discriminating gentlemen." The ad gave his voicemail pager of _____ as a contact number.

_____ indicated that he believed it would be possible to contact the _____ and obtain a copy of the ad as it had appeared in the past.

As a result of this ad, several customers responded. In Autumn of 1996 an individual left a message on his voice mail with regard to the ad. This individual was named either Tadd, Todd, or Tom. _____ could not recall the exact name that this individual had used at the time. Eventually, _____ called back and a meeting was set up. _____ was told to go to the corner located somewhere, in the area of _____ in the area of _____. He could not recall the exact intersection, but he remembered that he had parked his car near the _____. A time was set up in the evening hours and as agreed upon, he stood on the corner. Eventually a 2-door large auto pulled up. He described this car as being two tone in color, possibly a Cadillac or Oldsmobile. In the vehicle at the time were two occupants. The younger of the two occupants was driving the vehicle and would later be described by _____ as ANDREW CUNANAN. The older gentleman was seated in the front passenger seat and would later be described by _____ as LEE MIGLIN. _____ recalled that the vehicle was a 2-door, because MIGLIN had to bend forward and pull the seat forward so _____ could get into the backseat. They drove to the area of _____ and _____ Street. He believed they parked at or near _____ Street near the _____. They walked a short distance to a building described by _____ as possibly being a 12 flat. They went to an apartment which was located on the 1st floor above the lobby. It was a one bedroom apartment. Once inside, they had one cocktail and he _____ performed _____ to both the older gentleman, (MIGLIN) and the younger gentleman (CUNANAN).

The price had been set at $140.00 for what _____ described as "a 50 minute hour." He was paid cash and then given $10 or $15 to take a cab back to his car which was parked near _____.

_____ advised that in this type of business, he did not use his real name and used the made up name of "Daniel." The older man, however, was introduced to him as "Lee" and again the younger man had either the name of "Tom," "Tadd" or "Todd."

The second trip to Minneapolis could've gone better. The cold wavering sunlight hurt his eyes, the rime of frost on the morning windows nauseated him. Everyone drove a sports utility vehicle, everyone worked for a corporation, everyone had a caller ID on the telephone. The simplest social arrangements became byzantine through a mesh of defensive gadgetry, no one ever picked up a ringing telephone, everyone had a beeper and a voice mail—just like him, he reflected, but he had *legitimate reasons*—and no appointment was ever finalized on the first or second call, people left their options open right up to dinnertime. The ritual drive to the mall, the trip to the supermarket seemed to be the high points of everybody's week. The gay scene, he thought, could not have been more bland and unassertive in Montana. The most attractive people were also the most damaged, in "recovery," adjusting to a quiet set of colors after Hazelden. He overheard an absurd number of bar conversations about people "stalking" each other, people going to court for orders of protection. Thinking of David and Greg Nelson, Andrew considered that filing restraining orders had perhaps filled the entertainment void left by anal sex.

Tracts of empty space yawned between "neighborhoods," even the newest clusters of commercial architecture had a look of windswept vacancy. The buildings dwarfed the meager population, there simply weren't enough people to make the place feel like a city. Strangers had an unnerving habit of saying hello without following hello up with anything else. Personal information seeped out of people on a "need to know" basis, in stingy driplets. Bleak-looking strip malls scarred the major thoroughfares. Everything looked brown, or asphalt gray, and worn to a muddy disintegrative state by gritty winds. Jeff lived in a subdivision where the surrounding ponds and vegetation looked simulated. Jeff had broken up with his latest boyfriend and hardly knew anyone so Andrew's arrival had been more or less a happy thing, but several things occurred that left a sour taste. David gave a cocktail party before this Design Industry Foundation for AIDS benefit, at the party David's current beau, Rob Davis, was playing cohost, Rob Davis intercepted Andrew as he darted to answer the phone, saying something like, "That's my job now," Andrew couldn't help hovering close to David, didn't he have a prior claim on David, wasn't he closer to David than Rob Davis really, yet David did little to acknowledge him or to demonstrate to his friends from work and his other guests how close they really were, his friends seemed not even to know that they'd been *lovers*, on the contrary David got on his case telling him not to feed Prints from the buffet, and then when Prints vomited David blamed Andrew, then just when the party was winding down and everyone started leaving for the benefit Andrew as a goof decided to pile up these paper plates and napkins on the table and set them on fire, he'd had a bit to drink and he really meant it as a joke, what kind of joke he really couldn't say, Jeff called him an *asshole* and David acted completely pissed and the whole room looked at him as if he were some kind of freak, fortunately he knew the main organizer of the DIFFA benefit from some social events in Scottsdale and spent most of the benefit chatting with the most important person in the room which probably gave David's friends a slightly clearer picture of who he was, David himself obviously hadn't clued them in that Andrew traveled in pretty high circles, a lot higher than theirs, that they ought to consider a party like David's party cranked up several notches by the presence of Andrew, yes he was flamboyant and said whatever devastating thing came into his head, had they ever heard of Tallulah Bankhead or Truman Capote or anyone brilliant and witty or what? Anyway, whatever unpleasantness he supposedly caused he rectified at brunch the next day with JT and David and Rob

Davis, swallowed his sarcasm and his outrage that David could even imagine replacing him with Rob Davis, sure he was handsome and well-off and smart but the same sort of soul mate as Andrew? He stopped short of flattering their relationship but laid on the charm, by the end of brunch he felt certain they were all adoring him and kind of awed by his brains and he had a lot of private time with Jeff that he thought smoothed out the raggy edges, still he knew it could've gone better and he left for Chicago with that funny unsettled shame of fleeing a huge embarrassment, which of course made him furious with Jeff and David, who should have protected him from such feelings and made him special in other people's eyes.

Approximately 1 or 2 weeks later, he received a second call on his voice mail from either "Lee" or "Todd." He was told to come directly to the building, which he did. Once inside the lobby, using a cellular phone that he carried called up to the apartment and was buzzed in. _____ indicated that there was a doorman on duty at the building both times he went there.

On this second encounter, he related that they drank some white wine and talked more freely than in the first encounter. During the conversations this time, _____ mentioned that he was interested in going to college in Europe. "Lee" told him about locations that he was familiar with. In addition, "Lee" spoke of the fact that his wife was involved in some way with the "Home Shopping Network."

He eventually performed _____ on both "Lee" and "Todd" and left. This was the last time that he would have sexual relations with either of these individuals.

Possibly a month or two later, he ran into "Todd" at a gay bar called the _____ located at _____ and _____ in Chicago. _____ saw "Todd" inside the establishment and did not approach him, however "Todd" did buy _____ a drink. No conversation took place.

_____ indicated that he had only seen "Lee" one other time. He could not recall exactly, but believed it was some months later when he had an occasion to run into "Lee" in a store. "Lee" was with a couple and he did not approach him or have any conversation with him. When he made eye contact with LEE, he _____ simply nodded.

When asked to describe the individual he referred to as "Lee," he described him as a white male, approximately 5'10", medium build, being at least 55 years of age and having fat fingers. He believed he remembered seeing a gold "pinky ring" having a red or purple stone on "Lee's" hand. _____ indicated that since the news coverage with regard to CUNANAN, he has on numerous occasions seen photographs of LEE MIGLIN on TV and is positive that the individual referred to as "Lee" is in fact LEE MIGLIN.

When asked to describe the individual referred to earlier as "Todd," "Tadd" or "Tom," _____ indicated that he was in his early 20s, approximately 5'10", medium build and having no glasses. In the news coverage with regards to the investigation of CUNANAN, _____ indicated that the earlier photographs which depicted him with glasses and much thinner did not look like the person he referred to as "Todd." It was only recently when the news media showed the photograph dated April of 1997 in which he is not wearing glasses and his face is heavier did he realize that this individual was in fact the person with MIGLIN when they had sex.

18

Associates and friends Andrew saw between December and April: Michael "Shane" O'Brien, Stan Hatley, Bryan Smith, the lawyer Richard G., Steven Frederick Nauck, Don Setterfield, Robin Thompson, Norman Blachford, Erik Greenman, Kenneth Higgins, Ryan and Bryan, Tyler, Ethan-Michael, Adam, Philip Home, Tim Sanders, Simon Dando, Karen Lapinski, Evan Wallitt. Some had known him for several years, others a month or two, in Philip Home's case it was a matter of a few weeks, a mutual friend had put them together and Andrew claimed to be leasing a great apartment in the Marina District of San Francisco, an apartment he would be absent from for long periods because of his prodigious business travels, ergo he'd be willing to share the place with Philip at very low cost. Andrew's sister Gina lived on Octavia Street in the Marina, a half block down from Bay Street, it could have been Andrew's idea that if he moved in with Gina he might find a place nearby, or if Gina got married and moved out the apartment might become his, there is really no way of knowing what Andrew's idea was. On this latter question, what Andrew's idea was, about anything, none of the people Andrew mixed with between December and April have had anything illuminating to say. Every statement is vague, contradictory, colored by subsequent loose assertions that spread in the press like virulent bacteria; in this case hindsight, contrary to the cliché, has been blinding. More peculiarly, hardly anybody who spent time with Andrew during this period recalls a single verbatim sentence he might have uttered, or indeed a single thing he did. *He was all over David wanting sex*, Lapinski and Wallitt recalled of their

Easter Week idyll at the Chateau Marmont, yet the gross picture this suggests doesn't really describe anything. We have scattered reports of momentary bursts of aggression, putting people in headlocks in bars, complaints to selected friends about money, complaints to bartenders about not getting dates, reports of uncharacteristic heavy drinking, reports of Andrew smoking crack, reports of Andrew consuming epic quantities of S&M pornography, from the peripheral chorus of people who merely saw Andrew in public places there is some unanimity about his physical deterioration, remarkable if only because Andrew was getting *fat*. If you arrange the "many faces" of Andrew Cunanan (which appeared in strip form in virtually every news magazine in the Western world) into precise, chronological order, you will see that his amazing chameleon-like quality can be easily duplicated by any human being with a weight problem. (Andrew did like changing his clothes a lot, but so does Nancy Reagan.) The weight gain is remarkable for another reason, in light of efforts to explain events as having been triggered by the satanic drug du jour, *crystal methedrine*.

Despite the haziness of people's memories, we have a reliable witness in this matter: American Express. For the period in question, Andrew whipped out his credit cards on a daily basis. When he wasn't purchasing huge quantities of food from Ralph's supermarket, Andrew dropped anything from fifty to four hundred dollars at Montana's American Grill, Chef's Wok, Taste of Thai, Sushi Bar Kuzumi, Mixx, Wolfgang Puck Café, Ginza Sushiko of Beverly Hills, Valentino Ristorante of Santa Monica, *forty-six dollars at Denny's* on the same day he charged a meal at North China Restaurant. A food snob like Andrew doesn't chow down at Denny's unless he's really hungry.

These charges run straight through to the week before Andrew left for Minneapolis. One indisputable characteristic of people on crystal meth is, they don't eat. People on steroids, however, eat plenty. If we could put the crystal meth together with testosterone, we would have sufficient combustion for an even more prodigious string of homicides. But we can't. A mountain of sushi rules it out. What we have are firsthand sightings of Andrew injecting himself, the leftover phials of testosterone found in his travel bag, and the usual documentation of side effects and counterindications. What we have are mood swings, depressions, giddiness, diminishing funds, *loss of image.*

He made several trips to San Francisco, six-hundred-dollar rooms at Sherman House and the Mandarin Oriental, he rented cars, he looked people up, he drank, read books, watched TV, smoked cigars, masturbated to porn movies, shaved his head, popped downers, and ran up bills, lots of bills, he started the winter with nineteen thousand dollars in the bank, paying off his monthly AmEx shrunk it to ten thousand dollars, then lower, he didn't think about it and didn't think about it, when it did finally catch his attention he filed a petition for bankruptcy, but never registered his debts or notified his creditors, the application just sat there, he'd always found money and always would, he thought, better still it had always found *him*, and then there was this *plan*, for him and David and Karen and Evan to spend Easter week in Europe, a perplexing turn in the narrative, for David had been telling friends for months that Andrew was an unpleasantly loose cannon, fun at parties but disreputable, probably engaged in illegal activities, a compulsive liar, someone he never wanted to see again, and Karen and

Evan later gave essentially the same opinion to police, the European plan fell through but the four got together in Los Angeles, went around as a group in Andrew's rented car, ate meals together, Andrew and David slept in the same room at the Marmont, in the same bed, on the dresser were handcuffs and candles and other kinky sex paraphernalia, according to Karen and Evan, and the question, really, is how far one person's demonic party energy can be used to explain another person's reckless disregard, if that's what it was, if *Andrew was all over David constantly wanting sex* and David didn't want sex, if Andrew couldn't open his mouth without saying something questionable, the logistics to say nothing of the atmosphere of several days' cohabitation and conspicuous consumption among friends leave the imagination in an odd place, it is in fact hard to conceive why three close friends would go on vacation with someone they considered a creep in the first place, and the only answer that comes to mind, i.e., that the creep was paying for it, doesn't say much for the three friends. Someone who knew Andrew better than most said that Andrew's tragedy wasn't that *he* lied, but that people he spent money on never told him the truth.

Now the money was running out, in fact he had no money, now the *credit* was running out. Still he gave presents, bought meals, treated himself like the Queen of Sheba. He managed to install himself in Karen and Evan's apartment on Vallejo Street after David flew back to Minneapolis, one person who saw him there describes him as glazed, distracted, off in a world of his own. At the same time, he visited his sister Gina, who had Elena's daughter Jamie staying with her. To them he seemed not only normal but in high spirits. Brotherly. Avuncular. Whatever.

They did the tourist thing for Jamie, Fisherman's Wharf, Ghirardelli Square, rode the bumper cars in the amusement arcade, took the cable car, went shopping. Andrew bought Jamie hundred-dollar sunglasses and a slew of children's books. He got a buzz cut somewhere in the Castro. He bought cashmere socks.

He didn't look like someone whose inner structures were collapsing. A little out of shape, a shade preoccupied, fitfully surly, sullen, rough, phlegmatic, maybe a trifle stoned, but not the figure out the window screaming in a storm, far from it, you just had to give him a minute to put his face on, then you'd get the jokes, the sly patter, the routines. One part of his mind continually rescued all the other parts from any prolonged contemplation of reality. Reality was what he said it was. You could not believe a word he said, not because he always lied, but because when he did lie he would lie about *anything*, kill off his family, give himself degrees from the Sorbonne, tell you he spoke fluent Hebrew, inflate the price of anything he said he paid for by as much as a thousand but also as little as two dollars, claim he'd had three drinks instead of two or two drinks instead of three, five pills instead of four, or six, write that he was currently driving an *Audi* instead of a *Mustang*, report that the certified public accountants he'd met in Aspen were Courteney Cox, Lisa Kudrow, and David Schwimmer, all social relations, all histories, all facts were an infinitely malleable dream substance worked into transient shapes by the verbal process. The only element that resisted his sculptural ingenuity was money. His cleverness at getting it had evaporated. Andrew seems not to have understood this until the day he visited the travel agency on Market Street, the day his AmEx was refused.

He got an emergency extension of credit the next day, but it sank in that this would be the *only* extension of credit, and for the first time in his so-called adult life Andrew's eyes focused on the naked lunch at the end of his fork. After it all came down, LC shrewdly observed that what other people thought of Andrew "was more important to him than life itself." This preposterous fact is the purloined letter, hidden in plain sight.

FOUR

THREE MONTH FEVER

1

David Madson had started his day walking Prints, his Dalmatian, down Hennepin and over the bridge to Nicollet Island and back, then lifting free weights at the Arena Club, then taking meetings and phone calls at John Ryan Co., macromanaging various projects, then a desultory lunch with coworkers, and throughout the day he'd spoken to friends in his office and friends on the phone, giving various spins to the imminent arrival of Andrew, as his inner weather fluttered from dread to guarded optimism that Andrew's visit would be quickly over with and that Andrew would spend most of the weekend with Jeff Trail in Blooming-ton, even voicing at moments the improbable hope that it might be fun—because, after all, Andrew could be a lot of fun, in sparing doses and crowded rooms, like a bottle of poppers. It was only tête-à-tête, and vis-à-vis him, David, that Andrew's fun quotient dipped precipitously, and Andrew's maudlin delusion that he and David "belonged together" seeped forth from under its rock.

He'd talked about it with Darren Howelton the night before, subtly fishing for reassurance. David and Darren had broken off a romance that had run concurrently with David's and Rob Davis's affair, but they still kept in touch. The mystery of Andrew's "business" with Jeff Trail had come up, but David told Darren it was too complicated to go into. David did not remember exactly when and how the idea had arisen that Andrew and JT were involved in "something shady" together, or how this nebulous shady something had concretized via rumor into drugs, Andrew always had a small pharmacy in his luggage but David couldn't put JT together with drugs, you only had to meet JT to see how straight he was. And the drugs Andrew usually had on hand were prescription painkillers like Vicodin, stuff you got from a dentist, that a real drug dealer wouldn't bother with. It had crossed David's mind more than once that Andrew probably fed the rumor himself, to make his friendship with JT seem more of a dark entanglement than it was, the fact being that JT wanted to cut Andrew loose and hoped their connection would wither with distance.

David didn't care much for JT. They had nothing in common but Andrew. David had, at Andrew's urging, shown JT around the hot spots of Minneapolis, such as they were, and invited him to the occasional party; they quickly discovered that the only friend they shared was one they both mistrusted and wanted to ditch. Anyway, David led a stylish, well-heeled downtown life, the bourgeois bohemian trip, he had a visible career going, lent time to charities and civic functions, paid attention to his clothes and his food and the finer things—in Minneapolis, David was "a catch." Jeff, pleasant guy though he was, seemed a bit clueless and lumpen-prole, losing his looks to his appetite in some woebegone subdivision near the Mall of America and working a nowhere job for a propane company. He lacked the sort of push David looked for in friends.

Thankfully, though, JT had opened David's eyes about Andrew, or at least confirmed David's uneasiness. When someone's ostensible best friend is quick to call him a pathological liar, that tells you something. On the other hand, David couldn't shake a certain fascination with Andrew, and kept vacillating about him. David's friend Rich Bonnin had been horrified to hear that Andrew would be staying at David's place that weekend:

"David, why on earth are you going down that road again?" Rich had called to offer a seat in a sky box at the Twins game, which he swiftly withdrew. "I don't even want to *see* Andrew, much less go to a game with him."

David somewhat weakly offered that Andrew, besides being in a bad way and needing a friend, was really trying to turn his life around, and felt grateful to David for setting a good example.

"Turn his life around from *what?* He's never even given you a valid mailing address."

"Well he sounds like he's ... making some effort, anyway."

"I'm amazed you're making time for this person. Look how he behaved the last time he came here."

Rich tweaked David's conscience. David had downplayed his Easter weekend with Andrew to avoid Rich's disapproval.

"Well," David asseverated, "I ain't going out of my way for him."

But he was, of course. Andrew had picked up the check for everything over Easter in LA, and David was vain enough to let himself be courted by someone he didn't want. To his immense irritation, he felt indebted afterwards. Andrew would force you to take the shirt off his back, and then never let you forget it. David was even fetching him from the airport, because Andrew had maxed out his AmEx and couldn't rent a car.

All day Friday, David swayed from resentment to resignation to a blithe fatalism. He phoned Cedric Rucker in Virginia and told him for the second time that week of a "strong apprehension" regarding Andrew's visit, but turned sanguine in mid-conversation, as if to say *well, how bad can it be, he's leaving on Monday*. Cedric, who'd been seeing David sporadically on business trips, advised him to be careful. There was something alarming in David's perplexity, an icky quality embedded in all stories about Andrew that didn't make sense and didn't sound right. Suddenly David felt he was ridiculously casting himself as the maiden whose virtue is menaced by some swarthy barbarian. "I can handle myself," he assured Cedric. David struck a more assertive note in a call to John Walker, another current beau in Atlanta, dismissing Andrew as "an asshole" he didn't want to bother with.

And after all that palaver here he was, waiting for Andrew outside the airport gate, preparing a broad smile and a welcoming hug.

2

"I won't have scads of cash to throw around from now on, so I really wanted you to have this."

Andrew knew these weren't exactly the right words. He caught an odd flicker in David's eyes as he handed him the box. As if the transaction confirmed some suspicion David had been nursing in private for a while.

"But this is your watch, Andrew," he said, staring at the gold Cartier that he knew had cost eleven thousand dollars. A square-faced watch with Roman numerals. Andrew had worn it on his last trip to Minneapolis; David's friends had remarked on it.

"Listen David," Andrew said, keeping it light, "you've helped me a lot, to see … the error of my wicked ways, so I figured … David gets the watch."

"I don't know what to say," said David, meaning it. Andrew's gifts were what Andrew gave you instead of sincerity. Or a legible explanation of how he afforded them. So far as David could tell, nothing had changed about Andrew except his clothing: his Andrew Cross leather jacket was identical to one he'd given David in LA. A smudgy parallel between the watch and the jackets flashed through David's mind.

"'Thank you' would be good," Andrew teased.

"Well, obviously thank you." David smiled a fraction wider. "I still don't know what to say. I mean if you're having … difficulties, you could sell this, Andrew."

The queasy part for David was that he did want the goddamn watch, who wouldn't?

"Don't even think about it, David. It's for you, it's yours."

Andrew bussed him on the cheek. David revved the Cherokee and drove in the direction of 35S. Andrew read off the special features of the watch from a brochure that had come with it, his voice climbing above Sheryl Crow on the radio, *But now no joker, no jack, no king can take this losing hand and make it win, I'm leaving Las Vegas.* He'd put everything back in the original box, like someone returning a purchase. David said the minimum. Andrew effused about a party in Oceanside, about meeting the Boise Cascade heir, about meeting Lisa Kudrow. He talked about Gordon Getty, about running into "my first *master* from years ago, opening an antique store, don't you love it?," about Karen and Evan, David's friends, who'd put him up in their flat for a couple weeks.

"Karen is *sooo* exquisite," Andrew cooed. He had given her a thousand-dollar coat as a thank-you present. *Thanks for being you.* Karen had called David during Andrew's visit, worried that Andrew might be bringing tricks to her place when she was out at work. She just didn't trust him. That makes two of us, David thought.

3

David's brittleness mystified him. Andrew realized it would be tacky to say *Hello? I just gave you an eleven-thousand-dollar watch,* but it was even tackier to take the gift and continue acting reserved and uncomfortable. Even if there was some problem between them that he didn't know about, the caring thing would be to have it out and clear the air. Instead, David made small talk, showing how he was building the partition between the main loft and the kitchen area, pointing out little decor changes and asking him, almost as a formality, if he minded joining some of David's office friends for dinner. In gross contrast to their tepid hellos at the airport, David greeted Prints with ebullience. Andrew resented the animal as it lapped David's hand and pawed David's pant leg. He remembered that Prints had been run over as a puppy, leaving him with a strangely elongated head. David had nursed the thing like a mother, though an actual dog mother, Andrew considered, would've snapped its neck and put it out of its misery.

David's body language did not read "friend," and the silences that fell between them had a toxic heaviness. Andrew felt a mingy sort of relief when David had him lodge his duffel bag in the bedroom, indicating that they'd share the bed; from David's coolness, he'd expected to see sheets and pillows piled on the sofa. But there came no moment of comfortable rapport, just activity, David fussing around, putting on music, moving tools to clear space at the kitchen table. Right after mixing Bloody Marys, David strolled off to the bedroom clutching the mobile phone.

"Gotta phone Cedric," he said.

It struck Andrew as a deliberate insult, the same thing as David saying, *If you were waiting for Rob Davis to exit the picture, get in line.*

Andrew loathed the smell of suffering. Particularly his own. In his eyes, he deserved a lot from the world and until recently the world had come through, with a modicum of effort on his part. He wondered if David was instinctively drawing barriers between them because he dreaded the contagion of bad luck. Was David that shabby? His David? The intimate murmur in the next room was turning him into a pariah, a loveless geek. He nearly laughed at how completely his fantasy of arrival had been routed in every detail. He could appreciate it as farce if he ignored his emotions. All right, he thought, two can play this.

4

"I better call the Alpha Male," Andrew announced with an ironic air, as if his personal nickname for Jeff was a communal thing.

"Sure," said David, indifferently, handing over the phone. He consciously resisted adopting Andrew's pet names and signature expressions for things. He had seen people turn into Andrew after fairly brief exposure, and seen Andrew turn into other people, Jeff Trail in particular, and it gave David the creeps. "Listen, you need to call Jeff, I have to go meet someone around the corner. I told this person I'd have a drink with her—but like, fifteen minutes at the most."

Andrew raised an eyebrow. "Anybody I'd like?" He wanted to see if inviting himself along would rattle David.

"It's a work thing. I have to talk to her privately," David improvised smoothly. "A girl who wants to intern at John Ryan. I'm serious, fifteen minutes tops." He pulled on his coat and stood by the door. Perched on a sofa arm, Andrew cheerfully waved him away, the image of unconcern.

After JT came on the line, Andrew was bitterly grateful that David had left and couldn't see the spreading shock on his face. Andrew's voice registered none of it, for something told him he could only lose by screaming indignation and hurt, as he wanted to: Jeff was telling him that his boyfriend Jon and himself were leaving town the next day, possibly but not definitely returning the day after, that JT "really hoped" they'd have a chance to see each other but couldn't guarantee it, as Jon's birthday was Sunday and Jeff had promised to do whatever Jon desired all weekend. Andrew spared himself the humiliation of asking about the evening at hand. "Weekend," no doubt, included Friday, and Jon Hackett, Andrew surmised, resented the bond between him and JT. *I'll still be around when you're gone*, he promised Jon in his mind.

"What I'm gonna do," Jeff went on, stabbing him with each bland, matter-of-fact phrase, as Andrew, stunned, slid from couch arm to couch seat, "I'll leave the keys under the mat out front, I know we agreed you could stay here one night and I want you to." Duh. As if it made no difference. As if Jeff had a really opulent deal going out in Bloomington, well worth the travel time even if Jeff wasn't there.

"Wow, that's great, but I really wish you were going to be there, J. T., or at least I hope I see you Sunday." Andrew managed to sound like a robot, swallowing rage.

What might have been a carping voice shrilled in the background before JT muffled the receiver. Andrew thought he'd actually heard *giggling* follow the carping. Then Jeff's voice returned:

"I was just reminded, we're coming back Sunday for sure, because a couple of Jon's friends are coming for a little, uh, birthday thing, it's only Jon's friends, so—but you and I could meet up after that."

This, he thought, just in case he hadn't picked up on that "one night." Probably Jon the bossy bottom would throw a fit if Andrew were there when they returned. Andrew heard himself agreeing to these nebulous nonplans, sending Jon a happy birthday, making warm noises, while something like a speed rush shot up his back into his brain, an almost blinding impulse to smash something. He saw himself diminish in the lens of this awful city, becoming a despised, laughable creature whose feelings mattered to no one, least of all his closest friends. He thought of all the wonderful things inside him and the good things he'd done for other people and saw the shrieking outrage of their betrayal as proof that the world's heartsick evil can never be underestimated. He poured vodka into his glass and began pacing the loft's big central area, circling the sofa, taking in the smug inanimateness of David's belongings, and glaring at the dog, who kept coming up to sniff him and beg for attention with moist eyes. He forced himself to take a deep breath, swallow some vodka, deep breath, *Get this picture back in perspective*, he thought, *you told Jeff you were coming here to see David, and you told David you were coming to see Jeff,* maybe they weren't shunning him, maybe the steroids were making him paranoid, maybe Jeff and David were acting what they considered normal, or maybe each felt wounded thinking the other was more important to him, maybe all this cruel behavior was really a cry of pain, or not intended as cruelty, or nothing—for them, perhaps, this was just another weekend, and maybe he hadn't made it plain how rapidly all his life's contradictions were rolling to a boil.

5

David sat in the bar of the Monte Carlo scanning his blond reflection in the bar mirror, willing himself out of the rotten mood that he'd somehow gotten stuck in the minute he saw Andrew, realizing he could not go through the weekend this way and he needed to repair things, if only for seventy-two hours, and after that he would find some better method than lack of enthusiasm to make Andrew know he wasn't welcome next time he announced a visit. While sitting in the Monte Carlo, he struck up a conversation with a man two stools over, a guy roughly his age, maybe gay, maybe not, and they started chatting about *trail biking,* for some reason, the man had just bought a trail bike, David too had recently got himself a trail bike, Do you live around here? David asked him, Inver Grove Heights, the man said, this led into a long discussion about the prodigious system of bicycle trails in Minneapolis, David averred that this system of bicycle trails was perhaps the best in the country, indeed according to David Minneapolis's bicycle trail network was *the one piece of urban planning that hasn't run horribly askew in Minneapolis,* completely at odds with the insane Minneapolis habit of *ripping out its historical buildings* and replacing them with *monstrosities*, monstrosities furthermore which *have no logical relation to each other*, it's a grotesque scandal, David told the stranger in the Monte Carlo bar, that St. Paul has *preserved its architectural heritage*, whereas Minneapolis, its so-called twin, has *raped and destroyed every building worth looking at except the Forshay Tower*. Before long David offered to take this person, who introduced himself as Russell Long, on a bike-riding tour of *Minneapolis's architectural debris* on the coming Sunday, and only after they exchanged numbers and David left the Monte Carlo did David realize he'd planted this appointment in the middle of Andrew's visit, that if he were going to fix this trouble between them and keep relations amicable until he got rid of Andrew he'd have to cancel this bike-riding date and make a real effort with Andrew, the trouble was that, despite having won high praise in a college production of *The Music Man*, David was not a terribly convincing actor.

6

Andrew had noticed, on earlier visits, how perfunctory and incurious people tended to be in this frosty northern town, as if they begrudged any interesting qualities a visitor displayed and could only accept him as a grayish, peripheral blob. His other trips had happened in the dead of winter, so he'd written this off as seasonal malaise. But now in late April the thaw hadn't changed things. The group from David's office in Café Solo smiled at him meaninglessly, if they couldn't avoid his face altogether, locked him out of conversation with a numbing blizzard of shop talk. They seemed genuinely to prefer a discussion of the company's current, dreary-sounding projects to any loftier discourse on, say, the almost completed Frank Gehry Guggenheim in Bilbao, or Jean Nouvel's recent buildings, or the *No Place (Like Home)* exhibition at the Walker Art Center.

"They want a teller line kind of design."

"You think we'll get the go-ahead for prototyping by Wednesday?"

"We need to sit down Monday and look at a way to value-engineer this thing."

The company, which basically installed banking islands in supermarkets and other retail stores, thrived on jargon, job titles like "Creative Manager" and terms like "the isometrics of the space" and "spine situation" to brighten the mundane realities of interior design. Andrew felt like a black hole opposite David and this Laura Booher creature; somehow their glances slid across him, settling on Linda Elwell, David's boss, an acerbic woman crunching her salad beside this Kathy Compton person sitting next to him, and two other John Ryanites farther down whose names he didn't catch and wasn't going to bother with, they all looked pert and professional and full of *spunk*, he thought, relishing the word's double meaning, as they blabbered away about in-store signage and client job numbers. He attacked his southwestern chicken, finding the food preferable to the company, and studied David's ruminating jaw.

"Why don't you show them the watch I gave you?" Andrew asked loudly, making a slight nick in the general din.

David's jaw ceased its discreet grinding. "I didn't put it on yet," he told the group.

"And look what you did put on," Andrew needled, running his eyes over David's clothes as if his T-shirt were somehow amiss.

"I gave him this *fabulous* watch." Andrew's expression challenged them all. He licked his fork with the delicate self-absorption of a cat cleaning its paws. Silence rippled across the table; voices rearranged themselves into fresh patterns around the awkwardness. David blanched, took a sip of water, then, rescuing Andrew's outburst from the realm of embarrassment, produced the watch from his coat. He slipped it on. He began to carefully enumerate its finer points—the quartz movement, the sapphire cabochon on the stem, "water resistance to one hundred feet," whatever that meant—while angling his wrist in the light, his words like stitches closing a burst seam.

"What do *you* do, Andrew?" Laura asked as if she'd drawn the long straw. A loose scroll of multihued hair, harsh mascara, and dark lip gloss gave her stolid face an illusion of angularity. Andrew thought she resembled Picasso's drawings of Jacqueline. He sensed her casual dislike. That he did not fascinate these people continued to astonish him. Minnesota nice, cold as ice.

"I'm working on a number of projects," Andrew said. And he told her about the factory in Mexico, the sound-abatement panels that it fabricated for film studios, the labor costs differentials south of the border. He mentioned various materials, their relative utility in acoustical design. The factory had entered his mind one afternoon in Balboa Park, complete in every detail. He saw the white-smocked Mexican workers, the asbestos bales piled on steel tumbrels, cranes and scaffolding in continual motion. He saw himself dabbing his brow at a desk strewn with purchase orders, on the phone with Paramount, juggling the industry's byzantine equation in his head as his Learjet idled on a landing strip outside. This was not like his long apprenticeship in the family's vast sugar cane or pineapple empire, which stretched across dozens of small islands in his own private Philippines; its changeling commodity had never provided any entrée into Hollywood parties or movie sets. Sugar was used by everybody on earth, and pineapple ended up cloved to Christmas hams. Of course you always have to think money before you think glamour, but. More important, he'd started the soundproofing enterprise from scratch. No one had handed him Mexico on a platter, he'd put all the elements in place through his own admittedly eccentric synergy.

David was now looking at him in wonder, silverware frozen above his entrée. The others were looking at him too.

"Right now we're just waiting to reel in a couple more investors," Andrew concluded, drawing a line through his story with a folded slice of rye bread. His fingers compacted the slice for greater delicacy, and he began mopping sauce off his plate.

7

It had to be the vodka, David thought, suddenly noticing the frequency of Andrew's drink orders. Andrew had never been a drinker during their relationship (though he had popped pills, lots), not until this past winter, when the love affair was already over, and even then it hadn't been remarkable. Tonight, however, after Andrew had insulted him for the sixth or seventh time, sniping little barbs about his hair going back or his clothes not being chic or some less than genius statement he'd made, David realized that Andrew didn't hear himself and didn't think his verbal pricks were as nasty as they sounded. Andrew thought he was witty and urbane, thought his fishy stories about deals and investments and globe-trotting escapades impressed David's Junior League colleagues, trumping their tiny backwater lives and ambitions, filled them with envious dreams and wistful admiration.

In certain settings, David thought, the formula of Andrew's personality meshed perfectly with the surrounding pretense and superficiality. Andrew was designed for highly mobile situations where nothing said is really listened to and nobody depends on anyone else's words. Andrew was a "party person," a sort of human special effect—a walking gay bar, really. Yet Andrew had, for a long time, created an illusion of real substance, and watching it all break down was like watching a train wreck. David had never allowed himself to objectify Andrew to quite this extent before; it filled him with guilt along with a nauseous sense of freedom.

The drinking and insults continued in Nye's Polonaise, where they joined David's friend Monique Salvetti, a lawyer in the public defender's office, and two of her attorney friends from work, Deborah Russell and Charlie Clifford, though the peculiar atmosphere of Nye's took the edge off. Nye's hit you like a hearty outpost of Central European kitsch planted obdurately in the Yukon, the Ruth Adams Band ("The World's Most Dangerous Polka Band") bleating Zakopane summer favorites in one corner, large parties of working-class retirees noshing on pork hocks and sauerkraut in the banquet room, an assortment of solitary drinkers, college kids, and indefinable others ranged along an endless bar and three tiers of varisized tables. Monique and her friends and Andrew and David stood around the piano bar in the Chopin Room, Andrew again insisted David show off the watch, but seemed distracted from his conversational agenda by the wall-mounted accordions and stained-glass lighting sconces and the blunt offerings on a gravy-stained menu he kept opening and closing and fanning himself with, sirloin, T-bone, walleyed pike, frog legs, it seemed for a while that Andrew had met his match in Nye's highly calculated, boisterous weirdness. He managed to make everyone uncomfortable but not enough, David thought, for Andrew himself to notice it, and that was, perhaps, the best anyone could hope for under the circumstances.

8

They shoved on to the Saloon, parking near David's house and marching up Hennepin against an icy breeze. By that hour the bar was crammed with the usual gay motley, overwhelmingly local, fashion gamut ranging from L.L. Bean to Kmart, Otis Redding on the box and one tall, frowsy drag queen, frost-blue wig askew like half-eaten cotton candy, trying too hard beside the ice machine, a clutch of nondescript admirers egging her into lip-syncopation. Andrew switched to rum and Coke; David drank a beer. To David's surprise the mood turned easy. Andrew chatted up the manager, Walter McLean, then while David and Walter talked, Andrew introduced himself to Deegan Kennedy, a beefy, thirtyish, black-bearded guy David knew by sight, who did land-scaping for city parks, David vaguely recalled. He heard Andrew asking Deegan Kennedy all sorts of questions about hardwood transition areas and timber reserves, Andrew listening hard and coaxing a stream, then a torrent of expertise from the normally laconic Deegan Kennedy, who warmed to Andrew as if no one had previously bothered to ask Deegan Kennedy what he did in life or how he did it. As Deegan Kennedy talked with Andrew, his glassy eyes grew soft and something in his face opened. It was uncanny to witness. The abrupt concentration, the breathtaking subtlety of Andrew's charm. And with David, now, Andrew turned solicitous, flattering, even maternal, confounding him by saying kind, prescient things about the people they'd seen earlier, as if he'd carefully observed each one while playing his role as the Awful Guest. *How does he do that?* David thought, *how does he do that ...*

9

Walking north on Hennepin four bone-freezing blocks to the Gay 90s, and coming up the sidewalk, like a fata morgana, Stan Hatley, flashes of Hillcrest, *Hey Andrew far out,* flashes of the Manhole in Point Loma, hugging Stan Hatley, *Welcome to Siberia,* wishing he knew the hugging signals for *keep your lousy trap shut,* Morse code through the Eskimo jacket, shaking hands with Stan's friend, Bob something, *You visiting J. T.? We should get together, you me and JT.* Stan Hatley knows David, Stan Hatley knows Jeff, Stan Hatley knows me. Brain sorts and cross-references a thousand megabytes of dangerous information, like library microfiche spazzing across a screen, freeze-framing Gamma Mu shirt collars and rep ties and rent boys popping out of cakes, stoned trips to the La Jolla Dairy Queen, Stan belongs to the DeSilva life, the Top of the Park Friday evening El Caliph hot summer San Diego sugar daddy trip, Stan Hatley Shane O'Brien Bryan Smith Richard G., Richard G. knows about *Cunanan* because of the ticket he bought me for Vancouver, *David Madson doesn't know the whole Stan Hatley scene*, or did he, what Andrew had always told that bunch about the Mossad and the years they spent in the South of France before his father bought the parking lots, *or did Stan already tell him? Stan's living here he runs into David runs into Jeff. One thing leads to another.* Stan and Bob already with their backs to them shivering up Hennepin.

"Blast from the past," he tells David, as if it were nothing and of course it was nothing.

10

Or maybe, maybe it's our nowhere towns, our nothing places and our cellophane sounds—David in the Gay 90s, dancing with a black guy in a nondancing area, a light-skinned bodybuilding type not much taller than David sporting a rainbowy knit beanie on shaved scalp and John Lennon specs, Comme des Garçons gear, a black guy David didn't know but had seen and had often considered sleeping with, the Gay 90s a labyrinth of black walls, dark corridors, service bars, dance floors, a warren of tables where you could order dinner, kind of a tourist trap offering racy peeks at go-go boys and the chic gay set *just traaash, me and you, it's in everything we do.* RuPaul's MTV special and music videos on monitors, nothing too extreme, a haze of cigarette smoke wafting no whiff of dope.

Andrew worked the main bar while David danced, asking people who didn't look utterly clueless where the sex clubs were. When that proved futile, he found a toilet with stalls where he booted his last testosterone insulin spike, afterwards crushing and flushing it. It had no discernible effect but back in the club darkness he felt exalted, loose and sexy with alcohol, moving his body as if he'd dance if somebody danced with him. He bought another drink, a sex on the beach. As he swallowed he got the giggles, caught a wave of helpless mirth churned by recollections of his old Castro persona, *Commodore Cummings.*

In his mind, Commodore Cummings, riding crop tucked in armpit, stiff-marched before an inspection line of cadets. The cadets were naked except for their service caps and they all had David Madson's face. *That's* Commodore *Cummings of the Seal-test Naval Brigade, you men who stand bare-assed before me about to give for this nation that musky tender bud of which I would gladly relieve each of you as the lights go out over Europe, and if you absolutely must let a nigger fuck you darling why not throw a toss to your old comrade, bon vivant and raconteur, the Filipino-Sicilian wonder, Commodore Cummings.*

A blond kid wearing a nose ring watched Andrew mutter and laugh to himself. Andrew caught the look, struggled with his face, exploded into more laughter.

"It's because I—*I,* you see" Andrew rubbed his sore gut and tenderly kneaded the shoulder blade poking through the boy's ripped T-shirt. "I was educated by Jesuits," he gasped, "*I* am Commodore Cummings!" He really couldn't stop himself "You may call me ... *Cummy.*" The cackle from hell erupted from his diaphragm. "My friends do."

Andrew's laugh drew alarmed attention along the bar.

The stranger stroked Andrew's hair familiarly.

"Pleased to meet you," he said, "I'm Kevin."

"And the map of Ireland on yir wee face Kevin as I live and breathe. Know where a lad can cop a Valium?"

11

On Saturday morning, Jeff Trail drove Jon Hackett to his job at Old Navy Clothing in the Mall of America and proceeded along 494 into Inver Grove Heights, to his own job at Ferrellgas. He planned to expedite some paperwork, then he and Jon would drive downstate to a B&B in Kenyon. People phone-ordered propane over the weekend, and it saved him headaches to organize some of Monday's deliveries ahead of time, plotting routes for the drivers and setting up invoices. He was a fastidious, orderly worker, a product of Annapolis and several years' methodical, undramatic advancement at the Naval Amphibious Base in Coronado. He had seen "action," of a sort, serving aboard the *Gridley* in the Gulf War, or at any rate had inspected the mounts and trajectory specs for cruise missiles that were never fired.

Among other homosexuals, Jeff stood out as almost weirdly wholesome, an old-fashioned guy, who loved Sinatra records and sentimental—i.e., not campy—movies like *Steel Magnolias*, someone whose tastes lay so much in the American mainstream and so far from the ironic that he did not seem "gay" at all. The bent of his desires had only bitten him in his late teens, at the Academy; by then his personality had been forged in the culture of masculinity. Figuring out he was gay did not present so much a psychological problem as a logistical risk. Annapolis kept him depraved in thought but pure in deed. Later, living on base in Coronado, he discovered that other men were eager to fellate him in certain anonymous settings, on base and off. Though this usually transpired in total silence, he learned from one gratified supplicant about even better action near the naval reservation across the bay. That he was unusually attractive had never impressed him until then. He became a favorite lust object for numerous "military chasers" who haunted the Point Loma glory holes. Jeff loved the attention. He developed a specific taste for small, nubile, well-scrubbed men who looked way too young to be doing this sort of thing, and eventually moved off-base with one, into a Hillcrest apartment. A lot of navy men led double lives, closeted at work, out after dark. Jeff kept his predilections sub rosa for a long spell, freaking out if he saw a Coronado man in a gay bar. After a time, though, he perceived a great injustice in the military treatment of gays, being himself as patriotic, and certainly as manly, as any straight serviceman. Armed with this illumination, he became quite militant in his opinions, albeit careful where he shared them; he went on a tabloid news program during the gays-in-the-military debate, but appeared only in silhouette.

Jeff Trail was so open-handed and lacking in neuroticism that the defensive sophistication of the gay world eluded him, in some measure. He often felt, not stupid exactly, but lacking in cultural fluency and that verbal finesse so many gay men displayed as the prelude to a kiss, or, as he preferred, a blow job. If anyone asked how and why on earth he and Andrew DeSilva had become such intimate friends—and lately, people did ask—Jeff's answer was that Andrew had accepted him exactly as he was, and shown him that *as he was* was pretty damned incredible. Soon after they met, Andrew told Jeff that Jeff was precisely what Gore Vidal meant in speaking of "homosexuals"—red-blooded, all-American, totally *normal* men who happened to prefer sex with other males. It was, Andrew said, an entirely healthy thing that Jeff had no idea who Proust was and couldn't tell Maria Callas from Maria Shriver, what Jeff had long considered his lack of savvy actually meant he hadn't become a *distorted, self-hating fag*. Of course, Andrew sometimes hinted, it mightn't be a *bad* thing for Jeff to familiarize himself with the kinds of things fags routinely talked about, there was such a thing as being *self-defeatingly naive*, but on the primal level, the level where humans had sex, Jeff already had the great fortune to be what Andrew called *the alpha male*, referring, Jeff gathered, to some hierarchical sexual arrangement among chimpanzees.

Andrew was fascinated by the military, he could quote you Clausewitz and DeVigny and Caesar and all the great tacticians of history, he knew intricate details about the Battle of Waterloo and Hannibal's March on Rome and could tell you when almost any piece of weaponry was introduced and how it evolved from earlier weapons. Andrew made Jeff feel important in the navy and just good about himself in general. Andrew adopted him, really, initiating him into recondite areas of gay existence. At the same time, Andrew overtly admired him and liked to copy any little change Jeff introduced in his mannerisms or appearance: if Jeff grew a goatee, Andrew had one a week later. It went on for years that way. Andrew had never exhibited any yearning to *be together* with Jeff in a couple-type arrangement, even when it seemed obvious to Jeff that Andrew had fallen in love with him. The few times they had had sex, the sex had felt extraneous to their friendship, not a deepening emotional thing but almost an honorary proof of how "close" they were. Jeff had felt no real desire except for the release of coming, and he was sure it had been the same for Andrew. No, Andrew wanted to *be* Jeff, he *still* wanted to be. If he'd mentioned his pierced nipple or the ring he wore on his middle toe, Jeff knew Andrew would immediately copy them.

For years Andrew's emulation seemed just fine. And then it wasn't any more. If Jeff had learned a lot from Andrew, he'd also learned plenty about Andrew. Andrew's unsettling gift for mimesis, his habit of incorporating other people into himself, borrowing parts of their life stories. Jeff had always been a little bothered by Andrew's fabrications, the things Andrew prattled in bars, his flights of theater, yet Jeff hadn't seen any true harm in Andrew's mythomania, most often he told himself Andrew was merely *putting people on*, not malevolently, just testing to see if they could take a joke, but over time, especially after Jeff left the navy, he began to understand that Andrew didn't only lie to people whom he believed (rightly or wrongly) didn't matter, he also lied all the time to Jeff. What Jeff had taken for granted about Andrew, regardless of whether Andrew really was or wasn't a Jew or rich or whatever, was that Jeff's values and Andrew's were somewhere in the same ballpark, and Jeff at last knew this simply wasn't the case.

Jeff blamed himself for perceiving this so late in their relationship, and though their past smelled of poison now, he couldn't rid himself of Andrew easily. Jeff dreaded confrontations. They'd already had something like a showdown a month ago, an argument that blazed up when Jeff tried pinning Andrew to some facts about his recent doings, pointing out contradictions in Andrew's account of himself. Although Jeff never raised his voice, as soon as Andrew grasped that he was being criticized, a different personality took over and went on the attack. He began screaming the most pustulant, violent, ugly insults Jeff had ever heard in his life, a torrent of invective that sounded less like one side of an argument than the demented screeching of a creature *fighting for its life*. Trying to calm Andrew down was futile.

The more conciliatory Jeff sounded the louder and more blindly hostile Andrew became. Andrew attacked every vulnerable aspect of Jeff's life, past and present. Feelings Jeff had shared with Andrew out of deepest trust were flung at him in tones of icy ridicule. Jeff could not defend himself because throughout this insane episode *Jeff no longer existed.* If their friendship had been a house, Andrew would have smashed it to pieces board by board and incinerated the debris.

It had all gone down on the telephone. When Andrew finished screaming, he hung up. Jeff couldn't stop his hands shaking afterwards but he had thought, with disgusted relief, *that's that.* A week passed, he came home to find Andrew's message on his machine, *Jeff, I'm sorry you're not home, I'm calling to beg your forgiveness, I know you realize I didn't mean any of that crap I laid on you the last time we talked, I was completely out of control at the time, I don't know why I reacted the way I did, you have to know you're probably the person I respect most in the world and you had every right to confront me about those things you brought up*—Jeff quickly forgot most of it, he remembered thinking Andrew had timed the call and prepared this heartfelt speech specifically for the answering machine, so that Jeff had to hear him out without interrupting or hanging up. It did feel better to know Andrew was sorry, if only because that meant Andrew wasn't stewing in the same rage, but Jeff now had the problem of maintaining some polite ghost of friendship while secretly keeping Andrew at a safe distance from his life. Some days later, Andrew called when he was home, as Jeff had known he would, breaking into a reprise of the apology until Jeff hushed him, said it was forgiven and forgotten, and got him talking about other things.

Only days after that faux reconciliation, Andrew called to say he was flying in soon to visit David Madson and really, really wanted to see Jeff. Somehow it seemed exactly Andrew's style to force things back to normal instead of allowing a decent cooling-off period. Jeff agreed to let Andrew stay with him for part of the weekend, presumably to give David time to himself, but also for them to "catch up." As the weekend approached, Jeff's dread of it became excruciating and he decided to flee. He now recognized that letting Andrew use the flat was an example of his generous nature sabotaging his judgment, a dumb way of humoring someone whose wrath he actually feared.

At all costs, Jeff wanted Andrew never to turn on him again. He believed he could buy insurance with small gestures of friendship when necessary, the increasingly rare phone call, a meal or a drink when they happened to be in the same city. In Jeff's experience, Andrew was too self-absorbed to distinguish gesture from reality. With that in mind, Jeff decided that he would, in fact, squeeze in coffee with Andrew on Sunday; it might be a good idea to check in with him this morning, too, to reinforce the illusion that he found Andrew's proximity a happy circumstance.

David Madson answered the phone. Jeff held for Andrew. He heard Beck playing. *I'm a loser baby, so why don't you kill me.*

"How's your visit so far?"

"Great, just great, we … saw some folks, went dancing at the 90s."

"Get laid yet?"

"Well … technically. I did some cute punk in his car, but J. T., it was *freezing*. I swear to you my come formed icicles on his face."

He heard David laugh and bray something in the background.

"David says to tell you I woke him at four A.M."

"Was he pissed?"

"Well, he had to dress and come downstairs, he still hasn't got his buzzer fixed, but no, David was cool … pissed, but cool …" There was a long pause, Andrew moving to privacy. "He met this guy, J. T.—" Andrew's voice dropped. "David met this guy who turned out to have exactly the same *name* as that ex who was stalking him."

"The same name?"

"Strange, no? I mean maybe not *that* strange, Greg Nelson, I'm sure there are forty of them in the phone book, but David took it as a good augury. That his Greg Nelson troubles are over."

"That's the guy he got the restraining order—?"

"Right. The dipso lunatic."

"I thought that guy left town."

"Yeah, but see, David saw him like, recently, David was sitting in Café Wyrd? You know Café Wyrd?"

"In Uptown, sure."

"David's sitting there and looks out the window and sees Greg Nelson out on the sidewalk staring at him. So David leaves by the rear exit, and he's so spooked he actually *drives to a friend's house*, Monique, maybe you met her last year at the DIFFA thing, anyway, right after that, somebody keyed his car and broke one of the windows. Then he starts getting hang-up calls. He like, stayed at Monique's place for three days scared that Greg Nelson was going to show up here."

"Fuck."

Ambient sound, Andrew pacing into the main loft.

"We gonna see each other?"

"Yeah, I guess tomorrow evening? You know how to get out here tonight, right?"

"Thirty-five West going south, West Ninetieth Street off-ramp, west on West Ninetieth to Penn Avenue. Second right after the little bridge, right again and first left."

"How do you remember stuff like that? The keys will be under the mat. Listen Andrew, I'm sorry about the confusion with Jon's birthday, you know when you're *in a relationship* you have to kind of accommodate—"

"No *problem*, J. T." A long pause. "I've taken you into the bathroom with me. When are you leaving for the country?"

"Around three? Jon and I both need a break. Even for twenty-four hours."

"Fresh country air. Hearty farm breakfast in bed."

"Wake up with the birds chirping, someone young and pretty sucking your toes."

"That makes an image. Call me here when you get back, all right?"

They'd lapsed into the easy cadences of San Diego, Jeff thought. A cloudless continuum of perfect weather in which absolutely nothing ever happened. As long as he could sustain that, letting it fade and die when it would, there was nothing at all to be afraid of.

12

Andrew fixed their breakfast: coffee, whole-wheat toast, cereal, fried eggs, orange juice. David called Monique about dinner, she said she had plans, David gave the phone to Andrew and Andrew proposed that the three of them meet the following night, Monique said that might be fun. Then David lent him a spare set of keys he remembered Rich Bonnin had given back after dog-sitting Prints Easter weekend. David had a workout date with his gym partner, John Herbert, a guy Andrew'd met the night before in the 90s. As soon as David left, Andrew felt unbearable hope-lessness, a kind of claustrophobia inside his own body. He could feel the hours running out and none of what he'd planned had materialized. He hadn't thought it out, had conjured a vague fan-tasy of telling David and Jeff he was bottoming out and could never go back to San Diego. In his mind, he'd already abandoned everything in his room at Erik Greenman's; his life consisted of the clothes he had on and whatever he'd packed in his duffel bag.

He'd been so positive that David or Jeff would offer to let him stay as long as he needed to, as long as it took to find some way of earning money, that David, especially, would step in and take care of him, he'd hinted enough before coming here that his situation was turning precarious, but they both deflected him, he couldn't find a single opening to plead his case and ask for help. Okay, David had suggested selling the watch if he needed money, but the whole point in giving the watch was to signal that he needed more than money, he needed a stable environment, emo-tional support, a subsidized little corner in someone else's life for a while. The effulgent feeling he'd flown in with, that confidence that he could plant himself anywhere and instantly prosper, had carried him through the last weeks of using up his credit and through everything else, really, until this morning. Now he felt so desperate he couldn't sit still.

He went out, taking the stairs, walked across Fourth Street to Hennepin and down Hennepin to Schinder's. Schinder's was a trip, every paper and magazine in the universe, including every porno. Magazines for freaky lifestyles, biker mama digests, dick piercing quarterlies, 'zines on Xerox paper, the whole rich array of possible obsessions, possible interests, possible lives. Andrew imagined devoting weeks to building muscle at David's gym. He'd crunch off his spare tire, buy a beeper, and plant an alluring escort/masseur ad in *Lavender Lifestyles* or *Focal Point*. He preferred the idea of offering "erotic massage with release" over full-blown escort service, he'd never done escort and didn't know if he could, he wasn't confident about penetrating strangers on demand. "Massage with release," okay. The barre of beauty in Minneapolis wasn't set very high, probably even with the gut he could put together a sizable wad in a few months, enough to move to San Francisco or LA. His porno friends all lived pretty plush on their out-call takings and some of them only did massage. Of course they spent every penny on drugs, cars, and furniture, things that depreciated. Andrew on the other hand could take five or ten thousand dollars and grow it fast in the stock market, he kicked himself now for not doing that with his Norman Blachford mad money. He'd meant to. Pete had taught him everything about the market. Andrew tracked dozens of stocks in the paper every day. If he'd put in half what he'd spent on dinner for the past year he'd be rich now.

He also pictured working for much less, another descent into meniality à la Thrifty, as a coffeehouse waiter, or a clerk in a music store. Adjusting to a calmer set of colors. He could do that here without embarrassment, it wouldn't be like taking a job in San Diego. Andrew in a crisp white shirt and crisp black pants serving cappuccino to Laura Booher and Monique Salvetti. "How's that Mexican factory of yours?" He could just hear Laura now. He quickly opened an issue of *Fetish World* and focused hard on black-masked vixens giving Ron Jeremy an enema. No, hold the cappuccino. He skimmed some articles in *Cigar Aficionado*—Demi Moore, it appeared, enjoyed kicking back with a fine cigar—and *U.S. News and World Report*. Finally he bought *The New York Times* and took the free throwaway paper published by Sex World, the strip joint across from David's house.

13

They drove to Red Owl across the river, David detouring onto Nicollet Island, where he pointed out the bridge, the first one built across the Mississippi, then drove behind the massive Pillsbury silos to show him where railroad tracks ran straight inside the mill. He showed him the dynamo at the river's edge, hundreds of girders in byzantine grids, high-voltage burrs snaked across them, and he showed him the pylons supporting the bridge, showed him the river, the derelict warehouses turned into storefronts, the soap factory reclaimed as an arts center. David loved the ruined Gothic majesty of these places, the little parks and strips of woodland fringing the dead monuments of industry, the chill murmur of the past. He seemed to forget he'd shown Andrew everything before.

Andrew barely spoke, sunk in reverie or some thought tangle David couldn't penetrate, but David felt whatever it was had little to do with him, for Andrew smiled when David told him something and dutifully looked when David showed him something and at Red Owl Andrew helped him find things, cranberry juice and English muffins and 2 percent low-fat milk, apples, lettuce, dog food, *People* magazine, they carted this treasure to the loft and immediately left for the Target store on Broadway, where

David needed cleaning supplies, odds and ends, a roll of electrical tape, grout, prosaic substances and objects of various kinds, it was a method for filling a shopping cart and an afternoon that Andrew said he liked as well as any other. The day went by.

They ate dinner alone at the Monte Carlo, where Andrew thought the bar looked like the Overlook Hotel's bar in *The Shining*, festively aglow in witchy darkness. Andrew took pains ordering the wine, declaring that a 1992 Semillon would be surprisingly good because that year's white wine grapes had been harvested early, before the disastrous rains that ruined the red ones. They shared the Sample Platter of chicken wings, stuffed mushrooms, gulf shrimp, and Szechuan green beans; Andrew asked for oysters. Puget Sounds, big ones. He fed one, then another, to David on his oyster fork. Andrew had visibly pulled himself together since their shopping trip, having napped and showered and spent a good forty-five minutes grooming, putting on dress socks, dark twill trousers, and a smartly cut gray blazer over a Banana Republic T-shirt; his mood had lifted, and though he certainly had gained weight lately, he looked very handsome, David thought, like the old Andrew, nowhere near as manic, perhaps, but not emitting that troubled edginess David had sensed since his arrival.

No, tonight's Andrew seemed on point. A little detached, a little bemused, funnily pedantic, intellectual in the dry way that really suited him, not at all serious. He joked about Heaven's Gate, saying that the cult people had dropped their containers about five doors from where his family lived in Rancho Santa Fe ("there goes the neighborhood"), claimed that Hedy Lamarr had invented an electronic frequency device for torpedoes in World War II, and worked out an elaborate semiotic correspondence between *Shaft in Africa* and *Cleopatra Jones in the Casino of*

Gold—blaxploitation films were Andrew's specialty—between appetizer and entrée (Cajun pork chops for David, Andrew the whiskey peppercorn fillet). He was making himself lovable, David realized, and hiding the effort involved with amazing grace.

Could the hollowness of Andrew's composure be due to David's slightly grudging hospitality? Was there *so* much harm in Andrew's tendency to spin myths about himself? David guiltily reviewed all the badmouthing he'd done against Andrew since they broke up. Was it all justified? A lot of gay men reinvented themselves after leaving home, fearing rejection by their peers, having already been rejected by their families. David himself often painted a much rosier picture of his Wisconsin childhood than he recalled, routinely cranked up his family's economic status several notches and transformed their disapproval of his sexuality into an attitude of liberal enlightenment. If Andrew took this type of fibbing to extremes, it was doubtless because his scars cut much deeper than David's. *You really need to be a little kinder to this person*, David chided himself as espresso and brandy arrived. He dug out his car keys and pushed them across the tablecloth.

"When you go out to Jeff's tonight, I want you to take the Jeep," he told Andrew. "There's no sense paying twenty or thirty dollars on a taxi."

"I am your own forever," Andrew laughed.

14

Andrew packed his bag and stowed it in the Cherokee. They walked over to the 90s and had a drink. Tonight they danced together. Andrew was the kind of dancer who took his cues from the least complicated moves of those around him. David soon moved off in search of Mr. Blackbody. Andrew strutted to the back bar, where somewhere into his second vodka rocks Kevin appeared, wearing a sour expression and the same ripped T-shirt, jeans.

"Hey, sailor," Andrew greeted.

"Yeah, hi," Kevin mumbled.

"How's it hanging?"

"You son of a bitch," Kevin hissed, angry but not *permanently* angry. "You almost bit off my fucking nipple." He rubbed it through the T-shirt. "It *still* hurts."

"True love always hurts," Andrew sighed. "I can love you lots more if that's what you're into."

Kevin seriously considered it, despite his dour face. His eyes flittered around, sighting other prospects.

"Come to think of it no thank you," he said shakily, backing away.

15

Jeff's apartment was pure Jeff, neat as a pin, blandly tasteful furniture, muted colors, neutral fabrics, a few homoerotic touches in the form of Bruce Weber and Robert Mapplethorpe reproductions, Mapplethorpe *flowers*, nothing gross, a rainbow flag the size of a cocktail umbrella poking from a mug holding pencils and marking pens, souvenir magnets on the fridge, some snapshots in little frames, mainly family pictures, more of a tidy bachelor pad than a fag pad, Jeff's bedroom contained a good deal of navy memorabilia, Andrew noticed a few things that probably belonged to Jon Hackett, a pair of sneakers too small for Jeff and some clothes, quite a *nice* place, Andrew thought, poking about the kitchen for booze. He'd stripped naked and strode around masturbating while rummaging through every drawer and cabinet and container he could find, inspecting old letters, postcards, bills, notepads, he didn't expect to uncover any dark secrets but hoped he'd find some scribbled thought or incongruous object that would tell him something he didn't already know. He did find scotch, and drank some, fantasized making love to David, stroked himself more vigorously, when he got close he grabbed one of Jon Hackett's sneakers and spurted into it.

Within minutes the despair came back, the crushing sense of time flying past with nothing resolved and nothing to look forward to. Andrew started on the closets, fishing through Jeff's suits, shirts, pockets. As he did this he understood that what he wanted to find was some evidence of *himself* in Jeff's apartment. Some *reflection* of Jeff's affection for him. He could not find the letters he'd sent, the gifts he'd given Jeff over the years. A few postcards and whatnot but nothing that paid homage to Andrew's existence, nothing that said *cherished friend.*

At the back of Jeff's closet he found a large metal ammunition box and brought it out. In the box were safety goggles, earplugs, and Spenso padded gloves, along with a gun, several holsters, and a box of a hundred .40mm hollow point bullets.

16

The pistol had been cleaned and oiled recently. It had the smart lethal gleam of a cherished fetish. On Sunday morning, after showering and changing his clothes, Andrew loaded the magazine with ten bullets, sat on Jeff's bed, and closed his lips around the barrel, remembering that this particular pistol, a K9 Taurus semi-automatic, fired with about five pounds of trigger pressure, i.e., not much at all. He saw his brains splattered on the wall. Then saw Jeff and Jon Hackett frozen in the doorway. He knew the Jon Hackett part shouldn't bother him now. He thought of Jon Hackett walking around with Andrew Cunanan come in his shoe and couldn't help laughing. He lowered the gun. It would be tasteless to kill himself in Bloomington, if people learned of it at all they'd always associate his suicide with the Mall of America. He could do it at David's. At least he'd have bought the farm in a chic neighborhood.

17

Andrew drove into the city. The sky was greased with gray clouds that looked like a dropped ceiling. He got all messed around trying to get off 35 at an uptown interchange, Minneapolis had to have the worst freeway system in the world, full of left lane off-ramps and misleading signage, the whole city was skewed because Uptown was south and Downtown north, idiotic, he finally exited the freeway somewhere near the Hubert Humphrey Metrodome and wrangled his way back south on surface roads, ending up on Franklin somewhere east of Nicollet Avenue. He pulled into a White Castle that was full of blacks who looked as if they had spent the night there, arguing. He took six bacon cheeseburgers and a large white coffee to go and drove around Uptown eating. His last day in Minneapolis. His last day, period.

18

Just because he felt less bleak after eating didn't mean he wouldn't do it. He could phone up *Norman* and do it over the phone, *Hi you rotten old flick just thought I'd call and blow my head off*. His mother? She'd probably think she was having a bad dream. What else could he do? Ask for help from which faggots? Erik *Greenman*, perhaps? Family? He could not face Chris or Elena, they weren't that far away in Peoria but neither was his mother and she of course would step into it, and none of them would understand any of it, he hadn't seen them in years anyway and what would he tell them, how would you put this to God-fearing middle Americans, *I owe American Express forty thousand dollars that I spent on clothes and expensive restaurants and I'm gay*, what a winning formula.

19

Rain was spitting on the windshield. Andrew took Hennepin to David's neighborhood, circled the block three times looking for a space. As he parked the Cherokee, a thicker rain slashed the streets. In the loft, David had just finished nailing up Sheetrock and lay on the couch watching a news analysis program, shapeless old men discussing the tobacco industry. He sat up when Andrew came in and said he'd been waiting to hear what his plans were.

Andrew said he was so tired he couldn't even think as far ahead as dinner. He hadn't slept well at Jeff's, and he thought the rain might be giving him a headache. David made a concerned face. Andrew stared at David's high forehead, his faintly down-slanted eyelids, and pointed chin, unable to link them in his mind to the person speaking to him.

It's all over with you, Andrew thought, holding his duffel bag and dripping rain on the sleek wood floor. David was saying something about Buca or Boca, aping excitement over some type of lasagne. Andrew set his bag down and pressed fingertips into his temples. He kept hearing a line from a poem, *Labial gossip of night, sibilant chorals*. He wished David would shut up. David wanted to know if Andrew had had *brunch*, did you have a good *brunch*, David supposed that Andrew had eaten *brunch* with JT. Andrew's arms and legs felt heavy, his head felt too heavy for his neck, he moved his lips to say *JT went out of town, David*, but what came out was *really nice, eggs Benedict, Old French Café*, Andrew sat down and slipped off his shoes, *Labial gossip of night*, he looked into David's eyes, *Friday's ruling is definitely going to impact tobacco stocks*, one of the shapeless men said, Andrew pulled off his socks, he managed to say *I really don't feel well* before he ran for the toilet, he slammed the bathroom door and squatted and puked up all the White Castle burgers, the sight of chewed-up chunks bobbing in gluelike bile brought more gunk shooting out of his stomach, *Are you all right are you okay* through the door. Andrew flushed the john and thought it was over but when he stood up another wave hit him in the guts, he couldn't place the gory-looking things coming out of him, he told himself he was throwing up *Hillcrest* and throwing up *La Jolla*, vomiting out *Rancho Bernardo* and *East Bay* and *UCSD* and *Norman Blachford*, he was also puking away *David Madson Jeffrey Trail Lincoln Aston*, puking off the sugar plantations and the soundproofing factories and the fake Judaism and Commodore

Cummings and Andy DeSilva, it was all so much vomit, and it kept sluicing up inside him and splattering out of him until he felt ridiculously empty.

20

Darkness.

"Feeling better?"

"Mmm. What time is it."

"It's a little after eight."

"Oh, man." Sits up.

"They must have a new chef at the Old French Café."

"Can you get me the phone?"

Music in the next room. *Every day is a winding road*

"Thanks. I'll come but in a minute."

"I didn't book anything for tonight, I didn't know—"

"Just give me a minute David, we need to talk."

Every day is a faded sign

"This is Jeff, I'm not in right now …"

Beep.

"Oh JT, where are you? It's … eight-twenty, so please give me a call when you can. 339-9186. Okay, bye bye. Let me know if you're still coming; I really want to see you. Bye bye."

Stands up. Weaves slightly. *I get a little bit closer.* David curled on the couch, a section of the Sunday paper open in his lap.

Everybody gets high, everybody gets low, These are the days when anything goes

"I don't think I can eat, so if you want to go out and have something." If he would just leave. I could do it before he comes back.

David thinks about it. Shrugs.

"We bought all that food, I can fix myself something. You should have, you know, soup, something bland."

Andrew walks around the room. Stops at the table. Walks to the window. Walks back to the table. Puts on his blue baseball cap, gnaws his thumbnail.

Out of sight, out of time, out of patience and I'm out of my mind

"Did you want to discuss something?" David says it jokingly, as if nothing serious could possibly come up.

"I kind of do." Sighs. "Maybe it's not—"

Phone rings. David goes for the phone. Before answering he walks over to the Caller ID box near the apartment door. He comes back, hands the handset to Andrew.

"Jeff," David says.

"Hello?"

"Hey Andy, I had the phone turned down.… You wanna meet for coffee, like in an hour?"

"All right. Where do you—"

"I'll find something near where you are and call you?"

"Sure, that's fine."

Breathes. In and out. Maybe Jeff can pull me out of this. I'll tell him how real it is. How I even took his gun. David nervous.

21

"Things are a lot worse than I told you."

"How ... how so?"

"Well, I'm broke, for one thing."

A long pause. *Old James Dean Monroe hands out flowers at the Shop-N-Go, hopes for money but all he gets is fear.*

"Would you mind if I turned that off?" How to say it. What to say.

"What about … the, um, business with J. T.?"

Andrew draws a blank. He looks out a window. Night. Neon. Sex World.

"I don't really have any business with J. T."

"To tell you the truth I wondered about that. But I thought you did have all these projects, these investment things."

"I guess I exaggerated a little."

"You always do." It slipped out.

"What's that supposed to mean."

"Andrew don't take offense, but you know as well as I do that you tend to … embellish things."

It was coming closer. Something awful was coming closer.

"Embellish," Andrew said, as if a hunk of stinky cheese were passing under his nose. He shook his head, pushing the cheese aside. "I owe a lot of money."

"You mean—like, to drug dealers?"

"No, David, not to *drug dealers*, to American *Express*."

"Oh God, Andrew, lighten up," David laughed. "So do I. So does most of America. I mean it's usually to Visa or—"

"And where is this *drug dealer* shit coming from, I used to sell a few Percocets for like, cab money, in fucking *San Diego*."

From *you*, Andrew, David tried to say, and couldn't.

"I think I need a drink."

"So do I."

"Jesus, Andrew, I don't think so. You'll barf it up."

22

Andrew knocked back three vodkas, bam bam bam, David knew he should never have opened his mouth but how could anybody even begin to help Andrew when you had to scrape through all his bullshit even to find some little fingernail clipping of fact, apparently he didn't even have a return ticket to SD even though they extended his credit cards and he could've bought one, because he had some weird idea that he and David could hook up together again and Andrew could stay here and get a job, absolute madness, when David had told him a million times the sex part of their relationship was over and they were just going to be friends, of course David would buy him a ticket back to San Diego and under the circumstances, he said, it wouldn't be *right* for him to keep Andrew's watch, Andrew could sell it for thousands, but Andrew also had this screwy concept that he should stay in Minneapolis anyway, that he could live with JT for a while, But Andrew, David said, you still have a place in San Diego full of stuff, thinking the last thing he needed was Andrew living right up his nose, unfortunately David put his foot in it then partly to get himself off the hook, he said Andrew I'm not asking you this to upset you, but do you really know where you stand with J. T., Andrew got that funny look well not so funny and said What are you talking about and David really should've kept his mouth shut then but went ahead and told him all the stuff JT had said to Rob Davis last November at the party about leaving California because of Andrew and Andrew being a pathological liar, David said this not accusingly as if he agreed with it but humorously as if to say we sophisticated adults will say all kinds of extreme things about each other but we learn to take it with a grain of salt, the look on Andrew's face at that point made David realize he'd really committed a huge faux pas and to make matters worse the phone rang right then, Jeff was calling from Dunn Brothers coffee shop uptown and Andrew told him he wasn't feeling well and couldn't come out but wanted Jeff to come over to the loft of course Jeff couldn't see Andrew's face at that moment if he had he probably would've turned around and driven right back to Bloomington, or gone straight to the 90s to regroup with everybody who'd just been at his place for Jon Hackett's birthday party, after Andrew hung up he said something like I'm going to have to sort this out with him, in this really cold, precise voice, like he was the teacher and Jeff the disobedient pupil in some really strict German boarding school, David made this half-assed effort to rectify everything by saying he knew how much JT liked Andrew and cared about Andrew despite whatever problems, all friends have little things they don't like about each other, Andrew just nodded with his mouth all tight as if to say We've heard enough from you on this subject for one night, at that point Andrew poured himself another vodka and drank it fast, he even started on another one, then they talked about something else altogether, how long it was going to take David to complete the partition, the toolbox was still lying open on the kitchen table and that corner of the room had a lot of construction mess, David said he couldn't seem to find enough time to finish it off, then exactly at 9:45 the phone rang and David looked at the Caller ID, it had to be Jeff using the intercom phone downstairs, and since David or Andrew had to go down to let him in anyway David had the inspiration to say he needed to walk Prints, calling the dog and throwing on his coat in a hurry. He said he'd let Jeff in on his way out.

23

Jeff knew right away maybe it took five seconds Hey dude he said Andrew's open mouth made this unnerving mocking sort of smile he stepped away from the door a few steps Jeff saw he was barefoot Glad you could set aside ten minutes for the person who drove you out of California Andrew said Jeff knew right away the tone the voice now he could see what Andrew must have looked like when they had the fight on the telephone Jeff tried to handle it Whoa Andy what's that supposed to mean Jeff's heart started pounding Oh I think you know fucking well what it means No I don't pal Jeff said Jeff could hear the escalating sarcasm just like before he felt his blood pressure rising in his ears Pal, that's a new one, Pal, what *exactly* did you tell Rob Davis about me, Jeff was not going to play this, I have seen this movie before, Jeff thought, Who the hell is Rob Davis he said he really had no recollection of any Rob Davis Rob Davis David Madson's black ex-boyfriend Andrew snarled at that point working himself up, Jeff knew where this was going and said Hey, Andy, putting up his open palms like Stop right there, this was already too crazy, You know what, he said— and before he could finish saying You know what, I'm outta here, Andrew screamed GET THE FUCK OUT Jeff gave him a pitying smile shook his head turned around opened the door.

24

Andrew grabbed the hammer from David's toolbox. It was the first thing his eyes lit on, and gripping the rubber handle tight, with blurry visions of whacking Jeff's arm or maybe hitting his shoulder, fucking betrayer, he brought it down harder and from a different angle than he anticipated and it cracked across Jeff's head, exactly where the hair whorled to a tiny bald spot. A piece of Jeff's scalp flew off and another piece came away on the end of the hammer and stuck to the wall where the tool's impact sheared off a crescent of plaster, just below the light switch. A speck of blood spurted across the corridor and dotted the wall. Andrew crashed the hammer down again. Jeff slumped into the door. Blood coated the door frame as his weight slammed it shut. He wheeled to balance himself and spun on his heel flailing his arms in front of his face. Andrew slashed at Jeff's hands, knocking his watch off. He attacked first with the blunt end of the hammer, then went at the face with the claw end. Jeff's eyes went through awesome changes as parts of his brain were snuffed. Andrew tried gouging both eyes with the hammer blows but only grazed one socket. After the fifth or sixth blow Jeff's limbs didn't work and he dropped to his knees and finally smacked the floor with his face. Blood needled across Andrew's neck and scrawled weird messages on his T-shirt. He kept sinking the hammer into Jeff's head, amazed at the damage he was wreaking. Gouts of brain the consistency of custard clung to the hammerhead and dripped off it. Andrew flicked blobs of it off his arm. Each time the head struck the hardwood it sent a loud thunk through the walls. A crimson caul rippled around Jeff's ear, down his neck, forming an irregular pool beneath him. It spread to the fringe of a Navajo rug that Andrew's bare feet, sticky from sloshing in the tacky puddle, kept slipping on. He hopped around avoiding Jeff's spastic legs and arms, blood soaking into the cuffs of his jeans. As life drained away Jeff twitched like an appliance shuddering to a halt. His throat made a harsh clawing noise. Andrew attacked his skull as if driving nails through it. He felt it splinter through the hammer grip, the blunt metal squishing into exposed brain tissue, mushy now like rotten melon. Jeff ceased moving. Andrew continued bashing the lifeless face until his arm hurt.

25

Immediately after killing Jeff, Andrew slipped on the Ferragamo loafers he'd taken off earlier, in order not to track blood all over the house, then set about mopping up the mess he'd made everywhere, governed by a ridiculous impulse to hide everything before David returned from walking the dog. He started by running the taps in the kitchen sink and rinsing blood and brain matter off the claw hammer, next he tore open two of the six rolls of Brawny paper towels that David had purchased at the Red Owl supermarket the day before, Andrew had some notion of washing all the blood down the sink drain but quickly abandoned the idea of getting it all up with paper towels, setting to work instead with a purple terrycloth towel from the bathroom, which he first ran under the tap and squirted with dishwashing liquid. He soon realized that scrubbing away such a large quantity of blood would be impossible unless he moved the body, which continued, he believed, to leak all over the hardwood floor, increasing the likelihood of stains setting in before the boards could be cleaned, furthermore it disturbed him to keep stepping over the body, which had settled in a particularly garish attitude and was bound to become rigid and possibly harder to move, therefore he decided to roll the body up in the large Navajo carpet he'd almost tripped over during the attack.

Andrew went to the area between the body and the carpet. Grabbing Jeff's ankles, he pulled him across the floor, shifting his own weight to angle the body parallel with the lengthwise edge of the carpet. The floor squeaked as Andrew pulled. Jeff did not pull easily and seemed to grow heavier by the second. His black socks slid on his ankles in Andrew's grip. Andrew noticed white pebbles embedded in Jeff's sneaker treads and wondered where they came from.

Once Jeff was in position, Andrew draped the near end of the carpet over his middle. The rug wasn't long enough to cover Jeff's legs. Andrew fetched a smaller white shawl-like thing and arranged it lengthwise under Jeff's shins. He would just about fit. Andrew resumed sopping up blood with the towel, which soon became sodden. He gathered all the bathroom towels and set to work with them, managing to soak up most of the wet blood, though obvious spatters, already dry, ran all the way up the wall to the ceiling. Worse, patches of floor blood had dried, and everywhere blood had seeped into the wood and discolored it, fixing distinct footprints and shoeprints in a scattered pattern. Exasperated, Andrew got a T-shirt from his duffel bag, an "Amphibious Group Three" shirt that Jeff had given him back in San Diego, to swab blood from the wall. It left a huge smear.

26

Fear wrapped David Madson in a cloying hug, like a dream of premature burial. Fear first of the thing on the carpet which made no sense and second fear of Andrew, who said several things that were plainly crazy (including, at one point, "I didn't do it!") and was clearly capable of anything. David had a moment or two after walking in, when Prints pushed into the loft ahead of him, when he could have bolted and run screaming down the hall, if he'd put the picture together that fast, but his nerve went as soon as he focused the thing in front of him as *Jeff Trail's dead body*.

He tried dowsing fear with the fact that other people lived no further than a hundred feet away, outside his walls, that another moment would arrive like the one he'd blown, but Andrew dispersed the first moment's ambiguous residue by showing David a gun and telling him he'd shoot the dog if David ran. Prints was agitated, claws tapping an excited circle around the carpet, but not barking, perturbed by the body but interested, too, as if it could be food. Andrew called him and Prints went wagging over, it showed how effortlessly he could blow the dog's head off.

The gravitational pull of the battered head and the normally dressed body attached to it acted more powerfully on David than on Andrew. He felt paralyzed, as if his own brain had been knocked senseless. Andrew told him to put the towels and anything bloody in a bag: the hammer, Jeff's Swiss Army watch. He even had David pry a ring off Jeff's finger, for what reason he didn't say. Andrew laid the gun down several times but no way was David going for it, physically stronger he might be, but Andrew had the superior adrenaline. They rolled Jeff up in the two rugs, then pushed him behind the sofa, Andrew saying they had to *make Jeffrey disappear*, David nodding in agreement, aping complicity, they would have to get a floor sander, of course, and wall paint, right, and wipe out any evidence. Andrew seemed to abandon that idea as the hours went by, however, Andrew said Jon Hackett would definitely file a Missing Persons right away, the fact that they were all faggots would definitely buy several days' indifference from the police but people were going to come looking, no way around it, and an attempt to smuggle the body out, even at three or four in the morning, would stir a ruckus in this neighborhood, people came and went in the building all night, Sex World entertained customers round the clock. David tried to introduce the idea of *getting help* for Andrew, of Andrew turning himself in, getting *the best defense lawyers* to plead temporary insanity for him, but Andrew didn't think he was insane, that was the problem, this event with Jeff had just sort of happened, he said, *and frankly probably happened for the best*, he added, deciding then to move David's vintage rocking chair into the bedroom.

27

Andrew sealed David's mouth with tape. He cuffed him to the rocking chair, manacled his ankles together. He took a shower. The chair worked perfectly as a restraining device. If David rocked too hard he'd land on his face with the chair up his back. Andrew came back naked, wet, showing himself to David as he pleaded, *Why don't you love me, why why why don't you love me.*

28

Taurus under the pillow, Andrew slept. Snored. David beside him, wrists and ankles bound, more tape around his head below the nose, tape across his eyes. Andrew stripped him to make him even more vulnerable, David supposed, and he felt it. A window open despite the chill, to cut the stink of blood in the house.

29

They walked the dog, exactly when David had a critical team meeting scheduled at John Ryan. A warm day of low sky, boxy factory buildings around Second Avenue vivid in an unreal way. By now the gun in Andrew's coat pocket no longer stopped him from running; he was held by a kind of sick enchantment, the mirage of a fever dream, the feeling that something decisive would happen next, that when they returned to the loft the nightmare would be revealed as the illusion of a potent drug, of course it was the allure of this lymphatic helplessness that had drawn him to Andrew in the first place, the rituals with handcuffs, gags, leg irons, dripped candle wax, trusting the ritual's boundaries, expanding them incrementally until the amount of manipulation you could welcome was truly astonishing to the uninitiated. At the same time, he knew it was real, and what greeted them at the loft was a headier stench of decay, the rolled-up body. But he understood something that seemed valuable. He feared Andrew in a whole new way, as if Andrew's powers had become so formidable and uncanny that even if David were clever enough to get it away from him, the gun would be useless against this power.

30

Andrew was tender. Not in a fag way, tender like a concentration camp guard with his "special" prisoner. Especially when he handcuffed David to the chair again, smoothed a fresh strip of silver tape over his mouth. Andrew had brought the handcuffs and leg irons from California, David realized. Dreaming of this. Of me. To escape the putrid odor they took another walk at dusk, without the dog, in the spectral environs of the Third Street Ramp. Coming back, the elevator door was typically slow to close, and Kathleen, a neighbor in 405, stepped on, saw Andrew, smiled uncertainly, noticed David, relaxed, said Hi, David was beyond expressiveness and mumbled back. The eon of the void passed with the three of them in the elevator. David thought to start an innocuous-sounding conversation that would tip this woman to something worse than a bad mood. He couldn't find any formula for alarm that Andrew wouldn't hear before she did.

By Monday night Andrew had ceased discussing his plans, Andrew was letting huge blocks of time rumble past, occasionally he said the word *food* like he'd just thought of it, he fixed Spanish rice while David sat leg-cuffed to the kitchen table. He said the word *Canada* and David knew Andrew's thoughts were turning toward Canada. David considered repeatedly screaming the name "Jesse," which might carry to Jesse, the tenant in 401. If Jesse heard it, the category of trouble David was in might suggest itself, for all David knew a real effort of resistance might unnerve Andrew altogether, but David's best guess was, Andrew would shoot him and shoot Jesse and anyone else who interfered with him. Eating proved difficult. That night Andrew played a bondage porno he'd brought, blond boys on Catalina fisting each other with Crisco, David in leg restraints on the couch, head in Andrew's lap, Jeff decomposing in the rug. Andrew stroked David's face with the side of the gun barrel.

31

Time crawled, Tuesday morning brought another dog-walk, breakfast horrors, keeping anything down with that smell, then soon the phone started ringing. David knew these unanswered calls would have consequences, he began once more trying to get through to Andrew's rational mind, painting scenarios of minimal incarceration, psychiatric repair. David believed Andrew listened more attentively than before, more flexibly, then it started, someone knocked around 9 a.m., that was when Andrew began thinking hard, it seemed. Around noon they heard Linda and Laura from John Ryan pounding on the door, which set the dog barking, soon after that some sharp foreign-sounding knocks, Andrew and David crouching behind the door, they heard Linda tell some guy, a police officer from the sound of it, two police officers, in fact, that David hadn't shown for work in two days, couldn't they kick the door in. At that juncture a voice down the hall piped in with questions, Linda told the story again, then the cop said, If this man's been seen walking his dog today, we can't something something, probable cause, then something else about an animal control unit. Andrew's eyes were about to roll up into his head. Then the voices broke up, Andrew hustled him into the bedroom and gagged him again, instructed him not to move. A long time passed, but things were in motion, David thought, this would all be ugly history in another couple hours, he doubted Andrew would fire at police or keep up this hostage stuff or kill him if it looked hopeless, he might shoot himself of course, good riddance to bad rubbish, in a way David never loved Andrew more than when he hoped Andrew would blow his own brains out. David commenced framing what he would say to his friends and the media about his ordeal. *All the things you think you'd do in a situation like that, you don't do them. The fear just freezes you.* While they waited in the bedroom, breathing heavily and scoping each other like bonded accomplices, a completely unforeseen event threw all his calculations off. *Someone entered the loft with a key.* They heard steps. A woman groaned, "Oh God." The building manager. More steps, exiting. Prints shot up from his dog bed and ran barking into the living room. The door shut. Loud knocking down the hall. Steps. The door creaked open again. Heavier steps. The dog's paws clattered in the next room. Someone had to be inspecting the rug, no question, the rug was the first thing you'd see when the door opened. The heavy steps went out. Someone called the dog out of the loft. The door slammed. Footsteps up the hall, disappearing in the stairwell. Andrew prodded David up and pulled off the duct tape and pushed him into the living room, grabbing things up, his wallet, the spare car keys, *Get to the car*, he ordered, and then they were both out the door, scrambling down the fire stairs into sordid daylight.

32

Supplement of FS 11 CA Johnson/B Krause/ officer R Timmerman Identification Division
5–1–97

On 4–29–97 at approximately 1715 hours car 21 was called to 280 2 Avenue North apartment 404 by Sgts. Tichich and Gordon. After arriving at the scene we were advised by Sgt. Tichich that a concerned co-worker had contacted the caretaker of the building about the tenant from this apartment. The caretaker and another resident entered the apartment and discovered a body rolled in a rug. It appeared that the body had been there for several days and it was believed to be the tenant of the apartment. We were also advised that the only persons known to have entered the apartment prior to our arrival without protective footware were the caretaker, one tenant, and 3 uniformed officers.

The location is a former warehouse converted into a 5 story multi-unit apartment building. The front entrance faces 2 Avenue and has a functional security system. Apartment 404 is located in the north west corner of the building next to a rear stair well. Observed across from apartment 404 on the hall, wall were several splatters of BLS [blood-like substance].

Entering the apartment BLS spattering was observed on the inside of the door, the wall area on both sides of the door, and the hard wood floor. The first room of the apartment was a large open area. This room contained the kitchen, living room, and dining room areas. A small bath area was located just inside and to the right after entering. Next to the dining room table, about 5 feet inside the front door, was a plastic handle bag. Inside this bag were paper towels, bath towels, clothing, and a hammer all with BLS. (Later it was found to also contain a broken watch, ring, and a baseball cap.) On the table was a wallet containing a Minnesota Drivers License and other identification belonging to the tenant of the apartment.

Behind a couch in the living room area a body rolled in a rug was observed. This body appeared to be of a male with only the legs protruding from the rug. The legs were covered with a light colored smaller rug and clothed in blue jeans and the feet with socks and tennis shoes.

In the Kitchen area dishes were observed as if at least 2 persons had eaten. Also a plastic wrapped package containing 4 rolls of paper towels was found open. This package when full contains 6 rolls of towels.

Passing through the main room of the apartment, on the left, is a bedroom area. The bed was not made and blanket and top sheet on the bed were crumpled and lying on top of the bed. On a dresser against the south wall were a pair of handcuffs, leg cuffs, 2 handcuff keys, 2 empty drinking glasses, 2 partial rolls of duct tape, 1 bottle of "ForPlay" lubricant, and 2 packs of "Wet" formula. On the night stand next to the bed was another balled up piece of duct tape. On the floor in front of the dresser were 2 balled up pieces of duct tape.

Next to the dresser was a black duffel bag. This bag contained adult video tapes, clothing, a empty holster, a empty magazine, a box of .40 caliber ammunition with 15 live rounds and several other items.

After viewing the scene, color photos were taken by Timmerman, and a video was made by Johnson. These indicate all the above items and the rest of the apartment as it appeared upon our arrival. A rough sketch was prepared by Krause. When this was completed the Hennepin County Medical Examiner arrived and the body was removed from the apartment still rolled in the rug.

The rug was soaked with BLS and a larger BLS stain was left on the floor when the body was removed.

Items that were recovered form [*sic*] the scene on this date are listed on inventory number 97–010634. Processing of the floor for foot-ware impressions were begun using Commassie Blue. At approximately 2145 hours we were advised by Sgt. Tichich that we would need to continue our processing at a later time. We cleared from the scene at about 2200 hours.

Supplement of FS 11 CA Johnson/B Krause/officer R. Timmerman Identification Divsion
5-1-97

On 4–30–97 at approximately 1120 hours we returned to 2802 Avenue North. We were met at this location again by Sgts. Tichich and Gordon.

The processing of the floor with Cornmassie Blue was continued. Several foot ware impressions were discovered. These impressions all appeared to be of the same pattern. Several bare foot prints were also discovered. All of the prints were photographed. After photographing sections of floor that contained 3 bare foot impressions and 2 footware impressions were removed for inventory and comparison purposes. A pair of shoes found under the dining room table were also taken for comparison to the prints.

A red Plastic tool box from the dining room table containing miscellaneous tools, a [*sic*] earning statement for David, Madison and 2 BLS samples were also taken this date for inventory, see inventory 97–010755.

The bathroom was processed for fingerprints by Krause and a palm print was recovered from the sink. This print will be retained in the Identification Division secured small evidence file.

Supplement of Off. Rod Timmerman Ident Div.
5–1–97

Upon our return to the office on 4–29–97, I secured the grey plastic "Jarman" bag in our office for the night.

On 4–30–97 at approximately 1030 hrs, I brought this bag and contents to the MPD Property Unit/Blood Room. The following is a description of the items and the order that the items were inventoried:

1. A grey plastic string tie bag bearing the name "Jarman" Bls is noted on the bag. Later found at the botom [*sic*] of the bag is a $99.99 receipt dated 4–25–97 for this store at Mall of America.
2. A "Toolsmith" hammer with BLS. It has a black rubber handle, a red body and silver colored head with a flat surface for hammering and a "claw" end of the removal of nails.
3. A purple towel with BLS.
4. A white towel with BLS.
5. A large pink towel with BLS.
6. A small pink towel with BLS.

7. Two "crumpled" wads of what is believed to be paper toweling with BLS.

8. A light blue colored baseball cap with a white letter "H" with BLS.

9. A white T shirt with what appears to be a "muscular alligator" holding a torch and standing in front of the "Olympic Rings" Amphibious Group Three is also on the shirt. Also with BLS. *NOTE: When viewing Off. Calistro's photographs of the autopsy of the victim: I notice that the victim was wearing at the time of his death what appears to be an identical T shirt as the one recovered in this plastic bag.

10. A white T shirt with BLS "spatter" It is possible due to the spatter pattern noted on this shirt, that this shirt was being worn by an attacker rather than being used to clean up the scene as it appears was the case with the aforementioned towels, paper towels and shirt.

11. A "Wenger" watch with brown leather band with a "pin" missing. This watch has "hands" rather than digital display. It is noted to be stopped indicating a time of 9:55 and a date of "27" Also with BLS.

12. A gold colored ring with a "wave" type continuous pattern. Again, with BLS.

These items, as mentioned, were placed into the blood room and allowed to dry from 4–30–97 at approximately 1030 hrs until they were bagged or boxed and inventoried by me on 5–1–97 at approximately 1647 hrs.

33

Supplement of Sgt. Wagner on 5/2/97 Autopsy Report

On 4/30/97 at 0900 hrs I attended the autopsy at the Hennepin County Morgue. Also in attendance was Officer Calistro from the B of I. Conducting the autopsy was Dr. Eric Burton. (ME case #1068)

The deceased was rolled up in a rug containing much BLS. Prior to unravelling the body, Dr. Burton removed hair and fiber samples from the outside of the rug. The rug was then unravelled to expose the body. Calistro videotaped the process. More hair, fibers, and what appeared to be brain matter, was collected. Inside the rug was a white terry cloth towel with BLS next to the victim's chest.... There was also an off-white Afghan type blanket that was folded near the victim's legs with BLS.

The victim was fully clothed in a red plain shirt, white t-shirt, blue jeans, brown leather belt, black socks and black "Simple" tennis shoes, all containing BLS. Inside the right rear pocket of the victim's pants, Dr. Burton found a black nylon wallet. The wallet contained a California picture drivers license identifying the victim as JEFFREY ALLEN TRAIL, DOB 2–25–69, license #B5722864, 2224 Sunset Blvd., San Diego, CA.

Also inside the wallet were:

$42.00 cash
Trail's business cards
VISA 4600 0300 0350 6352 belonging to Trail
Misc papers, credit cards and receipts, all belonging to Trail

Inside the front pocket of the blue jeans was a key ring containing a Honda vehicle key, an alarm remote control, and two other keys. With that information the ME staff was able to contact the victim's family in Illinois.

External Examination:
A Sexual Assault Examination was performed for possible collection of evidence. A ring was removed from one of the victim's toes and a ring from his left nipple. Hair and fingernail samples were collected. There was a tattoo of the "Warner Brothers" cartoon martian character on the victim's left lower leg and a tattoo of the "Mighty Mouse" cartoon character on his right thigh.

There were several abrasions on the left wrist, a small puncture wound and a small laceration on the left hand. There were 2 contusions on the victim's upper back. All other injuries were to the victim's head. There was a cluster of 16 blunt force lacerations to the left eye socket, 1 in the scalp above the left forehead, 1 directly in front of the left ear and 2 behind the left ear. There were no other signs of trauma to the body.

The internal organs were examined and revealed no signs of disease. The skull was then exposed. Beneath the cluster of injuries to the top and back of the scalp, the skull was fractured and fell apart in pieces. There was also an indentation in the skull above the left ear. Examination of the brain revealed severe injury beneath the dura in the posterior area.

Dr. Burton stated the cause of death a homicide resulting from blunt force injuries.

For precise nomenclature and wound measurements, refer to the Medical Examiner's report which will follow. Color photos were taken throughout the procedure by both Calistro and Dr. Burton. I recorded the injuries on Hennepin County sketch drawings which are included with this report.

CASE OPEN
SGT. WAGNER
HOMICIDE UNIT

34

"Good fucking *grief,* David," Andrew cackled as the Jeep shot up 35W in brisk, heavy traffic. Andrew held the gun and the steering wheel and fooled with the radio all at the same time, weirdly exhilarated and talkative. "Is the only tape you have in this heap the sound track from *Love Jones?*"

Andrew had a lot to say about Willa Cather and Mount Rushmore and the bucolic emptiness they were headed into, *why do you suppose these wanky places like Minnesota and the Badlands are so full of monumental sculpture,* he demanded, David would've had a good answer at any other time but simply said *I wish I knew,* wishing actually that he had the fortitude to grab the wheel and send the car tumbling over in traffic. He'd missed another moment, several really, he saw that now. Exits for Mounds View, Blaine, Lexington, and Circle Pines flashing by, clumps of mall metastasis, Buick Mazda Chrysler franchises, plastic flags snapping in the wind, wintry garden suburbs, vernacular houses of slightly stale gingerbread, mile after mile of pious Midwestern getting-by, thinning out around Lino

Lakes into farms and fields, big sky, islands of conifer floating on prairie grass, expanses of denuded sugar maple and green ash and bur oak, long tracts of vacant thawing land punctuated by isolated houses, some with smoke puffing from chimneys, Lutheran Atonement churches, telephone lines, surly crows picking at roadkill.

Andrew pulled off the highway near Rush City, onto a narrow paved ribbon that circled one lobe of a pair of lung-shaped lakes. The water was mostly hidden behind trees. The properties nearest the paved road were subsistence farms; the inner access roads ran closer to the shore, where trailer homes and vacation cottages nudged the lakefront, flanked by propane tanks and tar driveways, many of which had cars in them.

"What are we looking for?" David asked him, struggling for calm neutral words and a trustful tone.

"An isolated place," Andrew said, steering back onto the main road. He followed this several hundred yards, turned down a new dirt road much scarred by weather. The Jeep lurched and bounced. "What I need to do, David, is drop you off where it will take you a while to get to a telephone."

Andrew slowed the Jeep, backed it up to a car track where a broken fence and a PRIVATE PROPERTY sign interrupted the vegetation.

The car track ran beside a burnt-out farmhouse and a rotting barn and ended in a grassy field beside the lake. Andrew drove over the grass. The soil was muddy and the tires churned up the grass. Just short of the water Andrew whipped the Jeep around in an ellipsis, pointing it at the road, and switched off the engine.

"I guess this is the place," he announced. He sounded happy. He motioned David out of the car. *It's over*, David thought. Then Andrew got out of the car. He threw the door-lock remote and the spare set of car keys over David's shoulder.

"For when you get the car back," he said. David almost went for them but Andrew walked forward, herding him to the water.

"I promise you," David said, sounding fatally craven to himself, "I'll wait here, I'll wait for the sun to go down, I'll walk to a town, and I won't even say anything. I promise, Andrew. I won't say anything until I'm back in the city." His voice shook. His whole body quivered.

Andrew smiled and pointed where to go along the waterline with his chin.

"Never kid a kidder, David," he said.

35

At the last minute David found his will and ran, but covered less than ten yards before Andrew fired into his back. The shot echoed across the lake. You could see the water was black under a thin sheet of sunlight reflecting the clouds and the blue sky. David collapsed on the marshy grass. It had a rich, mossy scent, and the blades felt scratchy like a cat's tongue. The bullet had hit something important, maybe several things, but he thought he might live. He shut his eyes and stopped his breath, playing dead. He heard nothing but a rush of wind and the quick call of an aquatic bird, what kind he didn't know. Then soft crunching footsteps sucked by the wet earth. Andrew grabbed his collar and pulled him onto his knees and then yanked him backwards. David's lids fluttered. He couldn't help it. He looked at the sky, and the sun.

Andrew dragged him face-up through the muddy grass. Jerked him to his knees, walked ahead a few paces. David begged for his life now, frantic, freaked to see blood coming from his mouth as he pleaded. This couldn't be real, it couldn't. He could not finish up this way. He couldn't imagine it. He put his hands up.

The first bullet tore through his fingers and ripped away part of his cheek, his ear. Andrew fired again, through the other hand into David's eyeball.

36

Later he remembered filling the Jeep at a Citgo in Lyndon Station, Wisconsin, stuffing down a greasy meal in Oconomowoc, scattered items on radio news about a body in a Minneapolis loft. Wisconsin was all road and no convenience islands and sinister dairy farms brooding in darkness. The idea of Canada somehow didn't compute. He was flying ahead of the wave, chewing No-Doz and swilling Coke, *I hitched a ride with a vending machine repairman*, by five-thirty a.m. the nether sprawl of Chicago swallowed him and by six he'd parked in the downtown Sheraton garage and stumbled sore-assed into the lobby, snagged a tourist map and *Chicago Where* magazine, stretched out in the rear of the Cherokee, and forced himself to sleep.

37

In the tenebrous precincts of the dream he began to inhabit, *here* and *there* were weightless constructs, he'd torn out the switches connecting him to any place and could only find safety wherever nowhere happened to be. For a few days nowhere ran along the Mag Mile, through streets of the Gold Coast, and up into Boys

Town, where he parked and napped and rambled the nighttime circuit. There was a bar called Spin at Halsted and Belmont that featured Drag Queen Bingo, a dance place full of shirtless gym bunnies called Manhole, an edgy burnout saloon across Halsted called Little Jim's. There was Rhumba, a tapas joint, attached to a disco, Fusion. He had two hundred something cash and two credit cards he couldn't use, some loose checks and a Versateller card linked to an empty bank account.

He showered away the road in a bathhouse in Andersonville. With the cubicle locked it was possible to catch five hours' rest amid the muffled suction of sex. Later, he left the door ajar, dim milky figures entered and slipped out one at a time, stopping to worship the thing between his legs. He felt incredibly potent, but only the bathhouse provided relief. Men checked him out wherever he went, but in Chicago there was always someone prettier over his shoulder, or someone who wasn't talking to himself. It alarmed him that he'd started conversing with cars that cut him off crossing streets, talking to his money when he bought drinks. When he saw the money getting thin he found a wrinkle room in the Rush Street area, the Gentry, where he drank himself nuts, courtesy of several prehistoric queens.

38

SCSD Inv. K. Hoppe
ICR 97-6462
Date/Time Statement: 050397/1331 HOURS
Taped Statement of Kyle Nathan Hilken, DOB 060370, 205
E. Viking Dr., Apt. 229, Little Canada, MN

IH: Is this information correct Mr. Hilkin?

KH: Correct.

IH: Ok, um, Kyle, could you tell me what uh, transpired today and what you uh, witnessed this morning?

KH: Yep, uh, we came up just to look for some places to fish, we heard it was a good area to fish, um, we had just came back from the other side of the lake, uh, we went by the boat landing, we were coming back to leave and go to, uh, to Pine City to look up there cuase we heard there was good fishing, uh, we came past here, and uh, we saw the house and uh, you know, we were just commenting how nice and open it was and then we kept going and I said you know, gosh, I wonder if someone lives there, maybe we can go ask them if they drop, you know, drop a line or maybe let us camp back, or drop a tent back there, so we turn around and came back and pulled into the, uh, approach, um, and then went up to the edge of the gravel, uh, where the driveway stopped and at that point I saw that, you know, at least what I thought nobody lived there, um, I did get out just to, just to look down and uh, look out over the lake and I took about 2 steps and I looked and saw what I thought looked like, uh, somebody laying down by the uh, bottom of the lake, um, I took maybe two or three steps forward more, just to kind of look, and at that point I said I'm getting out of here and we went to town and then, uh, called the police.

IH: How close did you get to the body Kyle?

KH: Um, I was probably 20 yards away, I didn't want to get too close of course, um, I didn't know if someone was sleeping um, I did notice, uh, what looked like some sort of uh, tracks, um, just when I first walked down or walked those few steps, uh, there were some type of car or whatever tracks, um, and then I maybe thought he was sleeping or something so then I looked and it didn't look like it um, from what, you know, the, uh, body or whatever the person looked like and then we took off.

IH: Do you recall the position that he was laying in?

KH: Yeah, feet towards the lake, um, arms by his side, just on his back.

IH: Ok.

Taped Statement of Scott Alan Schmidt, DOB 060770, 205 E. Viking Dr., Apt. 235, Little Canada, MN

IH: Scott can you tell me what you witnessed and approximately what time you arrived here on today's date?

SS: Ok, I would say um, Kyle and I arrived here probably about 10:30, quarter to 11, um, we drove into the yard, well first of all we drove past and we slowed down, then we turned around and um, came back, um, the reason why, we were just looking for a place to, um, either go fishing or pitch a tent and this looked like a nice yard here and we were just going to stop and talk to, if there was someone, you know, who resides here, we turned and we pulled in here and we realized it was kind of an old abandoned place and we stopped as far as the hill a little ways, um, to see what was below the hill, um, what the lake shore and stuff looked like and then he stopped and he started walking backwards towards the Jeep and the whole time I was in the Jeep and he motioned for me to get out of the Jeep, uh, I got out of the Jeep, I walked a little bit, ways down the hill, paused, and he pointed and then he showed me where, you know, this guy was laying there and, um, it looked like, I cannot, you know, what I saw it looked like there was someone laying there, um, I didn't know if, you know, the person was dead or what it was or if it was a dummy, or you know, stuffed mannequin or anything like that, um, Kyle, I stayed up top, Kyle walked down a little closer and he came back and said yep, you know, definitely looks like, you know, looks like a dead guy and, uh, so I said let's go call the authorities so then we drove into, uh, into, up to Tank and Tackle I think is the name of the place, um, stopped there, Kyle called 911, um, told them where we were at and then I believe the officer's name was Bob, finally came and met us there and then we drove back out here and we pointed out where, you know this guy was laying and, um, not much at that.

IH: Ok, how long have you know, uh, Kyle, then?

SS: I grew up with Kyle, he's from my same home town, I betcha I've known him for 22, 23 years about, um …

IH: Guys went to High School together?

SS: Went to, grew up together, went the same uh, elementary school, went to high school together, actually went to college at North Dakota State together, um, lived with him for like 3 years while we were going to college and, uh, he graduated before me, he moved down here to the cities and then after I graduated I spent some time on the East Coast uh, working for the Government, came back here just last year in May and, uh, actually I live in the same apartment complex as he did, he was the one who told me there was an apartment available and …

IH: Okay, what brought you up here today then?

SS: Uh, we were looking for a few places to go fishing, um, opener coming up next week and, uh, plus we get, you know, we knew, uh, we could throw a few lines in, because they're catching crappie and stuff up here, some guys told me about that.

IH: There's a no trespassing sign marking the driveway, why did you guys proceed even with that?

SS: Um, we saw that and that's when we went by the first time and we drove slow and I said, you know, we didn't know if you know, we saw the sign said no trespassing and Kyle said, well let's just go back and see, maybe there's someone there, we can ask them, you know, talk to the owner, maybe there's a mailbox, find out who the owner is and just ask them and so, um, we, that's why we came back and pulled in and once we got in there a little ways we realized it was, you know, it was just abandoned, nothing but junk laying around here and then Kyle got out and we walked down, we walked down a little bit further just to check things out and then that's when he motioned for me to get out of the Jeep and then that's when I went over there and we were standing on the side of the hill there just looking down and that's when we saw, you know, I saw the body for the first time ...

39

Lindsay Thomas, Chisago County Coroner

This is David Madson? Gunshot wounds to the head.

Some of the wounds were to the front, I'm pretty sure. How does a bullet pass through the fingers? We see it. I assume somebody puts up their hands, thinking—I mean you're not really thinking, but a kind of reflex, that it's a kind of defensive posture when someone has gunshot wounds on their hands.

It's hard to tell about distance. If something is a contact gunshot wound, you'll see soot. If it's from a short distance, you get what's called stippling on the skin. It's little pieces of gunpowder that get embedded, and that's probably up to about eighteen inches, something like that. But anything further away than that, you can't really tell if it's eighteen inches or a hundred yards. There's no really very good way to tell exact distance. And if there's clothing, or anything in between, like hands, then any evidence may end up on the clothing and the hands rather than on the actual entrance wound. So it's pretty hard to tell. It's also very variable from gun to gun. The only way to really tell is to use the same ammunition and the same gun and do some test firing, and if there's stippling or something like that then you can see how far the gunpowder travels with this particular weapon.

This was a peculiar caliber weapon. I don't know that much about this type of gun, I'd never seen it before. It's larger than normal. The usual calibers we deal with are .22s or .357, .38, something like that, .40 is a little bigger than that. Certainly from a police perspective it's helpful because it's easy to link the various people killed by the same gun.

Time of death is really hard. There's no good way to absolutely say time of death. What we do is, When were they found, and work back from there, When were they reliably last seen, and then that kind of gives us our parameters. Obviously a lot of things influence that, temperature is the main thing. In May it was cool, but sunny during the day, it was in a wooded area near a lake, there's a lot of factors that contribute to that. We look at the changes that occur after death, rigor mortis and liver mortis and things like that. We can use insect activity, there's an entomologist that we use, they can tell whether a fly has laid eggs, and whether the eggs have hatched into maggots, how big the maggots are, all that kind of thing; I would say in this case, because it never went to trial, we never actively pursued the issue of time of death, I think if the case had gone to trial that would've been a much bigger issue that we would've spent more time talking about and putting everything together. Since it didn't go to trial, it becomes more an issue of just interest. I never really talked to the entomologist and got the perspective of other witnesses who might've had a really accurate time line of when he was last seen. I've read in the newspaper that the car had a parking ticket in Chicago all day Wednesday, so that means he was in Chicago on Wednesday and came back, and then went back to Chicago, or—

Really, to figure out time of death you put everything together and take a best guess, is pretty much how it goes.

Since the beginning, it's been a real mystery to us what David Madson was doing all week. I mean Jeffrey Trail was killed sometime over the weekend in his apartment, so what was he doing after that? Did he know about that? If he knew about that, why didn't he leave, was he being held hostage? I think since the very beginning that's been the question. If he wasn't killed until Friday night, what was he doing all week? Unfortunately, I don't have a good answer for when he was killed. I've talked to the family about it, their theory makes as much sense as anybody else's theory. Certainly if the case had gone to court I would've spent more time figuring it out.

That's something you can use, stomach contents, if you have something in the stomach, but I don't think it was useful in this case. It's kind of obvious things, insects, stomach contents, postmortem things, to kind of narrow it, but unfortunately the best we can narrow it is one or two days. Which we kind of already knew, obviously. He was seen Monday or Tuesday and he was found on Saturday. So we knew it was some time during the week.

A body's found in the middle of nowhere. There's no—how much time passes between the time the body's found and the time you get the body? When a body is found on the weekend, a lot of times I don't do the autopsy until Monday anyway. So if a body's found on a weekend, the police and sheriff and those guys will do their investigation, and then after several hours the body would be removed and taken to the cooler at the morgue down in Hastings. But then if it's a Saturday afternoon or Sunday I probably won't do the autopsy until Monday. If there's a lot of evidence the body might stay there for twelve hours while they're figuring out what happened.

The temperature that weekend—the weather service keeps track, I know I've seen a printout, but I can't remember, certainly it was cool enough that a body could be fairly well-preserved, so it would look more fresh than it actually was.

Nothing unusual about the body. He seemed like a healthy guy, he looked very muscular.

Usually we see animal depredation when the body's inside with a cat or a dog that hasn't been fed, or if a body has been outside for quite a while. Usually that doesn't happen very rapidly outside, I suppose animals have other things to eat. Inside, animals will sometimes start in on their owner if they haven't got any other food.

Could someone be dead from these kinds of wounds outside for as much as four days and have it be impossible to tell if they were killed on the first or the last of those four days? I think that is possible, unfortunately. It's very frustrating, because as you can imagine that question comes up a lot.

(Interview with the author, 1997)

40

He *thought* he had met up with Lee in the piano bar, though he couldn't be sure, he might have phoned him from the bar and gone along to the townhouse on East Scott, Andrew was so fucked up at the time he might have walked up and rung the doorbell without even calling first, who could say? He knew he'd parked the Cherokee on North Astor and slept in it and hit several bars and wound up soused at the Gentry. Next thing Lee's two-building mansion, all white-on-white inside with a Lucite staircase and a real Monet on the wall and a golden Labrador, Lee seemed excited to see him, really horny, he'd apparently been checking out a bunch of porn magazines, getting himself in the mood, or maybe Andrew himself had collected these magazines in his peregrinations, anyway he remembered magazines, later, and Lee kind of thrilled about getting off, wifey off in Canada peddling her perfume. Lee went down full of enthusiasm and then realized Andrew wasn't getting hard, the next thing Andrew took the gun from his little backpack and held it against Lee's head, Lee mistook it as a sex toy at first, kept calling him Honey or the dog Honey, maybe he was calling himself Honey, go know, Andrew seemed to remember hearing *Please don't hurt Honey.* Next he recalled yanking the deaf aids out of Lee's ears, that segued strangely into a garage across a back alley, you went across a Japanese-type garden and a patio and the garage didn't quite correspond with the house, at moments Lee seemed to still think they were going to have sex and the gun was just part of "extreme S&M" or something. For some reason Andrew brought the porn magazines and spread them out on the floor. Then he taped

Lee's wrists and ankles and mummied his head à la David Madson in the loft, using a thick roll of masking tape in the garage, round and round the neck and twisting it under the chin, up over the scalp, making a sort of tourniquet for the jaw, then bound up the face somewhat savagely, pulling tight against the lips, the eyes. Everything that happened felt like a movie, all the moves seemed written in advance. It was a movie about "how far would you go." He stabbed out a ragged hole at the nostrils with a screwdriver, then pulling up Lee's shirt poked the screwdriver through his chest about twenty times, gouging out a nonsensical pattern of oozing gashes. At some point, Lee understood he was going to die, Andrew could read it in the way his body jerked and shuddered, Jeff's physical being had sort of given up in the same fashion. Andrew finally sliced through his windpipe with a small bow saw, blood ran all over the saw and all over his hands, sticky, the blood stank like a butcher shop. He wrapped the whole mess in garbage bags and the kind of paper you cover third-class parcels in. For his pièce de résistance, Andrew repeatedly dropped a fifty-pound cement bag on him until all the bones snapped. He returned to the house, cleaned himself in an upstairs shower, selected some shirts and suits from Lee's closet. He played with the dog for a while, sweet dog, rummaged through more closets, almost by chance went into Lee's study, where he jimmied open a briefcase and found four thousand dollars in cash. Another two thousand dollars turned up in an envelope and some gold coins in a desk drawer. He had to open the garage again and move a trash bin to hide the body and close it again after getting the car out, a two-year-old Lexus without much mileage on it. When he read about it later, Andrew didn't remember shaving in the sink or leaving any ham bone on Lee's desk, oddly enough he'd taken one of Lee's shoes and put it in the Lexus, but then the whole episode was blurry, a prime example of consensual encounters run awry, *Chicago*, he thought, *not my kind of town* ...

41

Homicide Squad (Minneapolis lead detectives, informal conversation with the author, 1997)

Madson died sixteen to eighteen hours before the body was found?

Possibly the previous day, Friday.

That would've meant that he'd spent four and a half days with Cunanan after Jeff Trail's murder.

Which doesn't make a whole lot of sense. I can't see him going down to Chicago, coming back up, and going back to Chicago, it doesn't make sense.

But there was a parking receipt dated the second?

No, dated the thirtieth of April, isn't it? Wednesday morning of that week, six-thirty in the morning, something like that? In downtown Chicago.

That doesn't make any sense at all, does it?

Not to us. It would make more sense to us that he killed David Madson Tuesday night, Wednesday morning, then went down, to Chicago and stayed down in Chicago until after the Miglin murder.

Chicago police supposedly had some unconfirmed sightings of a guy fitting his description in and around the Miglin neighborhood days before Miglin was killed. Whether or not it was Andrew Cunanan we don't know, but there were some people who felt quite sure that they had seen him in the Miglin vicinity. And the red Jeep as well.

He arrived on the twenty-sixth?

Andrew? No, he arrived Friday night, he was met at the airport by David Madson.

He spent Friday at David's—

And Saturday night at Trail's. Trail was spending the night with his friend at a bed and breakfast in St. Cloud, or down in southern Minnesota. Jon Hackett.

It's somewhere outside the city.

Trail came back on Sunday.

On the twentieth of April Trail talked to somebody on the phone, he said, "I made a lot of enemies this weekend, I've got to get out of here, they're going to kill me."

I think that statement, "They're going to kill me," could easily have been misinterpreted, that was my understanding, that he wanted to leave Minnesota, it's cold and nasty and ugly, "they're killing me, I've got to leave here," something that didn't have anything to do with this.

We're speculating that when the caretaker opened the apartment and looked in, they saw the body, and immediately exited, which means they were probably still in the apartment at that time and they decided they better get the hell out of there, and that's why they left in such a hurry, leaving a lot of significant property behind.

Trail was identified right away?

Not immediately. In fact, initially we thought it was David Madson, until the medical examiner took a look and saw dark hair instead of blond hair, at that point they realized, wait, this isn't the guy who's missing, then they went to get a search warrant, because if it isn't the person's body in his own apartment, then it could be the person who lives there that's killed them, and you need a search warrant.

He didn't have any identification on him?

He was rolled up in a rug.

There was also a report that on May second Madson's Jeep was spotted on Interstate 35, was that considered a good report?

Chisago County looked into that, I don't know what credence they put on it, I think there were some problems with the description, something about the bumper sticker—

The back of Madson's Jeep had a bumper sticker on it for Vail, Colorado, and it wasn't on the bumper itself, it was on the back tailgate of the Jeep where the back window would be, and someone reported seeing a vehicle of that description with a Vail sticker on it, however it turned out later that the sticker was not in the area it should've been.

We discussed the Full Moon Bar & Restaurant in Stark—

I think the people up there still believe David Madson and Cunanan were in there on Friday but that's been pretty much discounted.

When you were in San Diego, did anything emerge about him dealing drugs?

Erik Greenman thought that he may have been acting as a middleman for some pharmaceutical transaction.

Would that have put him in enough of a level, was this really small time, or would it have possibly involved him with people in the Mafia?

I wouldn't say so. Drug dealers are a dime a dozen in any large city, there's such a demand.

So the scenarios that maybe he had mob connections are not true.

I would not believe it.

I understand his mother now is saying he was killed by the Mafia. Did you have any dealings with her?

No. With the sister in San Francisco. The mother took it very hard.

He gave away a lot of his personal belongings. We talked to one guy he talked to about moving in with him, but nothing was firmed up.

So in a sense he was abandoning his past life—

One could draw that conclusion.

There was some mention of a diary he kept?

We never got hold of it.

"Investigators found a diary that said, 'If I have to get away I'm going to New York.'"

The book you're referring to, it's a terrible book, I picked it up yesterday—

The papers said "a ham bone" was left behind in Miglin's house—

I remember hearing that, that he ate a piece of ham—

Was Norman Blachford questioned by the police?

We talked to him, after Miglin was killed. He was just leaving San Diego, he was going on the Queen Mary to Europe. The FBI talked to him in some detail.

I don't think I talked to him about Gamma Mu. I did talk to one guy in Gamma Mu who was afraid to lose his job, but we know Norman and Andrew attended a gathering in Seattle ...

If David was killed Tuesday night Cunanan could've got immediately to Chicago—

It's an eight-hour drive.

42

He heard WAOR 95 out of South Bend, WXKE Fort Wayne, WRRK 95 FM Pittsburgh, *all classic rock all the time*, you could easily hit a hundred and twenty in the Lexus without even feeling it, though he mainly held the speed limit, he'd read enough true crime trash on airplanes to know that people like him were usually caught after being pulled over for a broken taillight, or speeding, some trivial traffic thing. Lee had this "creative thinking" tape in the tape player, a soothing voice full of these creative suggestions, mental exercises, how to visualize your goals. The black road and the yellow lines spun out before him, like poisoned licorice pouring straight from his forehead, that was all he could visualize. Every thirty or forty miles he switched on the CD player loaded in the trunk and heard "Days of Wine and Roses," "For All We Know," "The Shadow of Your Smile," orchestral renderings, somewhere outside Pittsburgh Andrew pulled over and opened the trunk. He looked for the box. *The Romantic Moods of Jackie Gleason.* He tried calling Rusty on the cell phone, he'd been employed by Rusty once upon a time in San Diego, his one and only waiter job that had lasted all of two weeks. He seemed to recall that Rusty knew some gangland type of associates in Nevada, perhaps he should offer his services for what they called wet work. Each time he punched Rusty's number he got a phone company recording. *Everybody gets high, everybody gets low.* Double you zee zee oh

coming at you from Allentown. A cognitive glitch put him on
380 north instead of south near Pocono Pines, east 84 through
Port Jervis, north 87 up to Saugerties. He found a diner in
Saugerties, ate some eggs, figured out where he was. He arrived
in Manhattan so buzzed he parked just anywhere and crashed.

43

Andrew hadn't spent any real time in New York since the summer
before when he and Norman stayed in East Hampton. Before that,
there'd been the stopovers with Norman and the Met and *La
Bohème* and the Globe Theater Tour he took with Norman and
Norman's gang of fifty- and sixty-somethings, New Year's '96, the
New Year's of *Miss Saigon* and *Phantom of the Opera* and that awful
piece of crap downtown where the audience had to schlep from one
location to another, *The Wedding of Ugly to Stupid* Andrew always
called it. The Chelsea district had already turned into Fag Haven
at that point, now it was worse, or better, he guessed, in terms of
anonymity. Every forty-watts with a gym card was on the street.
He found a gay bookstore, picked up the free gay rags, *Next* and
HX, bought the Fodor *Gay USA Guide*. Aside from the occasional cruisy once-over, he passed entirely unnoticed in the
restaurants and bars. He managed to stop talking to himself.

44

He tried the West Side Club, a bathhouse on Twentieth Street.
You could only get a private room if you bought a full year

membership. He paid for a changing room instead. The West Side Club had sleek wooden floors and somewhat higher lighting than any bathhouse he'd been to, it looked more like a dance studio that had been filled with lockers and cubicles. He showered and took a steam, but the bench in the changing room was much too narrow to sleep on. He caught a few z's in a dark chamber where men in towels sat on a carpeted ledge along the wall, jerking off to porn movies. He bought socks and jeans at the Original Levi's Store on Fifty-seventh Street, changed in the Lexus, went to the Chelsea Cinema. For three days he felt truly invisible. Manhattan was one restaurant after another with practically nothing in between, all full of rich nineteen-year-olds. He walked around Chelsea and the Village, ate and slept enough to stop hallucinating, saw movies: *The Devil's Own*, *Liar, Liar*, and *8 Heads in a Duffel Bag*, all garbage, his life story in film titles more or less. One night a bland-looking shlub approached him outside the Stonewall Inn. They drank a bit there and moved across the street to the Monster, things looked promising, but after a lot of chitchat Andrew sensed that he'd turned up a wrong card, Commodore Cummings must've slipped out or else some off remark about *bondage*, he was suddenly alone staring at bubbles in his Cuba Libre. At that point, he decided to hit the road.

45

By the time he went through Philadelphia they'd found the Cherokee and put him together with the Chicago slaying. He saw items in the papers. They'd found David at East Rush Lake.

A few miles outside Wilmington the radio picked up a police press conference in Philly, they'd tracked signals from the Lexus cell phone to Ridley Township. He was not far from Ridley Township at the time. Ameritech Cellular had already monitored signals from Union County and Philadelphia. Andrew cut the handset wires with pliers from the Lexus tool kit and tore off the antenna on the rear window mount. Still the phone kept emitting a signal, Andrew realized he had to ditch the car. He crossed into Jersey over the Delaware Memorial Bridge and left the highway at Pennsville.

46

Pennsville had a Revco pharmacy and a Family Dollar Store and a Food Lion and a bunch of auto dealerships. On the far edge of town where the houses thinned out, a side road branched to a state park on the Delaware River. The park had almost no visitors. Andrew hung around for a couple days, checking out the fort's cannon bunkers, a ghostly ferry slip at the end of a long pier, the Coastal Heritage exhibit in the visitor's center. He learned that the soil in the park was loamy, siliceous, semiactive, mesic Arenic Hapludults. That "New Jersey's maritime heritage is rooted in the interdependent stories of trade, navigation, and coastal defenses." The place had been fortified in anticipation of the Spanish-American War, without which event, he supposed, no Andrew Cunanan would ever have made his way there. From the ferry slip, he made out a grayish smudge upriver that must have been Wilmington, Delaware. The Civil War cemetery down the road, a walled quadrant of manicured grass, contained Union and Confederate obelisks and a two-story cottage of bluish-gray dressed stone. During the day, the grounds were tended and the cottage occupied by a solitary caretaker, a lanky, bearded man who drove a newish red pickup.

47

The caretaker, William Reese, had almost finished for the day. William Reese was forty-five, a Civil War enthusiast who visited battle sites on his vacations. He was married to a school librarian and had a twelve-year-old son. He'd recently learned that he had multiple sclerosis. He sat in his office listening to WAWZ, "a ministry of the Pillar of Fire International." The Bible on his desk was book-marked at Deuteronomy, a section of Deuteronomy that refers to "unknown murderers." Andrew knocked and asked for directions. He then showed his gun and asked for Reese's truck keys. He told Reese he would have to tie him up in the basement, that he needed time to leave the area. Then Andrew took him down. The basement ceiling was so low they both had to stoop. There was a worktable with a small vise on the end, some bags of fertilizer. Andrew told Reese to kneel down. It was awkward shooting him. Andrew didn't enjoy it at all. It was just something he had to do. It was nothing personal.

48

CCSD Inv. K. Hoppe
ICR 97–6462

Date/Time Statement: 05–14–97/1500 HOURS
TAPED TELEPHONE CONVERSATION BETWEEN GREGORY
SCOTT NELSON, DOB 072270, 1736 19TH ST NW,
WASHINGTON DC

KH: Hi Greg, uh, you're Greg, right?

GN: Yes I am.

KH: This is Deputy Keith Hoppe and I'm, uh, just, uh, doing some follow up on, uh, a homicide that we had in our county here.

GN: I'm very aware of it, I've been contacted, God knows how many times.

KH: I bet you have, uh, can I get some information, the information I have is your full name is Gregory Scott Nelson?

GN: Uh huh.

KH: Um, that's spelled N-E-L-S-O-N?

GN: Uh huh.

KH: You have a date of birth of 072270 is that correct?

GN: Uh huh.

KH: Ok, and uh, do you have a home telephone number there?

GN: 202-XXX-XXXX, do you know, do I have, do I have anything to be worried about with this Mr. Cunanan at all?

KH: Well do you know Andrew Cunanan at all?

GN: No but the only thing that started to worry me was during the, during the, when David and I were in court together, according to the papers that's when him and Cunanan were together and I don't know what this guy's motive is or what it's all about but ...

KH: I guess you know, we don't know exactly what area right now, uh, Mr. Cunanan's at, uh, you know the last contact was kind of the Philadelphia/New Jersey area, and you know I'm not sure you know where he's at right now and I'm not sure what his motives or what anybody's motives are you know, I guess what I'm doing right now is just doing some follow-up, I got your name, that, uh, that you and David Madson had been involved in a relationship is that correct?

GN: For 2 years.

KH: For 2 years, ok, and uh, I guess what I need to know is that you were just in Minneapolis uh, recently in uh, I believe April is that correct?

GN: Uh-huh, for business.

KH: Ok, do you remember Mr. Nelson when you flew into Minneapolis?

GN: I flew into Minneapolis on Saturday the 2—wait, have to look at my calendar.

KH: Ok, do you keep a calendar or anything of, of your activities, uh, I guess I'm under the impression that you travel quite a bit for MCI is that correct?

GN: Uh huh, I flew in Saturday the 19th for my niece's birthday and flew back the 23rd of April.

KH: Ok, 23rd, ok do you remember what airline you flew?

GN: Northwest Airlines, I have the tickets and everything.

KH: Northwest Airlines, ok um, could you do me a huge favor, at some point photocopy them and mail a copy of them to me and I could, uh, provide you with my address here at the office?

GN: Ok, what's this for?

KH: Well what I'm trying to do is just uh, eliminate you or you know tie you in any way that I can you know what we're trying to do is tie down any time frames that you were in the area um, of Minnesota, ok?

GN: Am I being implicated in this?

KH: No, you're not but uh, uh, what I need to know is, uh, uh, the information I have is kind of vague of when you were in Minnesota and what you were doing here, ok?

GN: Ok.

KH: Um ….

GN: Do you want my, what I, do you have a fax number, I'll fax it to you right now

KH: Um, just hang on one second, I know we do but uh, can you hold on one second please?

GN: Uh huh.

KH: I'm sorry for the delay, um, our fax number is 612 …

GN: Wait, wait one second, 612 …

KH: Ok.

GN: Hello?

KH: Are you ready?

GN: 612.

KH: Ok, it's 257 …

GN: Uh-huh.

KH: 9256, and uh, I guess basically what I needed to know is just the last time that you ever had any contact with, uh …

GN: With Mr. Madson?

KH: Yeah, with David?

GN: I saw Mr. Madson on a chance meeting when I was in Uptown on the 21st of April, before that it would have been in a court proceeding which would have taken place in March of 9—uh, March of 96.

KH: March of 96?

GN: Which I'm sure you have copies of.

KH: I do not but did you guys have like a violent relationship or something or what happened that he had a restraining order against you?

GN: Mr. Madson owed me a lot of money and within the State of Minnesota I found out all you need to do is go down to the Hennepin County Court Office and Mr. Madson working for a law firm understood this, that he wanted a protection order against me, there was never—

KH: Ok, did David do this before he became an architect, because I was under the impression that he was an architect.

GN: Yes, before he became an architect because he owed me about $17,000.

KH: Oh really, ok.

GN: Mr. Madson was very physically abusive to me and very psychologically abusive to me and he understood how to manipulate the court system and my lawyer can, can fully go into this and unfortunately I got caught in a case where I was too poor to not have, to have a free lawyer and made way too much money and I didn't make a heck of a lot of money just to be pouring out to lawyers so I just decided to cut my loss, the violation of the protection order came from a phone call that came from my house, there was never any conversation that took place, it was just simply a phone call that took place, it was traced from my home to his home and, um, Mr. Madson, well I guess you don't need to know the details of all this but it was basically a rigmarole over a lot of money and the court system never listened to me about, what I did wrong was when Mr. Madson hit, and when Mr. Madson did all these other things I didn't run down to the domestic abuse office, not being out in the community and everything and Mr. Madson being so heavily involved in what I ended up finding out in the S&M community and having this secret life, I mean an extensive secret life in the S&M community within Minneapolis where he, and it wasn't just something simple and it went nationwide where he had relationships with various people, um, through an underground system and I'm sure that they would find meticulous notes in the storage lockers and things like that, which I gave the police the combination to which I had because we had once lived together.

KH: You guys shared the residence at 280 uh ...

GN: Yeah, I actually, we had a joint uh, lease in there.

KH: You lived there for approximately 6 months is that correct?

GN: Well, we lived together for approximately 2 years in that building for about ...

KH: Oh, in that same building?

GN: No, previous to that we lived over, about 2 blocks from there.

KH: Oh ok, I guess the information I got Mr. Nelson is that uh, when you were in Minneapolis you stayed at the Marriott, is that correct?

GN: Uh huh.

KH: Um, do you remember which Marriott Hotel you stayed at?

GN: Marriott City Center.

KH: City Center?

GN: Uh huh.

KH: Ok, do you remember what room you were in?

GN: Here, let me try to find my expense account and I can answer all this for you, I was in Room 3002.

KH: 3002, okay, and you said you flew out on the 23rd, do you remember the time of your flight?

GN: Uh huh, 2:30.

KH: 2:30, do you know uh, where you went to after you left Minneapolis on the 23rd or ...

GN: I was in Washington DC the rest of the time.

KH: Ok, and that was uh, ok, what day was the 23rd, I'm just trying to see.

GN: A Wednesday.

KH: A Wednesday, so you worked through Friday then and then I take it you had the weekend off?

GN: And was in Washington DC that whole time ...

KH: Ok, do you remember where you were at around May 1st, 2nd, or 3rd?

GN: Washington DC.

KH: Ok, and that would have been also in your office?

GN: Yep.

KH: Ok, do you like time sheets or anything um, to validate your time there?

GN: No.

KH: Ok, how about anybody that I could contact to substantiate that you were ...

GN: Well I really don't like my personal life to get involved in all of this, I mean if you need to that's fine, but ...

KH: Well, the only thing that I'm trying to do is just try to eliminate any possibility of your involvement here ok?

GN: And is there anything more, am I going to hear from anybody else or?

KH: The only thing is I, you know, I don't know why you'd be contacted by like Chicago P.D. or, or any of the others ...

GN: And part of the reason I left Minneapolis is I was, just needed to get away from this man and unfortunately I think he's a complete victim of his own lifestyle.

KH: Ok, and I guess, you know I can't say what other people are doing or whatever happened but um, as far as for me I'm not releasing any names that I get and I just needed to, to verify your time frame because you were in Minneapolis real close to the time frame that uh, uh, Minneapolis had a homicide and then um, David was killed in our county here.

GN: And I had called the Minneapolis Police Department as soon as I had found out about it.

KH: Ok.

GN: And has anybody been charged in Mr. Trail's death yet?

KH: Pardon me?

GN: Has anybody been charged in Mr. Trail's death yet?

KH: Uh, that would be Minneapolis's case and as far as I know there hasn't been any charges filed in that death, ok, and do you think you have some knowledge or just …

GN: No, I find the whole story to be quite odd that Mr. Madson didn't have something to do with it from the fact that he was seen walking his dog Monday and Tuesday, having dinner with this gentleman and if he was indeed just a poor witness to the crime, I don't understand why he wasn't killed earlier.

KH: Ok, and I don't know any involvement uh, of what …

GN: All I can say is there's a very dark side to David Madson and David Madson was into a lot of weird things.

KH: Well to be honest I never met David and I know you …

GN: I'm just saying, if people do some research and look into it and I have told the police and I've told various contacts, as to people who they should contact with this underground S&M

thing and prostitution thing and such that none of this surprises me and he had a very Jeckle/Hyde personality.

KH: Well if, I guess if you think of anything that you really feel is pertinent to, uh, the homicide of Jeffrey Trail or to David's murder, please feel free to contact me or to contact Minneapolis, ok?

GN: And to be honest with you I haven't felt very cooperative because when I contacted the Minneapolis Police Dept. they still position it as "well, it sounded like Mr. Madson had something to fear of you, not of him," and I, I completely disagree with that and I, I mean I would like to know more about this Cunanan man and how this is all, and I'm sure you would too.

KH: Well and I think a lot of people are finding stuff out, I mean a lot of people now that this has been so public that have been calling with information on Cunanan, so.

GN: Ok.

KH: I guess anything that you can think of or help, and you've been a great help so far, ok?

49

He left an incredible mess in the Lexus, fast-food wrappers, soda bottles, Lee's shoe, a snapshot of Robin Thompson he happened to have in his wallet, slips of paper with his handwriting on them, Andrew had no thought of destroying evidence, not really, he kept moving in a trance, down through Baltimore, DC, he stopped in DC and picked up a date in the toilet at JR.'s, a blond guy with some passing resemblance to

David Madson, "I want you to do me right here," he told him in the men's room, but the man insisted on taking him home. The next morning when the guy asked, Andrew said he never gave out his last name, and quickly left. He drove through Virginia and North Carolina and in Florence, South Carolina, he pulled off 95 and lug-wrenched a license plate off a vehicle parked at Wal-Mart.

Alarms were going off, but not nearly as many as people later imagined. His name was out there, some bits of his story, the "high-class male prostitute" angle got out there right away, with the "AIDS revenge" scenario soon to follow, there was never much evidence to support either one of these notions but the press ran with both of them anyway, what the hell, you might not be able to print this stuff about every homo, but this "would-be jet-setter," this "flashy, smooth-talking gay man," "champion name-dropper," "hungry for the high life," could stand in for the rest of them, not so much incarnating the general view of gay people per se—they were, after all, sometimes wonderfully gifted persons, and many seemed sincere if not fanatical in their conformity with wholesome American values—but the general queasiness about what these gay people did with each other in bed, the ass-fucking and what have you. Even though Andrew was ready-made for the media, his victims didn't matter, not even the locally famed real-estate developer. By the time the first major story broke in the *New York Times*, in which he was rumored to be "heading east," Andrew had already checked into a hotel in Miami.

50

O
X
Y
G
E
N

One block north of the Normandy Beach Hotel, between McDonald's and Miami Subs, was a suite of shops with recessed entrances and twin display windows lit at night. Two shops particularly reflected the character of the neighborhood. One set of windows showcased rupture trusses, bedpans, motorized electric chairs, crutches, and oxygen tanks; the windows next door featured kendo rods, Japanese swords, punching bags, protective vests, and other martial paraphernalia aimed at Third World juveniles aspiring to samuraihood.

The Normandy Plaza was wedged between the Clarion Suites and the Port Royale. The Clarion Suites was partly faced in black glass and had a ground floor of vacant storefronts. As with many buildings in Miami Beach, it was impossible to tell if the Clarion Suites was being finished or undergoing an extremely languid demolition. The Port Royale was an apartment house that appeared to be exclusively occupied by couples in their early nineties.

If an oversize rotogravure image near the elevator was anything to go by, the Normandy Plaza had once occupied a large, neighborless patch of beachfront. It was hard to credit the claim that movie stars had flocked there long ago. The rooms were modest and even new could not have been terribly grand. The lobby had a bar with a row of stools, but no bartender and no bottles. Restaurant-style booths sat perpetually vacant at a street-level window. Over the bar hung a framed blowup of James Cagney peering at *The Racing Form* over Edward G. Robinson's shoulder; another showed Marilyn Monroe splashing on Chanel No. 5. In the center of the lobby, an oval glass table supported by an acrobatic-looking brass mermaid held a profuse, sickly arrangement of ugly flowers.

The hotel desk, a warren of tiny religious fetishes and outdated office equipment, was usually attended by a good-humored, middle-aged Hispanic woman whose desuetude and lack of curiosity were perfectly suited to the clientele. The clientele came in two varieties: tourists, usually foreign and in couples, traveling on grotesquely restrictive budgets; and people in some sort of complicated trouble. The latter only ventured out very early in the morning or very late at night. They wafted an odor of failure through the halls, a scent compounded of outstanding warrants and overdue checks and spousal abuse and alcohol, greasy meals improvised on hot plates, joylessly consumed drugs, and bad sex.

It was not the worst place in the world or even in Miami Beach, and Andrew felt secure there. He had checked in as Kurt DeMars, the name of a San Francisco acquaintance; he had not been obliged to produce an ID. He moved steadily up from the ground floor over two weeks, from room 116 to room 201 and finally to room 322. Room 322 had a primitive Zenith with no cable and no remote, a gas stove, a small Formica table, a brown refrigerator with a MIAMI NICE bumper sticker on the door. The window overlooked some patio furniture planted in sand and a lifeless chunk of beach. It had a comfortable double bed, a functioning air conditioner, and a tiny bathroom.

Andrew bought sandals from the Nike Store and shorts from the Speedo outlet and a hair-clipping set from Walgreen's, dressed and frapped himself to blend with the streets, but he hadn't drastically changed his appearance. He started finding articles about himself in magazines and out-of-town newspapers that referred to him as a "chameleon," even a "master of disguise." These articles usually included a lineup of bad snapshots taken over many years, chronologically jumbled to enhance the idea of awesome metamorphic skill. He couldn't really tell if he needed a disguise in Miami Beach, where very little fuss was being made about his so-called killing spree, and people seemed too preoccupied with their own pursuits to notice him or anybody else. He tanned in the morning on the hotel beach; he thought this darkened him enough to cancel resemblance to the photographs. Still, going into places scared him, going into South Beach in the daytime scared him, drawing anyone's full attention scared him.

He was only mildly surprised to see what various queens in San Diego had told reporters about him; it was probably the first and only time when anyone not placing a food order would ask their opinions about anything. It did bother him that certain articles suggested he'd gone to Minneapolis intending to kill Jeff Trail, but he could hardly call up and demand a retraction. And this Michael Dudley creature, claiming Andrew had more or less confessed to having AIDS, had gone to Michael Dudley for counseling, what an insane fabrication, you would go to Michael Dudley to unload a quart jug of Thunderbird maybe, and that sick queen Nicole Ramirez-Murray, *as if* Andrew had ever even met her. The funny part was, the only person Andrew could recall ever saying he'd like to kill was Nicole Rimjob-Murray, after reading her silly column.

51

The hotel was sixty blocks and a world away from South Beach. If you walked down Collins Avenue the zone between the Normandy Beach and the Deco District was a cancer of hideous development, high- and medium-rise condos and hotels so ugly Mussolini would have found them unduly oppressive. Among the monstrosities growing on the Indian Creek side was a vomit-pink edifice of something like a million units, identified on the hoarding as "Maison Paco Rabanne." Andrew passed it whenever he trekked to South Beach on foot, as he usually did—after parking the truck around the hotel for two weeks, he'd stowed it in a garage near the Versace Mansion. A cab ride cost twelve dollars one way, more than he wanted to blow with no foreseeable income. Anyway, he liked walking at twilight along Indian Creek where it turned into a houseboat marina, with party boats passing and cocktail ice clinking in bungalows across the water. His feet were always sore when he got to Ocean Drive, so he usually waded in the surf before hitting the bars.

He did blow money on books, he needed books in his room, he usually got them at Kafka's Used Book Store on Washington at Fourteenth Street, less often at Books & Books on the Lincoln Road Mall, bought them or stole them according to whim. The *Claudius* novels, Kenneth Clark's *The Romantic Rebellion*, Braudel's *A History of Civilizations*. A used copy of John Updike's book on painting, *Just Looking*. Thomas Cahill's *How the Irish Saved Civilization*. He snapped up biographies of Condé Nast and William Paley, the autobiography of Slim Keith. Beaumont Newhall's history of photography. At a branch library near the Normandy, he slipped Louis Begley's *About Schmidt* into his backpack.

During the day, when he kept to his room, with the heavy curtains drawn, Andrew devoured these books and lost himself in the act of reading. Someone, a woman, he thought, in the next room, had a horrendous cough, what he imagined a tubercular cough must sound like, as if pieces of the lungs were peeling off with every hack. And he heard little voices, not what they said, only the tones, so abstract as to sound idiotic. There were two Hispanic boys living down the hall. The younger and cuter one had acne and the slight build of a child on the verge of adolescence, but something in his eyes and his carriage suggested experience beyond his years. Andrew wondered what such a young kid was doing in this place, how he happened to be living in a hotel for grown-up losers. There were probably kids like that in every place like this, scary kids who looked as if they could do serious damage to other people without giving it a thought.

He collected porn magazines, *Urge, Manshots, Jock, Hard, Ram, Euro Boy,* and *Hunk.* He studied the faces of the models, faces going for "sexy," and wondered why they invariably looked like aliens struggling to look human.

52

South Beach drew him, of course, despite what his mind told of its dangers: that someone from *before* would spot him, that if he drank too much Commodore Cummings could pop out and blow his cover, that the panic he'd visited on four people—was it four? five?—might return if he picked someone up. And he was muttering again, sometimes volubly, if thoughts went a certain way he perceived himself as two entities, *Andrew Cunanan the fugitive* and *Andrew Cunanan the nice clever guy*, two competing voices trapped together. With part of his mind he was somehow becoming the person described in the media, even identifying with malicious gossip and ludicrous rumors that circulated as reported fact. At least part of the time, Andrew now believed he'd been *involved in the international drug trade*, that he had worked extensively as a *male prostitute*, had been, in a professional sense that his previous life actually belied, a *gigolo*; that he had recently tried to strangle a casual pickup named Schwegler or Shargill or Schwimmer in San Francisco; that he'd once shot a neighbor's cat, and had regularly tortured small animals as a child. The other Andrew, who didn't see himself as any type of *serial killer*, et cetera, disputed this contrived identity. Unfortunately, he tended to do this when both Andrews were walking on Espanola Way or Ocean Drive, and although what came from his mouth unbidden was a sort of gargle, opaque to any bystander, the performance itself invited perilous scrutiny.

But he needed South Beach, the sight of other young people, the tactile aura of other people's glamour and money and pleasure, he needed to talk, the hermetic silence of his days drove him crazy, the shabbiness of the hotel, the seedy businesses around it, it reminded him of the Philippines, of that dead-mice-and-mildew dankness that lurks everywhere in the tropics but really stinks where there's poverty. In South Beach, the smell seemed to dissipate, and at stray moments in South Beach he forgot who he was, his inevitable doom. All those cake-frosting facades, all those David Barton bodies, the places reeled against his eyelids, Lario, Pelican, Caffe Milano, the Breakwater, straight studs in white jackets, women with tits squirming out of their bikini evening wear, Majestic, Avalon, Johnny Rockets, the Colony, the primo Edsel station wagon in front of the Palace Bar and Grill, *I'd like to see the Riviera and slow-dance underneath the stars*, the white parasols on the terrace of the Ocean Front Hotel, the rich drunks on cell phones ordering cocaine, *I'd like to watch the sun come up in a stranger's arms*, limousines crawling through night crowds, this month's models tossing beer bottles on the lawn of the Clevelander, every night was a Cannes Film Festival for desperate wanna-bes, catamites, sycophants, fashion pimps and their ingénue camera whores, all mixed in with legible celebrities and authentic rich people. South Beach had an atmosphere of craven fantasy that Andrew felt he'd invented rather than walked into.

53

He checked out all the gay places, Amnesia Club on hip-hop night, Warsaw, the Paragon, a leather bar on Alton Road, he found he could go night after night without hitting a suspicious glance. He liked to pretend that people knew precisely who he was and weren't fazed. Twist was his favorite. A mixture of the old and the beautiful. The old were mainly downstairs in subdued lighting amid paintings of ibises and egrets. The back service bar was outside under a loose canopy of parachute silk, and there he often sparked conversations with boys who could have stepped out of *Manshots*, conversations that segued into dancing upstairs. In Twist, he was Kurt DeMars, an advertising account manager for *Out* magazine, with homes in Key Biscayne and San Francisco. In other places, he was Steven Nauck of Long Beach and Kew Gardens. He did, in fact, know a Steven Nauck, Steven Nauck had been one of Andrew's Hillcrest crowd for many years and considered himself Andrew's "baby brother," Andrew had considered calling Steven Nauck, as he was, in fact, calling people, Rusty and several others, using a Data Wave Long Distance card, sometimes to ask about passports, sometimes just to chat, he didn't always reach these people but often he got through. Everyone he called sounded surprised to hear from him. He told them he was calling from New Orleans or Boston or Texas, anywhere but there. He hinted that certain fancy older gentlemen would get outed if he didn't get help. He made some crank calls to Minneapolis, just to spook people.

54

Kurt DeMars said he had a South Beach pied-à-terre, hardly a lie, since Andrew kept a Pratesi shopping bag full of evening wear in the truck, changed there and occasionally slept there as well. The truck was filling up with socks and underwear and scattered toiletries. The garage charged when you left, Andrew always made sure he had enough cash on him to pay the mounting tariff if he needed to get out. Money was disappearing. He pawned one of the Miglin gold coins, signing his real name, writing his real address. Something told him to. He'd never been in a pawn shop before, he figured the paper got filed away and forgotten about. The black counterman in Miami Subs recognized him one afternoon, Andrew knew it, knew the look, but he wanted his tuna sub. He calmly paid a different cashier for it and strolled back to the Normandy while the first guy called the police. "How did you get so good?" he asked the bathroom mirror. "*I'll tell you,*" a voice in his head answered.

55

He overheard a lot of gossip in the bars, tales about Madonna, Ingrid Casares, George Michael, Elton John, a lot about Versace too, that Versace held orgies in his magnificent casa, that he had a procurer who auditioned escorts for Versace and his boyfriend at the nearby cafés. The procurer would order four or five men from St. Tropez Escorts, meet them at a café, pick the best-looking one and take him around the back entrance at Versace's place. The owner of St. Tropez Escorts called himself Sebastian, but his real name was Bret Hawkins. Andrew believed he'd met Bret Hawkins somewhere, maybe at a party in La Jolla. And of course he "knew" Versace, in the sense that he "knew" Lisa Kudrow and Matt Dillon and Gus Van Sant and Nicole Kidman, i.e., had met them at parties, or glimpsed them at parties, or imagined he had, and had so habitually exaggerated these real and unreal brushes with fame into close personal ties that he could not reliably recall if he had met Versace once or twice, if Versace had met him once and remembered him on seeing him a second time, or met him once and mistaken him for someone else he'd met before, or what. He wished he could talk to Versace. Italians understood revenge and rage and running amok a lot better than Americans.

56

He found he could order a coffee in the Eleventh Street Diner and sit with it for hours without being harassed. It was just down the street from the Versace house. Andrew liked being near the house, it was like being near a foreign country whose border he could slip across in an emergency. In the diner he first heard the voices, audible enough to mistake them for the voices of other customers. "We're here to help you," they said. "There are many things you don't understand but everything will be made clear." The voices began to point out the true meaning of things, the messages disguised as ordinary signs and objects. They directed him to look at certain people and explained who these people really were. They were not who they seemed. Neither was Andrew.

57

The same day the voices began helping him he developed a skin irritation on his stomach, which he scratched furiously all day without realizing it. Later when he lifted his shirt he discovered a tiny circular wound, probably from his fingernails, around what must have been an ingrown hair. He bought cotton balls and alcohol at Walgreen's and covered the wound with a Band-Aid, but he kept scratching it and it kept getting bigger. The voices identified it as the mark of his divine plan. His divine plan needed to be fulfilled in order to balance 51 percent of his karma. Once Andrew balanced that 51 percent the mark would go away.

58

The voices manifested with such subtlety. They slipped him messages through unconscious agents, for example a man on Washington Avenue handing out little cards for BEST CUBAN FLAME STEAK had no idea the one he gave Andrew read I AM

GOLDEN LIGHT! For the split second his eye caught it, a plaque on a hotel that said STANDPIPE AND SIAMESE ARE INTERCONNECTED was shape-shifted to read, CLEAN THE GUN. A few minutes later he saw Versace going into his mansion on Ocean Drive.

59

"Get out of here tonight," the voices told him in the room. "Leave everything behind. Leave the books, leave the clothes, the way will be shown, and the path will be made straight." He left by the fire stairs, taking only the gun and his backpack and the keys for the pickup. That night he was given a brief vacation from destiny, the voices subsided to a faint buzz, Andrew danced in Twist and drank g&t's until four in the morning, woke groggy at 8:15 in the pied-à-terre, took off his long pants and slipped into black shorts, swallowed some Vivarin tablets with bottled water, then went out to balance his karma.

60

Andrew supposed that the famous designer had been working on behalf of the voices in his head all along, that Versace's mental voice was directing all the others, what would happen was Andrew would make contact, a wordless understanding would be reached, Versace would usher him into the mansion and later spirit him to safety, Versace had already balanced quite a bit more of his karma than what was being asked of Andrew, Andrew in his new humility would learn much more of the invisible world through Versace, perhaps he would even have carnal relations with Versace if various spirit entities saw fit, but then when Versace's corporeal form passed Andrew's on the narrow sidewalk the form's eyes flickered with alarm even as its mouth gave a polite smile, right at that second as Versace crossed the road the voices whispered that *a malign current* had taken over Versace's body, the real Versace had been zapped right out of his albuminous container and this *current* had recognized Andrew's terrestrial incarnation, would return to Versace's house and call the authorities, casting Andrew forever out of the divine plan. He was directed to wait around the corner until the form returned, in hardly any time at all he saw the false Versace coming back, arms full of magazines, passing the corner, Andrew got the gun out and followed, he looked at Versace, Versace looked at him, *What if I'm completely crazy* flashed in Andrew's head as he fired the gun, fired again, he looked at what he'd done, people came running, Andrew ran, he ran to the alley and up the alley to the garage and in front of the garage, two cars were locked in a fender-bender, traffic cops were at the scene. Andrew slipped into the garage and up cement stairs to the truck, he couldn't drive it out with the police downstairs so he changed his clothes and ran up to the roof, ran to all four sides of the roof in search of a fire escape, nothing, found a set of back stairs on the ramp below and followed them down to Collins Avenue, up Collins to Lincoln Road, down Lincoln Road to the beach, Andrew covered thirty blocks in no time whatsoever. *I can't get off Miami Beach without a car,* he thought. Then his voices reminded him about the houseboat, he'd passed it a million times, never a light on or any sign of life inside, *wait until dark,* the voices said, and Andrew did. And after that he never heard the voices again.

61

Lt. Collins, San Diego Homicide

After the murder of Lee Miglin, the media from Chicago and Minneapolis came out here, I'd have two or three pages of calls from media people, one of those people asked me a lot of questions, I was surprised how much they got from law enforcement in those cities because a lot of that we wouldn't release, one of the reporters asked me some questions, and said, "You're not going to give us anything you don't want to give us," unfortunately one of my detectives failed to get one of the search warrants sealed, so when that got made public ten days later it was all over the news, that we'd seized a porn videotape ... just the cover for the videotape, we were looking for finger-prints on the cover.

Kelly Thornton ran that story about the guy in that coffee shop, this Michael Dudley who claimed Cunanan went to him saying he had AIDS, that he kicked the wall and so on, Kelly Thornton was calling every day—there had been a lull, nothing had happened for a while, first I had a reporter from Fresno down here who called and asked me, Do you have anything to verify this? And I said absolutely not, what I have is that Andrew did not have AIDS, I don't know where that's coming from. The next morning Kelly Thornton calls me and asks me the same thing, I said I don't know where you're getting this from, and she said, Michael Dudley said he called the police and talked to the police. He never talked to anybody in my office. He called communications and told them he had this information, and they were getting a lot of crank calls, and they never sent anyone out about it, he talked to one of the dispatchers who didn't believe him—this wasn't after a lull, this was right after the Versace murder, I think, because the FBI command post wanted to talk to this guy. I think when we contacted the guy on Friday, he said I can verify that this story was told to Kelly Thornton, but you'll have to talk to me right away because they're flying me back to New York to be on *Good Morning America* on Monday morning. And I knew at that time that the victims did not have AIDS, and I proposed to the FBI that they do a press release saying that none of these victims had AIDS, and take the wind out of this guy's sails and *Good Morning America* before they get it going.

(Interview with the author, 1997)

62

The horses were out of the barn. The narrative had been locked into place since the Kennedy assassination, *world's most important person slain by world's least important person*, and for a considerable time, beginning with the Menendez trial, an expanded cable range had refined the spinning of such narratives into a condition of defiant redundancy, a demand for "closure" which was, at the same time, an adamant refusal of "closure," filling the air with hyperanimated gargoyles, usually lawyers, in this case psychological experts and mavens of the fashion industry, the public would now have to swallow encomiums from fashion editors and supermodels, for whom the ultimate accolade seemed to be that the decedent had "lived like a Roman emperor," the ultimate disparagement of his killer being that

Andrew was merely a wanna-be, one of a million faceless nobodies who couldn't live like a Roman emperor, in other words couldn't live like Tiberius, say, or Caligula, or Nero, on the contrary, Andrew and people like Andrew "preyed on the rich," who became, in this narrative, the cream of the human crop, Versace very possibly the creamiest, an example of the free-enterprise system at its finest. "I can spend three million dollars in two hours," *People* approvingly quoted. "I go shopping one day in Paris buying things for my house in Miami. That night, I come back home, and I see the figure I spent—oh, I start to dance ... I want to kiss myself." On *Rivera* the killing was referred to as an *assassination*. The display of obscene wealth on the part of Versace's friends and associates assumed an entirely benign and even delightful innocence in contrast with the event's horror. It became possible to show, for instance, photographs of Elton John, frapped by Versace to resemble Marie Antoinette, as exemplary of the enviable and altogether merited frivolity obtaining among our show business aristocracy. The obdurate conventions of the narrative required that people whose lives were passionately devoted to appearances should suddenly exhibit depths of feeling. Some lip service was inevitably paid to the four previous victims of Andrew's rampage, but the narrative made it absolutely clear that only celebrities have real lives. Paradoxically, the same narrative rendered all the figures in the story, including Versace, completely unreal, since all the worrisome inconsistencies and missing pieces needed to be shaved off or ignored.

63

Officer reporting: Detective P. Scrimshaw.
Officer reviewing: Sgt. G. Navarro
Case assigned to: Detective P. Scrimshaw

18 July 2200 Hrs I met with F Nauck to attempt to glean more
information about the subject. Causey and Estravez were present during the interview.

The following observations were solicited from Nauck;

The only employment that he knew Cunanan to ever have had
was as an assistant in a pharmacy.

He knows of no romantic affairs engaged in by the shooter. Any
affair would be based on financial reward, from an older
benefactor.

He is not a sensual person.

His fantasy involves bondage and "fucking somebody to
death." When asked about sexual activities, he would
respond with, "I just pay a guy to have sex with me."

He did not think Cunanan is capable of romantic love.

Is conservative about visible display of affection in public.

Prefers leather bars and masculine but "not over muscled"
men. With facial hair.

Cunanan becomes easily angered by the inattention of fickle
friends.

Cunanan was always flush with cash and always paid when out
for dinner drinks etc. Very generous with money.

Shooter is a busy body, in the extreme, with an excellent memory.

Cunanan is alleged to be a college graduate with a degree in
history, a desire to get an advanced similar degree and teach.

His history interest is that of the WWII era and is apparently
    fascinated by the regime of Adolf Hitler.
Is an avid reader and "quoter of the stock market."
Is not interested in sports as either a spectator or participant.
Cunanan is neat and particular about his surroundings but is
    not described as "anal."
His sense of humor runs to sarcasm at some one else's expense.
At social gatherings he is always the life of the party, loud and
    boisterous.
Although Cunanan never said, Nauck feels that he is probably
    a "top man."
Investigation continues:

64

In the narrative, *celebrity* and *being* were the same thing, the
wish to be famous was no less than the *desire to exist*, it was
assumed on the strength of fifth-hand bar chatter culled by
reporters that *Andrew always wanted to be famous*, it was inferred
from this that shooting Versace was Andrew's *last chance to
become famous*, meanwhile Erik Greenman revealed to the
National Enquirer that photographer Herb Ritts was "No. 3" on
Andrew's "hit list." It was suddenly chic to be "targeted" by
Andrew, Harry de Wildt bragged that the FBI considered him a
possible target. It also became chic to claim a deep personal
friendship with Versace, to infer that one might, but for a trick
of fate, have been *with* Versace at the very moment of his "assassination," as it had once been chic to reveal one's invitation to

Cielo Drive on the evening of the Tate slayings, an invitation only declined because of *car trouble* or a *previous engagement*. Versace's friends no less than Andrew's friends were helpless not to make hay off the carcass, for the narrative itself excluded from *existence* all relevant persons who *failed to appear*, to put their two cents in, to *deplore* and to *grieve* and to advertise their sense of *shock* and *loss* and *outrage* as publicly and bathetically as possible, and because the narrative had the force of a psychic avalanche it provided the segue from the previous narrative, extricated the public eye from the previous keyhole, the Andrew narrative, in effect, *solved the JonBenét Ramsey murder case*, as that case had finally *wrapped up the O. J. Simpson case*, which in turn had *closed the Menendez case*, the Andrew mystery would ultimately be *solved by the death of Princess Di*, which in turn would achieve "closure" in the form of Monica Lewinsky.

65

Officer reporting: Detective P. Marcus
Officer reviewing: Sgt. G. Navarro
Case assigned to: Detective P. Scrimshaw

… While at the Normandy Hotel, I received a telephone call from Crimestoppers. A call was received from a caller, stating that he overheard a conversation that CUNANAN was seen at the Crystal Beach Club at 71st & Collins Avenue. Agent Evans and myself responded to this location and checked with the clerk. No information was found via name, and the shown photographs were also negative.

Upon returning to the C.I.D. I received a telephone call from Crimestoppers. A male caller was transferred to me who had seen CUNANAN at Twist Nightclub. The caller told me that on Friday Night, 7/11/97 he was at Twist with some friends. He saw CUNANAN there and they even danced. The caller indicated that his name is "BRAD" and he was calling from West Palm Beach. During the time they danced, CUNANAN had his hands "all over him." He said that he was grabbing and rubbing him. They were talking and exchanging information about what each did for a living. He indicated that CUNANAN told him he was a serial killer, but then said that he was into "investment banking."

The dance ended with a kiss, and he disappeared into the crowd. He never saw him again that night. He indicated that the photograph being shown is not totally accurate, indicating that CUNANAN had a thinner face.

66

Gay serial killer Andrew Cunanan is madly in love with Tom Cruise! The sick monster talked openly of killing the superstar's beautiful wife Nicole Kidman so he could have Tom all to himself to tie up, torture and humiliate for pleasure. And if Cunanan can't ensnare the actor, he wants Tom dead!

JonBenét Murder Weapon Found! ... Cops Say Daddy's Golf Club Matches Death Blow (*National Enquirer*, August 5, 1997)

67

Officer reporting: Detective P. Scrimshaw
Officer reviewing: Sgt. G. Navarro
Case assigned to: Detective P. Scrimshaw

1116 Ocean Drive is a 3 story structure of apparent finished coral rock, brickjoister construction. The residence is the only such private residence on the length of Ocean Drive. It is situated on the west side of the street facing east. The grounds of same cover fully 1/3 of the block surrounded by concrete and steel decorative walls/fences reaching heights of 12 feet above the sidewalk. The southern boundary is delineated by the convergence of wall and sidewalk in the 100 blk of 11 St from the west Ocean Drive sidewalk to the eastern edge of Ocean Court. The western side of the building runs to the north along Ocean Drive and may be accessed by both rear west facing delivery entrance/garage and a west entrance leading into the central courtyard. The northern boundary is similar and unremarkable, while the eastern boundary may be breached by double steel gates of a decorative design. These gates are secured by a keyed dead bolt in the northern half of the gate. A perimeter security video camera system is in place but was not turned on at the time of the offense.

In order to gain access to the eastern gates there are 5 steps leading up from the street, placing the base level of the gates approx 30 inches above the level of the sidewalk. The northern half of the gate opens inward and was so configured at the time that I arrived on the scene. It was open approx 1/3 of the way.

A pair of black sandals are arrayed on the lowest step, the southern most being approximately 8 feet north of the southern end of the step and the other being an additional 5 feet further north. Pooling of blood and some possible brain matter is noted on step 1, 2, and 3 toward the northern end of the steps approx 6 feet from their northern ends. There are various other smears and transfers on step 4 and 5. A second set of smears and transfers occur on the sidewalk directly to the east of the main pool. These probably represent the position of the victim's body as he was moved by FRU. There is some FRU debris in the same immediate area.

On the walk way area at the gate level in the open gateway is a paper bag containing magazines and to the north of it within 1 foot, a pair of sunglasses with black frames.

Two .40 silver colored expended casings are located, one on the sidewalk near the curb line approx 7 feet north of the northern end of step 1 and 4 feet west of the curb, the second is in the street approx 1 foot north of the first and 3 feet east of the curb line.

Between the two casings in the street with its head oriented north and in a supine position, is the body of a dead mourning dove. Blood coming from a wound in the dove's head appears to be of the same temporal freshness as that of the victim.

68

From "The Electronic Funeral" by Daniel Harris, an analysis of Internet postings regarding the Versace killing:

"In fact, it is not just Versace who is disguised as an artist, 'a dream weaver, a story teller through fabric,' who 'was to fashion what Michaelangela was to art,' but capitalism itself, which is characterized throughout the tributes, not as the money-grubbing enterprise of corporate price gougers, but as a vast philanthropic organization, an altruistic cultural institution that 'bequeaths'—not sells—beauty and elegance to our aesthetically impoverished society. Versace's merchandise is almost invariably referred to as a 'legacy' handed down to us by a selfless humanitarian who 'gave alot to his community' and who did not 'endow' the world with the 'visional grateness' of his 'oeuvre' out of sordid profit motives but for the pure, high-minded 'passion of designing ... such wonderful clothes that were showy but will always be classy in a sense.' Just as corporations like Benetton now attempt to disguise shopping as a political act, a way of giving to a cause, of expressing compassion for the poor put-upon people of the Third World, so buying clothes is recharacterized in the Versace tributes as an act of 'collecting' art works handcrafted by a beneficent genius who 'graced us' with his 'beauteous objects.' The subtle transformation of the fashion industry into a charitable public interest foundation shows capitalism in the process of purifying itself, rendering itself clean in the eyes of the public who, as these anguished cries from the heart reveal, takes at face value the propagandistic efforts of corporate America to foster a kinder, gender image of itself as the great champion of culture, the fierce, uncompromising advocate of exacting standards of taste."

69

Officer reporting: Sgt. G. Navarro

In the early evening hours, I interviewed a source by the name of Alex. Present during this interview was S/A Evans and Detective Marrero. The interview was conducted at the CID interview room. Alex stated the following:

Alex worked as a male escort in the early to mid 1990's. During this time, Alex was listed in various gay publications and went by the name Kyle. One day, he was called to meet with a white, Latin male at the Palace Grill named Jaime. The Palace Grill is located at 1200 Ocean Drive. Alex went to the Palace Grill and waited for Jaime.

While he was at the Palace Grill, he realized that other escorts were also waiting there. Alex did not like that and was ready to walk out, when he was approached by Jaime. Jaime picked him over the other male escorts and took him to the rear door of the Versace Mansion with specific instructions to go directly up the rear staircase leading to Mr. Versace's and D'Amico's rooms.

Alex followed instructions and met with Mr. D'Amico and Versace in one of their rooms. They had a brief conversation and proceeded to have sex. Alex stated that he had sex with both Mr. D'Amico and Mr. Versace, but felt that the whole scenario was more for Mr. D'Amico's needs than for Mr. Versace's. Alex exited the residence the same way he entered it, after his services were complete.

Alex went to the Versace residence four to six times. The first two times, he was called by Jaime, but all other times was called directly by Mr. D'Amico with no middle person. Alex was paid by Mr. D'Amico every time.

The information provided by Alex regarding his contacts with Mr. D'Amico and Mr. Versace, was later collaborated by Jaime Cardona. Mr. D'Amico also collaborated some of these activities at a later date.

Mr. Cardona stated the following:

Mr. Cardona met Gianni Versace in late 1991 or early 1992 through a modeling agent named Richard Paulman. Mr. Cardona became friends with Mr. Versace and acted as a guide and social director for the Versace household when they first came to Miami Beach. Mr. Cardona also did some modeling work for Mr. Versace.

After a long line of questioning and a lot of denial by Mr. Cardona, it was obvious that Mr. Cardona was not being totally truthful with investigators. Finally, after consulting with his lawyer, Mr. Cardona admitted to activities that were confirmed by Alex, prior to this interview.

Mr. Cardona stated that he planned various parties and as part of his duties, he hired male dancers as entertainment for Mr. Versace and Mr. D'Amico. Mr. Cardona also admitted recruiting and hiring male escorts for Mr. Versace and D'Amico on several occasions.

Mr. Cardona would use various gay publications that list male escorts or he would contact male escorts that were recommended by people he knew.

Mr. Cardona would have the male escorts meet him at the Palace Grill, located at 1200 Ocean Dr. where he would conduct a short meeting. He would then take them to the back door of the Versace residence. This would happen until

Mr. D'Amico would feel comfortable with the escort. Once that occurred, Mr. D'Amico would call them himself and have them meet him at the back door of the residence.

The only names that Mr. Cardona could recall were Carlos and Kyle. The name Kyle has come up during a previous interview of a source, as a person that visited the Versace residence on a regular basis.

Mr. Cardona verified information that was gathered from a previous source. Mr. Cardona stopped hiring male escorts for Mr. Versace and Mr. D'Amico in 1993. Mr. Cardona does not think that Cunanan ever met Mr. Versace, but was not sure. He based his opinion on the fact that Cunanan was not their type and did not appear to move in their circles.

70

Did he or didn't he leave the boat at any time once he was on it? No one seems to know. The police received two phone calls from the same informant in New York, who claimed that Andrew called him twice and said he was in Newton, Massachusetts, had flown into Boston from Orlando, of course, by that time, Andrew had been spotted on a flight from Orlando to Dulles, sighted at roughly the same time in Oklahoma; he'd also been seen at the Crystal Beach Club at 71 and Collins; in Ft. Lauderdale, in women's clothes, entering a supermarket; and at a sports trading-card establishment in Lebanon, New Hampshire. People resembling Andrew were being detained at airports all over the country, according to the news he could be anywhere and even in several places at same time.

71

The first thing Andrew had to contend with was the *incredible bad taste* of all the houseboat furnishings, quite beyond anything, porcelain elephants and plaster dolphins, some type of Buddhist or Hindu shrine set up in front of a room divider made of wooden frets, Oriental throw rugs over white shag carpeting, hideous vases all over the house stuffed with dead flowers, bad pictures everywhere, fifth-rate decorator items of a sleek generic "prettiness" Andrew had sometimes run across in the homes of porn actors, an office with ugly modular furniture. Some nouveau riche with no aesthetic sense at all had thrown this place together, someone named Reineck, figured, a kraut; in the office he found ledger books on a high shelf, Sealand Investment, Inc., Signature Power Boat, Inc., New Queen Condominium Hotel, Inc., Dockside Rental, Inc., fishy-looking ledgers that were all of a piece with the decor, the companies sounded like shell corporations and the tinny "luxury" of the place was a shell, too, Andrew found cigars and promotion watches and boating magazines and a paperback copy of *Hawaii* by James Michener but almost no real food in the place, bags of Doritos and chili lime tortilla chips and a box of Better Cheddar crackers, a pound of walnuts, a tomato spoiling in the fridge, a lettuce turning brown, and a jar of Hellmann's mayonnaise, as if this wasn't bad enough there was no running water, only some large plastic bottles of Publix drinking water and Coca-Cola and Minute Maid Orange Drink, and the ice trays in the freezer ...

72

On a large square projection-style TV, Andrew followed the gathering tsunami of news about himself, the so-called outpouring of grief at the steps of the Versace mansion, endless clips of models on catwalks, Naomi Campbell in tears, cops examining the pickup truck, pictures of David Madson and Jeffrey Trail, Lee Miglin and William Reese, though it was mostly about Versace, Versace and him, whole afternoons and evenings of CNN were devoted to public séances where weird guys exhumed from outer academia argued whether he should be classified as a "serial killer" or a "spree killer," FBI profilers on Larry King, classmates from Bishop's School, waiters from California Cuisine, and of course Nicole, the so-called Andrew Cunanan expert, all trying to sound like these sanctimonious talking heads, Andrew considered that his whole life was flashing in front of his eyes, a sour version of his whole life, anyway, and flashing in front of millions of other people's eyes at the same time, Andrew thought *spree killer* was a touch too exuberant-sounding for this lousy acid trip, the so-called spree itself hadn't been that much fun, more of a compulsion really and furthermore one that surprised him as much as anybody else. Audience participation shows invited people in the studio and people on the telephone to decide whether he should *get the death penalty* or simply *be locked away for the rest of his life*, of course the so-called gay community jumped right into it, he was not *representative of most gay people*, a person like himself *gave an unwarranted bad name to gay people everywhere*, gay people were concerned, gay people were outraged, gay people were frightened, this particular assortment of gay people were a bunch of assholes as far as Andrew was concerned, one fag in Hillcrest said he'd like to see Andrew *hung by his testicles*, these so-called spokespersons for the gay community went as far as saying that *Andrew Cunanan is not one of us*, a great many fags in South Beach claimed that he'd cast a shadow over *the one place in America where gays can feel safe to be themselves*, that Andrew had *ruined a wonderful party*, but as far as Andrew could see the party had just started shaking loose, people were being themselves all over the place on cue, pillaging through every Versace boutique in the country for a relic, sobbing for reporters, striking noble poses, deploring the everyday violence in our society. Andrew was smart enough to see that the TV was fashioning a *homosexual golem* to absorb every scary fantasy about *the gay community*, imputing supernatural powers to Andrew, suddenly he spoke five languages and maybe killed a bunch of other people thus far undiscovered, they staged reenactments of his so-called *spree*, complete with sinister disco footage and even more sinister peeks into leather and bondage emporiums, backrooms, torture clubs, it was touted that Andrew *wanted it all and didn't want to pay for it*, that he killed Versace to *make himself famous*, that he was just like whatshisname who shot John Lennon. *Yeah, you assholes, and I killed the Lindbergh baby too*, Andrew told the television.

73

Andrew lost track of time. He read part of *Hawaii*, the first part about the formation of islands and plankton and the beginning of life in the great sea. A bird would shit a little seed on the barren island. Ten thousand years later another bird would shit another seed. A million years later or whatever a hurricane deposited some living insects. And so the rich mosaic of life in Honolulu began. Wonderful. He ate the walnuts and took some of Torsten Reineck's penicillin for the angry little wound in his stomach. The boat was turning into a pigpen, he just tossed his garbage into the bathtub, no point in cleaning for company, though company would, he figured, inevitably come. He waited for a sign. One day someone knocked downstairs, he looked out to see an obvious police detective walking away from the house-boat. The news said police were sure he was still in Miami Beach, Andrew didn't quite believe that but didn't disbelieve it, either. They were showing more and better pictures of him around the clock, plastering his image all over the country. The story was so sexy he knew it would never let up until they caught him, people were now speculating that he'd *go out in a blaze of glory, surrender, kill himself* or *keep on killing people*, wonderful options, there seemed to be this insatiable curiosity about his motives, *as if I had any*, and a lubricious general terror about *where he might strike next*, Andrew heard Madonna, he heard Sly Stallone, these might have been good suggestions, he thought, if he'd had more than the one drop of energy he needed left, but why take out the Material Girl and Rambo when you can kill Public Enemy Number One?

74

He gave a lot of thought to how he wanted them to find him, rehearsed getting to the bed from other parts of the houseboat. He would look terrific on the black satin sheets. He was not going to weaken and he wasn't letting any State of Florida electrocute him, the last one they'd done spent twenty minutes frying before time of death. He had his gun all ready and he waited for a sign. When the sign came, and Andrew sprinted for the upstairs bedroom, he passed a poster Reineck had over his desk: "I Survived Hurricane Andrew," it read *Yeah, well, I didn't*, he thought, then went up and laid down and ate the gun. *Such a muddy line between the things you want   And the things you have to do I'm leaving Las Vegas*

75

The bullet bounced around in his skull and came to rest without damaging his face, contrary to all reports. In fact, Andrew looked really, really pretty.

ABOUT THE AUTHOR

Gary Indiana is a writer and artist.